Are We Nearly There Yet?

LUCY VINE

ORION

First published in Great Britain in 2019 by Orion Books,
an imprint of The Orion Publishing Group Ltd
Carmelite House, 50 Victoria Embankment,
London EC4Y 0DZ

An Hachette UK company

1 3 5 7 9 10 8 6 4 2

A CIP catalogue record for this book is
available from the British Library.

ISBN 978 1 4091 8088 3

Typeset by Input Data Services Ltd, Somerset

Printed and bound in Great Britain by Clays Ltd, Elcograf S.p.A.

MIX
Paper from
responsible sources
FSC® C104740

www.orionbooks.co.uk

Lucy Vine is a freelance journalist based in London, who regularly writes and edits for the likes of *Grazia*, *Heat*, *Cosmopolitan*, *Stylist* and *Marie Claire*. Her debut *Hot Mess* was an eBook Number One bestseller.

Follow her on Twitter @Lecv

By Lucy Vine

Hot Mess
What Fresh Hell

Prologue

20 April – 2.15 p.m.

ROUGH DRAFT
NOTE TO SELF: DO NOT PRESS PUBLISH YET!!!

Welcome to my new travel blog, dream chasers,

My name is Alice Edwards and I have quit my very important and glam job and my really fulfilling life back in the UK to spend the next three or four months travelling the world. I shall be going to many exciting and unusual places like LA and Thailand. I will be out here all on my own, as I feel that is important for my spiritual journey. *#Brave.* I have just arrived in Los Angeles, known as the City of Dreams and it is really, really nice. The sea is blue like a gleaming sapphire and the sand is pure white and soft like creamy Country Life butter but without any of those toast crumbs in the corner.

So far, my new friends, I have only been here in this city of dreams for one day, but I can already feel the bohemian, relaxed vibe changing my very soul. I am quickly realising that American people are v tanned and v good looking. It is like the sun sees into their very being and then it shines out from deep in their hearts. I am excited to see more of these strange and foreign people, and what effect they will have on me. I will be staying briefly with my friend who is a very famous actress – I cannot name names – and we will be mingling and vibing with some very cool people like YouTubers and Instagram influencers. I have met a few already and one was wearing a top hat. V cool, I'm sure you will agree.

Goodbye for now, my new friends. I have many more adventures ahead of me, many roads to travel, many beaten paths to get off – and I will share it all with you, if you will join me. I look forward to going on this journey with you all and I shall end my very first blog post with a famous quote that I feel is very apt here:

'A journey of a thousand miles must begin with a single step.' Sir Albert Einstein.

#TravelBlogger #Travels #Travelling #Wanderer #GoneAWOL #Hashtags #AliceEdwardsBlog #OffTheBeatenTrack #Blogger-Life #Blessed #Brave #DreamChaser #ComingBackWithATan #ConstanceBeaumontWannabe

0 Comments · 0 AWOLs · 0 Super Likes

1

One Month Earlier

What's on your mind, Alice?
2 hrs · London · Friends only

I can't believe it's my last night of being twenty-nine! Wish me luck for tonight, everyone. I think this evening is going to be truly wild and MESSY.

Checked in at: **The Gherkin, London**
Like   Comment
4 likes

Alice Edwards: No one's reading this, right? Because Facebook is over, yes? What is the point of anything, why am I here, what am I doing?

Alice Edwards: But if Facebook is ovah and Twitter is ovah and Instagram is ovah, where am I meant to do all my attention seeking?

Alice Edwards: Why am I still asking questions when no one is listening?

Mark Edwards: Jesus Christ, Alice, commenting on your own status is a new basic bitch low, even for you.

I am thinking about sex. I mean, I've had two double gins, so *of course* I'm thinking about sex. But it is also because tomorrow I will be thirty, and therefore used up, dried up – unappealing in all the *up* ways – according to everything I hear from the internet. And so I am thinking about sex.

I mentally paw through my phone contacts. Who can I text? Who would be available for shagging my brains out later tonight but then also pretending to care about me afterwards?

No one.

Honestly, most people in my phonebook are there so I know not to answer when they call.

Across from me at the table, Amelia suddenly barks a happy birthday in my direction. She is a socially awkward barker, always has been. When there is a momentary silence of any kind at a gathering, she will nervously start barking things. Usually I love that about Amelia, but tonight it makes me want to claw at my own skin. To be honest, right now everything makes me want to claw at my own skin.

I laugh heartily for a second too long, clinking my drink to hers and nodding politely at the beige boyfriend beside her. I can't remember his name, what is his name? I look around at the sea of plus ones I don't know around me. Who are all these extra people here at my birthday? When did all my friends couple off?

I stare down at the empty plate in front of me and feel my misery crank up a notch. I suddenly feel intensely disappointed.

Dinner. Dinner? For my thirtieth birthday? A fancy dinner, sure. A fancy dinner in a tall building, but still, *dinner*.

For the last ten years my friends and I have had the same messy, sticky routine for my birthday, which has gone as follows:

Disgusting pre-game shots over at mine and Eva's South

4

London flat with our friends Amelia, Karen, Slutty Sarah, Isabelle (when she's in the country), my brother Mark, and his best friend, Joe, plus any other casual acquaintances I happen to have accumulated that year.

Then disgusting pink drinks at bars called, like, Strawberry Moons, or Infernos, or basically anywhere where they play appallingly cheesy nineties music (Ideally East 17 and the Honeyz).

Followed by a lie-down on the sticky floor at around 10.15 p.m.

Followed by screaming at each other because we've lost a member of our group – usually Eva – and then a bit of angry crying in the loos.

Followed by finding Eva asleep outside on a pile of bin bags and everyone happy crying, which – from an outsider's perspective – is not that different from angry crying.

Followed by someone suggesting we get a kebab as the whole lot of us scream *eating is cheating* and then the arrival of too many Ubers because no one coordinated.

Followed by getting refused entry at a club for being too drunk.

Followed by offering to sleep with the bouncers and getting humiliatingly rejected in front of a long queue of people wearing designer clothes.

Followed by getting home en masse and binge-ordering leopard print maxi dresses from ASOS that will need returning but will never be returned.

Followed by burning sausages under the grill (kitchen fire optional).

Followed by group-passing out in my room because it is slightly bigger than Eva's.

Followed by three hours of sleep and then hangover fear

so bad that picking at the dried-out, charred sausages to block out all feelings seems like a good idea. And because there is nothing else to eat.

But now, because I am turning thirty, it has apparently been decided that I am too old for fun any more. Now we must be *adults* who eat *food*. And there aren't even any sausage options on this menu.

So that is why I'm thinking about going to see a man about some sad comfort-sex. And come on, there must be someone.

Correction: there must be someone *who is not him*. Surely there is more than one option?

But there is not. There is only one person: TD.

I loathe him, I *loathe* him. But at least it would be easy. He will be free, he will put it in me without much fuss and then he will scratch my back afterwards. I will hate myself enormously afterwards, of course, but what other option is there? Yes, I could go on Tinder right now and find a shiny new man to do it with. That part would be easy, but, oh the *effort* of getting naked with someone new.

Plus, I'm feeling very insecure about my vagina after my smear test last week. I had an idea in my head – since I'd had it done once before and was obviously therefore an expert – that I would be very cool and laid back and, I don't know, *French* this time round. I would casually whip off my cigarette leg trousers (v French) and be like HERE IS MY VAGINA, DO WHAT YOU WILL. But then I got into the nurse's room and climbed up on the bed – immediately ripping the thin tissue paper with my sweaty buttocks – and was suddenly seized with panic about my socks. Like, I know you don't wear socks for sex, but a smear test isn't sex, is it? Don't answer – I know that for a fact.

So, I kept them on but suddenly felt very silly. I was also very aware of my hairy legs. I was worried the nurse might be offended I'd made no effort before getting naked for her. Then she got down there with her scalpel (I know it's not a scalpel but come on, it feels like it is a scalpel) and muttered, 'It's too small'.

And lads, I was momentarily DELIGHTED with my tiny vagina. My vagina, that is too small for inspection. Too small for insertion. So small it is basically sewn up! No wonder I never get any sex – it's because men sense I am too charmingly delicate down there.

Then the nurse spoke again, tutting as she declared, 'Yes, it's too small, I need a bigger one. I'm not sure they do them any bigger though?' And I realised it was not my vagina that was a tiny fragile flower, but the device. My vagina was, in fact, a giant gaping monster. A wide, pink cave that eats speculums for breakfast.

And so.

You understand.

Right now, it's my ex-boyfriend, Twat Dan, or no one.

The waiter passes my chair and I swipe at him, catching a fistful of shirt sleeve.

'Three more double gins just for me,' I hiss, and when he looks appalled, I smile blankly, adding, 'And four shots of tequila please.'

I watch him glide towards the door and I blink hard several times, hoping I can magically make Eva walk in.

Where is she? I miss her so much suddenly. She's my best friend and my flatmate, it's her actual job to be here first, holding flowers or something. She texted an hour ago to say she would be a little late but had 'a big surprise'. And she used a bunch of emojis she specifically knows amuse me – the octopus will always do it for me – so I expect she's been picking up my present. Late as ever. Late as Eva.

I kinda hope the present is a taxi away from here.

The waiter is back, and he lines up my drinks judgementally before me. Amelia barks *cheers* nervously across the table and I grin at her as I do the first shot. The warmth of the liquid coats my throat but the rest of me feels cold. I do another one. If I have to be thirty and if I have to be here, eating like a cheat, then I'm at least going to make sure I get really, really drunk.

'Can I have one?' my brother Mark asks, leaning across from his seat on my right.

'Get your own,' I mutter belligerently, and he raises an eyebrow as I pound my second shot.

My brain begins to swim nicely as I stare broodily at the door.

And finally, she is here. I smile widely as Eva walks in, jumping up and scraping my chair loudly across the floor.

Ooh, I'm drunker than I realised.

Eva is here! Yessss, Eva is h … Oh fucking what! She's brought *Jeremy*. Ugh, yuck, *Jeremy*. Why did she need to bring him, he is awful, I hate him so much. Nobody used to bring partners for our sticky nights out, and now – look around – it's a sea of beige boyfriends and even beiger husbands as far as the eye can see.

Eva and Jeremy have only been dating for seven months, but Eva's, like, obsessed with him. I don't get it, he's so dull. I do not understand why she's chosen *him* over me. She's fully replaced me in every aspect. She's even replaced me in her Facebook profile photo, which was, until recently, a picture of us cross-eyed drunk from our holiday to Cornwall last year. Right after that picture was taken, we decided Justin Trudeau was in the same bar as us, so we spent the whole night following him around until he told us to shag off in a very distinctive Cornish accent and we realised it probably wasn't him. Now her profile picture is of her and Jeremy from last Halloween. I have been literally replaced.

I hate Jeremy.

'Alice!' Eva screams, throwing her arms around me, 'Happy birthday!' She hands me a gift bag and a very large helium balloon that says 'Birthday Wanker' on it.

OK, that is a great surprise, well worth waiting for. Things are looking up at last.

'I missed you so much, Eva, it was rubbish here without you.' I sigh into her coat.

'Rude,' Mark mutters good-naturedly beside me, but we both ignore him.

'I'm sorry Al, I had to stop off after work to get the balloon. I brought it on the tube and these middle-aged white people glared at me the entire length of the Piccadilly Line.' She giggles, delighted. Jeremy leans over, interrupting our moment, and I fight the urge to scowl at him.

'Happy thirtieth, Alice, are you having fun?' He smiles and it is such a boring smile. It's the only way to describe it: boring. Even the adjective I choose for him most is a boring one: boring. Bleugh. I nod vaguely and pick my drink up from the table, taking a large gulp. My head is starting to swim. I wave at the disapproving waiter, gesturing for him to come over.

'Yep, loads of fun, thanks for coming, Jeremy . . .' even though you weren't invited, you fish-faced weasel, '. . . let's get the two of you drinks.' I pound another shot. 'I'm already well on my way to being wasted. You'll have to do some doubles to catch up.'

'Hum, well, actually Al,' Eva puts her hand on my arm and looks at Jeremy, who gives her one of those coupley supportive nods.

Fuck you Jeremy, Eva and I used to have a secret language too.

She looks back at me, and shifts the weight from one foot to the other, awkwardly. 'Please don't be annoyed, Al, but I'm not going to drink alcohol tonight.'

'What!' I say too loudly, outraged.

I catch Mark rolling his eyes beside us and Amelia barking a laugh. 'But you have to drink,' I say lowering my voice, but still distraught. 'It's my thirtieth birthday, Eva! I know that last hangover was awful and I'm not saying you should get so bad you puke on a gravestone again, but just start your sober thing from tomorrow or whatever.'

Eva pulls me away from the table and the Birthday Wanker balloon hits Jeremy in the face. I smirk as she pulls me out into the hallway.

'Listen Al, you know I said I had a surprise?' she says breathily.

'I thought the balloon was my surprise?' I say, giving the string a pleasing yank.

She laughs but it has the edge of hysteria to it. 'No, Al, it's . . . I can't believe I'm saying this, but . . .' she trails off. I shake my head, and later, when I think back to this moment, I cannot believe I was so unprepared.

'Alice . . . I'm pregnant.'

I wait.

Pregnant with what? Anticipation? Pregnant with the evening's possibilities? Because of course she cannot mean she is pregnant with child. No sir, that is not an option.

We stare at each other.

She giggles. 'Alice, I am pregnant. *I'm pregnant.*'

Again, my brain searches for an alternative meaning. She can't be *pregnant.* That is impossible. Ridiculous, silly. No no no. That's not what the plan is. Not now. Not yet. Not with fucking Jeremy. We were going to wait until we were both forty and dicked-out, and then she was going to marry her old neighbour, Reuben, and I was going to marry Adam from Year Nine. We hadn't even made a plan for the kids part. It seemed so far off and unlikely.

Not Jeremy. Not now.

I am lost for words. I don't understand how this can be right, how this could have happened.

Something in the pit of my stomach aches.

The silence goes on a beat too long before I can muster a smile.

'Wow, Eva!' I try to say as genuinely as I can. 'That's so . . . exciting! Is it . . . um. You're . . . keeping it?'

She giggles. 'Honestly Al, I don't think your Uber rating could take another trip back from a Marie Stopes clinic.'

I have not been able to get above a 3.5 since I escorted Eva home from that abortion, four years ago. The driver was deeply unimpressed with our backseat conversation, particularly the part where I said that our trip was 'at least proof she'd been getting some'.

'Wow!' I say again, as enthusiastically as possible, adding quietly, 'Oh my God, I can't believe it.'

'Neither can I,' she says a little shakily. 'It wasn't planned, and I know we haven't even been together that long, but I don't know . . . It sounds weird, but I'm . . . I'm happy.' I look at her properly and she does indeed look happy. She is bright and shiny in a way I haven't seen before. She keeps going. 'I know it's out of the blue, but you know how I feel about Jeremy. I'm in shock, I am, but I swear, we're both really happy.' She pauses. 'I know this wasn't the plan, Al, but he's The One, and he's going to make the best daddy ever . . .' The sentence chokes her up, and it chokes me too, as I remember the last time I heard Eva say 'daddy' – in reference to a hairy older man she wanted to get off with.

We both swallow hard as she keeps going, '. . . And when we had the scan this morning Al, and I heard that tiny heartbeat, I can't . . . I don't even know how to describe the feeling . . .'

I interrupt her. 'Wait, what, the scan?' I am puzzled. 'Why would you have the scan so early?'

'Oh,' she smiles wide. 'It wasn't early. It was the three-month scan. That's why we can finally tell people!'

My head spins. Three months. Three months?! She's kept this from me all this time? For months? She has kept this thing inside her, literally and emotionally, for weeks and weeks and weeks. Was she *pretending* to drink all those times we've been out? When she vomited on a grave, was that all a morning-sickness-related LIE? Every day we chatted and texted and FaceTimed, she didn't say a word. Eva and I have never hidden anything from each other, ever. I know everything. Every single thing.

But not any more, apparently. Not only has she gone off and taken a giant step without me, she's done it behind my back. She and Jeremy are having a baby, and that means they have a private, secret life that I'm not allowed into. The stomach ache becomes a tight ball of pain.

I can feel tears stinging my eyes, and she takes my emotional display to be a good sign, hugging me as Amelia approaches.

'Eva!' Amelia barks happily, as my best friend, who's been

keeping this secret for months, whispers in my ear, 'Don't say anything to anyone, I want to tell them!'

She and Amelia bustle off conspiratorially, and I stand there for a few more seconds. I don't know what to think, I can't believe it. I mean, of course I'm happy for her. Of course I am! Aren't I? I mean, if I wasn't happy for her that would make me a Full Monster and I'm not Full Monster, am I?

Yes, I'm happy for her! She's happy, so I'm happy. Everyone around me is having babies and getting married and bringing their husbands whose names I don't know to my birthday dinner and having lives and moving on and I am totally, absolutely, completely happy for everyone.

Happy happy happy.

I look down at my hands and they're shaking a bit. All the information jumbles around my brain like a washing machine.

Eva and Jeremy are having a baby. Eva didn't tell me. Jeremy will now be around forever. Even if they break up – which obviously they will at some point because they're so wrong for each other – he is going to be in our lives for good. He's going to be the dad to Eva's child. Eva's going to have a child.

Then the rest of it hits me: Shit, I'm going to have to move out. It's Eva's flat – her parents own it – and she'll want it for her, Jeremy and the baby. After eight years of living together, Eva will throw me out, to make room for her new family. Her new gang, which I'm not a part of.

Fucking hell.

I knew everything was going to change when I turned thirty, but I thought it would be more along the lines of hand wrinkles and body confidence. Instead, I've lost my best friend and my home all in the space of a few minutes.

I feel so lost, standing there at the edge of my own birthday party, and a sudden intense longing for my bed overwhelms me. I wish I was there right now. I wish I was under my duvet armed with a five-pack of Creme Eggs.

The thought makes a single tear dramatically roll down my face. It's my birthday and it's such a small want, but I can't even have that.

Fuck this, I'm texting TD.

Dan Heam – also known as Twat Dan or TD – and I have been on/off for the last four years. I say on/off, but he 'doesn't really like labels' so we were never really officially 'on' or properly together. Even though of course we were! We were mad about each other at one point. I know he loved me and I know I was his girlfriend. Nobody else really understood our relationship, but I did, and he did. We got it. It was us against the world. And there were times it was so good. So good. And also bad. But that's any relationship, isn't it?

Either way, we are definitely off right now. Except I keep sleeping with him because I'm an idiot and I hate myself. There's no point trying to fight it though. I am who I am. And that person is an idiot with no self-control or willpower.

'You awgknf?' I type. Shit, I'm a bit blurry with the emotion, and also probably all the shots.

I try again: **'You around?'**

His reply is instant: **'Yep cum over.'**

Not even a question, just a command. Twelve characters of non-affection. He didn't even invest the effort it takes to write 'come' properly. Because obviously an 'o' and an 'e' require so much more time and care. Maybe if he'd added a comma after 'Yep', maybe I could've seen some kind of yearning in that, some kind of sign of love. Commas are on the other keyboard, so that would've signalled intention and interest.

But no. I cannot find any evidence of actual effort.

14

God, I hate him and his presumption – as if I am powerless to his demands! As if I will obviously do what he says, without question!

And, OK, fine, yes I will come/cum over. But not yet because I have *some* dignity! And also, I need to eat dinner, which is just coming around now.

An hour and a half later and I am sitting under the table. I can hear Slutty Sarah stage-whispering about 'attention-seeking' but she can bloody talk. Who even uses the word slut any more? No one, that's who. It's an awful nickname but she insists we keep using it. We've tried casually calling her just 'Sarah' – we've even tried to explain how sexist the word 'slutty' is – but she is adamant. She made a speech about empowerment and reclaiming words but everyone knows that is all patriarchy double-agent bullshit, she's doing it for the shock value and because she thinks it's funny when she introduces herself to new people and in-laws.

Anyway, I don't care if everyone – even Slutty Sarah with her nipple-ring party trick – is judging me. I'm drunk, it's my birthday, I've lost my best friend and I have nowhere to live. I have a right to throw a tantrum and hide under a table.

Obviously I would hide in the loo, but then people might not notice I'm throwing a tantrum?

The legs wobble around me as Mark lifts the table cloth and climbs under to join me.

'Feeling a bit sorry for yourself, are you?' he says nicely, as he plops himself down. 'What is it?' he says patiently.

I sigh. 'Everything is changing around me, Mark. Why is everyone else doing stuff with their lives? What's wrong with keeping everything the same? What's wrong with staying put for ever?'

He looks at me hard. 'You haven't texted TD have you, Al?'

'No,' I lie, hating how well my big brother knows me.

'Give me your phone, Al, I'm not letting you do it,' he says, hand out.

'You are not the boss of me,' I shout-slur. 'I can texcht TD if I wanch. You dunt tell me what to do. I'll text him whenever I want, I'll do it right now.'

I pointedly pull out my phone and squint at it.

'Don't, Alice,' Mark says, a warning in his voice

I exaggeratedly pull up a new message, and begin typing elaborately.

'You . . . are a dickhead . . .' I write, reading it out loud as I tap. **'I've wasted all my best years on you. But I still want to hump your stupid brains out just to prove a point to my dumb brother. Even though your penis has a weird bend in it that like hurts my kidneys.'**

Mark sighs loudly. 'Fine, great message, send it.'

He is calling my bluff, which he shouldn't do when I'm this drunk.

'I will send it,' I say, waiting for him to take my phone.

He doesn't.

'FINE,' I say louder and scroll through my contacts for TD's name.

'SEND,' I shout, fake pressing it, but – in my blurry state – actually sending it.

Shit.

Oh well. I've sent worse to TD. I'll still probably go back to his in few minutes. If I can just stand up.

Mark only examines his cuticles in response. 'Are you done fake texting morons?' he says.

'No, I actually sent it. Look,' I say shoving my phone at his face, proudly. He rolls his eyes again but nonetheless examines the message. Then looks again.

'Who is Tony Danes?' he asks, confused.

'What?' I say, puzzled.

I take the phone back. No, no, no. I can't have. NO NO NO. I haven't? I can't have? How have I . . .? Oh God oh God OH GOD NO.

'Who is Tony?' Mark asks again, louder, clocking the horror on my face.

'My boss,' I say in a tiny voice.

He snorts, and then looks awkward. 'Oh, Alice.'

I reach for the tablecloth. I need to get out from under this table and fix this. I can fix this, can't I?

I quickly try to stand but in my panic I misjudge the distance and fall backwards.

The noise is loud and unfamiliar. It takes me a hazy second to realise I have pulled the cloth off and am lying tangled in a sea of white table, surrounded by broken glass and plates, bits of leftover birthday food in my lap. Mark is standing above me looking mortified.

The silence in the room is deafening and I remain seated in the centre of it, still and numb. All these plus ones I don't know stare down at me pityingly. Look at the drunk thirty-year-old making a fool of herself, yet again.

Single. Alone. Pathetic. Birthday cake on her foot.

Eva's lovely worried face fills my vision, and horror fills me as she takes my hand and I slowly stagger to my feet.

'Are you all right, Alice? Are you bleeding?' she asks me kindly. Too kindly. The humiliation burns as I try to laugh, shaking my head, and trying not to burst into tears.

'Shall we go to the loo and get you cleaned up?' Eva says in a low voice, holding my hand as the waiter arrives through the door. He stops short, appalled at the mess in the middle of the room.

'I'm so sorry,' I whisper in his direction, the crushing weight of shame burrowing deep into me. I can feel everyone's eyes still on me.

Behind Eva's shoulder, Mark is staring at his phone, his face lit up by a message he's reading. He doesn't look embarrassed any more, he looks frightened. This isn't about my night turning into a nightmare, this is something else. His grip is white, his knuckles almost yellow, as he makes eye contact with me. The mess around me and the alcohol and the burning humiliation is suddenly a long way away.

'Alice.' Mark is pale and sweaty as he reaches for me. 'It's Mum – she says Steven's in hospital. It's really bad.'

Los Angeles

2

20 April – 6.43 p.m.

Welcome to my new travel blog, dream chasers,

Apologies for my blog post earlier today. It was prematurely published because of a fault in the system and not because I pressed publish without thinking. And I do not totally understand how this website works, so I don't know how to take it down. While I work this out, please may I ask you not to read that one and please do read this one instead. Ignore what was said about toast crumbs in butter, that was stupid.

So, assuming you are doing what I have asked, let me now introduce myself to you. My name is Alice Edwards and I have quit my very important job and my really fulfilling life back in the UK to spend the next three months travelling the world. I shall be going to many original places like LA and Thailand and many other brilliant places that I haven't decided on yet because I am an incredibly spontaneous person. I will be out here all on my own, as I feel that is important for my spiritual journey, which some have called brave, but is simply what I must do. I have just landed in Los Angeles, known as the Sunshine State, and it is really, really nice. The sea outside the plane window is blue like a gleaming sapphire and the sand is pure white and soft like an expensive M&S pillow.

So far, my new friends, I have only been here in this sunshine state for a few minutes, but I can already feel the bohemian, relaxed vibe changing my very soul. I will be staying briefly with my actor friend Isabelle and then on to other adventurous adventures.

Goodbye for now, my new friends. I have many more roads to travel, many beaten paths to get off, and I will share it all with you, if you will join me here. I shall end my very first blog post (apart from the other one, which again, please don't read), with a famous quote that I feel is very apt here:

'A journey of a thousand miles must begin with a single step.' Sir Charles Dickens.

PS. If I get murdered, please don't let the *Mirror* use any Facebook photos pre-2012.

#PleaseDon'tReadTheOtherBlog #TravelBlogger #Travels #Travelling #Wanderer #GoneAWOL #AliceEdwardsBlog #OffTheBeatenTrack #BloggerLife #Blessed #Brave #Dream-Chaser #ComingBackWithATan #ConstanceBeaumontWannabe

5 Comments · 3 AWOLs · 2 Super Likes

COMMENTS

Karen Gill
| You'll be grand, but mammy says she's got dibs on the Irish *Sun* if you do get kidnapped or wot not.

Eva Slate
| I'm counting down the daze until you return. Feeling v v dazed already honestly :(

Danny Boy UrMum

| UR FAT AND NO 1 CARES

> **AWOL MODERATOR**
> **Replying to Danny Boy UrMum**
> | We know it's just bantz, but please be respectful to our users :) I'm here if you fancy chatting more or want to chill. Luke

> **Danny Boy UrMum**
> **Replying to AWOL MODERATOR**
> | fuck off luke

I step off the plane looking like absolute horse manure. I'm starting my LA adventure feeling like I've been kicked for half a day – because I literally have. After more than eleven hours in the air, we then sat on the tarmac for another hour, waiting to be allowed off the sweatbox tin plane. I've had no sleep and the guy sitting behind me spent the whole journey kicking the back of my seat.

I say *guy*, but I actually do mean tiny, tiny child – which I found out around hour seven, when I finally lost my mind and started swearing in every direction and shrieking that I would aim my vomit across the whole row behind me if they didn't 'fucking chill'. It was only when I made eye contact with the crying three-year-old responsible for my discomfort that I calmed down.

Those last five hours went really slowly, I can tell you.

Either way, I'm finally here, and the buzz of the airport and the early evening heat on my face is slowly starting to invigorate me.

I can't believe I'm actually in California.

Honestly, it's been a weird few weeks. After *that* night – my thirtieth – I woke up with the worst hangover I'd ever had, and a terrible case of the paranoias.

Except, it's not paranoia if you really have ruined everything, is it? Everything about the night before was hazy but I knew a lot of bad shit had gone down. It took me a full hour to even look at my phone, knowing the awfulness that would be waiting for me.

There were, predictably, a string of WhatsApps from Eva asking if I was OK and to come into her room when I was awake. There was also a 3 a.m. message from Slutty Sarah asking where I was. Another one was from Amelia asking why I kept barking like a dog at her. There were also a few missed calls and voicemails from Mark and my sister Hannah. And – most horrifyingly – an awkward couple of emails from my boss, Tony.

Ex-boss, I should say.

I can't even think about it, it's too mortifying.

So, being the adult I am, I hid in my room for another four hours straight, before I finally rang my brother back. I asked after our stepdad, Steven, and I knew it was bad because he was actually really nice to me. He told me not to worry about anything and just get some food in my belly. He carefully mentioned that he'd booked his flight to Australia to see Mum and Steven, and that he was stable for now, but he didn't ask if I wanted to go with him. Thankfully.

I know it sounds heartless, but I couldn't face any of it, it's too much.

Then I crossed the hall and got into bed with Eva, where she just stroked my head and asked if I wanted her to put *Saturday Night Takeaway* on from the planner, so I could watch 'Anton Du Beke' – which is what she thinks Ant and Dec are called. She also thinks they're brothers, but so does everyone, right?

Eva is so clever in lots of ways – she's a corporate lawyer and she went to one of the best universities in the country – but she's also the dumbest person I know. Her family are super rich and she grew up in the poshest area of Surrey, where there are six-foot metal gates and golf courses everywhere. She didn't get drunk or even watch any telly until she was about eighteen because she was too busy riding horses, hanging out with princes, and, like, learning the rules to water polo (I don't know? What do rich people do with their time?). She's not an arsehole about it though, she's really generous and lovely. She's just sheltered, y'know? And it meant when we met at work – aged twenty-two – I got to corrupt her.

We watched telly together in bed like that for ages, while I wondered what the hell I was going to do with my life. I'd lost my job, I had to move out, and ... well, all the Mum and Steven stuff I couldn't even let myself think about. I was feeling so weird and alone and confused, absent-mindedly scrolling through my apps – and then I found the note on my phone.

It was addressed to 'Future Alice from Drunk Alice', which I must've written when I was in the taxi, crying all the way home.

It was long and incoherent, but it was actually super wise – if you discount all the messy typos and segues into *Friends* episode critiques. Basically, Drunk Alice was telling Future Alice that her awful night needed to be a wake-up call; that it was time to change her/my life. I couldn't keep bumbling through, waiting for stuff to happen. I needed to figure out what I was going to do, find my own path without relying on

Eva and Mark – and stop messing around with TD. I had to find my own answers and change everything. Throw my life up in the air and see where it landed.

The important part went like this:

It is timed to figggure ooout <u>WHO YOU R</u> and also <u>FIND TE FUN.</u> When was the last time you had fun??? When did you last let yourself have an adventure? You are so stuck in this rut, pretending to be happy – but are you actually happy? What is happiness to you anyway? Is this everything existence has to offer? Shouldn't you be asking for more? Wat r u actually DOING WITH your life?? No friends, no job, no boyf, ducked up family. You need to change everything. start agin. Go travelllin!! Go and run around for a year like Forrrest Gump (might get free trainers?????? Get more followers on socel media??? Can I post on Instagrm and run at same time???). You could Climb a mountain! Sale around the world in TEN DAYS???? Is that posibl? Buy drugs, take drugs. Hve sex with LOTS more people or like lits anyone. U need 2 be more lik constance. Go find the joy.

<u>INSPIRATION BRainstorme:</u>
-BARE GRYLLS
-DAVID ATTENBRUH
-BLOGGER CONSTANCE BEAUMONT
-BUY DRY SHAMPOO AND ALSO BREAD BECOS YOU NEED BREAD

<u>MOOD BOARD:</u>
-dchbjvdhhvdwch

Which is when I think I must've fallen asleep in the taxi.

It was mostly silly nonsense, but, bizarre as it sounds, I was inspired by Drunk Alice's enthusiasm. She gets me in a lot of trouble but I know she only wants the best for me. And

I knew she was right. I had to change things. Of course I did. Everyone else around me was moving on, having babies, getting married; ticking off the life goals you're supposed to. Why was I the only one who hadn't figured things out yet? Don't I deserve to be happy? Happiness comes so easily to everyone else, why haven't I pinned it down yet? And, knowing how unhappy I am, why have I been so set on staying in this one place; so determined nothing can ever change? It was time to choose something else. And either way, I couldn't stay there, getting left further and further behind.

I spent that whole next day thinking and thinking. I thought about everything that was going on, and everything hanging over me. I thought about the rut I was being forced out of by other people changing their lives around me. I thought about how it was time to take control of my own life.

And so I went online and I booked my flights to LA. It was an impulse decision but for the first time in ages, I felt *excited* about my life. Everything seemed clearer and more hopeful. I even deleted Facebook! Well, I mean I didn't *delete* it because I'm not a fucking idiot, but I'm not really looking at it that much any more. I've started a blog on AWOL.com instead, so I can be like those cool chicks online, being spontaneous and happy.

I'm evolving, you guys.

So yes, coming to LA is the first leg in a three-part plan for changing my life.

Firstly: fun. I plan on spending my time here laughing and having as many silly adventures as possible. I want to sunbathe and party and chase celebrities around in circles – it will be as shallow and mindless as possible. I want to find the joy here; that's the plan for this section of my trip.

After some mindlessness in LA, I'll give the mindFULness

thing a go, with a month in Asia. There will be hostels and backpacking, because that's how a person finds themselves, right? By not showering for a month and crying themselves to sleep on a cement mattress?

After that, I'm going to take a third, spontaneous adventure somewhere else. I haven't decided on that bit yet. Maybe I'll get on a sailboat for a month. Maybe I'll climb a mountain. Maybe I'll become a scuba diving instructor. I'm leaving it up to fate to decide where I end up for the third part of this trip.

Fate, or Lastminute.com.

The idea is: three trips to change my life. Just like Elizabeth Gilbert in *Eat, Pray, Love*. But not enough like her to, say, get sued.

I've never done anything like this before and I'm so scared and nervous.

But excited.

Obviously none of this is coming cheap, but I've decided to use the money I got when my granddad died last year. I had planned to put it towards a deposit on a house one day, but since I'm only a temp (and now not even that), I couldn't get a mortgage that would cover even a broom cupboard in London. So I figured I might as well spend it running around the world, making memories and changing my life.

I officially gave Eva a month's notice on the flat. She protested weakly, but we both knew she'd need me out soon anyway, what with Jeremy and The Foetus moving in. But she couldn't believe it when I said I was going travelling for a few months. Mark was really shocked, too. They both kept saying they couldn't picture it. Mark said I'd give up and be back within the week and Eva said nicely that she'd keep my room empty just in case.

I get why they were both so surprised. Because the thing

is, I'm not really a travelling type of person. At least, I never thought I was. Because I have always had a very specific idea of those *types* of people, and it just isn't me. Travelling Types are naturally thin, tanned and don't need to wear make-up. They wear denim hotpants like they are comfortable and don't cause chub rub. Travelling types just naturally wake up in the morning without an alarm clock on their phone. Actually, they don't even have a phone because they are too free-spirited. Or maybe they just have one of those Nokia 3210s because they're retro and ironic, and don't have the internet. Because Travelling Types don't worry about the internet. They're secure enough in themselves without the validation of strangers. But at the same time, they make friends easily, with, like, the guy sitting opposite them on a train. They have hair that doesn't need 'doing' and they don't get too tired to do anything after 9.30 p.m. They like sunsets and they're not afraid of the ocean. They like all different kinds of food and don't need to know exactly what is in this dish and who made it and did they wash their hands properly. They don't get travel sick. They don't write bin collection dates on their calendar or get excited because Boots are doubling their Advantage Card points this month. They are laid back and spontaneous and go-with-the-flow.

And, see, I am none of those things.

Plus, my massive, speculum-eating vagina would consume denim hotpants in one bite.

Genuinely, my body isn't built for spontaneity. I need to be wearing the right underwear for spontaneity. I can't just take off running in some new direction – not without wearing at least three sports bras. And my back rolls are made – and I say this with genuine fondness – for fetish websites, not string bikinis that disappear into my folds. My hair gets frizzy in heat and if mosquitoes were on Tinder I would finally be a guaranteed right swipe. I burn and boil and sizzle like bacon in the sun.

Now, don't get me wrong, I love a normal holiday – lying on a beach in Tenerife for seven hours straight, not realising I have burnt immediately, then spending six full days in the shade complaining about the sun. Taking eight hundred filtered selfies in sunglasses that all look the same. Drinking weird-coloured cocktails with umbrellas and screaming 'EYES EYES EYES' at Eva when we do a cheers.

But *travelling* is different. It's where you're supposed to become one with the world. Where you learn about and embrace exotic new cultures. Where you try and speak the language and eat deep-fried spiders. None of it has ever appealed to me.

But I'm going to try.

I've spent the past couple of weeks immersing myself in the travel-y internet, researching places and things to do, staring at photos on travel agent websites and ordering every single thing Amazon Prime recommended – including an oddly tall rucksack with seven hundred buckles, and a mosquito net that could realistically cover an entire four-poster bed.

I've even been to my GP to ask about jabs! But then failed to get them because you have to do them all a hundred years in advance. Adulting fail, but oh well.

I've become obsessed with travel blogs, and Constance Beaumont's blog, in particular. She makes it all look so serene and laid back and sunny, with her beachy waves and seamless tan. She's got it sussed, so why can't I? I can't wait to be just like her. That's what I'm doing with my AWOL blog. I want it to be just as deep and cool as hers.

Actually, she's the reason I've decided to make LA my first

stop. She was blogging from Venice Beach recently, using words like 'bohemian' and 'quirky', which sold it for me because I have a bunch of floaty skirts and off-the-shoulder tops that sound like they will be perfect for that kind of place. The photos all looked so lush and there were topless men on scooters everywhere. I am here for all of that. And here I literally am, just a few weeks later. Five and a half thousand miles away from my life and my flatshare in London. A life and a flatshare that isn't even mine any more.

And I couldn't be more ready for it.

3

AWOL.COM/Alice Edwards' Travel Blog: Living My Dream and Feeling Very #Blessed

20 April – 8.13 p.m.

Good evening, dream chasers,

I have just arrived back at my friend Isabelle's luxury apartment here in the Sunshine State of LA. She picked me up from the airport in a limo, and we enjoyed champagne in the perfectly regulated air-con, as we drove back to her incredibly impressive home in Santa Monica.

She is the very same Isabelle I remember from the UK. But – if it is possible – she is even more serene and wise with the benefit of a little age. I can confirm she has not been changed by her huge success in the movie business, despite admitting – when I pressed her – that she now knows Leonardo DiCaprio!! I feel confident we are going to get on very well during my stay with her.

All in all, it has been a wondrous first few hours here, and we are about to don our best attire and hit the hottest bar LA has to offer.

Oh, also, sorry about that picture I just uploaded. We drove past Owen Wilson and I was trying to get a photo and share an insight into this world I now inhabit. But I don't understand about re-sizing so it came out upside down and too large. I don't know how to delete, so please just ignore it.

All my love and peace to you all,

Alice x

1 Comments · 0 AWOLs · 1 Super Likes

COMMENTS:

Karen Gill

| I'm staying up for the jet lag craic to set in, then you'll be less smug.

Hoiking my massive backpack further up my shoulders, I am swimming in sweat by the time I finally spot Isabelle across the car park.

Sweating: another thing Travelling Types don't do.

She's picked the furthest away spot and I trip over myself as I pick up speed to reach her. I'm feeling hot and cross, like some kind of Easter bun.

'Hello!' I shout jovially from a distance, trying to communicate that I need help with my bag. She waves back, but doesn't move, and I almost stop in my tracks as I take in how different she looks. She's platinum blonde, dressed head-to-toe in yoga gear, and even from twenty feet away, I can make out the tight sheen of a face full of Botox. She looks good, don't get me wrong, but very . . . different.

Isabelle was our family's neighbour when we were little, and the pair of us were quite close until we started secondary school. That was when she – a brunette back then – turned into an uppity heinous bitch just because Karen with the cool Irish accent started paying attention to her. The two of us didn't speak for, like, five years, but then we reunited in sixth form, which is around the age you realise uppity bitches can be brilliant. After that, Isabelle, Karen and I were pretty close – along with Amelia and Slutty Sarah from our year – until Isy moved to the US about eight years ago. That was around when I met Eva while I was temping for her legal firm and we moved in together. I can't believe how long ago that is now. And how much has changed, and maybe no one more so than Isy.

Anyway, when I told her I was coming over to LA for a while, she got super excited and insisted I stay with her for the first week. Which sounded really generous in theory, but then she casually mentioned that she'd need me to pay rent and was quite specific that I'd have to move out after a week because she needed the space back to use as her dressing room.

I love her, but there's always small print with Isabelle.

'Where's your car?' I huff, out of breath when I finally reach her.

She waves at something odd-looking beside her.

'It's a hybrid?' she says, climbing in and pressing buttons. I open the passenger side, throwing my giant bag in and climbing in after it. The plastic-y floor quivers under my weight.

Isy continues, speaking in her delightful new upspeak accent. 'I paid double because I care about the environment? But also because it used to belong to Leonardo DiCaprio? You're sitting where Leo would've banged at least a half dozen blonde twenty-year-olds?'

'Is that why it smells weird in here?' I say, crinkling my nose.

'No, that's probably the gem-infused protection mist I've sprayed everywhere?' she says, nodding authoritatively. 'It is a psychic vampire repellent, to stop any bad energy infecting my aura?'

'Um . . .' I have nowhere to go with this and yet I am over-whelmed with questions.

She continues smoothly. 'I'm a subscriber to the life-style website Gloop. They talk a lot about the importance of staying on top of these things because there are so many people around here who want to suck away your life energy.'

We pause at traffic lights and a man who looks like Owen Wilson crosses in front of us, stopping in the road to flash us. Isy doesn't react.

'Wait,' I say, pausing in the act of taking a picture. 'Did you say Gloop? Do you mean *Goop*?'

Isy tuts. 'Gloop is way better than Goop and far more open to alternative medicines? Like the regular at-home coffee enemas they recommend? I'm detoxifying while also stopping myself getting any and all cancers ever?'

'By squirting coffee up your anus,' I mutter, deliberately without a question mark.

'I'll send you some links?' she says, her face unmoving.

'Fantastic!' I reply, enthusiastically, waving cheerfully at Owen Wilson still in the road. The vampire repellent doesn't seem to be working.

Isy lives in a three-bed flat share in Santa Monica and as she unlocks the door and pulls me inside, still not helping with my bags at any point, she tells me there's a pool in the complex.

But – she adds superciliously – she doesn't ever use it because it's 'full of actors with fake pecs'. Which, conversely, is the exact reason I want to check it out.

'Aren't you an actor?' I say, confused.

She waves her hand dismissively at me because I clearly just don't *get it*.

'Yeah, but I'm a *proper* actor,' she explains, rolling her eyes. 'I'm a stage actor. They do adverts and shit like that. That's why I used air quotes when I said actors.'

'Aha,' I say, nodding my head, resisting the urge to point out that she definitely didn't do any air quotes and does she actually know what they are. Usually I love pointing out Isy's pretention, but I'm too tired right now.

It's a small, sparsely decorated apartment, and as she shows me round, Isy keeps shouting the words 'rent control' at me. I don't know what it means, but my noughties telly brainwashing remembers it as the reason Monica had that really huge place in New York. I still don't get how they were allowed a monkey though.

I have a whole entire room to myself, which is nice because I was expecting a sofabed at best. And there's a handy little washbasin in there, that I plan to use as a tall bidet, don't tell Isy.

'OK!' she says suddenly, clapping her hands. 'Dump that bag in your room, change into something nicer and let's go.'

Go? Oh God, we're going out?

I nod enthusiastically, determined to be fun, even if it kills me. And it might? I got no sleep on the plane and it must be close to 5 a.m. in the UK by now. I briefly wonder how long it will be before I stop translating US time, and then I wonder if I should be bothered by that 'change into something nicer' comment. But Isy's already moved on. My jet lag has me existing in a universe about a minute behind real time.

'We're hitting up Chateau Marmont,' she says, already picking up her handbag.

'Chateau Marmont!' I say, as jovially as I can. 'Wow, even I've heard of that place. A-list celebs love it, right?' I pause. 'Is that nearby then?'

'Yep!' she says cheerfully, then pulls a face. 'Well, no, not technically. It's about a half-hour drive from here, but it's really glam and you'll love it! Plus, it's just where I have to be *seen*, y'know? For work?'

'Gotcha,' I say, even though I don't gotch anything, and obediently go change.

'Oh my God, be cool, but that's Brad Pitt over there,' Isy is saying an hour later, as we arrive at the glitzy restaurant-bar in Hollywood. She is barely containing her own un-coolness as she nods over my shoulder.

Fucking hell, Brad Pitt! On my first night in LA! I can't believe this, it is *so* . . . nope, that's not Brad Pitt. Not even close.

'Isy,' I sigh. 'I may be jet-lagged to buggery, but I'm pretty sure that is in no way Brad Pitt.'

'It definitely is,' she insists, 'and I would know because he auditioned for a movie in a room near me one time.'

I cock my head at her, waiting, and she adds quietly, 'Not at the same time.' She glances over again and this time she fully squeals.

Several super cool fellow patrons look over judgementally.

She leans in, trying to compose herself as she hisses, 'And shitting hell, Alice, that is Jennifer Aniston with him. I'm not kidding, it's Brad and Jen, back together at long last. The press is going to have a field day with this! They're going to want to interview me! You can see the chemistry between them from over here. I'm totally calling TMZ.'

I turn around and squint at the pair in question properly. There is no doubt at all. It's definitely not Brad and it's definitely not Jen. It is, in fact, two men in their mid-thirties, who are sipping wine and having a quiet chat by the bar.

'Isy,' I say slowly, trying not to slap her in the face. 'I am a thousand per cent sure it's not either of them. There is zero chance, I swear.'

She tuts, then sighs dramatically. 'Dammit, really? I *knew* my laser eye surgery was too cheap. OK, fine, maybe it's not Jennifer Aniston, but it *really* looks like Brad, doesn't it?!'

'No.'

She ignores me. 'We should go over there and say hi! Imagine if the paps made the same mistake I did! We could totally end up on E! Online as the "mysterious girls flirting with Brad Pitt in front of Jennifer Aniston".'

'We are women, not girls,' I say robotically. 'Stop infantalising our gender.'

'Come on,' she says, grit in her voice, ignoring me.

'I really don't think . . .' I try, but it's too late. She's already aggressively flipped her hair over her shoulder and is striding towards the non-alike who, honestly, looks more like Goldie Hawn than Brad Pitt.

I follow after her, kind of intrigued as to where this is going.

'Hey! Hey!' Isy is trying to get not-Brad's attention, her voice an octave higher than usual. Isn't it weird how we get all reedy and sing-song when we're flirting with men? Like we think sounding more like a kid is sexy?

Actually, maybe E! Online will mistake her for a 'girl' after all.

The men turn around, surprised.

'Um, hi?' the second not-Brad says, hesitantly.

Isy smiles coyly, 'We're British,' she says, as if that's all they need to hear. And apparently it is, because they turn fully towards us then, smiling widely now.

'Brits, huh?' the first says, delighted. 'My sister visited London last year, she went to a bunch of *pubs*. She says they're everywhere over there, you can't throw a stone without hitting a Red Lion or a Royal Oak! You Brits are hilarious.'

Isy flips her hair again. 'What can I say, we love a pint of beer over there,' she says coquettishly, eyelashes fluttering, voice still paedo-friendly.

'I'm Noah, he's Ethan,' the less annoying of the two says nicely, offering his hand to me.

'Hello Noah and Ethan, how are you?' I say, shaking Noah's hand.

Ethan chuckles. 'You Brits, with your weird sayings! I love it!' he says, taking my hand, too, as I peer up at him.

'Sayings?' I repeat, confused. '*How are you*?'

'I'm great babe, I'm great!' he says, misunderstanding me. 'Hey, do you know my pal John Windermere? He used to work with us and he's from England, you must know him.' Isy pretends to think about it and then exclaims, 'Oh wow, you know what, I definitely think I do know John – British accent, right?'

The pair nod happily and the group suddenly feels more intimate. OK, I may not approve of her techniques but Isy is good at this.

Ethan takes a tiny step back, giving Isy the once-over.

'You're so hot! You must be an actress?' he declares.

'And you have great teeth.' He pauses before adding a little unnecessarily, 'For a Brit.'

He looks at me next, goes to say something and takes a polite sip of his drink instead.

Oh well.

'I am an actor, yes!' Isy says, beaming. 'My name is Isabelle Moore.' She flicks her hand at me without looking away from Ethan. 'She's Alice.'

He leans in. 'Listen, we're producers, and I gotta say, you really have something. You ever do commercials? You'd be great in something I have coming up.'

Isy makes a gargled noise. She can barely contain her excitement as she bounces up and down on the spot. 'You bet I do!' she says. I snort and she glances briefly at me with irritation before continuing. 'Er, I mean, I've mainly done stage work up until now, but I really respect the process in adverts these days. There's so much talent involved. All the big-name writers are doing commercials, right? It feels like really ethical and important work. You're influencing a nation.'

Ethan chuckles again, 'Sure babe, and there's just so much cash in advertising. You gotta number I could call you on?'

She roots around in her bag, pulling out a crisp white business card, and hands it over, beaming.

'How about you?' says Noah nicely to me. 'Are you an actor, too?'

'Yeah, are you, like, a *character* actress?' adds Ethan pointedly.

'No, I'm not,' I shake my head, directing my response to the much-nicer Noah. 'I'm just over here for a few weeks for the fun and sunshine. Back home in London I wasn't really anything . . .' I trail off. 'I mean, I worked, of course. But I was just a temp in an office with this English politician. I guess I was kind of a troubleshooter – his PR, almost. Whenever the tabloids called up about his latest sex addiction, or whatnot, I was the buffer – threatening to sue and persuading them it wasn't in the public interest if Tony wanted to have a three-some with a former prime minister and a pig.'

Noah laughs, incredulous. 'For real? That sure sounds like an intense job for a temp.'

'Yeah, it was,' I say, laughing too. 'But I'd been there for over a year, so I guess he trusted me. I started out on recep-tion doing a few days of holiday cover, and ended up behind the scenes, working alongside the boss. They offered me a full-time position, but it wasn't what I wanted to do long term, so I just stayed on a rolling contract, battling for the forces of evil.' I stop and look at my feet. 'Actually, I quite enjoyed it and probably would've stayed on, but then I also sent my boss a text that talked about his bent penis on my thirtieth birthday.'

Noah nods, looking a little unsure about that last part. 'So,' he moves on. 'What do you want to do long term? Or is that a boring question to ask right at the start of your vacation?'

I laugh and then I'm silent for a full ten seconds. 'I don't know,' I shrug. 'That's part of why I'm here. To figure things out. I've kind of always just . . . temped. It's been quite fun over the years, going from office to office, meeting new people, challenging yourself with whatever madness gets thrown at you. But without worrying about any of the commitment. You don't get sucked into the drama or dumb office politics. You don't have to contribute to anyone's leaving present, and every day is different. But I don't know . . . maybe I'm ready for something more.'

An hour later and I am crashing hard. We're still chatting to the producers, and it turns out Noah is really nice, in addition to the hotness. Ethan and Isy are full-on snogging in the middle of the bar, while Noah and I sit in a corner, people watching. We've laughed a lot and now we're getting onto more serious subjects. Noah is telling me about his divorce and how he has to take on commercial work he doesn't enjoy to pay for his ex-wife's summer house. But he doesn't seem too bitter about it – he's not being horrible about her – he just sounds a bit sad. Life happens, doesn't it? Everyone has baggage and everyone has their story. I feel bad for him.

'It's been a tough road,' he says, in a low voice. 'And of course it's been a knock to my confidence. It's hard to get out there and meet people.'

'I get it,' I say sadly, because it seems like the only answer.

There is a pause in the conversation and I squint at him. 'You know, you do actually kinda look like Jennifer Aniston.'

'Huh?' he laughs.

'Sorry, nothing,' I clear my throat. 'All I mean is, I think you'll do fine on the dating scene.'

He laughs and sits up straighter.

'Well, on that note, Alice,' he says. 'I'd love to see you again while you're in LA.' It's not a question, it is a statement. He is confident. The men here seem very self-assured. It's attractive, but a bit intimidating when you're used to the English brand of flirting, which mainly revolves around hiding in a corner and avoiding eye contact. But this trip is all about fun and trying new things, right? And I have always had some confusingly sexual feelings for Jennifer Aniston, so . . . yeah, why not?

'Sure,' I say, smiling. 'But I don't have a business card,

so I'll have to just give you my number like this is still the noughties.'

He laughs, and I get a hint of butterflies.

Ooh. Imagine having sex with someone who isn't TD. Imagine that.

4

23 April – 10.13 a.m.

Good morning, dream chasers,

I write this latest blog lying beside a crystal-blue, sparkling azure pool of deepest cerulean. The sun is beaming like a happy face down on this really nice place by this swimming pool. I am surrounded by natural stunning beauty everywhere I look. It is very calming and nice. I've had a lovely first few days in LA. I have already hung out at the renowned Chateau Marmont with a couple of very famous people I cannot possibly name, and that was really good. I have spent my mornings walking along the perfect beach on Venice Beach which is also nice. I have also been shopping along LA's famous boutique road, Abbot Kinney, which I thought would have more of a church theme, but it's mainly pop-up shops. They are all very very cool and hip and I can definitely afford all the clothes available. It's really good and I am embracing the boho chic vibe while also making many new friends. My host, Isy, is so kind and generous, we are getting on beautifully and I don't know how I will bear to leave her in a few days. But before then, we have many more adventures to go on, side by side.

Sending you good thoughts, followers,

Alice x

#NaturalBeauty #LAPools #AbbotKinneyHasNoAbbots
#AListSpotsAtChateauMarmont #TravelBlogger #GoneAWOL
#AliceEdwardsBlog #OffTheBeatenTrack #BloggerLife #Blessed
#Brave #DreamChaser

7 Comments · 3 AWOLs · 6 Super Likes

COMMENTS:

Karen Gill
| Have you had Botox yet though?

Eva Slate
| You're awake! Can we Skype?

BLOG HOST PICK A USERNAME
Replying to Eva Slate
| YESSSS, will call you at half past.

Mark Edwards
| Alice, no one has said 'boho chic vibe' since 2005.

Hannah Edwards
Replying to Mark Edwards
| P*&"

Mark Edwards
Replying to Hannah Edwards
| The important thing is that you keep trying with AWOL,
Han.

NaughtyLad678
| Get a life whoever u r

'Yeah, it's really fun!' I'm shouting, as if the Skype connection will improve with volume. 'I got super sunburned on day one, because I am hashtag-British, but I am still going down to the pool every day just to stare at all the hot people. All the tits are fake, which makes my wonky boobs feel a bit sad and jealous but that's entertaining too. Also, is it just me or is chlorine a really sexy smell?'

Eva laughs on a delay but her reaction is a little downbeat. 'Aww, I'm so jealous. I really miss you, Al. I'm feeling so fat and weird. My boobs hurt.'

'They always hurt,' I grin. 'You've got to stop fiddling with them.'

She sighs. 'I know.' She looks sad.

'Oh, Eva,' I say, suddenly worried about her. 'I miss you too. Are you OK though? Really? Is it super weird, being pregnant? Are you feeling ill and being, like, sick everywhere all the time?'

'I'm mostly over that bit,' she says, rubbing her nipples again and looking pained.

'Stop it,' I scold and she drops her hands.

'Sorry.' She pauses. 'No, I'm not being sick any more, although I am exhausted all the time. I've never known anything like it. It's like having a fuzzy blanket wrapped around my brain. I thought I was meant to get all glow-y and full of life, but this is more like having a tapeworm stealing all my nutrients and energy.'

It's a great analogy.

She sighs, before going on. 'It's just such a super weird idea to get my head round. I can't get over the fact that I have a person growing in here,' she gestures to her stomach like it's separate to the rest of her. 'It also feels a little bit like Jeremy gets all the fun bits. He gets taken off for celebratory drinks and claps on the back, while I'm not allowed to get drunk or even look like I'm having too much fun. Strangers feel up my belly and tell me judgementally that I shouldn't take any drugs or have any help during labour. And God forbid I have a sip of wine. Oh Alice, I really miss wine.'

I nudge an empty bottle on the desk beside me out of camera shot.

'That does sound really tough,' I say sympathetically, trying not to leap on the chance to slag Jeremy off. It's interesting to hear Eva being the tiniest bit negative about him. They've always been so glossy and shiny as a couple.

They met last year on Tinder – yes, Tinder! They were literally the last people on earth to ever meet someone they really liked on Tinder – and Eva said she knew straight away that he was *it* for her. There were no games, she kept saying it like that was a good thing and not just boring. I mean, when did games get such a bad name? Games are great! Who doesn't like Monopoly or charades, after all? Anyway they spent basically every day together after their first date. He might not be my cup of tea, but I suppose I have to give him credit for how thoughtful he always was with their dates. He always went that extra mile, cooking three-course meals for her and whisking her away on mini breaks. And he did make a pretty big effort with her weirdly huge family. There are about forty-five first cousins in the Slate dynasty, who are all so posh you can't even understand what they're saying. Eva said Jeremy spoke to each and every one of them at the bi-annual Slate family gathering – and that was only a few weeks after they first met.

But just because he's nice to a bunch of braying cousins, doesn't mean him and Eva are right for each other. Because they're not.

She inhales deeply. 'It'll be worth it, I know. That's what everyone keeps telling me anyway. Everyone keeps saying it'll be worth it and how the love is magical, and then in the same breath telling me the most awful horror stories about labour.'

She pauses and we both picture something bad.

'But never mind all that,' she adds quickly. 'I'm just feeling sorry for myself. It's the hormones. Please cheer me up, Alice. Tell me about the cool things you've been doing since you arrived.'

And so I do. I tell her about the excess of food and the excess of drinks. I tell her about the sandy morning walks along Venice Beach, which are full of exhausted-looking Instagram husbands doing photo shoots for their partners, who insist on eight hundred versions of the same pose to perfectly capture that casual caught-unawares angle. I tell her about LA's famous boutique road, Abbot Kinney, where I can only assume I couldn't afford anything because there are no price tags. Not that it mattered either way because all the sizes go up as high as a whopping *four*.

I also tell her about my funny texts from that producer guy I met on my first night – Noah. They've been coming in non-stop, and they're great. I think I actually quite like him. I mean, I know I'm only here a month but it's nice to have those butterflies when my phone buzzes. But I'm also very aware the messages don't seem to be going anywhere. He hasn't said any more about going on a date. I've casually mentioned meeting up a few times and he just changes the subject.

'Do you know what his star sign is?' she asks suddenly, dead serious. I roll my eyes. 'No, Eva, I do not.'

'I'm just saying, I could help you a lot more if I could do his star chart. That's how I knew Jeremy was The One.'

Fucking Jeremy.

Something occurs to her and she adds in a worried voice, 'Also, just to warn you, I did see the name Noah on a Facebook meme the other day. It was a list of men most likely to be commitment-phobes, and his name was, like, number seven.'

I laugh. 'You believe in such crap, Eva.' She looks sad again as the Skype connection fizzes. I raise my voice over the interference. 'NAH, I THINK HE'S JUST ONE OF THOSE REALLY HOT FUCKERS WHO ONLY WANTS TO CHAT FOREVER AND NEVER WANTS TO ACTUALLY MEET UP. YOU KNOW THAT TYPE? THEY JUST WANT THE EGO BOOST WITHOUT ANY OF THE . . .'

'BABE,' an angry-sounding Isy interrupts us through the wall. 'CAN YOU STFU PLEASE? I'M TRYING TO SLEEP.'

I cringe because she actually did say the letters S-T-F-U, which is no more syllables than 'shut the fuck up', and did not save her any time to say.

'OK, BUT NOW YOU'RE SHOUTING, TOO,' I shout back, trying not to laugh. I really enjoy winding Isabelle up. It's so easy.

'I KNOW I AM BUT ONLY TO MAKE A POINT,' Isy yells.

'POINT MADE,' I yell back. 'SORRY DUDE. I'LL TRY TO KEEP IT DOWN IN FUTURE, YEAH?' On the screen in front of me, Eva is covering her mouth, trying not to snort. She knows Isy well.

'THANK YOU,' she screams back.

'ISY?' I bawl, enjoying the noise. 'BABE? COULD YOU ALSO KEEP IT DOWN NOW THOUGH? I'M TRYING TO SKYPE EVA?'

'STFU, ALICE, YOU'RE NOT FUNNY.'

'SHHHHHHUSH,' I shout, and then collapse in giggles. Eva is wiping tears away and I give her an exaggerated shrug.

'Is Isy being really annoying?' she stage whispers.

I nod, 'Yes, but I do appreciate her letting me stay here. And to be honest, I've barely seen her. She's been out every single night with that producer friend of Noah's. The one who didn't look at all like Brad Pitt and was a bit of a knob. The two of them have been at it like horny rabbits since that first night I got here. I bumped into her in the kitchen yesterday where she was making them kale smoothies with 'sex dust' she bought online. I asked if sex dust is rohypnol, but apparently it's something Gloop sells to make you horny. As if they need help.'

I giggle as the connection fizzes again. When Eva's face returns, she looks contemplative.

'So listen Alice, how are you, um . . .' she pauses and I know what's coming, '. . . how are you feeling about the Steven stuff? I texted Mark about it a bit the other day in Australia, and he seems OK. He says not much has changed with Steven's condition. Have you, um, been in touch with your mum at all?'

She knows this is dangerous territory with me.

'Um, no.' My answer is short and brooks no further discussion.

'Mark said the doctors don't think he'll last much lon . . .'

'Eva,' I sigh deeply. 'I love you and I know you mean well, but I'm not really ready to talk about it yet. I don't want to talk about it, please leave it alone.'

She nods, hearing me. 'OK Al, but you know where I am if you do ever want to talk. I know it's a difficult situation for you. And I'm sorry.'

'Thank you,' I say brusquely, but meaning it.

She clears her throat. 'By the way, have you heard anything from TD since you've been there? He must be able to see online that you've left the country. We all know how he orbits your social media.'

I laugh, relieved she's not going to push me into a difficult conversation I don't want to have. Not that she ever really would, she's so nice.

'I got a text last night, actually,' I say, giggling. 'He sounded really annoyed I'd gone. He was demanding to know when I'd be back, and asked why couldn't I pop back for a few days. He's livid that my vagina is currently unavailable.'

She squeals, horrified. 'Ew, he's so gross. Did you ignore him?'

I make a face. 'Well, no. I did reply. And don't tell me off, Eva, I know I shouldn't have. But I was just being polite, I don't want to be rude! Being nice is the, like, higher ground. And obviously I told him I'm not coming back for a while, so it's not like I'm going to see him.' She doesn't look convinced so I add, 'I didn't ask any questions, either, so it was obvious I didn't want to chat!'

'Alice!' She looks stern. Eva is rarely stern and I struggle not to laugh. 'You've really got to cut him off completely. Responding at all makes him think he still has a chance with you. You've got to be totally done with him, block him! You made me do it with Xerxes, remember? And it worked because then I met Jeremy!' I snort at the mention of Eva's ex, the poshest moron to ever live. He once asked me what a Woolworths was. She ignores me and continues. 'That's what this trip is about, right? A fresh start? Knocking yourself out of these bad habits and unhelpful patterns. TD doesn't deserve a second of your time or consideration, you know that, Alice. He's an idiot and a user, and you are too good for him. And, look, you've got Noah now.'

'I haven't *got* Noah,' I roll my eyes. 'He's avoided all mentions of meeting up again. It's all just texting forever and ever and ever.' I pause, then add defiantly, 'I'm going to be too busy for men, anyway.'

She smiles. 'What have you got planned for your second week of LA living? More of the same?'

'There will definitely be more extreme drinking and eating,' I confirm. 'But I also want to do some more typical LA-type stuff. I want to feel culturally awkward in a pedicure place. I want to go to a Soulcycle class. I want to get my palm read by a fraud on Muscle Beach. I want to wander the streets trying to get recruited by a cult. I want to do everything Constance Beaumont did when she was here.'

Eva is now equally obsessed with Constance Beaumont. Back in the UK we spent a solid week sending each other her glistening sunny Instagram pictures while it rained outside. Just to make sure we fully hated ourselves and our lives.

I pause, then add, 'Also, I totally want to get Botox.'

'You don't mean it?' she looks at me agog.

'Yeah I do,' I insist. 'I stopped a woman yesterday to ask for directions and she was like, "Sure hon, I can tell you how to get to the Whole Foods, but then I'm giving you directions to a place that will get rid of your elevens".'

'What does that mean?' says Eva, looking perplexed. I point to the parallel lines between my eyebrows. 'These are apparently my elevens,' I tell her. 'I didn't know they were something I should be ashamed of, but now I do and I'm obsessed. I keep staring at them in the mirror. Plus, why not? I want to try new things. Why not try some poison in my forehead? Everyone else does it. You should see Isy's face. It didn't even move when I told her I'd never had my vagina steamed.'

She laughs, long and hard, and I can tell she doesn't think I'm serious. I don't even know if I'm serious. I did say I wanted to try LA stuff? Have adventures.

Botox the Adventure!

It sounds like a Lady Gaga music video.

'OK,' she is still laughing. 'But if you get it done, I have to get it done, because you can't cheat ageing unless we're all cheating ageing, otherwise it's not fair.'

'I don't think they'd let you have poison injected in you while you're prego, Eva,' I point out.

She looks down at herself surprised. 'Right, of course not. I forgot for a minute.'

I change the subject. 'Oh, and Isy's getting us into some fancy awards show thing on Sunday. So that should be exciting.'

Eva squeals, 'Ooooh that IS exciting! Is it the Oscars? The Emmys? The People's Choice Awards?'

'Er, no . . .' I say, a little embarrassed. 'It's something called The Teddy Awards.'

Eva tries and fails to disguise her disappointment. 'Ah, um, right, I think I've heard of that one!' she says, mustering fake enthusiasm.

'No you haven't, and I hadn't either,' I reassure her. 'But it's still an awards show! An awards show in downtown LA!'

'That is amazing,' she enthuses. 'Do you know which celebs will be there?'

I shake my head. 'No idea. But if I don't Netflix and Chill with an actual Netflix star on this trip, I will cancel my subscription and write a stern letter.'

5

26 April – 2.14 p.m.

Good afternoon, dream chasers,

I am sitting down to a large chai latte after a very chilled morning spent truly embracing #LA life. I enjoyed an early Soulcycle class, which was very easy for me because I am very fit. I then went for a #SelfCare pedicure where I very much bonded with my podiatrist and she suggested I enjoy the cultural hub of Muscle Beach and Sunset Boulevard. Which is what I'm doing now. The natives are so very welcoming and happy, it is warming my soul.

After all my #LA #SelfCare, tonight is the top secret AWARDS DO I am attending with my actor friend Isy!!! I cannot possibly tell you anything about it, except that it is set to be very very glam and full of celebs (coughMerylStreepcough). Before then, however, I shall be having some ME time to myself, enjoying the sights and delving deep into this new world around me.

Sending good thoughts,

Alice x

#CrushingSoulcycle #PamperSesh #LAPedicure #LovingLife #CelebsDeadAhead #TravelBlogger #GoneAWOL #AliceEdwardsBlog #BloggerLife #Blessed #Brave #DreamChaser

COMMENTS:

Noah Deer
| You're amazing surviving a Soulcycle class, they're brutal!

Karen Gill
| Send me a selfie with Meryl.

Morgan PatriotsRule
| Why are you in my country dumb bitch!!!!

AWOL MODERATOR
Replying to Morgan PatriotsRule
| Hey Morgan mate, we know it's just a bit of a 'LOL', but please be respectful to our users :) I'm here if you want to chat!! Luke

Morgan PatriotsRule
Replying to AWOL MODERATOR
| go suk a dick luke

Hannah Edwards
| d

Alice Edwards
Replying to Hannah Edwards
| Thanks Han.

I have found a cult and I am THRILLED.

I spent all morning in a state of sweaty terror thanks to my determination to spend the day being as LA as possible. Which meant getting up at 5 a.m. for one of those Soulcycle classes, so beloved by celebrities. Except I overslept, arrived really late, then tripped over a bike as I tried to sneak in the back. The instructor then stopped the music so everyone could wait for me to find the only spot available, which was inevitably front and centre. I only made it through ten minutes before I started seeing stars and had to pretend I needed a wee. Everyone in the room knew I was off to the loo to puke but it was better than passing out on the instructor.

And I didn't see a single Beckham in there so it was an absolute waste of my time.

After that I went to get a pedicure to calm myself down, but that experience was even more embarrassing. The woman spent an hour ignoring my attempts at small talk, as she sawed at my yellow soles, making noises like she was competing at the women's Wimbledon final. She then made me leave wearing lurid green flip-flops in a man's size eleven.

Since then I've been trying to pull the day back from the brink of terribleness by limping around Sunset Boulevard looking for a Scientology building. Mark dared me to get recruited, and I'll be damned if I fail at that one thing.

I was just about to give up hope when a lady, wearing what could only be described as *robes*, stopped me in front of a nondescript building, holding out a leaflet.

'I sense you need to find yourself,' she said, smiling through dead eyes. 'We can help you. In fact, we are the only people who could ever truly understand you.'

I nodded enthusiastically, completely delighted. 'That's good,' I told her. 'Because my brother says no one will ever understand me, or my haircut.'

'We can help you solve your haircut and all other problems

with the art of Sheathology,' she continued, smoothly.

'Oh, don't you mean Scientology?' I said, trying to hide my disappointment.

'Those con-artists have no idea,' she scoffed, waving her hand dismissively. 'Sheathology is the only real method of self-discovery. We dig deep inside you, down below, to determine what terrible spirits are holding you hostage and preventing you from reaching your sheath potential.'

'So, you are still a cult, right?' I asked, anxiously.

'Of course we're not a cult!' she replied, cocking her head at me. 'We only ask that members commit themselves fully to our cause, turning their backs on non-believers and giving themselves and their ancestors to the Sheathology cause for the next thousand years. In exchange, we can help you release your demons and become the sheath bearer you were meant to be.'

'Sounds great!' I said happily, following her inside.

Which is how I find myself sitting in a circle of nervous-looking females, all sitting on the floor of a large hall, clutching leaflets.

'Er, what do you know about Sheathology?' I whisper to the young woman on my right, because I'm starting to worry there is a small chance I've made a mistake.

She leans across enthusiastically. 'Oh, it's . . .' she begins, just as a beaming ringleader – wearing the same robes as the woman outside – strides in and plonks herself down, cross-legged, in the centre of us.

'VAGINA,' she shouts, still smiling inanely. I jump.

'Welcome, my fellow sheath-owners,' she continues, making steady eye contact with each of us, one-by-one. 'Today you have taken the first step towards reclaiming your vagina from those who would keep it from you.'

Oh God.

She gestures at her groin, smiling maniacally. 'Sheathology is all about releasing the power of the vagina. We must, each of us, embrace our collective vagina – our magic muff is one – and exorcise her demon. Today, I will show you how this can be achieved.' She stands excitably, her robe flapping around.

I start sweating. This is not what I signed up for. I wanted Tom Cruise secrets, not taco talk.

'For those of you who don't know,' she continues, speaking way too loudly, 'vagina is the Latin word for sheath. It is where those worthy can place their sword. And the one true king is the one who can remove it again.'

Wait, is that a Sword in the Stone reference? What was I thinking doing this? Spontaneity is a terrible idea.

Merlin moves around the circle, stopping in front of me and we stare at each other. A bead of sweat runs down my face. Godammit, Mark won't be impressed by this cult at all – he doesn't like vaginas. Honestly, I'm not even a fan of my own. Maybe if I tell them about my awkward smear test they'll let me leave? They won't want my terrible vag ruining their collective hoohah.

Merlin is still talking, waving her hands some more and talking about how our group flower needs room to blossom.

'We shall now watch a short film about the rise of the rosebud,' she announces, as one of her whisker biscuit minions pulls down a projector screen and dims the lights. 'The movie will be followed by a discussion on what type of animal your vagina is,' she announces, eyes bulging as she walks off. 'Mine is a chinchilla.'

The room gets darker and the woman beside me leans back into me.

'Holy shit, this is amazing,' she breathes in a European accent. I grimace in the gloom. I was going to try to sneak off, but I have a believer beside me. She continues in my ear, panting. 'Isn't it though? I mean, I wanted mad, but this is absolute batshit nonsense.'

I suppress a relieved giggle. 'What kind of animal is your vagina?' I say in a hushed voice and she considers it.

'A mosquito, probably. I'm small and cause an itch.' I giggle and someone nearby tuts.

'That's not an animal!' I say, scolding.

'That is a good point,' she looks thoughtful. 'In that case, is a pussy too obvious?'

I shake my head. 'No, I'll let you have that, but you'll have to be more specific. Sphynx? Siamese?'

'Garfield,' she says baldy. 'Because my vagina hates Mondays.' I giggle again as she adds, 'You?'

'I think . . .' I squint, knowing this is very important. 'Mine is a giraffe. Because it's yellow and spotty with a long neck.'

We both laugh again, but silently. 'Why do you think she's a chinchilla?' I whisper, pulling out my phone and Googling them.

We regard the picture. 'They are very hairy,' she says at last, in a serious tone.

'And grey,' I add thoughtfully. We look at each other for too long a moment and simultaneously snort. An older woman on our right angrily shushes us.

We turn back to the film, which seems to be a detailed – and highly inaccurate – biology lesson. My phone lights up with a message from Mark and I click away from the poor, hairy chinchillas.

'How's LA? Miss you.'

I reply quickly. 'I have accidentally joined a vagina cult, which would be fine, except they don't even know the difference between vagina and vulva.'

His reply is quick. 'Who does? Have you signed over all your money yet?'

'I would've but they don't accept Paypal,' I type back. And he gives me a LOL for my troubles.

I suddenly really miss my brother. I want to speak to him, to hear his voice. I slip away from the group and press call.

Mark is two years older than me, and then we have a sister, Hannah, who is a few years older again. The Early Mistake, as we call her, and which she very much enjoys.

I'm closer to Mark, but I am very fond of Hannah. Mostly because she's such an oddball. Truly. Whereas Mark and I have grown up with the internet, she was just a little too old to ever fully accept or trust it. She is convinced it is watching her and monitoring her every move – which duh obviously it is doing that, but Millennials mostly don't care, do they? She loves any kind of conspiracy theory – you name it, she believes it. Elvis isn't dead; the moon landing was faked; the government is a secret race of lizard people; Princess Di was murdered by her in-laws; Finland doesn't exist; Peppa Pig is Illuminati brainwashing propaganda.

She sends round a monthly family newsletter sharing all her amazing thoughts on these topics – as well as tedious and embarrassing factoids about our relatives – but never ever click on a link she sends round. Your computer will never recover. Actually, I should send her the details of this place, she'd love it.

Mark, meanwhile, is an enigma. He is the world's most

evasive best friend. He loves gossiping about me and my life, but he gives me almost nothing back. He just shrugs and smiles when I try to get him to open up. He's been like that for as long as I can remember. Sometimes when I'm drunk, I grill his best mate to find out secrets, but Joe laughs and says he doesn't know anything about Mark either. And they've known each other almost as long as me and Mark. Joe lived one road over when we were little and is the happiest person I know. He's one of those people who is always looking on the bright side of things and giving motivational speeches over brunch. Him and Mark actually make quite a strange, night and day-type of pairing, but it seems to work because I've never seen them fall out. Maybe being evasive and constantly turning things back around keeps a friendship safe. Or maybe not. Either way, it frustrates the hell out of me. Honestly, the only way I know Mark loves me is that he keeps getting in touch.

'Hello dickhead,' he answers quickly, sounding happy.

'Hello yourself,' I say, pleased. 'Sorry for calling, I know you don't approve of phones being used for calls.'

'That's fine,' he laughs. 'I don't mind when it's you.'

'How is your sunburn?' I say, not sure how else to reference his trip to Australia without getting into specifics.

'Even, dark and non-burny,' he replies smugly. 'Sorry Al, I know you burn in stripes. It's really sweltering here.'

The moment – and the *here* – hangs in the air.

'What non-vagina-y things have you been up to?' he says, when the silence has stretched on too long.

I clear my throat, staring off at the group on the other side of the hall, watching the brainwashing propaganda closely.

'I went shopping where a woman shouted, "Have a great day" at me so aggressively that I am now really afraid of not having a great day,' I say. 'I feel like she will somehow know and she will find me and she will gouge out my eyes with expensive oak coat hangers.'

'And you would deserve it.'

'I know right. It's strange, I'm just not used to everyone being so nice and friendly. And everyone speaks therapy. I sat in a coffee shop this morning listening to a man having a brilliant argument on the phone. He was saying, like, "I do appreciate you communicating where you're at, but I do not feel valued by you." I thought it was some street theatre at first, it was so great. My coffee got cold while I eavesdropped.'

'I'm so jealous, I love listening to people's conversations. It's the only reason I go outside.'

'I also visited Muscle Beach, which has got a very Blackpool-in-October vibe. It's such a strange place. On one side you have this very real, very stark homeless problem – and then on the other side, you have an entire shop dedicated to, like, toe rings. And there are extremely rude pants for sale everywhere you look.'

'Sounds hot.'

'They all say things like "All you can eat", "Lick me until ice cream" and "Slippery when wet".'

'Aw, did you not get me one?'

'I was actually very tempted. But I got my palm read instead. There are hundreds of psychics who all happen to be dotted along the sea front. I think the sea must be a psychic energy conductor.'

'Oh my God, tell me everything.' Mark sounds breathless. 'Did the psychic mention me? Am I going to be rich? Famous?'

'Very. You were all she wanted to talk about. But really, it was actually hilarious. This bored-looking woman just held my hand for ten minutes and spoke at high speed about how I was going to live a long life, but I was chasing something right now. She also said there is a man in my life who doesn't treat me very well. Like, LOL, who ISN'T that going to apply to?'

'She is right though. I hope you haven't been in touch with TD lately.'

'I'm sorry, I can't hear you, the connection is bad.'

'Ohhhh, Alice! At least tell me you haven't sexted your boss again though.'

A pulse of humiliation burns through me. I do not want to be reminded of that terrible night. A beat passes and Mark speaks quickly, probably sensing he has hit a nerve.

'So no more progress with that Noah guy you met on your first night?'

'Nah, but that's fine. He was super good-looking but I don't know, I think he might be really boring.'

'Fair enough. Did the psychic say anything about other men coming your way?'

I pause.

'Nothing about men. But she said . . .' I am not sure whether to tell Mark this. '. . . that sometimes I can be unkind to people.'

There is another pause and I add hastily, 'But I think that was just because she was upset I was laughing in her face.'

A few more seconds pass and I feel myself getting cross. I'm not unkind! I'm a straight shooter! Honest! I'm not unkind! That's unkind to say!

'But are you finding The Fun like you wanted?' he says.

I jump on the change of subject.

'I kinda think I am,' I reply. Despite my current discomfort and boiled feet, I am actually having a great time in LA. It's not anything like I expected, but everything is so new and exciting. And I can't tell you how affecting it is to have the sun on my face every day. I had no idea how much the grey gloom of London was dragging me down.

'Project Find The Fun is definitely coming along. Maybe I'll just stay in Fun mode, here in LA. I don't need to Find Myself in Thailand if I can Find Fun forever instead, do I?'

'True, but I think the novelty will wear off all your Finding Fun soon. You like being able to complain and shout too much. Plus, they're bound to chuck you out soon. Have you not heard of a BUI?'

'No, what the fuck? Is it like a DUI?'

'Yep. But for biking under the influence. It's an actual crime, and they take foreigners straight to the airport if they're caught. And frankly, Alice, I cannot see a way around it. You are bound to end up hiring a bike one day while you're drunk. It's just too YOU not to happen at some point.'

'Oh shit, that is true. I'm going to get a BUI. They're going to chuck me out.'

'Try to wait until your last day, because that could work out quite well. Hey, I saw Hannah earlier.'

'Oh? How is she? Wanting more tips on how to use AWOL? She's almost as bad at it as me.'

'Ha, no,' he says, his voice a little tight. 'She wondered if I would try to talk to you again about . . . Mum.'

My breathing gets shallow but before I can reply, the lights in the room come back up and I hang up, throwing my phone back in my bag, and rushing back to the circle.

'Here comes the chinchilla,' mutters my new friend, as the Sheathology leader sweeps back in.

'Right,' she shouts, smiling benignly as she regards each of us. 'Time to remove our robes.'

6

AWOL.COM/Alice Edwards' Travel Blog: Living My Dream and Feeling Very #Blessed

26 April – 5.24 p.m.

Good evening, dream chasers,

I have had an intriguing afternoon at an animal sanctuary, where I saw a range of creatures, most notably chinchillas. Unfortunately, I had to leave early when many of them almost escaped from their cages. I did not want to see that.

This is just a quick one to update you, as I can now reveal that I am merely moments away from attending the very exclusive Teddy Awards!!! I know it's going to be a life-changing experience and I am very grateful for my life. I will embrace these moments and also live in the moments. Look out for me in the audience on the telly.

Peace and love,

Alice x

#TeddyAwards #MerylStreep #NotTheOscarsButCloseEnough #TravelBlogger #GoneAWOL #AliceEdwardsBlog #BloggerLife #Blessed #Brave #DreamChaser

7 Comments · 9 AWOLs · 13 Super Likes

COMMENTS:

Hannah Edwards
| .gu

> **Alice Edwards**
> **Replying to Hannah Edwards**
> | Gu? Like the chocolate pots? That is a great idea, thanks! You are such a wise big sister.

Sarah Sommers
| You better catch some celeb dick or I'll never forgive you.

Piers Ned
| Whore slut.

> **AWOL MODERATOR**
> **Replying to Piers Ned**
> | Sorry to be a boring dad type, Piers – AWOL is cool, I promise! – But please be respectful to our users :) I'm here if you fancy chatting more. Luke

> **Piers Ned**
> **Replying to AWOL MODERATOR**
> | luke u bellend wot u sayin bout my dad

Noah Deer
| You going with your English friend? Have a good time. I can get you into an afterparty if you need? Message me.

I have grown quite attached to my green flip-flops by the time I meet Isabelle, who is waiting for me outside the theatre.

She looks down, fear making her eyes all bulgey.

'What on earth are you wearing on your feet? We have to go in!' she says, panic in her voice.

'The pedicure woman stole my shoes, Isy, what can I do?' I shrug helplessly, secretly delighted. 'Don't you think they

68

almost work, though?' I look down and wiggle my toes, pleasingly.

I was going to tell her about my afternoon with the vagina cult, but it's clear Isy's not in the mood. She sighs impatiently, hopping from one foot to another. Despite the warm early evening temperatures, she must be freezing her tiny ass off in the smallest, tightest dress I've ever seen. I love it and completely approve. I think women should be as cold – or as hot – as possible, at all times, just to prove a point to those judgy types who temperature-concern-troll you about your outfit choice.

You know what I mean? 'My goodness, aren't you *cold* in that?' is a comment that is only ever intended to make you feel insecure. Likewise, when I've still got my jacket on at a party and someone's like, 'Wow, you must be boiling!' It is never the heat making me uncomfortable, it is YOU trying to make me remove my clothes. And, honestly, fuck off mate, I paid a hundred and forty quid for this Zara coat, it goes with my shoes, so I AM KEEPING IT ON YOU WILL NOT MAKE ME FEEL SHIT ABOUT THIS.

Isy flicks her perfectly coiffed hair over her shoulder and regards me critically. Her make-up is expertly applied in that way that makes her look like she's hardly wearing any, even though I know for a fact she is wearing all the make-up that exists in the known universe.

'Wow,' I breathe out. 'You look stunning.' She smiles widely and I see the tension leave her shoulders. 'Thanks, I only used ethically sourced, organic manure-based make-up,' she says, trying not to look at my feet. 'You look nice, too.'

I've pretty much only brought one Really Nice Dress along on my travels. It's long and yellow and makes my boobs look momentous. I've been carrying it around all day so it's nice and crumpled, but I'm still enjoying feeling dressy.

'Cheers,' I say, cupping my chest proudly. I reach for Isy's arm. 'So how did you get us into this tonight?' I ask as we head slowly inside. 'Are you nominated for an award or something?'

Her stride falters. 'Um, no. Maybe one day! But not this time.'

'How then?' I ask, suddenly suspicious. I've just noticed there are no other people in fancy outfits around. No red carpets, no paps screaming for attention.

'How, Isy?' I say louder this time. 'Did your new boyfriend, Ethan, get us in?'

She shakes her head. 'Um, don't be mad, Alice, but we're actually . . . seat fillers.'

I stop. 'Wait, what?'

She continues in a rush. 'We're seat fillers. When the actual attendees go for a wee or to take coke in the bathroom, we have to sit in their seat. It's so the auditorium never looks empty on camera. You have to be on hand during the show to run in if a celeb vacates their chair. It's actually a huge honour and you have to know all the right people to even be asked to do this. I had to pull so many strings for this.'

I consider it for a second. A *seat* filler? 'This is . . .' I pause and she looks worried. 'This is the COOLEST THING I'VE EVER HEARD!'

She laughs, relieved by my reaction.

'Isy, this is so epic! Not even Constance Beaumont got to do something like this when she was travelling around California! I could be sitting in for Meryl Streep. I could feel the warmth of Meryl's bum on my own. I bet Meryl has lovely warm buttocks, y'know? Not too hot like she's farted, but just comforting and cosy levels of warm. Will I be able to take a picture of Meryl's bumcheek imprint before I sit on it?'

Isy shakes her head. 'No, definitely not. You have to be cool, Alice. Seriously, or they'll chuck us out. No pictures, no AWOL updates, and you'll have to sign a non-disclosure agreement as we go in. Plus, there is no way Meryl will be here.'

'Oh. Well, still.'

'I mean it,' she insists. 'You can't be . . . well, *you*. You have to be polite, no backchat to the men upstairs. You have to be nice, quiet and discreet.'

'Great,' I say sarcastically. 'It's 1954 in there.'

She rolls her eyes at me. 'Fine, yes, tonight you are a Handmaid, got it? And it's all top secret. What happens in seat-filler club stays in seat-filler club. Not that non-disclosures really mean that much to anyone any more. Not since Harvey and Donald.'

I nod. 'I'll be cool, I promise.'

I'm thrilled. After failing to get recruited by a cult, this is exactly the kind of celeb silliness I was hoping for from California. A seat filler! This is going to be so much fun.

OK, it's not *that* fun. We're currently huddled in a corner of the main hall with the rest of the seat fillers: a large group of confident-looking regulars. A stern man has already shouted at us not to talk to anyone, not to behave badly, not to have any fun at all, actually. He keeps singling me out to scream about how I'm not paying enough attention, but dude, I get it. We are not allowed to drink or eat, we are not to speak to any invited guests, and even eye contact with celebrities is fiercely discouraged. Our job is to blend in, to avoid drawing any kind of attention at all, and smiling is outlawed.

I made that last bit up, but it feels that way.

There was a moment of awe when they eventually lead us into the arena where the ceremony is happening – the high ceilings and glittery décor has clearly cost serious big bucks – but then we were dumped in this dark corner. Out of view, out of the way, with orders from the dickhead seat-filler conductor not to speak. Isy and I do anyway, breathing out in low whispers whenever someone important-looking arrives, but we are well into the show before I spot anyone actually famous. If I'm being honest, I am fairly bored.

Until. Suddenly there is action.

'Go. YOU, go,' the boss is violently hissing at me, grabbing me by the elbow and throwing me towards the audience. I glance back and he smirks at me like he knows something I don't. What is his problem? He's probably jealous I get to join the celebs while he's stuck in the corner on his power trip.

Oh my God, an actress I recognise from one of my favourite telly shows is gliding out of her seat in the second row. We pass each other and she is dazzling up close. For a moment, I forget the instructions shouted at me mere minutes ago, and I look her full in the face. She is irresistible, she is a goddess, I cannot resist her celebrity pull. We make eye contact and she winks.

'This is the bad place,' she murmurs as we cross paths, and I nearly pass out.

Her seat is still warm – it is just like I imagined Meryl's bum print would feel – and I feel the buzz of celebrities surrounding me on all sides. The bad place? This is the best place ever! My stomach fizzes happily. I don't care how shallow it is, this is *amazing*. Well worth standing around for hours in the shadows. Even worth the dickhead boss screaming at me to take this seriously.

The actress has probably only gone for a wee, I likely only have a couple of minutes, and so I close my eyes and bask in the few moments I have among the B-list. The stage is overwhelmingly close and the clapping is noisy. I open my eyes and glance around. Across the room in the gloom, I can just about make out Isy, who gives me a quick wave. She still looks a bit jealous. Which I'm fine with.

'How are you doing? I like your flip-flops,' a half-whispered voice interrupts my glow. The man on my left is leaning over and smiling. He is wearing a tux and looks vaguely familiar.

Oh God, I'm not allowed to talk to guests. But the boss didn't brief me on what to do if guests spoke to me, did he? So I can make up my own rules.

'Hiya!' I whisper cheerfully, offering him my hand to shake. 'I'm Alice!'

He takes it, smiling. 'You're one of the seat fillers, right?' he says, cheerfully. I smile and nod, hoping I'm being watched by the seat-filler dictator. I have celeb mates now, he can't tell me what to do.

'Do you know what's going on backstage?' he continues. 'Have you been there all this time? I'm nominated in the next category and I wondered if you'd heard anything while you were waiting around back there?' I shake my head slowly, giving a helpless shrug. He slumps down in his seat, despondent.

'Never mind, it doesn't matter,' he says, speaking too loudly. 'I don't stand a chance anyway. I'm up against that guy who overdosed last year and just got out of rehab, so clearly he's got the sympathy vote. Plus, one of the other nominees has been sleeping with literally everyone on the voting panel so I'm way down the list.'

Shit, this guy is loud. Let's hope the other nominees aren't sitting around us. I grimace at him in what I hope is a supportive – but not encouraging – way. Maybe I shouldn't have engaged after all.

'Oh fuck it!' he exclaims even louder, and the presenters on stage just a few feet away glance down at our row, looking startled. My face is beetroot, as I stare straight ahead, trying to pretend nothing is happening.

Behind us a reality housewife angrily shushes us and I sink lower in my chair. When am I going to be relieved? My actress must be doing multiple number twos in the loo. The two times table maybe.

'Sorry,' he shouts hazily behind him, and I realise he is drunk. 'Heyyy,' he leans into me again, 'you know who I am, right? You watch Netflix, don't you? Of course you do, everyone does.'

I give him a sharp nod, as subtly as possible, even though I still don't have a clue who he is. He takes this as encouragement, continuing, 'I knew you had! I could see it in your eyes. The star-struck thing. I see it all the time. I can't walk down the street without seeing that desperate look in people's eyes.'

I consider this. How intently must you have to look at people as you walk along, to be able to spot them spotting you? And if you're staring at everyone to see if they're staring, no wonder they stare?

'It's hard to have a proper life, y'know?' he sighs now. 'Because of people like you always bothering me, Alice.'

I bite my tongue to prevent it calling him a dick – and

also to stop from laughing. There's no stopping him though, despite the angry shushing around us getting more intense.

'I just think I deserve a bit of recognition from my peers, don't you think?' his volume has reached a truly uncomfortable level. 'I know I'm talented, everyone says so. Everyone says it. I am extremely talented – a genius – not my words. Why shouldn't I get some accolades for that?' He reaches under his chair and swigs from a bottle he had hidden, while I continue to stare steadily ahead, my face radioactive with shame.

'Can you please keep it down?' A very famous US telly presenter has turned fully around from the front row and is directing his waggling finger at my new best friend – and me. I'm in this now, I'm part of it. It's not just him, it's *the two of us*.

Oh God, the cameras have arrived. There is a guy with a camera on his shoulder, and the wider pan attached to a crane swings down near our faces, zooming in on my green flip-flops. But my new pal is oblivious, continuing his rant unabated.

'I've had enough of hearing how great I am from the general public on Twitter,' he shouts. 'And yet that greatness never being recognised or validated. I don't *need* validation, you know? It's not even about that. I just think it's only right. When all these HACKS around us have got a Teddy Award and I haven't, it starts to make the whole thing look like a bit of a joke, doesn't it, Alice? Like it's all a fix, and just because I haven't given the right blowjobs in this town, suddenly my genius on screen doesn't matter. It's a JOKE.'

The glowering around us is hot on my neck and I cannot sink into my seat any lower. Suddenly he grabs my arm. 'Come on Seat Filler,' he yells, standing us both up and bustling me along the row ahead of him. 'Let's rush the fucken stage! If we can't be award winners, we will be internet heroes instead! It'll be so much FUN!'

OK, well I did ask for fun.

7

AWOL.COM/Alice Edwards' Travel Blog: Living My Dream and Feeling Very #Blessed

29 April – 2.19 p.m.

Good afternoon, dream chasers,

Apologies for not updating this blog for a few days, everything is excellent and fine and I am still very #blessed. The Teddy Awards were truly wonderful and went off without a hitch. I mean, apart from that one tiny hitch which I am legally not allowed to talk about. But I know many of you have seen it on YouTube by now. I am not legally allowed to say anything, but I do just want to say again that I had nothing to do with what happened. It was not my idea to rush the stage, I was swept along in the moment. He made me do it. I say again: it was not my idea.

In particular, I had no clue at all that he was going to defecate on stage.

And whatever it may look like in the video, I did not deliberately flash, it was a total accident. One of the security men who grabbed me caught my bra strap with his gold signet ring. And despite all those YouTube comments, no, my bra isn't grey and stained, it was the lighting. My bras are all v expensive and well maintained. Of course I cannot legally talk about any of this, but I will just also say that I wasn't thrown out, I left by *mutual agreement*.

And otherwise it was a really wonderful evening that went off without a hitch. And I got a goodie bag!! Which I didn't steal. It was just sitting there going spare as I left. You are meant to help yourself. Do not believe those YouTube comments, I was a victim in all of it.

Anyway, with that out of the way, I am excited to report that I'm now moving out of my friend Isy's place. And for the record, that was always the plan, it's not because she pretended not to know me at the Teddy Awards. I do not blame her for that, I would've done the same. But to say again, I was innocent in all of it. Anyway, we have had a truly bonding experience living together and learning about each other's intimate foibles. We are closer than ever, and thank you Isy, again, for my Gloop subscription. I will definitely use it. Now I'm off to a really lovely AirBnB in Marina del Rey.

Having the BEST TIME, sending my good vibes,

Alice x

#TeddyAwards #OfficialStatement #DontReadTheYouTube-Comments #NonDisclosureAgreement #SecurityGotRough #WardrobeMalfunction #Travels #Wanderer #GoneAWOL #AliceEdwardsBlog #BloggerLife #Blessed #Brave #DreamChaser

7 Comments · 102 AWOLs · 65 Super Likes

COMMENTS:

Isabelle Moore
| I would also like to say here that I didn't pretend not to know you, I was just hiding from NAME REDACTED BY MODERATOR because he started throwing his poop at the audience.

Alice Edwards
Replying to Isabelle Moore
| We've all seen the YouTube video Isy, let's not go over this

again. Thanks for having me to stay anyway!

Isabelle Moore
Replying to Alice Edwards
| Thanks for coming! I'm sad I didn't get to see enough of you though. Blame @EthanWinklemanProducer

Ethan Winkleman
Replying to Isabelle Moore, Alice Edwards
| Hey, don't blame me! I can't help it if I'm just so distracting ;)

Isabelle Moore
Replying to Ethan Winkleman, Alice Edwards
| Oh, you know it's all your fault, big boy. I'm looking forward to being 'distracted' again later tonight . . .

Ethan Winkleman
Replying to Isabelle Moore, Alice Edwards
| I'm looking forward to getting distracted all over your face . . .

Alice Edwards
Replying to Isabelle Moore, Ethan Winkleman
| Please God, why am I still tagged into this conversation. Make it stop, for the love of Christ.

The most important part of any new place is, for me, the bathroom. Or *loo* as I'm deliberately calling it in front of every American I encounter, just because it confuses them so much.

As far as I'm concerned, that particular room can make or break a holiday. A weak flush, or a cold, leaky shower can be the difference between a happy start to every day, and an angry, annoying one. The perfect bathroom needs a strong toilet, an effective shower, a readily available air freshener, good ventilation, nice towels, and most importantly – especially when it's an en suite like I have here at this AirBnB – a good solid, sound-proof door. The insulation between sexy boy visitors and my morning poos could be the difference between me getting some, and me very much not getting some.

And after all the false starts with Noah, not to mention the texts still occasionally coming in from TD, I really need to get me some hot strange soon. Which means this new loo has to be up to scratch.

As the AirBnB host, 'Patrick', shows me around, I'm impatiently waiting to see the bathroom, and whether it will pass muster. We wander down a short corridor and he stops. 'Here's your room and there's a restroom,' he says, waving off to the left.

'The *loo* is through there, huh?' I say, emphasising 'loo' out of English spite.

'Huh? The what?' he says.

I ignore his confusion, surveying my space for the next few weeks. The bedroom is small and functional – acceptable. I hold my breath as I pass through to my favourite room – and breathe a sigh of relief.

It's perfect. Small enough so farts don't echo round the flat, and the shower head looks clean and new, with controls I actually understand. There's even a little shelf in the shower, for me to put the balled-up blob of hair I will peel out of my bumcrack. It hits me now how much women need a hair shelf to save us wasted hours trying to get the hair blob to stick to the wall. Maybe that could be my new career when I get home – a range of hair shelves?

I reach for the towels. They are soft and made of a material that will actually dry my hands. Wonderful. What is with those posh towels that just seem to spread the water around?

I'm happy. It passes all the amenities tests.

To be honest, my bathroom obsession isn't just about having a nice showerhead. It's more than that. The loo has always been a kind of sanctuary for me. It's a place to be alone. Somewhere to run away from whatever your situation is. Whether it's work, arguments or a boring party. It's the small room to hide in when you're on a bad Tinder date with a guy called Quentin who won't stop licking his lips. It's somewhere to sit quietly when you've had a long day with your dick boss. And sure, it was somewhere to escape as a kid. A place to disappear to when Mum was crying, or Steven was staggering around drunk again. Everyone needs to shut their heads down for five minutes in the chaos, don't they? And everyone needs to wee. It's a legitimate escape when you need that alone time.

I turn around and Patrick is watching me with a slight air of amusement. Fuck, how long was I fondling his towels?

'Would you like a tea?' he says, nicely. 'I got some in when I realised it was a Brit staying with me.'

I am so touched, I could cry. And I might.

'That is so thoughtful, thank you. I would love one, you have no idea,' I say, following him out into the kitchen. 'Got milk?'

He laughs. 'Got milk! Like in the ad!'

I laugh nervously along, but have no idea what he's talking about. And he hasn't answered my question. I decide against enquiring after sugar.

I sit down on his sofa and Patrick puts water on the hob to boil.

'Don't you have a kettle?' I ask, bewildered. He laughs

again and I huff. Why do Americans think everything I'm saying is a joke? It's this dumb accent I have, that's what it is.

Handing me my cup of tea, I sniff it suspiciously. He has added milk, but it is a terrible colour and I know this will be bad. Tea colour is sacred – he might as well have set light to the British flag. But I must not be ungrateful, he's gone to a lot of trouble and not being polite would be just as unBritish.

'Thank you very much!' I say as enthusiastically as possible, pretending to take a sip and trying not to gag.

'What have you got planned for the rest of the week?' he says sweetly, blowing on his own cup of vile mud-water. 'Need any tips for local bars or anything?'

'Ah that's really nice of you,' I say politely, already bored of being polite – GOD, isn't making new acquaintances so tedious? – 'I'd love that. I'm going to do some tourist stuff on Friday – visit the Walk of Fame, that kind of thing – but otherwise I haven't got much specifically planned. Actually . . .' I laugh, 'I've kind of got a date tomorrow.' I make a face so he knows I know it's weird.

He looks amused.

But I don't care. I'm well into week two of my LA adventure, and this leg was definitely, definitely, definitely meant to include sex. I mean, could 'Fun' have been any more euphemistic? The closest I've come so far was when the vagina cult wanted to compare bushes. And Isy promised to help me, but she's been too busy non-stop fucking that moron Ethan. I still kinda hope Noah might be a possibility, but I'm officially sick of waiting for things to happen naturally. So I have taken matters into my own hands. I have opened Bumble.

I had the dating app back in the UK, but it was mostly just for people-watching. I never actually met up with anyone for dates, I just went on there to look at humans and get the odd dopamine hit and ego boost from matches I never bothered messaging. Truthfully, I've been going through a major dry spell this past year. I haven't made eye contact with a man in at least nine months. The last night out I had where there were attractive men present – all taken – I actually thanked one of them for standing near me. That's how bad things have been. Honestly, I think I used up all the men in London in my mid-twenties. And then of course, I was trapped in the TD vortex for far too long.

But I am meant to be having fun on this leg of the trip. And surely sex with strangers – or at least snogging strangers – has to come into it somewhere.

And so, yes, I went online and I'm actually super impressed with LA Bumble. Everyone is much hotter, more tanned, and more naked than on the UK Bumble. After an hour of swiping on the beach, I narrowed it down to 'Robert', a sexy dirtbag type, who loves a selfie, and 'Emre', a sensitive musician, who was a clear hatfish.

A hatfish – if you're not familiar – is a guy who wears a hat in every single photo, because they have bad or no hair, and they don't want you to know. Which is weird to me, because I love a bald dude. Be bald and proud, I say, because at some point, we're going to figure it out. Unless you're planning to wear a hat in bed, and I don't know many people who are into that.

In the end, I went with Robert. Mostly because a sexy dirtbag is exactly what I'm looking for right now.

My new friend Patrick laughs. 'Dating in LA is kind of strange,' he says, thoughtfully. 'I only moved here a year ago, from Michigan. Over there we just kind of went on a date and if we liked that person, we made a go of things.' He sighs a little dramatically. 'That is not the way of things here. I think LA dating is a perpetual state of being for many natives. They have to be forced or tricked into actually committing. I'm not really into either of those options, so I'm staying single. Actually I quit dating a few months ago.'

I make a sympathetic face, but I'm delighted by all this information. I am so not looking for commitment right now. I just need a wipe clean after TD. Casual is ideal.

He clears his throat. 'So, where are you going on this date tomorrow?' he says.

'It's a themed restaurant,' I reply, thinking about it. 'And apparently it's great. It's pirate themed! So I guess we'll have a drink and if we don't hate each other, we'll get some food after.'

'Pirate themed?' Patrick says, looking amused again. 'Sounds like it could go either way. Whose idea was that?'

'His,' I confirm.

Which, I realised later, should really have been my first clue.

8

AWOL.COM/Alice Edwards' Travel Blog: Living My Dream and Feeling Very #Blessed

30 April – 9.25 p.m.

Good evening, dream chasers,

I have come to LA to meet humans from all walks of life, to connect with other souls from around this big wide world. And to that end I am currently on a date. This will be a very quick blog post as he is in the loo and will soon return. I was feeling very excited about the date because I sensed he could be my soulmate, and now we are here, I can report that he is very handsome and lovely. But sadly, I can now also sense that he is not The One, and we must all trust in our instincts, must we not?

Now I am left with the sad problem of what to say in order to soothe his hurt, to apply balm to his wounds. How do I leave without upsetting this person? These are questions I must contemplate.

Also, the food is really nice.

Wishing you all love,

Alice x

#HurtFeelings #FirstDate #Kindness #Bumble #MillennialProblems #TravelBlogger #Wanderer #GoneAWOL #AliceEdwardsBlog #Blessed #Brave #DreamChaser

5 Comments · 6 AWOLs · 12 Super Likes

COMMENTS:

Isabelle Moore

| Oh Al! You need to find a good man like @EthanWinkleman

Ethan Winkleman
Replying to Isabelle Moore

| Aww babe! You are so cute. You're going to get so much good man later on tonight . . .

Danny Boy UrMum

| B GR8FUL ANY1 WANTS TO FUCK U FAT BITCH

AWOL MODERATOR
Replying to Danny Boy UrMum

| Hey Danny pal! We know you're just trying to have some lolz in life, but please be respectful to our users :) I'm here for some chilled out bantz if you fancy. Luke

Danny Boy UrMum
Replying to AWOL MODERATOR

| luke u r an absolute mug

I am feeling like some kind of superhero for still being here. I think Robert the dirtbag might be the worst person to ever exist. He's just so awful. Like, the worst. But that's underselling it. I'm pretty sure he is what would result if someone got Hitler and Donald Trump to have a baby together – but he has worse hair than both.

He's gone to the bathroom and I am contemplating making a run for it. But I don't think I have time. He wees weirdly fast, and he's definitely not washing his hands in there.

It's been two hours of tedious hell so far. I arrived five

minutes early to the date and he was already there, a large whiskey in his hand, taking up an entire booth with his ego. It looked like some kind of chauvinism tableaux – like Leonardo da Vinci had painted *The Last Supper* but there was no room for disciples because Jesus was manspreading in every direction.

When he spotted me, he – and I can't believe I'm saying this – *clicked his fingers in the* air to get my attention. As every decent, non-Hitler-Trump offspring knows, there is no situation where it's acceptable to click your fingers at another human being. That is, unless you are literally demonstrating the rudest way to get another person's attention. I slowly made my way over to him, stopping short of the booth to work out how exactly to slide in with his stupid giant legs in the way. He openly looked me up and down.

'You're fatter than you look in your photos,' he said in this ugly, slow drawl.

I stared at him for five full seconds. 'Are you serious, man?' I said, ready to walk straight out again.

He nodded, before continuing, 'But it's fine, because you're also hotter than you looked, so it's cool.'

He actually negged me before I'd even had a drink. Unbelievable.

'Sit down,' he waved his whiskey at me. 'I've ordered you a pink cocktail.'

'A *pink* cocktail? Any particular reason you thought that was what I'd want?' I said, eyebrows raised.

He shrugs. 'That's all you chicks ever drink, isn't it?'

I took a deep breath, just as the waiter arrived, carefully placing the drink down on the table in front of me.

I stood there for another few seconds, breathing hard at the outrageously sexist and offensive generalisation.

Never mind casually ordering for me without asking what I'd want, it's SO offensive to assume all women want some pretty, pink sparkly thing, just because we have more oestrogen.

I was absolutely livid.

And the fact that I do actually drink a lot of pink cocktails is very much beside the point.

'Sit,' he barked again, and for some inexplicable reason, I did. I don't know why. Maybe I'm just a trained monkey. Maybe I was too embarrassed to go back home to Patrick so soon. Maybe I didn't want to waste the six hours of make-up and hair prep. But whatever my warped reasoning for staying, I was immediately trapped, and the conversation has been much of the same ever since.

Robert insisted we order food, demanding off-menu steak-type items from the waiter because clearly a vegetable would threaten his masculinity. And all without once making eye contact with the poor beleaguered waiter, who definitely went away to spit in our food. Robert then spent the starter reciting entire scenes from *The Godfather*.

I've never seen it, and I can tell you with some sincerity I definitely never will now.

Then, when the main course came, he started screaming that his meat was too well done, and they needed to give him the animal 'still squealing in agony'. And then he smirked at me as if that was sexy. The chat since has mostly revolved around his work (his boss is a moron), his car (it is fast) and his gun (it is a gun). But I've only been listening just enough to know when to nod in the right places. Otherwise, I've been getting through this evening by playing episodes of *Rick and Morty* in my head. And believe me, no one is getting squanched tonight.

Oh God, he's coming back from the loo. He's walking slowly, looking around the room, like he's waiting for everyone to recognise him. He sits down, barely glancing at me.

'Look, it's getting late . . .' I begin. He holds up his hand shushing me with one finger on my lips. I fight the urge to bite it off – he might find that sexy.

'Be upfront, girl,' he says in a husky voice. 'If you want to come back to mine, just say it, girl. I won't judge you for giving it up on a first date, I think we should just give in to our animal urges.'

I almost puke in my mouth. 'Um, no, that isn't what I meant,' I say slowly. 'I mean, it's late, so I should be getting home. I'm tired and . . .'

He snorts. 'It's not late, don't bullshit me, girl. If you want to give up on this, then that's on you, but don't bullshit me.'

'I'm not . . . it's not . . . *giving up* on anything,' I say, bewildered and trying not to openly snarl over '*girl*'. 'I just think it's time to call it a night. We've had dinner, it's time to go.'

He shrugs, mutters 'fine' and clicks his fingers at the waiter, who is midway through taking an order from another couple.

'*Garçon*,' he shouts across the room, making the international prick mime for the bill. I catch the waiter rolling his eyes as he turns back to his customers.

'We'll just go fifty-fifty,' he says and I nod, repressing a sigh. I'm fine with going halves, I would've insisted if he hadn't suggested it. But I reserve the right to be resentful over the fifty-dollar steak and seven whiskies he's mainlined throughout the meal, while I nursed one pink cocktail I didn't want, and an orange juice.

'Although . . .' he says, pausing as he pulls out his wallet. 'You had that extra juice, didn't you?'

You fucking wot?

'Do you want me to just pay the whole thing?' I say, the sarcasm dribbling from my mouth.

'If you think that's best,' he says calmly, deliberately putting his wallet back in his pocket.

Oh my God, he is unbelievable. I feel the boiling rage fireworking in my belly, but I breathe deeply and swallow it. I suddenly really miss TD.

We leave together and I pull out my phone ready to order an urgent Uber. Please, please let there be one available within a minute.

That's when he leans in to kiss me.

'Woah!' I say, pushing him away.

'Come on, you know you want it,' he says, smirking. Ugh, why did I think this was a good idea? Why did I want to meet up with a dirtbag? He is gross, and Jesus, his breath smells like he has eaten a burp.

'I definitely do not want it, thank you,' I say, firmly, frantically tapping my phone – why don't I have a signal?

'Don't be so frigid, Alice girl. Let's go back to mine, get high and I'll give you a taste of my groin yoghurt. My groghurt.'

What?

Groin yoghurt? Groghurt? What in the name of all that is holy is groin . . . Oh God, I get it. I feel the sick burning in the back of my throat.

And get high? That is outrageous! It is *disgraceful*! Offering me drugs! On a date! How dare he!

I mean, obviously I want to do drugs on a date, but only with a guy I fancy. Duh.

'Please go away, right now,' I say firmly, and he shrugs – his signature gesture – but does leave. I watch him go and only finally breathe out when I'm sure he's not coming back. Reassured, I turn back to my phone, which has found its network and I tap 'request Uber'. It's four minutes away and I quickly WhatsApp Eva, filling her in on my dreadful night.

Her reply is instant: 'That sounds rubbish! Sorry Alice. But don't worry. As they say, there are plenty more fish in the sea.'

I take a second to breathe.

I am annoyed. Really annoyed. It's such an *annoying* reply. Such a dismissal of how shit tonight was. She thinks some clichéd platitude makes it all better? She has no idea how crappy the dating world is. She's so smug over there in her lovely home, paid for by her parents, snuggled up on the sofa with her beloved Jeremy. The image fills me with jealous rage. It's so easy for her. I didn't even want anything from Robert tonight, just some fun and maybe a bit of casual sex. I didn't need him to be The One, just not The Dick.

'Eva, that's bullshit,' I fire back, tapping the screen with irritation. 'Yeah, there might be plenty of fish in the sea, but believe me when I say, the dating-water is so contaminated and polluted, it's not possible to actually swim in it. There are too many sewage works around, siphoning their green sludge off into the water, and making all the sexy single fish in the sea mutate into arseholes with three eyes and ex issues.'

I press send and she replies quickly, regretfully. 'Sorry Alice, didn't mean to piss you off :(. He really does sound like a total wanker, I hope you're not upset? I hope it hasn't spoiled your trip? Sorry. Xxxx'

A second later, she sends another message. 'Really sorry. How is Project Fun going otherwise?'

I sigh, feeling a little guilty for taking my bad mood out on Eva.

'Sorry for snapping, Eva, love you. And yes I'm fine,' I text back. 'I'm having a good time. It turns out my AirBnB host is totally brilliant. We got drunk last night on 'frozé' – or is it 'frosé'? It's frozen rosé and we had an argument about how it should be spelled.'

My car pulls up.

'Car here, love you xx', I type out quickly.

'I'm glad he's nice. When are you free to Skype?' she replies, but I am gone.

9

AWOL.COM/Alice Edwards' Travel Blog: Living My Dream and Feeling Very #Blessed

30 April – 10.15 p.m.

Good evening, dream chasers,

   Just a quick philosophical message because I am feeling philosophical for no reason, to remind you all to follow your heart. For you know not what might happen tomorrow. What if you were to wake up dead in the morning? What would you say if you were dead? If you were a charred corpse right now, what would you do??? Think about that!!! Have you told everyone you love that you love them? We are all so #blessed to live this life, remind yourself of that EVERY DAY. Be kind to yourself and others. Enjoy every moment of your existence in the sun. Look up, look around, embrace life – and also please stop watching that YouTube video from the Teddy Awards. I mean FFS don't you people have better things to do? There are 900 comments on it now and some of them are really mean.

#EmbraceLife #HugLovedOnes

2 Comments · 0 AWOLs · 1 Super Likes

COMMENTS:

Hannah Edwards
| luv u 2 sis

Alice Edwards
Replying to Hannah Edwards
| Cheers for the support, Hannah.

Here is my last will and testament:

I bequeath everything I own to my brother, Mark, my sister, Hannah, and my best friend Eva. Because there is really no one else in my sad empty sad life. And actually, I don't really have anything to bequeath so why am I doing this? I have no home, no savings, no valuable antiques. Even my iPhone is cracked to fuck and would cost more to fix than it would be worth.

So, actually, I'm not sure my loved ones will want the bother. Sure, Hannah and Eva can have my jewellery, but I doubt they'll want that either, since it's mostly from Accessorize and my favourite ring turns my finger green. The most expensive thing I own is a bag from River Island, but the lining is ripped. Oh well, tell Eva she can have that because Hannah won't know the difference between that and the other Primark ones.

Tell TD I hope he is sad that I am dead, and I hope this teaches him to treat women better in future because my premature end is all his fault for being mean to me. And actually, also tell him not to date anyone else or I'll haunt him.

This last will and testament feels like it got petty?

So, my Uber driver is trying to kill me. He's driving with one hand and texting – while also singing along loudly to Lionel Richie. And everyone knows that's not safe driving music because you're singing too loudly to concentrate.

This is so unfair! I have so much to live for! I should never have left England! Everyone told me to download Lyft, they TOLD ME. But did I listen? Obviously I did not and now I'm in a death trap with a driver who has nearly crashed four times in the ten minutes since he picked me up. I am actually genuinely terrified. He is a lunatic, driving well over 100 mph and swerving in and out of other cars on the motorway. I'm clinging on to the door handle for – and I don't say this lightly – dear life.

I am fully about to lose my shit with him.

But I must not.

My Uber rating is an already-dire 3.5 because of my inability to not be shitty with drivers. If it goes any lower, I'll never get picked up. I need my rating to survive at least another few weeks while I'm here.

I must not say anything.

Even if it costs me my life.

Sigh. How come other British people are so much better with the stiff upper lip thing?

The mad driver suddenly veers across three whole lanes with one hand waving his phone, where his satnav is offering directions that he is ignoring.

I can resist the pull of my inherent shittiness no longer.

'Can you slow the fuck down please?' I say loudly, my English accent crisper with rage. He whips round and I fear for a second he will kill us both out of spite.

Instead he throws back his head and laughs maniacally.

The car slows – marginally – as he replies happily, 'I can see why you're a 3.5.'

I breathe out, relief filling me and my adrenaline slowing. But then I am outraged. What does he mean by calling me a

3.5? It is the Uber rating system that is the problem, not me.

And anyway his rating is no better. I yank out my phone, finally able to let go of the handle.

'Hey! You're a 3.5 too,' I say a little too aggressively. He nods happily. 'Sure I am, because I am a terrible driver. But that's why I was the only one to pick you up. We are both trapped in the lower echelons of Uber, we are a uniquely shitty subsection, stuck with each other because no one else wants us. I'm doomed to collect shitty passengers; you are doomed to being driven around like this and risking death. We are stuck with each other.'

He grins at me in the mirror and I ponder this for a moment. Am I a shitty passenger? I thought the drivers liked feedback while they drove? If their car smells weird, surely they want to know about it, so they can get an air freshener? If they're playing crappy music, wouldn't they rather I shouted over it until they put Beyoncé on instead? And who doesn't love Queen Bey? Sure, I talk a lot, but isn't that the best thing about an Uber driver? It's like free therapy. You can tell strangers things you can't tell your friends. Especially when it's 3 a.m. and I'm coming back from a night out where there have been a lot of pink cocktails even though they are mildly sexist.

I sit back in my seat, feeling sulky.

'Hey, don't be blue,' Uber Driver says, meeting my eyes in the mirror. 'I don't mind you being shitty. And I don't mind that you're going to give me a bad rating, I'm going to give you one, too. It's freeing being down here in the mid-threes, trust me. I know what to expect, and so should you.'

'But I don't deserve to be in the threes,' I say weakly, and he chuckles again. 'You're adorable,' he tells me, and I can feel his speed is picking up again. We're going to be back at mine in half the time it usually takes.

'So, where are you going tonight, 3.5?' he says, his voice teasing.

'Home,' I reply, shortly, hoping to convey my hostility towards the nickname I have somehow acquired.

'What!' he says, with mock horror. 'But you look so great, you should be hitting up a club or something.'

'Well thanks,' I say softening ever so slightly. 'But I've just been on the world's worst date and I'm looking forward to eating chocolate and pasta in bed. In that order.'

He throws his head back again and laughs. He has such a huge laugh. All encompassing. A laugh that takes up his whole being, his Adam's apple bouncing in his throat. It is a laugh that is hard not to join in with.

'I see,' he roars, because he apparently does everything loudly. 'Well, bed-pasta does sound tempting, I will admit.' We make eye contact in the mirror again, and I notice myself noticing how nice his face is. He has big, thick eyebrows, bushy and feral, like Sandy Cohen's.

'But,' he continues, thoughtfully. 'Have you had the chocolate over here? It's garbage compared to your British chocolate.'

'Oh damn, yes, I've heard that,' I say, genuinely upset. I lean forward against my seatbelt. 'But do you go to Whole Foods here?'

He laughs again, 'Sure, sometimes.'

'It's like how I imagine heaven must be,' I breathe. 'Rows and rows of imaginative, beautiful food. There are like six olive bars, how is that possible? I don't even like olives, and I still spent forty minutes examining them all. And the salad bars have macaroni cheese! That's not salad! But I could tell myself it was healthy because it was part of the salad bar! It's wonderful. I am planning to spend every day next week in a Whole Foods.'

'Don't you have Whole Foods in the UK?' he asks, still watching me in the mirror. I'm not sure he's looked at the road once these past five metres. I grip the door handle again, as his speed creeps up once more.

'Um, well I guess we do,' I say. 'But not many. We're more into Tesco and Boots.'

'What's Boots?'

I sigh heavily. 'Uber Driver, our countries will never be able to get along until you embrace a Boots over here. Or at least a Superdrug. Where did you go to shoplift mascara when you were fifteen?'

'CVS,' he confirms. 'Aged fifteen was my drag phase.'

'Really though?' I say, forgetting to hold on and getting thrown across the seat as he crosses two lanes without warning or indicating. But I'm no longer annoyed. Actually, all this dangerous driving is starting to feel a bit sexy.

He nods. 'Actually, yes, I did wear a bit of mascara as a teenager. I thought it was punk. Obviously I got the shit kicked out of me regularly at my high school, but that just made me wear more.'

'I am obsessed with *Drag Race*,' I say excitedly.

'It wasn't exactly drag,' he says, laughing again. 'More . . . rebellion. Against my parents, against the teachers, against the other kids, and against gender norms.'

'Fuck yeah,' I punch the air, and then add, 'Drag is really sexy though.'

He nods, looking me dead in the eye. 'Good to know.'

The eye contact suddenly feels a bit heated and I clear my throat, glancing out the window. I realise we're almost back at mine. I am a little disappointed.

'Well, enjoy your pasta and shitty chocolate, 3.5,' he says, playfully, as we turn into my road.

'Ha!' I say, a little sadly. 'Um, thanks. And you enjoy being a godawful driver out there. At least please try not to kill anyone tonight. I'm not over here long enough to waste time being interviewed by the police.'

He laughs his barrel laugh again, and pulls over. I reach for the door.

'Unless . . .' he starts, a little shyly. 'Unless you want to go for a drink instead? I'm going off duty, and it's rare I meet someone in the Uber subsection as mean and cute as you. I promise I'm not a crazy stalker, and if you say no, I'll still give you a solid four stars.'

I can't help laughing. 'How do I get that up to five?' I say and I am flirting.

'A drink would get you to five,' he smirks.

I smirk back, thinking about it.

Of course I must say no. Duh, of course, no. I am not a stupid person, and I grew up hearing the stranger danger mantra. I cannot go off into the night with this large, reckless man who has been given such a bad rating from other people. I picture defence lawyers holding up my underwear in court and declaring me 'asking for it'.

No way, man.

I open my mouth to politely decline, when my phone lights up. A message from TD flashes up and the message is short and salty.

'When r u back? Cum on I'm horny.'

I am suddenly sickened by the idea that his was the last penis I had in me. The last sex-sweat I tasted. Ugh. I can just picture his leering, unappealing face, his face slick with desire. Ugh.

I throw my phone back into my bag, I don't want his text touching me.

'Come on then, Uber Driver,' I say impulsively. 'There's a bar round the corner, we'll go get a drink. I want my five stars, but please don't murder me.' He grins in the mirror and un-buckles his seatbelt. We both climb out of the car and oh boy, he's good-looking. We face each other for a moment, smiling widely about what is happening. I am dizzy with spontaneity and buzzing with adrenaline from my near-death experience in the car. Or maybe it's at the thought of sleeping with this large, sexy human.

He offers me his hand to hold, and I take it, leading him away from the car.

Here we go, it's finally happening. I am going to have sex at long, long last. And I am confident it will be at least a 3.5.

10

AWOL.COM/Alice Edwards' Travel Blog: Living My Dream and Feeling Very #Blessed

6 May – 6.12 p.m.

Jkbfedbkh%

7 Comments · 0 AWOLs · 1 Super Likes

COMMENTS:

Kirpa Saul
| Oh hello, somebody just butt-blogged.

Karen Gill
| We haven't heard from you all week, been having too much fun?!

Ayo Damiunse
| Yeah! Fuck you, AWOL! Let's all post nonsense until we bring down The Man!

Eva Slate
| Miss yooooooooou, where have you been?! Answer my texts so I know you're alive.

Ryan T
| WTF is this? Dumb cow

AWOL MODERATOR
Replying to Ryan T

| Hey Ryan! Luke here! I'm sure you're just having fun but please be respectful to our users :) Cool chatting to you, bro. Luke

    Ryan T
    Replying to AWOL MODERATOR
    | am not ur bro luke u dickhead

'Owwww, ow, ow, ow, ow!' I shout, wriggling around in the bed sheets. 'Pins and needles, ow, ow.'

Dom reaches over and rubs my hairy legs. 'Better?' he asks, but it's not. 'I think maybe I need to get out of bed,' I say reluctantly.

'Nooooo,' he booms, grabbing me round the middle. 'I won't let you. Nobody is ever leaving this bed.'

'Well, you know, that is technically a kidnapping,' I point out, wincing at the shooting pain in my left foot. 'And I should warn you – other people are fight or flight in those situations – I just lose bladder control.' I point down at my stomach. 'Especially when I'm being squeezed.'

He laughs and lets me go, rolling away across the crumpled sheets.

Me and the Uber driver have been in a sex bubble for nearly a week now. We had one drink in that bar, before the horn took over. I wasn't sure about the AirBnB rules pertaining to shagging strangers in your room, so we raced back to his in the Uber – only nearly dying three more times – for a night of shagging. I was a bit alarmed when he took his clothes off, because – much like everything else about him – his penis was really upsettingly large. He presented it to me in this delighted way, like I should be ecstatic about this massive, unwieldy implement. But honestly, I didn't want it anywhere near me. There is a lot of talk about women preferring large willies, but in my experience, that is only the case because they quite like terrifying their pals with stories afterwards. Personally, I prefer anything coming that close to my internal organs to be as average as possible. But after some heated discussion, we agreed to make an attempt and, thankfully, Uber Driver made suitable efforts to ensure I was, er, ready for landing. All went as it should.

It's been fucking lovely. And lovely fucking.

But I have also not really been able to poo in, like, a week. His bathroom is right next to his bed, and I couldn't risk it. At this point, I am worried it has reabsorbed. Reabsorbed poo has got to be bad for you, hasn't it?

'Uber Driver, I think I may have to go home,' I say, sitting up slowly. My back creaks from too much lying down. 'I am in a bad way, and the bed sores are starting to get infected.'

He laughs, long and hard. 'You are so unusual, Alice. Very different from other women.'

I hate this line. I'm a human being, humans are all different from each other. It is one of the very first things they teach you at school: that people are all unique. Saying that line just feels like another way to set women against each other. We are encouraged to be different to 'other women', as if most women are awful and their personalities must be avoided at all costs.

I give him a look. 'You mean different from the other tourists you pick up in your Uber?'

'Exactly right,' he says grinning. 'You are so rude and you

don't care what I think. Most women in the US get bounced from the state for eating carbs but I've seen you eat a whole loaf of bread in two days. Not to mention that large bar of chocolate you ate for breakfast.'

I harrumph. 'That was only to prove a point,' I say defensively. 'How dare they call it a "Sharing bar"? I don't want to share. They don't get to police how I consume my snacks, with their politically correct, diabetes-friendly messaging.'

He laughs again.

'Also,' I say, 'You are not my elderly grandparent – you do not get to comment on my eating habits. This is a verbal warning, I don't want to hear anything else about me eating carbs or I'm out of here for real.'

'Fine, but I'm just saying I like it,' he smiles and reaches for me again, pressing his erection against my leg.

'Keep your likes and dislikes to yourself, you are a seven-night stand, that is all.' I roll away.

'Seven nights?' he says, coyly. 'That means I get one more night with you?'

'Oh,' I reply distractedly, looking around the room for my underwear. 'No, I just don't know how to count. Maths was never my strong point.'

'Math,' he corrects me.

'MATHS,' I say, giving him my undivided attention again. 'We invented the language, we get to decide if a thing is plural or not.'

I pull on one sock but he takes the other one, hiding it under the duvet. 'Don't go, Al, I want you to stay!'

I sigh. 'Really, I do have to go back to my AirBnB. My host, Patrick, will have called the police by now. He hasn't really seen me since that first night. And I'm meant to be seeing Isy for lunch tomorrow. I have to shower properly and I need a change of pants.'

'These are fine,' he says, picking up my jeans from the floor and sniffing them. 'You've hardly even worn them.' I roll my eyes. 'No, *pants*. Underwear. Oh God, you lot really have ruined the language. Although, I do very much enjoy what you've done with the word "fanny".'

'Well, I very much enjoy your fanny,' he says, scooching over, squeezing my bum and tugging at the top I've just put on.

'Look,' I say, giggling. 'We will compromise. I'll stay with you for one more evening, but we have to actually go outside. I want to see the world out there, I want to taste something that isn't takeaway pizza, leftover bread and chocolate you found in a cupboard that was so old it was turning white.'

'You still ate it,' he points out.

'What did I say about commenting on my eating habits?' I say loudly, standing up. He leaps up, too, and I feel my stomach flip a bit. He's so tall and big. I forgot about his bigness while we were horizontal for days on end.

'OK,' he is suddenly eager like a puppy. 'What would you like to do? What haven't you done in LA yet?'

I smile up at him. I already know what I want to do. It's been on my list from day one, but I didn't want to do it on my own, and I definitely didn't want to do it with that dirtbag Robert.

'I want to go visit a Green Doctor,' I say, grinning and taking his hand.

He cocks an eyebrow back at me by way of an answer.

An hour later, we are going through airport security.

It's not actually airport security, but it feels like it. We are in a place called WEED LOVE TO HAVE YOU AT THE BEST JOINT IN TOWN, where we are going to buy some totally legal marijuana. This could only be more exciting if it were still illegal.

'This is so *awesome*,' I loudly hiss, as I show a stern-looking woman my passport. Dom elbows me to shut up. 'It is though!' I say, my voice not really any lower. He pulls me closer as the woman nods us through and we enter the spliff shop.

So my original idea was to visit Muscle Beach for this. I'd walked past a bunch of totally legit-looking places selling the good stuff from 'Green Doctors'. They all had t-shirts with the name and everything. But Dom said we should go somewhere a bit more reputable.

The fact that marijuana shops have reputations to consider blows me away.

'This one has really good Google reviews,' he says conversationally now, leading me through a short corridor and into what looks just like the inside of an Apple Store. There are young, cool staff everywhere, wearing lanyards and showing customers around the room, explaining their products and making recommendations.

'More importantly, the name is pun-tastic!' I add, helpfully. 'A bit convoluted, sure, but I do love a pun.'

He snorts, confirming, 'That is what matters most, of course.' He glances down at me. 'You doing OK, 3.5? Have you really never smoked a spliff before? What were you even doing with your time at high school?'

I shake my head, still awed by the rows of options before us in fancy glass cases. There are edibles, drinks, and a vast array of pre-rolled spliffs. I bet they even have a genius bar somewhere around here.

'No, never,' I say, absent-mindedly. 'I was too busy not

studying at secondary school, and also not getting laid.' I turn to face him. 'So, what should we get? Any suggestions? What do you usually buy?'

'I think let's stick with a straightforward spliff for your first try,' he says, trying not to laugh. 'They have three options on the menu. One that makes you hyper, one that mellows you out and one somewhere in-between, like a mix of both.'

'Won't the one in-between just even you out?' I ask, only half joking.

'You could do with a bit of evening out, actually,' he says, smirking. 'You are quite the rollercoaster ride.'

I'm not sure if this is a compliment or not, but I'm too excited to care. We buy two pre-rolled spliffs, for fourteen dollars each, and I'm fascinated to discover that I am allowed to pay with my debit card. I even add a tip – because dollars are not real money anyway – and briefly wonder how this will appear on my bank statement. I am suddenly seized with worry over what a mortgage advisor would make of this purchase, were they reviewing my spending. But then I remember I'm wasting all the money I have in the world anyway, and will never be a home owner. But, let's face it, no one my age will – not without a parent to help. It's a real shame about my parents being so poor and complicated.

The cashier hands me a receipt, smiling. It has information about tax on there. I stare at it, enthralled. It's a receipt for marijuana that talks about *tax*. I am keeping this for ever. It occurs to me that I am one of the last generations who will find this a novelty. There are kids out there today who will grow up with it always being legal. Isn't that funny? They will grow up thinking of it as nothing to buy marijuana from their local Med Men or Green Doctor. It will be like Oddbins was for me when I was a kid.

Life is changing too quickly for me. I don't know how much I like it.

'Can we go smoke it on the beach?' I say when we get outside. I am bouncing up and down with excitement.

'Sure,' Dom says, handing me the plastic folder with our purchases. 'But FYI, that is incredibly illegal. They treat it like murder one here, so we'll have to be very careful.'

'Oh, excellent!' I breathe out. 'This wasn't going to be nearly as much fun without it being illegal in some small respect.'

He takes my arm and we wander down to the shore, choosing a spot on the sand near the creeping tide. The light is starting to fade as Dom shows me how to inhale. I am unsurprisingly bad at it.

'Are you going to be OK?' he asks me nicely, patting me on the back as I cough up my lungs.

'I'm fine!' I say weakly, genuinely quite enjoying the burning sensation in my throat. 'It's great! Because this is how it is in the films, Uber Driver,' I explain. 'The idiot virgin coughs up internal organs the first time she tries drugs, thus learning her lesson for ever. She never does drugs again but her best friend becomes an addict of course, later dying in a tragic car accident after taking too many hallucinogens. The survivor guilt haunts our heroine but ultimately, she goes on to have a great life after marrying her high-school sweetheart who teaches her the true strength and courage of saying no.'

He looks at me contemplatively, 'It's a good job you're not a virgin then, isn't it?' he says. 'Because that life sounds tedious as fuck.'

'Indeed it does,' I agree, looking around at my beautiful surroundings. Everything suddenly feels a bit smooshy – but that might just be all the coughing – and I stare up at the sky, fascinated. Somewhere out there, the sun is setting, but the evening cloud is too thick to see where.

'Where is the sun?' I say and my voice sounds far away and gravelly. 'It must be over there. That's west, right?' I point in a random direction.

'How would you possibly know that?' Dom says affectionately – and he sounds far away, too. 'You haven't got a clue where west is.'

'I sensed it,' I reply, self-importantly.

'You *sensed* it?' He does not believe me.

'Yes, I think that psychic I saw a couple of weeks ago gave me special powers.'

He still sounds sceptical, which I do not understand. 'Do you indeed? You know what I think, 3.5? I think that maybe the drugs are kicking in.'

'I don't think so,' I protest. 'How am I supposed to know if they are, anyway?'

'Well, how do you feel?' he says, turning to me.

'I feel great,' I say, adding quickly, 'but I don't think I'm high, I think I'm just great.' I pause. 'Wait, I have an important question.'

'What is the question?' faraway version of Uber Driver asks.

I think about it. 'I can't remember.'

'OK.'

'Wait, I remember now,' I say suddenly. 'It's important. When do you think The Rock will be president?'

'Isn't he president already?' Dom says and we both think about it for a long time.

'Help me stand up,' I say impulsively, as he takes my hand. But neither of us stand. It feels very funny to be holding his hand, sitting on a beach, and so I start laughing. I'm holding the hand of this stranger I have known less than a week. A stranger I met in a taxi, whose penis has been inside me. How funny life is. He is giggling now too, and I cannot imagine life gets any better than this. How could it possibly?

Then – off in the distance – I notice the funfair on the pier. The Ferris wheel lights up the night sky. I stop giggling and grip Dom's hand tighter.

'We have to go to that. I want to go on a ride,' I say and it is the most vital mission I've had so far on this life journey.

'Yes!' he shouts and he is on his feet, taking me up with him.

My legs feel funny and I am glad to still have hold of his hand. I take out my phone and I take a photo of our hands, locked together. I have to remember this lovely moment with a near-stranger. I want to look at this photo forever. I want to look at it every time I am sad and not sure if things will be good again.

'How far away is that?' I say, looking off at the sparkly pier and I am giggling again.

'I think it's almost certainly too far to walk,' he says thoughtfully. 'Particularly because I don't know if you can walk.'

'That's ridiculous,' I say crossly, 'of course I can walk!' And then I fall over in the sand and I lie there laughing, until he picks me up.

'We don't have to walk, but we do have to be able to stand,' he tells me, and I think he may be right.

'We will uder an ober,' I say, inspiration striking me. 'Wait, I mean uder an *orber*. Wait, what am I trying to say?'

'Do you mean uder an ober?' he says and we both start laughing again.

'You are an ober driver,' I point out, helpfully. 'Can I uder you?'

'I'm not picking you up,' he says and we are moving across the sand somehow. 'You are only a 3.5.'

We walk a few steps. 'Are we nearly there yet?' I say, and I think I mean in life.

'Not even close,' he says, and I think he means in life.

'I have an idea!' I say, stopping. 'We can get a rickshaw along the sand. That way we don't have to leave the beach. Because Uder Briver, I don't want to leave the beach, ever.'

Dom agrees this is a better idea, and we haggle with a passing driver in yellow shorts. For twenty dollars he will take us the three miles along the sea front, and he says we can shout as much as we like because we wanted that included in the price.

We climb on board and the man starts peddling hard. The warm wind in my face feels amazing as we fly along, passing glowing bikes and tourists and pedestrians and people on those scooter things. And I feel really happy. I know I am high, and also full of sexy hormones, but I think I really am happy.

I sit back and stare up for a minute.

I feel so far away from everything. So far away from my old, pathetic life. So far away from everything that needs resolving. I wanted escapism here; I wanted shallow silliness; I wanted fun; and that's what I've found. That's a good thing, isn't it? It is. Because escaping is not the same as running away. Escaping is fine. And even running away is fine, too, I'm sure of it. Getting a rickshaw away is even better.

I think I was right to come here, to do this. I think this is going to be OK. I think that *I* am going to be OK. Everything is going to work out how it's supposed to. I just have to stay on the beach, and I just have to get on that Ferris wheel.

'Which way is west?' I ask our driver and he points out in front of us, over the landscape full of people and life. I turn to Dom to tell him I was right, and he kisses me.

'Uber Driver,' I shout, pulling away and looking deep into his big brown eyes. 'This is important, you have to listen to me. You have to listen.'

We are silent as we stare at each other intently.

In a whispered voice I say it – I say the important thing.

'Uber Driver, let's play thumb wars with our tongues.'

And we do.

***

from: Mark Edwards <markedwardscityboy@gmail.com>
to: Alice Edwards <SimplyTheBestAlice2003@hotmail.com>

Here you go, Alice xx I know you love these!!

---------- Forwarded message ----------

from: Hannahtruthseeker@protonmail.com
to: Hannah Edwards
cc: Hannah Edwards
date: 6 May at 22.15
subject: APRIL FAMILY NEWSLETTER: TOP SECRET
mailed-by: ProtonMail

EDWARDS FAMILY NEWSLETTER/APRIL RECAP

Good evening, assorted family members,

Hannah here. I identify myself to you all with this month's code word so you know it's really me and not the government co-opting my family newsletters.

MOIST

I hope everyone is very well. First up this month, Mum has requested that I thank you all for the cards and well-wishes. Steven is still in intensive care at the hospital and when we have more news, we will update everyone.

Next: for those asking, Alice is currently in LA, where I have been a little concerned as we all know the CIA are listening and watching her every move, but she has reassured me she is keeping a low profile. She is writing a 'travel blog' on AWOL.com where you can read all about her adventures. Don't worry, I am in the process of infiltrating the website to ensure its security is top notch. I was concerned her most recent blog post was a coded message, but I have spent the past week trying to work it out and I think she maybe just sat on her phone.

Other investigations I am currently working on are:
-How the Y2K bug DID REALLY HAPPEN!!! We just didn't realise until now.
-The truth about how Finland is FAKE NEWS.
-Why are we not being told the truth about how Donald Trump's hair style is linked to Roswell and Area 51????? This is one Mark flagged up to me and asked me to look into and I am very intrigued.

In other family news:
-Uncle Ned has asked me to let you all know he has started a Crowd-funding page to raise funds for his gastric bypass operation. Please donate what you can here.

-Cousin Leon is having a big party for his dog Gertie's 17th birthday next month! All welcome, but just be aware that Gertie is having more digestive issues, so you may want to wear shoe covers.
-Aunt Charlotte is pleased to say her youngest, little Jemima, is starting to develop into a woman! She would like any old bras you can give away? Jemima is already a size B, so I'm mostly looking at you, cousin Jo?

Until next month, fellow Truth Seekers.
Hannah xx

AWOL.COM/Alice Edwards' Travel Blog: Living My Dream and Feeling Very #Blessed

12 May – 8.11 a.m.

Good morning, dream chasers,

Apologies for my previous blog post, I tried to delete it, but it just duplicated four times. Anyway, it was not a butt-blog, as one comment suggested, it was an elbow-blog. I was in bed a lot that week because of a little cold and my elbows got in the way of me trying to watch nature documentaries. But I would never complain, and it gave me much time to reflect and examine my place in the universe.

Either way, I am all better now and out of bed. I have been busy having a truly wonderful, fulfilling week. I have been on sunshine-filled bike marathons, visited the stunning Venice Canals, and travelled to the glorious Silver Lake for a picnic. We also took the fascinating Universal Studios tour, where I really lived in the moment and took the time to absorb the genius surrounding me. We then visited Madame Tussauds in Hollywood, where I took a picture with Gandhi and other important figures.

Today, I am extremely excited to say I AM GOING TO DIS-NEYLAND!!!! This is indeed a dream come true. Do I dare chase other dreams now? I am going with three new pals, Dom, Patrick and Ethan, and one old friend, Isy.

She's not old though, not according to her IMDb page.

I was inspired to buy Disney tickets after visiting a wonderful funfair last week. I shall upload a picture of the tickets in a moment, so that you, too, may enjoy the thrill of this experience (just in case you were wondering about the time stamp, yes, I did buy them at 3 a.m. but I was not drunk or high, it was just a coincidence).

I know we're going to embrace so much magic and wonder at the park, and I cannot wait to converse with the true star of the franchise: Minnie Mouse.

Yours sincerely,

Alice x

#DisneyLand #ARollercoasterRide #OverlyExcitableHashtags #TravelBlogger #GoneAWOL #AliceEdwardsBlog #BloggerLife #Blessed #Brave #DreamChaser

7 Comments · 8 AWOLs · 53 Super Likes

COMMENTS:

Isabelle Moore
| Me and Ethan are so excited, too! We'll see you by Mickey's Fun Wheel!

> **Ethan Winkleman**
> **Replying to Isabelle Moore and Alice Edwards**
> | Mickey's Fun Wheel sounds so sexual . . .

>> **Alice Edwards**
>> **Replying to Ethan Winkleman and Isabelle Moore**
>> | Guys, please, please don't.

Paul ProudDadtoDaughters
| Wot bout Mickey Mouse? U fuckin feminists are trying to kill

of anythin mail

AWOL MODERATOR
Replying to Paul ProudDadtoDaughters
| Hey Paul mate! I know it's an important convo about equality, but please be respectful to our users :) I'm here if you fancy chatting more. Luke

Paul ProudDadtoDaughters
Replying to AWOL MODERATOR
| luke you turd

Eva Slate
| Have fun Amazing Alice! Are you free to Skype later? Miss yoooooooou.

'DUDES, ONLY A FIFTY-MINUTE QUEUE FOR THIS ONE!' I am positively screaming, and people are staring, but I don't care. I'm wearing official mouse ears and a Disney jumper, and I've never been happier.

Dom smiles, but Isy looks bored already.

We are in actual Disneyland, and on a sort of pseudo double-date with me, Dom, Isy, Ethan and an enthusiastic fifth wheel in the form of my AirBnB host, Patrick. He is almost as excited as I am.

So OK, we have spent most of the day so far in queues, but it's worth it! And it's definitely been a high point after a busy week of trying to be A Good Tourist.

Since that night getting physically and literally high on the Ferris wheel with Dom, we've spent much more time interacting with Other People and doing Actual Things.

I wanted to tick off the list of stuff Constance Beaumont said on her blog that you have to do in LA. So we went on a long bike ride, which ended in the bad kind of hysterics when I face-planted on the pavement, grazed my knees and wept on the side of the road. Then we went to see the Venice Canals, which Constance said were 'spectacular', but were only OK. It was kind of cloudy and they just looked like muddy streams to me. We have better canals in the UK, and I will fight anyone who says otherwise. We also planned a day at Silver Lake with a picnic, like Constance did, but then got stuck in traffic for four hours and ended up giving up and going home to drink gin. It wasn't all a let-down though. We took the Universal Studios tour, and it was fun snapping a few thousand pictures like true tourists! But then I had to delete most of them to free up space on my phone for our visit to Madame Tussauds in Hollywood. I got a selfie with the Rihanna waxwork and then I cried again, but that was happy crying.

Dom has been very patient with my endless thirst for tourist attractions. And AirBnB Patrick has become a bit of a partner in crime to the pair of us. He's such a lot of fun, I'm so glad I'm staying with him, and delighted he's here with us today, too. Isy and Ethan were a last-minute addition this morning, finally emerging from their sex bubble, and now we are all here and I cannot stop screaming. We're at actual Disneyland! I've been to the one in Paris with Eva, Karen and Slutty Sarah, and it was the best long weekend ever. So I know today is going to be awesome.

I am very aware of my time in America running out, and I feel slightly panicky about it. I'm stuck in Fun Mode. I really don't want to leave. I don't think I'm ready for too much self-discovery in Thailand. I don't need to know myself better, I like this fun-myself just fine. And I've made friends here. I've got too used to the clear skies and all-day sun. I like my routine of morning yoga, a walk along the beach, lunchtime sex with Dom, followed by a touristy adventure. In Asia, I will know no one and I'm hopping from unglamorous hostel to unglamorous hostel.

From my current position of perpetual joy and sex, I am less than excited about that prospect.

But it's booked, and I can't stay here for ever. Life goes on. And I do still have nearly a whole week left! I'm trying to stay in the moment and make the most of what's left. And I have my picture to remind me. The one of me from last Wednesday. The one of me holding hands with near-stranger Dom, walking along the beach, high as a kite from my first-ever spliff, giggling like I would never stop, over 'oders' and 'urbers'. I keep looking at it to remind myself it's good to let go, to try new things, to jump on the spontaneous adventures. It's a reminder that everything that's happened lately has been worth it.

We join the queue and I shake my fists in the air happily. I can't wait.

'Next, I want to go on The Little Mermaid Undersea Adventure ride,' I say, a bit too loudly, and the little girl in the queue behind me shouts, 'ME TOO.' I turn around and we nod at each other with respect.

'Oh God, really?' Isy says, half laughing, but looking a bit exasperated. 'Haven't we done enough? Can't we just go on, like, this one ride, and then go get some booze?'

'Does Disneyland even sell alcohol?' I say, surprised.

She nods in a direction off to the right. 'In the hotels they do. Let's just get some selfies with the cartoon characters for Instagram, then go get drunk. Rides just get in the way of the actual fun.'

I am intrigued by the idea of getting drunk at Disney. I have heard reports of Disney jail and a big part of me wants to see it for myself. I want to see if the handcuffs have ears. But I am also desperate to get a proper go on the rides. I want more adrenaline.

'What do you want to do?' I turn to Dom and Patrick. Dom shrugs. He has been in a bit of an odd mood today. Patrick is more decisive, and shouts, 'RIDES' at me, grinning.

'Me and Patrick could go on a few more rides, then meet you guys later, if you like?' I suggest to the group.

'Sounds good to me,' Ethan says neutrally, examining his perfectly manicured nails.

'Typical,' Dom mutters and I frown at him. What's that supposed to mean? Typical of what? I don't understand.

Before I can ask, Isy pulls out her phone. 'Let's get a picture together in the queue!' We pose as she shouts, 'HASHTAG BEST TIME EVER AT DISNEY I CAN'T EVEN!'

I roll my eyes. 'Isy, you give Millennials a bad rap.'

The little girl behind me sniggers. I like her.

Dom leans over, resting his large head on my shoulder. 'Can we take a selfie, just of us?' he says quietly. I giggle. 'Sure thing, Uber Driver.' I pull out my own phone, and I see him flinch as we simultaneously register the text message waiting on there – from TD.

I've told Dom all about TD because why would I lie? This is just a twelve-night stand after all. So yeah, of course I told him about the tortured back and forthing and the never-ending drunk texts. He laughed and teased me about my stupidity in wasting so many years going back to an idiot. In fact, just yesterday, I was telling him about the last birthday present TD gave me. Some cheap, nasty lingerie. Lingerie. I mean, that is a terrible present anyway because it's not really a present for you, is it? It's for him, and I think it's a weirdly controlling and creepy move. Like you're telling someone what to wear and how to be sexy for you. But, to make matters ten times worse, the lacy thing he got for me was three sizes too small. The bra wouldn't have fit around my nipple.

Dom laughed a lot at the story and promised he would never buy lingerie for a woman he was seeing. But today he doesn't seem to have a sense of humour about anything, including the TD nonsense.

'Oh, it's that moron!' I say, as jovially as I can. Dom looks away, he seems pissed off. So I keep talking. 'Hey, I know! Let's send him a picture of us together. That'll fuck him off and also make him fuck off!'

Dom looks straight at me, but he's not smiling. Was that the wrong thing to say? I thought he'd be amused. We've joked about winding TD up before. Dom even offered to send him a cock shot. Which I would've allowed, had I been any drunker.

After a too-long silence, Dom pastes on a clearly fake smile and says a little too forcefully, 'Yes, let's send that shit-for-brains scumbag a picture of us, why not eh?'

He takes the phone from my hand, his long arms better than a selfie stick, and clicks the shot. He hands it back to me dismissively, without examining the picture, turning immediately away to talk to Patrick.

I feel a bit stung. I really don't know why he's being weird. I don't think anything's happened, has it? I thought he was at least marginally excited about today as well. Maybe he's annoyed that Isy and Ethan are here? I didn't have a chance to warn him beforehand. It can't be a problem with Patrick being here. They get on super well because of something about American football and the Super Bowl, which no

British person will ever understand. The only thing I know about the Super Bowl is that the adverts are really important, right?

Feeling weird, I read TD's message. For once, it contains proper words and multiple syllables.

It is surprising.

'Hey Alice,' it reads. 'I hope you're having a fun time out there. It feels like you've been gone ages. I know I don't deserve it but maybe we can grab a drink when you get back and have a chat about everything. I miss you.'

For a second, something in me leaps: hope.

I force it back down again. No! Ugh TD. I know he isn't for real – that *this* isn't for real. I've seen him do this before. He'll treat me badly; I'll swear off him. He'll call; I'll go back. He'll treat me like shit again; and I'll swear off him for definite this time. Maybe I'll last a few weeks; then he'll say something charming and apparently heartfelt – like this – and I'll give in.

But not this time.

Not. This. Fucking. Time.

But maybe . . .

What if . . .

Maybe he means it this time? Maybe this is different. Maybe me being away has genuinely made him look at his life and change his ways. Maybe he's realised I am what he wants – that I am The One – and everything will be good between us again, like it was at the beginning. Maybe the last few years haven't been a waste of my time. Maybe maybe maybe.

I hate the way my brain and heart are different people. I hate it so much. I hate that I – my rational me – knows, *knows*, that me and TD are not meant to be together. I absolutely know this, and I know that every time I reply or go back to him, I am making myself into a fool. I am being used, and being a user. I *know* it makes me just another stupid lovesick idiot. So why does the other me still want him? How can the other me still have this vain hope?

It makes me hate myself, which makes me more vulnerable, which makes me more inclined to give in. It's a vicious circle or cycle – I never know which – that I wish I could escape.

We are nearing the front of the queue and in a quick-flash decision – a moment of strength – I delete TD's message and I block him.

I breathe out. A weight falls away from me. I've done it. I know it's the right thing. It has to be. I can't waste this brain space on him any more. Do I really want to still be having these arguments in my head in another four years? I can't do it, I can't.

I take another gulp of oxygen and it is like new air in my lungs.

I reach for Dom's hand. He lets me take it, squeezes mine, but then pulls away. I guess, whatever I've done to upset him, I'm not forgiven yet.

Our group files onto the ride, and I find myself sitting opposite Dom in a circle. He looks off into the distance and I kick his shoe gently as the attendant makes his way round checking everyone is strapped in safely.

'Are you OK?' I mouth silently when he looks over at last.

He gives me a dismissive thumbs up and looks away again. I reach over, the belt straining against me, and put my hand on his leg. 'What is it?' I say, out loud. I feel Patrick glance over at us, but I don't care.

Dom shrugs, as the ride attendant passes our way.

'Have I done something?' I say, louder this time.

'Nope,' he says, aggressively.

The ride starts.

'Why are you being so moody, then?' I say, anger in my voice as we begin to move.

He's ignoring me! For no reason. I don't deserve this, I don't even know where it's all come from!

'I'm NOT BEING MOODY,' he shouts, looking away again as we start to swing into the air.

'FINE,' I shout back, and slump into the seat, determined to enjoy myself despite the sulking child across from me. If he doesn't want to talk to me, that's great, I'll just ignore him and have fun. I don't need his weirdness.

But suddenly he is talking again. 'I just think you could be honest with me and say if you're done with this, rather than making it so obvious. It's a bit of a shitty way to treat someone,' he says loudly, as we turn upside down.

'You fucking WHAT?' I shout, over the roar of the roller-coaster. What is he talking about? Done with *this*? With what? With this fling?

'I mean, we've had fun, Alice, but we both knew what this was,' he is almost screaming.

'I DON'T KNOW WHAT YOU'RE – ARRRRRG-GGGHHHHHHHHHH – TALKING ABOUT,' I shriek back, thrown around in my seat like a rag doll. It's like being back in Dom's Uber car.

'WHATEVER AL – ARRRRGGHHHHHHHHHH-HHH – YOU ARE CLEARLY DONE, YOU CLEARLY DON'T LIKE ME ANY MORE.'

'I AM SO CONFUSED, DOM – ARGGGGHHHHHHHHH.'

'YOU CLEARLY DON'T WANT TO BE ALONE WITH – WAAHHHHHHHHHHH – MEEEEEE.'

'BECAUSE PATRICK AND ISY ARE HERE?' I scream, still baffled.

Ethan waves angrily at me, flailing in his seat. 'ER, EXCUSE ME, I'M HERE TOO,' he shouts irrelevantly.

'OK, SORRY,' I concede, still yelling into the wind. 'YOU THINK I DON'T WANT TO BE ALONE WITH YOU BECAUSE PATRICK AND ISY AND ETHAN ARE HERE TOOOOOOOOAAAAAAARRRGGGHHHHH?'

Dom's hair is all over his face as his reply hits me in the face.

'STOP PLAYING DUMB, ALICE. I CAN SEE YOU FANCY PATRICK, IT'S FUCKING OBVIOU – WAAHHHHHHHHHHHHHHHHHHH – IT'S OBVIOUS YOU DOOOOO.'

We go into a tunnel and our group falls silent in the pitch black. I am panting with adrenaline and fury. I fancy Patrick? Where is this coming from? I think Patrick is brilliant as a new friend, but I have no designs on him. It hadn't even occurred to me to try anything. Sure we get on really well, but I thought Dom got on great with Patrick, too. We've spent the last few days with him, but I could swear Dom invited him along as much as I did. And ultimately, it's Dom I've been going home with at the end of every day.

We emerge from the tunnel and Dom looks angry and sweaty. Patrick is staring awkwardly upwards – which is soon downwards as we flip over again.

I am seething. This is so uncool. What right does Dom have to tell me who I should or shouldn't be fancying, anyway? It's not like he's my boyfriend. I have so much I want to shout at him, but we can't keep having this argument on a rollercoaster. It's awkward, sure, but it's also just really difficult and my throat is starting to hurt from shouting over the noise.

But Dom isn't done. 'AND IT'S NOT JUST PAT-RICK. YOU THROW YOUR EX SHIT IN MY FACE ALL THE TIME. I KNOW YOU'RE NOT OVER TWAT DAN.'

I almost laugh. 'OH, HOW COULD YOU POSSI-BLY KNOW THAT, DOM?' I shout. 'IS IT BECAUSE I SPECIFICALLY TOLD YOU THAT I'M NOT OVER HIM? MANY TIMES? IS IT BECAUSE OF THAT? IS THAT HOW YOU CAME TO THAT CLEVER DEDUCTION? CONGRATULATIONS YOU FUCKING POIROT PRAT.'

I think the Poirot insult might've been lost on the wind, but Dom responds immediately anyway. 'DID YOU SEND HIM THAT SELFIE THEN? DID YOU MAKE HIM JEALOUS? WAS I OF USE TO – WAHHHHHH-HHH – YOU?'

'I DIDN'T ACTUALLLLLLLLLLLY.' We veer off to the right. 'I BLOCKED HIM *ACTUALLY*. BUT IT'S REALLY NONE OF YOUR BUSI-NESS EITHER WAY. YOU KNEW WHAT THIS WAAAAAAAAAAAAAS BETWEEN US. I'M LEAV-ING IN LESS THAN A – ARRGGHHHHHHHHHH – WEEK! IT'S NOT LIKE THIS WAS EVER SERIOUUUUUUUUSSSSSSSSSSSSSS.'

'SOUNDS LIKE IT'S COME TO AN – WAHH-HHHHHHH – END THEN DOESN'T IT, ALICE? I'VE SERVED MY PURPOSE FOR YOU HAVEN'T IIIIIIIIIIIII? WHAT A SHITTY SAD END TO THINGS. YOU GO OFF AND FUCK PATRICK THEN AND I'LL GO FUCK MORE OF MY PAS-SENGERS – WARRRRGGHHHHHHHHHH!'

I am thrown back in my chair suddenly, as we pull up, back where we started. All five of us are breathless and silent. I yank at my strap, impatient to get out. I want to get away from this fury. Away from this humiliation. Away from Dom, away from Patrick, away from Isy, away from the pretentious dick on her arm. The belt around me comes loose at last and I climb frantically out of my seat.

As I storm away, I make eye contact with the little girl from the queue. She gives me a pitying look and I mentally order her to never grow up.

12

AWOL.COM/Alice Edwards' Travel Blog: Living My Dream and Feeling Very #Blessed

14 May – 6.03 p.m.

Good evening, dream chasers,

I have but a matter of days left on this LA journey, and I am all set to finish on a high – with a #spontaneous trip to Palm Springs. It is a place rich in history and culture, with humans first settling there two thousand years ago and living in isolation for hundreds of years. I found this out from Wikipedia because it is important to dig deep and research a place before you go.

Anyway, I am not expecting much to have changed in this peaceful 'desert resort city in Riverside County' (source: Wikipedia). I cannot wait to get away from the tourists to explore this place full of quiet joy and locals. I am going with my wonderful friend Patrick, who is very cool. We are going horseback riding, swimming and we plan to play tennis (recommended by: Wikipedia). It will be a very sedate, health-filled final few days here.

Peace be with you,

Alice x

PS. Did you know there is also a Palm Springs in Hong Kong? (source: Wikipedia)

#PalmSpring #SpringRoll #SpringAwakening #ThanksWikipedia #TravelBlogger #GoneAWOL #AliceEdwardsBlog #Blessed

#Brave #DreamChaser

8 Comments · 12 AWOLs · 19 Super Likes

COMMENTS:

> **Kirpa Saul**
> | Is it Spring Break? You have to somehow get yourself on camera dancing for an MTV show.

> **Mark Edwards**
> | You are such a cliché, Al. If you post a photo of yourself in jodhpurs, I will never let you live it down.

>> **Hannah Edwards**
>> **Replying to Mark Edwards**
>> | dont tease your little sister mark we miss u alice txt me

> **Sarah Sommers**
> | Been there, done that, copped off with a college student, lol!

> **Noah Deer**
> | You should check out the Cabazon Dinosaurs! They're great. If you're a geek like me.

> **Karen Gill**
> | I'm desperate to go to Coachella. Group trip next year?

> **Eva Slate**
> | I'm ready on my computer whenever you are!!

>> **Alice Edwards**
>> **Replying to Eva Slate**
>> | Signing in now xx

'I'm so happy to see you!' Eva is squealing through my

computer screen. 'I've hardly heard from you lately, are you having the best time ever?'

I laugh, turning up the volume on my Skype. 'I really am! I'm so buzzed to check out Palm Springs tomorrow.'

'Are you going with your sexy Uber driver friend?' she leans in excitedly. I bite my lip. I haven't spoken to Dom since our fight at Disneyland. After I stormed off, Patrick came to find me and the pair of us half-heartedly went on a few more rides, before eventually heading home, where we got drunk and watched *WrestleMania* boxsets for twenty-four straight hours.

Obviously, I was pretty upset about what had happened – no one enjoys a loud, humiliating break-up on a rollercoaster – but I am also determined to remain positive. Me and Dom were only meant to be a short-term, fun thing anyway, and I'm leaving on Monday. It had to end some time. I'm just disappointed it imploded so dramatically, instead of with a wave and a hug. So, oh well, really. And Patrick's been really nice and cheerful, it's helped a lot. We have not mentioned that part of the fight where Dom accused me of crushing on Patrick, and have focused instead on distractions and fun. He suggested taking this trip to Palm Springs for my last few days, and I jumped on the opportunity. He has a car and a friend down there we can stay with. I'm really excited.

Pretending to study my nails, I say carefully, 'Um, no. I'm going with my new pal, Patrick.'

'Ooh, the surfer dude AirBnB host?' she says, clapping her hands.

I nod, suddenly feeling weird that I haven't told Eva about the argument with Dom yet. Usually we text all day every day, but I haven't messaged her properly in days. Weeks. Not since I left the country, really. I know I've been distant since

I got here, but I wanted to saturate myself in this other life. I wanted to get away from all reminders of home, which – sorry Eva – includes my pregnant best friend. It also includes my brother, who's messaged me several times these last couple of weeks asking for a chat, and who I've repeatedly given the major brush-off.

'So how are you feeling?' I say, changing the subject before she can ask any more questions.

She makes a face. 'Tired, miserable, hungry,' she says, sighing. Then she pulls up her jumper to show me her belly, where there is the tiniest hint of a bump. 'Look, she's starting to make herself known.'

'She?!' I say, my voice high.

'Oh!' Eva laughs. 'That's just a guess. We don't know yet, obviously.'

We. *We*. It still jars with me whenever she talks as a 'we'. I hate the way couples do that. Like they can't be an 'I' any more. Everything has to be responded to together, as a pair.

'Will you find out the sex?' I say, trying to sound interested. She looks thoughtful. 'We're not sure,' she explains. 'Jeremy says we shouldn't. But I don't know. It's funny. I'm not sure he is quite *there* with me in this pregnancy yet. I don't know how to explain it, but I don't think it's real for him yet. Like, for me, I can feel this thing inside me. I can't avoid how real it is. My body is literally changing. I'm different already. But it's all still the same for him. I guess parenthood won't be real for him until she – or he – is physically here with us . . .' She breaks off, and I wait for her to continue. 'I feel a little . . .' she stops and laughs awkwardly. 'Sorry,' she says. 'I'm already being boring about pregnancy stuff, sorry.'

'No, no, you're not!' I say hurriedly. 'I want to hear about it. Are you . . . are things . . . OK between you guys?'

She nods, but it is not as effusive as I would expect. 'Yes!' she says, nodding some more. 'It's great, it just, I don't know, it just feels . . . different.'

'Well,' I say slowly, unsure. 'Things are bound to change a little. And they say men don't ever get it until they can hold the baby in their arms, right?'

She nods again, her eyes wide. 'Honestly, we're fine – we're brilliant! It's just the hormones. You hear all the warnings about it, but you never really believe how weird you feel until you're in it. But really, I'm fine!' She chuckles, and her bravado is not very believable.

'OK, Eva,' I sigh. 'You know where I am if you want to talk about any of this properly. I'm here for you.'

She laughs. 'Well, you're not really here for me for another couple of months yet!'

'What do you mean by that?' I say, feeling a little defensive. I'm still there for her. Just because I'm travelling doesn't mean I'm not a good friend.

'Oh, nothing! I didn't mean anything by it, I promise,' she says, smiling nicely. 'I am just sad that you are so far away. It feels like we haven't had time to talk properly since you've been gone. You just seem a bit . . . distant.' She goes on quickly. 'And I know you're having the trip of a lifetime, so I totally get it! And I'm so glad you're happy.' She pauses and then adds, 'I just really miss you, Alice.'

There is a pause and I am not sure what to say. 'I miss you too, Eva.'

After we say goodbye, I find myself feeling a bit cross. I'm having my very first big adventure out here. Eva doesn't have to make me feel bad about it. I haven't been distant, I'm just on a holiday! And even if I have been a bit, it's only because

I've been busy. And it's not like she needs me anyway. She's the one who went off and got herself a new family – a new boy best friend – behind my back. If I've gone and found myself a life that doesn't involve checking in with her every five seconds, whose fault is that, really? If she hadn't swanned off into the sunset with Jeremy and got herself knocked up, she could be out here with me, having this trip of a lifetime, too. But instead she's settled for some bland loser, just because she thinks she's reached the proper age and proper time to start Real Life.

But then, that's what everyone seems to do. They decide it's the right time to start their grown-up life, and whoever happens to come along next is suddenly The One.

I call bullshit.

And either way, I don't have to sit around waiting for the friendship scraps from the table.

Fuck it, I can't waste my last few days worrying whether or not Eva's being funny with me. I'm going to pack for my Palm Springs trip.

AWOL.COM/Alice Edwards' Travel Blog: Living My Dream and Feeling Very #Blessed

17 May – 5.17 p.m.

Good evening, dream chasers,

Well, here it is. After four long weeks, tomorrow evening I will depart my new home, here in the US. I shall be heading onwards and upwards to Thailand, even though I don't think Thailand is technically upwards according to my globe.

I am happy to say my last few days here have been wondrous and magical. My friend Patrick and I travelled to Palm Springs, where we met very many deep people and had many fun times. Transparency is key with blogging, so I must admit to you, dear followers, that we didn't quite get round to horse riding or playing tennis though. We nearly played golf at one point, but that was sort of an accident when we got trapped on a golf course after hours. Instead of trying to play sport, we decided to focus on meeting and connecting with other people, and so tonight, for our final evening, we are hitting up a very exclusive club to meet talented and inteligont people.

Goodbye LA, farewell, *sayonara, adios, hola*, so long.

Adieu,

Alice x

#FinalNightOnTheTown #PalmSpringsJoy #AccidentalGolfing

#TravelBlogger #GoneAWOL #AliceEdwardsBlog #BloggerLife #Blessed #Brave #DreamChaser

5 Comments · 14 AWOLs · 53 Super Likes

COMMENTS:

Karen Gill
| It will be great for you to meet like-minded intoligent people

Mark Edwards
| Text me when you've landed safely. I do care a little bit.

Noah Deer
| Can't believe you're leaving already! Seems like you just got here :/

Isabelle Moore
| Byeeeeeeee!

Eva Slate
| Have a fab final evening in America!

'Over here, babe! Babe!' Patrick is waving at me from across the room, trying to get my attention. 'BABE,' he shouts this time, grinning from ear to ear. I clear my throat, my face red as I slide off my bar stool. I slowly make my way over, clutching my undrinkable whiskey sour. I made the mistake of trying to flirt with the sexy bartender by telling him to 'surprise me' with a drink of his choosing. And then I didn't want to seem uncool by spitting the disgusting forty-five dollar cocktail in his face. Even though he deserved it.

'BABBBBBBBBBBE,' Patrick yells, even louder this time, even though I am fucking coming.

Patrick has taken to calling me 'babe' because I accidentally said it the other day when I was drunk, and he is now fully leaning into the joke. It's one of those nicknames I never used to say, and then I said a few times with Eva *ironically* – but then my brain forgot it was ironic and started saying it all the time and at inappropriate moments: on the phone; at work; to the postman.

Either way, it's embarrassing, and especially so here in this venue. 'Shut up,' I hiss, reaching over to swat at him while simultaneously checking over my shoulder to see if any of the suave, understated clientele around us are taking any notice of this oaf. Luckily it is way too dark in here for anyone to be aware of anything. The US president could be getting a blowie in the booth next to us and I wouldn't be able to see. Thankfully.

This is maybe the fanciest place I've ever been in my life. And you know it's fancy, because from the outside, you wouldn't even know it's a bar. There is no name or sign or bouncers, just a random door built into a wall. We needed a password to get in, and you just know everyone in here is big time because no one's really talking, they're just *existing*. They are rich shapes in the darkness.

It's wonderful.

I'm pretty sure Patrick had to pull some major strings to get us on the guest list for this place, and I know it's because he's trying to cheer me up.

I've had a nice few days in Palm Springs, but I also know I've been a little . . . distracted. I've been blue about what happened with Dom and I'm all too aware that this part of my trip is coming to an end. Plus, I've been dwelling a little bit on the awkwardness with Eva the other day. We've exchanged a few messages since our Skype chat, and we're both pretending all is normal, but there's an edge to it. And I don't know how to feel. Eight years of living together and we've never had a cross word. Now, this.

'Look,' Patrick nods excitedly at the bookcase before us.

'What?' I frown, perplexed. He smiles mysteriously. 'It's a *bookcase*!' he says, tapping it. 'You know what that means. That means it's a *door* – a secret door, babe!'

'Shut up, it's not!' I scoff. 'And please stop calling me "babe", it's not funny.'

'It is very funny, babe, and you shut up,' he is still smiling. 'We have to find our way in. Help me.' He starts pulling at random books and I roll my eyes.

'You are such a dweeb, Patrick,' I say affectionately. 'You've seen too many Indiana Jones films.' He ignores me, yanking at pretentious tome after wealthy moron autobiography. He stops to swig from his drink and a few books fall noisily to the floor. We look at each other, startled by the loud clatter. The president in the booth next to us looms up in the darkness.

'Just keep goi—' Patrick begins, sounding a bit panicked, but we are interrupted by the stealthy arrival of an angry-looking waiter. Oh crap, we're going to be chucked out. Haven't I been ejected from enough places in LA by now? And I haven't even had my BUI yet.

He regards us in the dim lighting, we look back at him. There is a three-way slow blink and I clear my throat, ready with my poshest royal family English accent.

'Erm, good sir, we do beg your forgiv—' I begin, but he cuts me off. 'Every night,' he hisses. 'Every. Single. Night. Every stinking night one of you does this.' He waves at the books on the floor despairingly. 'You know the owner likes them in a special order? So after we finally get rid of you rich leeches at 3 a.m., I have to stay behind to pick up the books people have thrown on the floor, and sort out the ones you've pulled out.'

'We're not rich,' I mutter sulkily. 'I am a bit of a leech, but I'm not rich.'

The waiter ignores me. 'Every night!' he continues. 'Which pretentious garbage monster came up with the whole bookcase-secret-entrance-in-a-bar thing anyway? Because I want to find them and water-board them.'

We hang our heads, ashamed of ourselves.

'I told you,' I nudge Patrick. 'I *told you* it wasn't a secret d—'

The waiter interrupts, sighing, 'Anyway, it should've specified which book it was on your invitation.'

Hold on.

'But everyone ignores that, don't they? They come in just grabbing at any old Trump biography.'

Oh?

He sighs, exasperated. 'It's *Lolita* to get into the West event.' He nods towards the Vladimir Nabokov book at the top corner end of the shelf.

Patrick and I sneak a look at each other; he's trying not to smile.

The angry man gives us another aggressive sigh before moving off. I catch a faint, 'Douchebags' in the wind.

Patrick reaches up and there is a click as the bookcase nudges ajar.

'Holy mackerel, Batman!' I gasp and Patrick snorts.

'We have to go in,' he says, gripping the edge of the door.

'Can we though?' I whine, excited. 'It must be a private party; they'd clock us straight away. And, er, hello, *Lolita*? What kind of disturbing shit is that? It's probably some kind of sex ring in there with underage slaves.

'Even more reason to crash it!' Patrick looks a little too delighted. 'We could be heroes, saving them all.'

'Or get murdered,' I giggle, thrilled. 'Ooh, what if it's a secret celebrity party? He said it was the "West party", right? That could be Kanye! We could be about to crash Kanye West's birthday party! I've always wanted to crash a VIP A-list party! I have this theory that me and Khloe Kardashian would be best friends if we were only given the opportunity to hang out. I just *get* her, y'know?'

'Come on!' Patrick grabs my hand, interrupting what would've been a lengthy monologue about reality telly, and we slip inside. 'This is going to be EPIC!'

It is super lame.

An hour later and we haven't seen any celebrities or sex rings so what is even the point. It is almost exactly the same situation as the main bar – rich-looking white people dressed in dark, expensive clothes. Everyone is standing around in small cliquey huddles, not talking to each other. In fact, everyone looks miserable AF. There is a DJ deck in the corner, but it's just playing some tinkly lift music rubbish. The only reason we're still here is that this secret VIP-type area seems to have free alcohol. So Patrick and I have been pounding the prosecco like teenagers.

'Do you think there might be canapés coming round?' I whisper from our position in the corner, people-watching. 'We should stand next to the kitchen door just in case. So we can have first option on everything. I want some kind of fancy, tiny mac 'n' cheese.'

'But that's the other end of the room from the bar,' Patrick looks rightly worried. Food v. booze is the eternal question on a night out. I nod agreeably. 'Maybe we should split up?' I slur thoughtfully. 'Divide and conquer. I'll go forage for food, you forage for drinks? We'll meet in the middle with supplies.'

'We should also forage for fun,' he says grumpily. 'This night was supposed to be really silly and spontaneous. It's supposed to be your last big adventure in America! I wanted this to be a mad night. I wanted you to have a story to tell when you got home.'

'I am having fun!' I insist half-heartedly, but he doesn't look convinced, mostly because I am also fiddling with my cuticles.

'We need to liven this party up a bit,' he says, suddenly perking up. 'Let's make it a secret mission. A dare.' Inspiration strikes him. 'I know! Right, I dare you to go take over the DJ decks. Put a banger on, and I will start talking to people and get a conga line going! Come on Alice, it will be excellent! Everyone here is dying for things to kick off, look how miserable they all are. Between us we can save this dire night.'

'DEAL!' I shout, suddenly excited. There is something in me that cannot resist a dare. It is juvenile, but irresistible. He's also right, this place badly needs a conga line to happen. Everyone is so dour and bored-looking, making small talk in corners and ignoring the dance floor. I have just the playlist to get everyone moving.

Patrick and I discreetly high-five and splinter off in different directions. I eye him joining a small group of men, all dressed in dark suits. He looks so out of place in his bright green shirt. Ugh, don't rich people have any imagination?

I sidle up to the DJ booth. There is a woman standing there looking bored, playing with her phone, which is plugged into the system. She must be responsible for this tedious background music. For half a second I wonder if this is a good idea. I could still make a run for it. She looks up, surprised by my closeness. 'Hello,' she says coolly.

'Um, hi there,' I say and for some reason, I am talking in an American accent. Not even a good American accent. She looks puzzled.

'You OK, hun?' she says half nicely. I nod enthusiastically. We fall silent and I swallow hard. This was a bad idea. This isn't going to work! How do I even get her away from the decks so I can plug my Spotify in? I glance desperately over at Patrick, but he is fully immersed in his rich-suits chat. He looks a bit serious, maybe he wants to chicken out, too?

'Do you know Sam well?' the woman murmurs, and my head snaps back towards her. Shit, is Sam the host? He must be. No Kanye or Kardashian family then, bummer.

'Quite well,' I hedge, matching her low tone. 'Great . . . person.'

I nearly said bloke, but Sam could easily be a woman, couldn't it? That is quick thinking. I am so good at this! Out of nowhere the adrenaline – and alcohol – kicks in. I need to take more chances, that's why I'm here! For God's sake, I'm in this country for one more night – this is it – my one chance to be silly. Constance Beaumont makes a big thing about taking risks and being spontaneous on her blog. Plus, Patrick dared me and I want to pretend to be a person who is brave, a person who does things.

I'm doing it.

'Mind if I have a go?' I say to the woman, gesturing at the DJ system. She narrows her eyes at me. There is a beat. 'I guess . . .' she starts, sounding unsure, but I am already moving in, triumphantly unplugging her phone. She steps back, still looking confused. No problem, she will be on board in a minute because I have just the playlist for this evening.

It's the one I put on ahead of big nights out with my mates. When we're going *out-out*. It is guaranteed to get everyone moving. I hit shuffle and crank up the volume. The booming sound of The Pussycat Dolls' *Don't Cha* fills the room. En masse, everyone turns in my direction. Clearly they were sick of the tinkly background music, too. Here we go! This is really happening! My belly fizzes with the joy of spontaneity. They are going to *love* this!

Nicole Scherzinger's distinctive warble fills the room, singing about how sexy she is and how no other woman comes close.

I grin widely at all the shocked faces in front of me.

I meet Patrick's eyes. Time for the conga.

Oh, here's the part of the song where she says men should all cheat on their girlfriends if there is a hot freak available. I love this bit.

Patrick is ashen.

My smile falters.

He is mouthing something. I can't make it out. Why is no one dancing? Or . . . smiling?

Nicole screams from the sound system some more stuff about being sexy, and I momentarily picture her with yoghurt on her nose.

What is it Patrick's saying? Wait, '*phew*'? It can't be phew, what is it . . .

Oh God, I think I know. I think I know what it is. I know what he's saying. I glance round at the woman next to me. She looks back at me, horrified. She is in all black. So is everyone.

Wait a minute, what did she say a minute ago? It suddenly clicks in my brain. She didn't say, 'Do you know Sam well?' – that wasn't what she said. She said . . . she said, '*Did* you know Sam well?' She said DID. This is a . . . this is a . . . I turn back towards Patrick who has his head in his hands but is still mouthing the same words. It is so clear now.

'THIS IS A FUNERAL'.

Later, when we are both hiding in the unisex loo, trying to get the window open so we can sneak out, Patrick just keeps repeating the same thing.

'It might not have been so bad if the incontinence advert hadn't come on afterwards. Why, Alice, why couldn't you at least have sprung for Premium Spotify?'

14

18 May – 7.15 p.m.

Good evening, dream chasers,

I know I made it sound like yesterday's blog was my final blog in LA, but this is actually the last one. I am writing this on my way to the very luxurious LAX, which they should re-name LUXE, because I have been upgraded to business class #blessed. And I know I said yesterday that I cannot believe my journey in LA has come to an end at last, but today I *really* can't believe it. It has felt both endless and also very quick. I have learnt much and also learnt nothing. It has been spiritual.

My final evening was wonderful. We went to a very exclusive bar, where there was almost certainly a president in a booth but don't tell anyone. We were invited to join the VIP section down a secret passage. There, my musical talents were recognised and I was asked to DJ. I am now seriously considering a career in music when I return to England in a few months. You can contact me on the tab above should you like to book me for gigs.

Goodbye to my dear new friends, thank you for sharing so much of yourselves with me. Until we meet again.

'Parting is such sweet sorrow.' Aristotle

Alice x

#Goodbye #MusicalVibes #FeeltheMusic #DJSkills #GoneAWOL #AliceEdwardsBlog#BloggerLife #Blessed #Brave #Dream Chaser

7 Comments · 4 AWOLs · 17 Super Likes

COMMENTS:

Hollie Baker
| Wow!!! Do you have a YouTube account for your music? I would like to listen!

Isabelle Moore
| WHICH BAR? WHY WASN'T I INVITED?

Karen Gill
| Who did you sleep with to get an upgrade?

Randy Howels
| Fukin women shit at music, is a mens job stooped bich

> | *AWOL MODERATOR*
> *Replying to Randy Howels*
> | I get it, Randy, mate, it's a tricky chat, but please be respectful to our users :) Let's all just take a chill pill!! Luke

>> *Randy Howels*
>> *Replying to AWOL MODERATOR*
>> | u r such a messy prick luke

Mark Edwards
| Hope you've got your neck pillow ready. Long flight ahead.

So LAX airport has a shop dedicated entirely to novelty magnets, at least twelve perfume outlets, and an iStore – but not one place that sells tampons. MY KINGDOM FOR A TAMPON.

This is definitely not my finest hour.

I'm stuffing my pants with airport-loo toilet paper, so thin it disintegrates in my hands. But it's the best I can do. My period arrived three days early, just as I was leaving for the airport. I think my body knew I was about to spend eighteen hours on a plane and wanted me to be as physically uncomfortable as possible. I assumed one of the biggest airports in the universe would have some variation of a chemist, but apparently not. I have now circled this bastard three times, and I'm on to last resort options.

And honestly, it's not even a tampon I really want. I want sanitary towels. Big, fat, night-towels with giant wings that make you feel like you're wearing a nappy. That's all I want for day one of my period, when I'm bleeding like an episode of *Santa Clarita Diet*. Especially when I'm getting on a long-haul flight. I just want to be securely strapped into my nappy and eating chocolate.

Sigh. What's a woman with a pointlessly functioning uterus to do?

At least the flight itself should be fairly badass. I got an email this morning reminding me it was my last chance to upgrade, and I had a hangover, so I HAD TO DO IT. I basically had no choice?? And anyway, I've spent such an insane amount of money in LA, I figured I might as well spend even sodding more. This is likely going to be my final luxurious hurrah before things get a bit dirtier and hostel-ier, so I wanted one last chance to use a real fork on a plane. If I'm going to spend four weeks trekking around East Asia, I wanted to feel the cool tang of metal cutlery on my tongue one last time.

Weirdly specific last request I know, but there it is.

And having spent so much money to ensure my LA exit was fancy, I'm frankly a bit pissed off about having a breakdown in the airport toilet calculating the long-lasting effectiveness of toilet paper. It's just not how I pictured this going.

Maybe the air stewards will be able to help me? I limp towards the BA lounge, steeling myself for a whispered conversation with an uncomfortable stranger.

'Hi there!' a BA employee greets me enthusiastically as I approach and I pull out my boarding pass. The woman waves me in, encouraging me to 'have a nice day'. I feel tearful thinking about how long it will likely be until someone else wishes that for me and decide not to ruin the special moment by asking her for a blood plug. The tissues will have to make do for a bit longer.

Once inside, I am immediately overwhelmed, and immediately lost. It's like a fancy bar in here, but without bartenders. There are rows of plush-looking seats lined up everywhere in front of floor-to-ceiling windows, looking out on to the giant planes tootling along the runway. And there are buffet tables of food everywhere.

It's thrilling, but I didn't bone up on the rules. What do I do, where am I supposed to go? Is this free? It can't be free. So where and how do I pay?

I stand frozen with indecision in a corner, fearfully clutching my carry-on luggage. Thousands and thousands (tens) of white men in suits stroll languidly by me, looking more at home than I do at literal home. One particularly sweaty businessman stops by the coffee machines, grabbing a fistful of those packaged biscuits I thought you could only get when you donate blood.

'Would you like a hot towel?' a voice makes me jump. It is another smiling BA automaton passing by, holding a basket and a pair of tongs.

'How much?' I ask suspiciously.

She looks confused. 'It's free, hun,' she says, shaking her head and holding out a steaming white hand towel with the tongs. I slowly take it, watching her carefully, waiting for something else to happen.

What is her game?

She walks away quickly and I examine my free tiny towel.

What the fuck is the point of this? Does she know I'm on my period? If so, white seems like a bad decision. Am I meant to use it when I go to the bathroom? In which case, shouldn't they hand them out in there?

A small kid sitting nearby pulls expertly at his own hot towel, dabbing his face and hands with the cloth.

Is that it? Is that the whole point of this thing? It's so rich people can wipe off any vestigial evidence of the world outside this lounge? Wipe off the poorness? Wipe away any skin cells of other passengers who can't afford to be here?

In which case I AM SO IN.

I give my available skin a good scrub, and sidle up to the biscuits, emptying the whole basket into my bag. Mine now. These will get me through my long flight.

What about the rest of the food?

I text Mark, he'll know.

'I'm in the BA departure lounge, it's so intimidatingly fancy.'

He replies fast. 'How are you not out of money yet?'

'Money is just a social construct,' I type. 'Stop trying to overdraft-shame me, it is not relevant to this conversation. I need your help because I don't know what's happening. I've stolen all the biscuits and also a now-cold tiny towel, but what now? Can I eat anything I want? I'm hormonal and really need food.'

Mark laughs at me over WhatsApp. 'Still a cliché, Alice.'

'Please help me, I want the food but I'm afraid. You remember how traumatised I was by shoplifting from Woolworths.'

'Yes, Alice the pauper,' I can hear the amused sigh across the airways. 'You can have anything you want. It's all included. Joe says to say have a safe flight and he misses you.'

'Amazing, thanks! Aw, tell Joe I love him more than I love you.'

'He knows,' he writes.

I am only half joking. I really do love Joe a lot. He's just genuinely one of the nicest people ever. He's one of those overly enthusiastic people you can't help smiling around. You spend ten minutes in his company and leave feeling like you've taken speed. He's a walking energy drink and I adore him. I'm so glad Joe's gone with my brother to Australia; I know he will look after Mark, he always does. Even when we were kids, I remember Joe coming over to ours after school with a black eye and Mark whispering that Joe had stepped in front of a fist meant for him. That happened more and more as Mark got older and camper. Sometimes I get jealous of how close they are, but mostly I'm just happy to have Joe around.

I am about to put my phone away when another message from Mark pops up. 'Are you about to get on the plane? I was hoping we could maybe have a chat on the phone? Do you have a few minutes?'

Shit. I know what this is. He wants to talk about Steven. He's been trying a lot these last few weeks. He'll try to persuade me to come to Oz.

'Sorry dude, I'm going to stock up on supplies then I have to make a run for the gate,' I lie, because I have hours yet.

'OK, Alice. Have a nice flight, we can speak another time. Go eat everything. Except the hot towels, don't eat any hot towels.'

I slip my phone in my pocket and regard the buffet. Triangle sandwiches, salad, pastas, crisps, cake, chocolate – all free. I feel like Princess Markle. Anything I want, I can take. And I want it all. It's a lot but I can do this. I believe in me. I am going to be so loaded down with food for this flight. And if I still can't find a tampon, I'll just use sandwiches in my pants. It'll be almost as good as a night-towel and probably more comfortable.

This is going to be the best flight ever.

Thailand

15

AWOL.COM/Alice Edwards' Travel Blog: Living My Dream and Feeling Very #Blessed

21 May – 8.53 a.m.

Good evening, dream chasers,

I have landed in the wonderfully atmospheric Bangkok. I can feel the culture seeping into my pores, like some kind of Asian facial but all over. I will admit I am a little bit tired after my long flight, but this thrilling new place is already invigorating me. I must experience everything this world has to offer, there is no time for lying around! Luckily I am excellent at shaking off jet lag, so watch me go. I do not have long in this fair city so I must get straight out there and make the most of every second.

Until next time, my friends,

Alice xx

#JetLagSurvivor #NewPlace #Thailand #TravelBlogger #GoneAWOL #AliceEdwardsBlog #BloggerLife #Blessed #Brave #DreamChaser

3 Comments · 1 AWOLs · 25 Super Likes

COMMENTS:

Karen Gill

| There is no way you are not jet-lagged to buggery. You can be honest on here you know!

Hollie Baker

| Wow!!11 Your life just sounds soooooo wonderful.

Isabelle Moore

| Miss you already! Hope you enjoy Bangkok. Come back soon.

My mouth tastes like glue and my brain is also glue and the air is extra glue. I am deep into a jet lag state of mind. It's a bit like an Empire State of Mind, but with less Jay Z. Staring at the ceiling of my Bangkok hotel room, from under the dark-blue sheets, I am obsessively contemplating time. More specifically, the fact that I have caught up with UK time, and overtaken it. During the flight from LA, I have gone from being younger than people, to older than them. It is time travel. And time travel is not sitting well with me. My head is mush.

I'm spending my first few days here in a fairly spenny hotel – in Thai terms, at least. After the sleekness of LA, I thought it would be better to ease myself into hostel living with a bit of niceness. Plus, I'm a spoilt brat who some idiot gave credit cards to. I am considering making this whole thing a flash-packing experience, and then spending the next forty years paying it off. That doesn't sound so bad, does it?

Either way, I'm going to spend this week wandering around the capital city and immersing myself in this brand new culture. Which, if the airport was any indication, will be mostly people with neon signs shouting at me about Wi-Fi and international sim cards.

After Bangkok, I'm going to be travelling about a bit more. It's a fairly stupid time to be in Thailand – just at the start of rainy season – but there it is. If only my life crisis could've come along around New Year. That would've been so much more convenient.

Either way, a beach is still a beach, even if I'm getting intermittently rained on. I picture myself standing in a bikini, back rolls bronzed and gleaming, the sand between my perfectly manicured toes, as the warm rain lightly grazes me. I am whoever played Leo's love interest in *The Beach*. I've never seen that film, but obviously I'm going to check out Maya beach on the island of Ko Phi Phi Leh where it was filmed. That's if it's open. Authorities keep closing it down because tourists insist on ruining it. Which is so out of order! It's not fair that I should be the only tourist not allowed to go along and ruin things.

That's just one of many things on my list to do over here. After Bangkok, I'm going to head down to the lower Gulf islands of Ko Samui, Ko Pha-Ngan and Ko Tao. And even though there are warnings about storms around Phuket, I wouldn't be a proper Westerner if I didn't go there, right? Then I'm going to fly up to northern Thailand for my last week. I want to take a boat along the Mekong river to explore the Golden Triangle, where Thailand meets Laos and Myanmar. My Googling informed me it's 'one of the biggest tourist traps in the country, and is best known as the world's most prolific opium producers back in the 1920s, until it was eclipsed by Afghanistan'. And honestly, they had me at *tourist trap*. Plus, the CIA came up with the name 'Golden Triangle', which is so totally badass, right? There's also a restaurant up there called 'Cabbages and Condoms'. So that whole thing is an Absolute Must in this soul-searching quest.

*

I really shouldn't be in bed right now. It's a terrible idea. I need to get up and survive the day. I have to try and right-way-up my head. But I'm so tired. But I also can't sleep. But I have to.

There is a knock on the door and in a daze, I wonder if I have ordered room service. Or did I dream it? I definitely considered ordering food, so maybe I did? Before I can work it out, I am opening the door and, when I see who it is, I know for sure I am dreaming.

'MARK?!' I scream, my voice sounding raspy but real. He is laughing as he sweeps me up and we spin round in circles. I cannot stop shrieking, and someone yells, 'Shut the hell up' behind a door across the hall. I guess this hotel is not at the fancy levels I hoped.

'Is it really you?' I say pulling him in and shutting the door behind us. 'Am I definitely awake? Is this happening?'

I cannot believe it. This is the strangest feeling. Someone you know so well, completely out of context. It's like seeing a teacher down the pub. He laughs and hugs me close again.

'It is me, Al, I'm really here. We got here yesterday, I wanted to surprise you.'

'WELL IT FUCKING WELL WORKED, MARK,' I scream again, so happy. 'I can't believe you're really here. How long do I have you?'

He shrugs, grinning. 'As long as you want me. I can stay here the whole four weeks if you like, or I can bugger off with Joe if you get sick of me.'

'Joe's here, too?' I shriek. This is so wonderful. I can't believe it, I really can't.

I didn't want to admit it, but I've been a bit worried about this part of my journey. America wasn't that scary, y'know? Because I knew people in LA, and there was an element of familiar, shared culture. I grew up on US telly – we speak a common tongue, herbs/'erbs aside – and I had Isy if I really needed help. Thailand is so different, so loud, so foreign. I had no one to break in case of emergency. I didn't want to admit how nervous I was about coming here.

But now Mark's here and there will be someone to raise the alarm if I disappear without a trace. YAY.

We dance around the room some more, giggling our heads off, before we finally have a sit down on the end of the bed. 'So talk to me,' I say, still struggling to believe it. 'I don't understand. I thought you were in Australia?'

'Well, I was,' he says, side-eyeing me carefully before continuing. 'But there's not much I can do while Steven's still out of it in hospital. He's had another couple of minor strokes since the first major one, so they're keeping him sedated. I've done nothing of use being over there these last few weeks, so Mum told me to get back to my life. I think she was getting sick of me.' I look down and there is a silence before he continues. 'But I didn't want to go all the way back to the UK just yet. I want to be nearby in case . . . in case there is *news*. So I thought I'd come see you for a bit.'

'So there's . . . the doctors . . . they don't think there's much hope, then?' I say slowly, looking away. Mark shakes his head. 'But Alice, can we . . .'

I clear my throat, standing up to interrupt the forthcoming speech about hospitals and Mum and Steven.

'What about your work?' I ask quickly. 'Don't they need you back by now?' Mark is a high-up badass in the City. They love him and he makes his company a butt-ton of money.

'I've taken a sabbatical,' he explains. 'They said it was fine given . . . everything that is going on. They're keeping my job open for a couple of months, but I can return sooner if I want to. I'm going to see how things go here and how Mum copes. She's still got Hannah with her, of course, so I think she's probably fine. Things are just a bit in limbo while he's still in intensive care. If we just knew either way . . . I don't know. I don't know what I'll do next. I might head back to England, or go back to Australia . . .'

I give him a small nod, as non-committal as possible.

'You could always come with me,' he drops casually as I stare out the window. 'I would really like to . . .'

I sigh. 'Mark, don't start,' I interrupt again. 'I just got here, I'm so jet-lagged and I just want to enjoy the fact that you're actually here. I still can't believe it. Where are you staying? Are you coming down to the islands with me?'

Mark's had my itinerary with a list of places I'm going all along – in case the police needed to look for my body, obviously. I guess that's how he knew where I would be today. I still can't believe he's actually here right now, in my hotel.

He sighs, but leaves the Australia chat alone. I have a feeling he won't let it be for very long though. I don't know how many times I have to say that I'm not interested in seeing Mum or speaking to her. Not right now. I am not a cold person but I can't just get over everything that happened between us.

'Me and Joe are in a hostel round the corner,' he says, smiling. 'Can you believe how polluted this city is?'

'Mark, that is racist,' I say, outraged.

He snorts. 'What are you talking about, Alice? Of course it's not racist. It's a fact.'

'Oh, OK,' I say, unsure. I suppose it does seem quite smoggy.

'All I'm saying is,' he says, still smiling, 'I don't think you should spend the whole week here. Bangkok is cool for a couple of days, but then you, me and Joe are heading down to the party islands for some full moon, full-tourist craziness. Let's shake up Asia while we have time.'

I consider this. Maybe soul-searching can wait. 'OK, I'm in.'

We high-five.

AWOL.COM/Alice Edwards' Travel Blog: Living My Dream and Feeling Very #Blessed

24 May – 5.40 p.m.

Good evening, dream chasers,

After a few intriguing days in Bangkok, I am now heading to the infamous Phuket with two surprise visitors from home – my brother Mark and his BF, Joe.

Leaving the city so soon was sad, but my few days there were a truly transcendental experience. We immersed ourselves in the local life, taking scooter taxis from temple to restaurant to the stunning Grand Palace. We met many interesting people and I hope to stay in touch with every single one of them.

The three of us are now planning to fully embrace the joys of the famous islands and the locals, while also connecting with one another on a deep spiritual level.

Sending good thoughts,

Alice xx

1 Comments · 4 AWOLs · 19 Super Likes

COMMENTS:

Joe Downe

| Come out of the loo already, I've got shots ready and Ne-Yo on the stereo.

Right, I know that I said I wasn't going to have any sex in Thailand while I focused on myself – but kissing is tewtally allowed, right? And maybe a bit of dry humping?

Because, too late.

Very too late, actually. I have kissed three men in the last hour and I'm thrilled about it. I got no names and ten minutes later, I could not identify them in a line-up. Except maybe in a tongue line-up. WINK. I am drunk, but nicely so, and basking in the feelings of being here and y'know being ALIVE. It is just so exhilarating. I am a million miles away from anything, feeling the sand beneath my feet and the atmosphere fizzing around me. My mind is nicely blank and empty. I really don't know why everyone is so obsessed with mindfulness – mindlessness is much more satisfying.

Mark, Joe and I landed last night – buzzing and bouncing – on the Phi Phi Islands. I was permitted to enjoy Bangkok for just a few days before Mark insisted we head off to Phuket. The three of us spent our days walking around the city, staring at the architecture and sight-seeing. The local people are so nice and friendly, but there's also such a vast ex-pat, international community, we couldn't go many steps without waving at fellow Westerners. We all stick out like a sore thumb, and therefore tend to gravitate together. We bumped into a group of Irish Americans on our last night, who insisted on taking us with them on their group dinner to this incredible rooftop restaurant. We've all exchanged numbers, and there's talk of meeting up on one of the islands in a couple of weeks. I have a feeling there's going to be a lot of that kind of thing on this trip and lots of then never speaking again.

But to be honest, great as it was, I was OK with leaving. The city was a real culture shock after the carefree lifestyle of LA, I can tell you. And if you thought the driving over there was dangerous, you should see the small children driving scooter taxis all over Bangkok. They are everywhere.

It was kind of fabulous though. There's something freeing about everyone's languid attitude to all the danger. And, look, we all made it out alive, so it's fine.

Either way, we're here now, and first stop: Full Moon Party, because obvs.

We got drunk at our hostel, dancing around the room like we were fifteen years old again, getting ready for the local disco at the Rec Centre. And now we're here at the beach, surrounded by fellow clichéd Western tourists, and I've continued on that same teen-type theme; flirting shamelessly and gradually hiking my skirt up higher and higher as the hours pass. Honestly, this could only be more Friday night teen disco if someone released some foam from the sky and a tit fell out of a Jane Norman or Bay Trading dress.

Oh, actually there are a few tits out over there.

Despite the youth club atmosphere, the setting couldn't feel more worldly and grown up. It is ridiculously beautiful here on the beach. The water is a colour I have only seen in films, and assumed was touched up in post-production anyway. The sand is so clean and white and soft. It's like no beach I've ever been on. And I never want to leave this spot, feet slightly buried, shoulders warm, face buzzing from kisses from strangers. It's glorious.

Ooh, I should save that kind of cheese for the blog.

*

Mark suddenly grabs me round the middle from behind. 'Hello amazing sister,' he says, kissing me on the cheek. He is drunk. 'You smell like boys.'

'You don't,' I say, giggling. 'Met anyone nice tonight?'

He shakes his head, giving me a mysterious half smile. 'Nah, I'm having too much fun dancing and drinking.'

'Don't you want to meet anyone?' I sound a bit exasperated and he rolls his eyes. 'Don't start with me, you're as bad as Mum.' I wince at the mention but we both let it go.

'Where's Joe, anyway?' I say, dropping the romance topic and looking around. Mark shrugs. 'Probably getting off with someone here, like everyone else,' he says without emotion. He grabs my hand, pulling me into a group of dancing men nearby, faces adorned with intricate animal-face paints. They are all high as kites, pupils solid black, and I wonder which one I should snog next. It's like a sex buffet here, it's such a delight.

We sway along to the distant music and Mark leans over to shout in my ear. 'Speaking of boys, any word from TD lately?'

I shake my head. 'No, actually!' I say enthusiastically. 'You know I blocked him on WhatsApp after that weirdly sentimental message he sent me in LA? But he could've contacted me some other way. I haven't had any emails or calls or texts – nothing. Which I think proves it was just a fleeting moment of emotion for him. Maybe he was drunk or lonely. Or, most likely, horny. Either way, I honestly feel fine about it. You know . . . I think I might finally be getting over him, Mark. I've hardly thought about him lately. And I have to say, all this snogging other people really helps.'

He nods importantly. 'That's excellent. And you should do more of that then.'

'So should you,' I say carefully and we eye each other warily for a second.

'Hannah sent me the latest family newsletter today,' he says, tactically changing the subject.

'And you haven't forwarded it to me yet!' I gasp, laughing. 'Any highlights?'

'So many,' he confirms. 'Apparently Hannah finally has absolute proof that the world is flat. Who knew? She has been swapping messages with some, er, "experts" she met on AWOL. They told her they're whistle-blowers from NASA and the round Earth thing is all a lie to keep us from investigating the aliens who really run the government.'

'That is so totally amazing,' I laugh again, as he continues.

'Yep, she is now officially referring to herself as a Flat Earther and included a number of YouTube and sub-Reddit links on the email, for those of us who want to know "the truth".'

I clap my hands together, delighted. 'Please forward it on to me immediately,' I say. 'Because I need more information. Do these people also think the sun is flat? And the moon? Why are there are no Flat Sun-ers or Flat Moon-ers?'

'I can show you a flat moon right now,' Mark says dryly, pointing at his own admittedly shapeless bum. We both giggle. I am so happy. Hannah's conspiracy theories are my favourite thing.

'It's a very good point about Flat Sun-ers though,' he adds seriously. 'Maybe I will raise it with Hannah and she can address her thoughts on other stars and planets in her next newsletter. But the whole thing is your fault, anyway. She's been looking into the Earth shape because you've been travelling to such faraway lands. She's really worried you're going to get to an edge and fall off. She's also asking the two of us not to go up any mountains while we're in Thailand, as the other side is often a drop-off point into outer space. Obviously. That's why we can't see the edges, they're up high. This whole Earth thing is essentially a valley.'

'That makes SO much sense, she is so clever,' I nod enthusiastically along. I love it. But I guess that puts paid to the mountain-climbing plan, at least. How useful because I didn't really want to do that anyway.

A man with a tiger painted across his face leans into our space.

'You with him?' he shouts at me, gesturing rudely towards Mark.

I look at my brother, my eyes wide. Outrageous! Interrupting us, barging into our conversation, dismissing my beloved Mark with a wave of his hand! No one talks to us like that! I will tell this idiot where to go.

'Nope, I'm not with him,' I say instead, smiling up at tiger face, all heavy-lidded and flirty. 'Why, are you interested?'

Mark winks at me, understanding that he could be falling into a vat of acid right now and I would not care or save him.

'See you later, loving *sis*,' he says with emphasis, and wanders off to find Joe. I turn back to the tiger, who is grinning at me.

'I'm a firefighter,' he says in an Essex accent, puffing his chest out. And it is a nice chest. 'Fancy a shag?'

'Does that line ever work?' I say, genuinely curious. Firefighters are sexy, sure, but is saying the word one time enough to make all pants in the vicinity drop en masse?

'About eighty per cent of the time,' he says, nodding, still waiting for my answer.

I consider it. I am definitely up for getting off with him – it would break my one-night snogging record, currently held by sixteen-year-old me when I got off with Adam, Giuseppe, Fazli and put half of my tongue in Aaron's mouth. Slutty Sarah said that only counted as three and a half – even though I actually went back and snogged Adam a second time later that night. So, snogging four people tonight would be a nice round number to reach, fourteen years later.

But it would also break my Thailand rule to actually shag him.

Hold on—

'How many cats have you saved from trees? Do you keep count?' I ask, carefully.

'Four thousand and seventy-two,' he says confidently.

'That many?' I am surprised and turned on. 'Who is putting all these cats up trees? Is it the arsonists, hoping to keep all you firefighters distracted while they set alight to the world around us?'

'Is that a yes?' he says, smirking.

Oh, you bet it is.

AWOL.COM/Alice Edwards' Travel Blog: Living My Dream and Feeling Very #Blessed

26 May – 6.22 p.m.

Can someone let me know in the comments section if the monkey photos are loading? I can't see them and I really want to post these incredible pictures I took of monkeys. You will be super amazed by all the monkeys, I PROMISE.

Will update properly in a bit, but we're having a great time. Who knew there were monkeys????

Alice xx

8 Comments · 1 AWOLs · 13 Super Likes

COMMENTS:

Karen Gill
| Yep, all 86 of the monkey pictures you took are on here.

Hollie Baker
| Wow!! Monkeys!!

Isabelle Moore
| Can you Skype me and @EthanWinkleman so we can see the monkeys!

Ethan Winkleman
Replying to Isabelle Moore and Alice Edwards
| Fair warning, Alice, we will be in bed, so you might see something you shouldn't ;)

Isabelle Moore
Replying to Ethan Winkleman and Alice Edwards
| We really should get out of bed sometime!! But it's so hard when you're such a sexy boy . . .

Ethan Winkleman
Replying to Isabelle Moore and Alice Edwards
| I'll show you something else that's so hard, babe . . .

Alice Edwards
Replying to Ethan Winkleman and Isabelle Moore
| BLOCKED AND REPORTED

Ayo Damiunse
| Wow, you are the first person to ever see monkeys in Thailand. Thank God you exist.

Joe and I are snuggled up in a hostel bed together eating an early, wholesome dinner of crisps. Many, many crisps. We were at a street market earlier and dared each other to try some deep-fried spiders – and now we feel predictably sick. The crisps are an attempt at masking the awful taste, but we also agreed that we just really needed to spend an evening lying around eating junk food and trying to illegally download some English telly.

It's really nice actually. Doing nothing for an evening. There's quite a lot of pressure when you're away travelling, pressure to make sure you fully *experience* everything. Pressure to *make the most of your time*. So a night of doing nothing – a night where I could easily just be at home in England, dreading having work in the morning – is exactly what I needed.

'Have you heard from that tiger fireman you had a special, adult cuddle with after the Full Moon Party?' Joe says, giggling through a mouthful of crisp.

I make a face. 'Yep, and it was gross. I should not have given him my number. He tried to sext me last night – it was hilariously bad. Hold on, I'll read it to you.'

I pull out my phone and find the message. '"Peep this, you naughty bitch,"' I read aloud in a posh accent, trying to keep a straight face. '"I'm horny. Where do you" – spelled with just the one letter – "want me to put this?"' I pause dramatically. 'That's what he's written, and then he has kindly attached a picture of his very average cock.'

Joe bursts out laughing as he takes my phone and reviews the image. 'Stunning. And did you reply?'

I nod, 'Yes. I wrote: "Hello. Your penis looks a bit herpes-sad." He didn't reply. But ugh, Joe, it was such an awkward, crappy one-night stand anyway. He wanted to have a bath! When are people going to get the message that taking a bath together is not sexy? Especially not in grotty hostels. Like, how do you take your clothes off? When you're just having normal sex, you can take them off while you're kissing and that. But he suggested getting in a bath the moment we got back to his place – we'd just walked in the bloody door. It ended up feeling like I was getting ready for bed. And then I accidentally took my bottom half off first, which just made me look like Winnie the Pooh with my belly hanging delicately out of my top.'

Joe spits out some half-chewed food, and bends forward laughing.

I sigh, continuing on with my woe-is-me tale of bad sex. 'It got even worse when the two of us tried to cram into this small, dirty bath. Of course I got stuck with the tap end because he's a selfish prick – which I found out later when he made absolutely no effort with my genitals. He seemed to think foreplay is just aggressively rubbing his dick against my leg before sticking it in. And he's one of those blokes who's watched way too much porn, so thinks we all want to be called a dirty bitch and sprayed across the face with sticky semen. It's not like I'm a prude, it's just so deeply, genuinely unsexy, and also makes such a mess.'

'Sounds like you could've done with another bath afterwards,' Joe laughs again, squeezing my hand.

I lie my head on his shoulder. 'Well, I did go back in the bathroom to have a wee after the crap sex, but he immediately knocked on the door. Is there anything more horrifying than someone knocking on the door when you're perched on an unknown toilet? And what are you supposed to say? "Occupied? I'm in here? Sod off, I'm weeing?" I've always wondered if there's a toilet etiquette involved, because mostly I just make a loud frightened noise and fail to wipe myself properly.'

Joe agrees noisily just as Mark stomps in.

'Shut up whatever you two are saying,' he shouts excitably.

'That's not very polite,' Joe begins teasingly, but Mark cuts him off.

'No time for politeness, we must pack!' He is bouncing up and down. 'We're going to Koh Chang in the morning.'

'We are?' I say, surprised.

'Yep, we're going on a retreat.' He smirks mysteriously, and I know there is more to it.

'A . . . retreat?' I say, deeply suspicious. 'Like, with boot-camp exercises and a week of eating spinach smoothies?'

Mark snorts again. 'Something like that, Al. My guru friend runs an Ayahuasca retreat.'

'Not Gary?' Joe says suspiciously.

'*Gary the guru*?' I say, my voice high. 'And what the hell is, er, I-have-a-whisker?'

'Ayahuasca,' Mark says with emphasis, rolling his eyes. 'It's a tree bark or a vine or something.'

'Sounds like you've done your research,' I observe dryly.

'Actually, it's a life-changing experience, Alice. And isn't that what you're looking for from all this?' he says, grinning. 'You spend a week hallucinating and vomming everywhere.'

'Sounds wonderful,' I say sarcastically but feeling intrigued, despite myself. I pause, considering it. 'But I already did my drug experimentation thing in LA.'

Joe hides his smile behind his hand nicely and Mark less nicely throws his head back laughing. It is the sort of deeply unkind, mocking laugh only siblings can get away with.

'You smoked half a spliff with a dickhead on a beach,' he exclaims, still unkindly. 'You cannot call that your once-in-a-lifetime drug experience. And this isn't recreational anyway, Ayahuasca is a truly important and spiritual entheogenic brew that will return you to the womb and help you see God and the universe. It's a deeply respected ceremony – a medicine – used by the indigenous peoples of the Amazon basin.'

'But we're nowhere near South America,' I protest weakly. 'How did your guru friend even get it over here?'

He nods importantly. 'Gary smuggled it in up his bum.'

Joe cheers and I reach for the crisps.

18

27 May – 2.58 p.m.

Hello, dream chasers,

We have left Phuket after a dreamy time, and we're on our way to Koh Chang! We are getting trains and ferries and taxis, which is all very, very enjoyable. Luckily I don't get car sick, and we have played I Spy all the way, and it has given us a chance to really take in the very impressive views and bond with each other even more. There is nothing like travelling to bring out the very best in people and bring you together. We are getting on really, really, really well. Despite seven hours in a car together. We are great. Closer than ever.

Anyway, now we are on our way to a spiritual retreat!! We will spend a week taking a very mythical form of tree bark called Ayahuasca. I shall hallucinate and connect with the universe and find out who I truly am. It is not always a pleasant experience and there may be bodily fluids as it is a drug, and I will not sugarcoat this, but it shall be worth it!!

Wish me luck on this journey,

Alice xx

#Ayahuasca #LegaliseWeed #DrugMules #TravelBlogger #GoneAWOL #AliceEdwardsBlog #BloggerLife #Blessed #Brave #DreamChaser

7 Comments · 6 AWOLs · 18 Super Likes

COMMENTS:

Karen Gill
| Sounds like your brother is driving you round the bend!! Eh? Eh?

> *Alice Edwards*
> *Replying to Karen Gill*
> | What exactly are you driving at?

>> *Karen Gill*
>> *Replying to Alice Edwards*
>> | That you've been driven to distraction.

>>> *Alice Edwards*
>>> *Replying to Karen Gill*
>>> | You drive a hard bargain.

>>>> *Alice Edwards*
>>>> *Replying to Karen Gill*
>>>> | PS. I know that last one didn't work but I'd run out of driving puns.

Eva Slate
| Al, is it a good idea to put the drug thing on here where anyone can see it?

> *Mark Edwards*
> *Replying to Eva Slate*
> | I want to publicly distance myself from this blog. I would never take drugs. Ever. Outrageous. Smh.

Here's a fun challenge: how long can you spend in the back of a car with your sibling without murdering them in cold blood? The question is not rhetorical – really I am looking for methods of execution.

I don't know whose idea this was, but I am going to destroy Mark because it was his idea. We have just spent an unfathomable number of hours in a taxi, and I've thrown up in a bag at least seven times. My stupid brother arranged the whole thing last night, and kept waving his hand at me this morning whenever I asked how long the trip was.

It reminded me of being little, when Mum, me, Mark and Hannah would go on long car journeys to Cornwall in the summer holidays. It was always awful – arguing and elbowing each other in the backseat while Mum shouted that she would 'turn this car around' – but the awfulness was also part of the fun. We knew adventures and the seaside were ahead. Even the lunch stop at Little Chef was magic. Then it was all about who could see the sea first and then crying because Hannah – being the tallest – always won. It was nice.

But right now, the three of us are running to catch a ferry, so we can spend a week in a national park, taking a drug that sounds like some kind of stripper.

I am looking forward to it.

I've been reading up on the Ayahuasca thing during the car journey, and I've decided it's going to be really interesting. I am going to eat only healthy, wonderful things and meditate every day. Then go puke my guts out drinking tree bark so I can have visions.

I want to get in the Turiya state, which is a complicated thing I read about, where you're very awake, but also sort of semi-unconscious. It's all about bringing discipline to bliss-ipline, which is a cool tagline I just made up and have decided to make my motto. Maybe I should get into advertising when I'm back in the UK? I think I have a knack for it.

Either way, I am going to look deep inside myself on this retreat, and truly *see me*.

And I am going to be one of those awful people who talk like that all the time.

'Come the fuck on, Bridget!' Mark shouts at me as he and Joe run to board the ferry. I hitch my enormous rucksack further up my shoulder and half-jog after them.

On board, we are greeted by a bearded Westerner, who introduces himself in a broad Welsh accent as Gary.

Aha, the much-revered drug-smuggler cum guru.

'Hello there, Alice, I've heard a lot about you,' he says cheerfully, and I briefly wonder what that Welsh tongue is capable of. You need a lot of muscle memory in your mouth to pronounce that language. I wonder what would happen if he went down on me and said that famously long-named Welsh train station, Llanfairpwllgwyngyllgogerychwyrndrobwllllantysiliogogogoch.

I give myself a shake. No more sex on this leg of the trip, thank you. Particularly not after that awful one-night stand. This is about soul-searching, not fun. Soul-searching is not fun, I'm certain of that much.

'Hello Gary, nice to meet you,' I say primly.

'You look like that actress,' he says, looking at me searchingly. 'That superhero woman, what's she called? Jessica Jones!' he snaps his fingers.

I nod stoically, determined not to be dragged into any flirting nonsense, even though it is the best compliment I've ever heard and I am in love with Krysten Ritter.

'Thanks very much,' I say, puffing out despite myself. 'I am also surprisingly strong.' I pause before adding, 'You look like . . .' I am lost for a celebrity look-alike. 'You look like . . . um, Jesus?'

'How do you know what Jesus looks like?' he says, bemused.

'It's just the beard,' I say, trying to sound confident. 'It's very Jesus.'

'Do you feel very surrounded by Jesuses when you're in East London?' he says, as Mark grabs my hand.

'Stop embarrassing yourself,' he says, yanking me away.

'See you later,' Jesus shouts after us, as we go find seats at the front of the boat with the rest of the 'retreat' guests.

'What do we actually know about Gary then?' I ask suspiciously, sitting down in the wet plastic seat. I can feel the engines beginning to roar beneath us and a surge of excitement pulses through me. We're officially on our way to the island. It's really happening.

Joe leans in. 'Call him Shaman Quam,' he says in an excitable, confidential tone. He's reverberating with joy – typical Joe.

'Why?' I whisper back.

'*Quam* means "shaman" in Turkish, and Gary just got back from Turkey,' Joe explains, confusingly.

'So you want me to call him Shaman Shaman?' I ask, carefully.

Joe nods, wisely. 'He's a medicine man. A healer. A life coach.'

Mark leans in. 'He's also an accountant. He used to do my accounts, that's how we know him. So if you need any tax advice while we're out here, he's your guy.'

Joe and I giggle, and a man in his mid-fifties within earshot shuffles closer in the row of plastic seats. 'You guys here for

176

the Ayahuasca retreat?' he says in a Texan accent.

'Yep,' I confirm, eyeing his big hat. Seems a bit of a Texan cliché, but who am I to judge.

'I'm darned excited,' he says loudly. 'I was gon' go to Peru, but this was cheaper and seemed a little more – how do I put it? – *laid back*. Plus, I could fit it in around my latest business trip to Bangkok.' When he says the words 'business trip' he winks at Joe and Mark. Mark openly grimaces and Joe looks confused, but the Texan continues oblivious. 'I think Shaman Quam is the real deal, too. He has, y'know, that transcendental energy about him, and that mysterious, mystical accent.'

'Welsh?' I say baldly.

He ignores me. I think he is mostly speaking to himself.

'I am here for the retreat, as well!' a woman calls across to our group in a European accent. She joins us, continuing, 'I am Clara, from Denmark.' She reaches out to shake my hand and I leap up.

'It's you!' I shout.

Her mouth gapes open. 'No, it's YOU!' We both laugh out loud and I catch Mark and Joe exchanging confused looks.

It's my friend from the vagina cult in LA. I can't believe she's here. This is madness. I giggle again and pull Clara in for a hug.

'Mark, Joe,' I say, pulling away. 'This is Clara and her little friend Garfield.' She sniggers and curtseys. 'And how is your giraffe?' she asks politely.

We both descend into laughter again.

'How are you here?' I say, bewildered.

'I've been travelling all over Asia for the last couple of months,' she explains, taking a seat next to us. I had just finished a few months in America when I saw you at the Sheathology class.'

'The sheath-*what*?!' Mark interrupts and Clara turns to face him. Her mouth and eyes open a little too wide. He smiles nicely, but glances away quickly.

This will sound gross, but my brother is really hot. He's tall and dark and brooding, all that Mr Darcy stuff. I have seen too many random humans turn to gloop in his wake not to have noticed, so there's no point pretending it's not a fact.

Clara and her pal, Garfield, don't have much of a shot though lololol.

Actually, to be completely honest, nobody really does. My brother never seems to date. Or, if he does, he doesn't tell me about it. He is decidedly not a sharer when it comes to his romantic endeavours. As far as I know, he's never had a boyfriend at all. He came out to me way back at his twenty-first birthday and I was like, yeah doi, no shit, but he's said almost nothing about his love life in the eleven years or so since. For the first few years I just thought he was a slow starter and I didn't want to push him into talking about that side of his life if he didn't want to. It had clearly been a big thing for him to come out at all, and I didn't want to rush him into conversations he didn't want to have. I thought he should go at his own pace and figure things out, without my big fat face leering over his shoulder or my downloading Grindr onto his phone. Much as I wanted to. But time went by and nothing happened. *No one* happened.

Sometimes I wonder about Mark and Joe. They would be so brilliant together – they *are* so brilliant together – but it's always been completely platonic. I once mentioned the possibility to Mark, years ago. He laughed his head off and then accused me of being one of those cis idiots who assumes just because two people are gay that they will automatically fancy each other. Which is fair enough. People can be just friends for God's sake! Except sometimes when I'm really drunk I want to kiss Eva a lot. But I think that's just some kind of complicated, confused cross-contamination of adoration. Sexuality is all on a spectrum, right? I'd say I'm like an eight out of ten on the side of fancying men.

Either way, I've never seen anything flirty going on between Joe and Mark, and Joe always seems to have a boyfriend so I don't think it would ever happen. I don't understand why *nothing* happens for Mark though. I have tried to get him to talk to me about his love life. Believe me, I've tried. I am always fishing, always saying unsubtle things like, 'How's life? Any gossip?' And sometimes more pointed things like, 'Is there anyone on the scene?' And a few times literally, 'Please tell me about your love life. Please Mark, I'm desperate to know.' But he always either laughs my questions off, or gives me a vague answer about being too busy with work for a love life.

It makes me sad, but I am also aware that not everyone is as obsessive about oversharing as me or, say, Slutty Sarah. So maybe he's just not that interested in talking about it. Or maybe he's having a rampant sex-filled mad secret life that I'm not privy to. I hope it's the latter, but I would also be sad if that were the case. I want him to feel like he can share all of that with me. Even though my brother having a sex life would of course make me puke.

'Well, it's amazing to meet you properly, Clara,' I say, shaking her hand and laughing again. 'I can't believe you're here. We are obviously meant to be friends. Sorry I ran out of that place in LA so fast, I did not want to see anymore chinchillas.' She throws back her head and laughs, as I add, 'Anyway, this is my brother Mark, and that's Joe over there.'

The Texan leans in. 'I'm Craig,' he says, and I freeze. I can never tell if Americans are saying Greg or Craig and it is my worst thing. We all nod at each other, and excitement buzzes around us.

'WELL then,' Gary booms, suddenly joining us. 'I expect you're all excited to hear what awaits you.'

'Is there anyone else joining our special group, Shaman Quam?' Mark asks, and you really have to know him well to hear the amusement in his tone.

Gary surveys the gang. 'Oh, wait, hold on, there should be a German couple around here somewhere.' He looks around until he spots an elderly pair huddled together in the furthest corner. 'Aha,' he says striding over to them. '*Hallo, Marie und Anna?*'

The women look startled but leap up. They must both be in their late seventies, but seem spritely enough.

'*Willkommen in Koh Chang*!' Gary says happily.

'You must be Shaman Quam, we are delighted to make your acquaintance,' one of the women says in perfect, formal English. The pair follow him over to our group and we all wave awkwardly.

'Hello everyone!' Marie and Anna say simultaneously. They laugh at the synchronicity, looking at each other affectionately.

I scoot over, making room for them to sit. They are already my favourites in the group. They have a nice energy and kind faces. When I'm puking my guts out in a couple of days, I want them to be right there next to me. I will even let them have first pass at the toilet.

Oh God, there probably won't be a toilet, will there?

19

AWOL.COM/Alice Edwards' Travel Blog: Living My Dream and
Feeling Very #Blessed

27 May – 8.11 p.m.

Good evening, dream chasers,
   I would just like to clarify about my most recent blog post. I
know I mentioned taking drugs but that was a misunderstanding, I would never do anything like that. I would never ever
jeopardise future employment by publicly writing about taking
drugs, because that would be foolish. There are definitely no
drugs.
   Anyway, we have just arrived at the spiritual retreat but as I
mentioned there will be no drugs. Just spiritual chat and medi-
tation. There might be some gongs or something, and probably
quite a lot of vegan food. But no drugs. Despite what I said before,
I am not going to do anything illegal.
   Do not break the law,
   Alice xx

#KeepingItLegal #FutureJobProspects #CallMyLawyer #Trav-
elBlogger #GoneAWOL #AliceEdwardsBlog #BloggerLife
#Blessed #Brave #DreamChaser

7 Comments · 6 AWOLs · 37 Super Likes

COMMENTS:

Karen Gill
| I would give you a job.

Eva Slate
| Haven't heard from you since you got to Thailand!! Call me! You are the missing link in my life!

> *Mark Edwards*
> *Replying to Eva Slate*
> | She sure is the missing link, Eva.

Danny Boy
| VAPID CUNT

> *Alice Edwards*
> *Replying to Danny Boy*
> | YOU'VE GOT ME THERE.

>> *AWOL MODERATOR*
>> *Replying to Danny Boy and Alice Edwards*
>> | We love to see people connecting, but please be respectful to each other :) Chilling is better than trolling, right guys?!!! Luke

>> *Danny Boy*
>> *Replying to AWOL MODERATOR*
>> | LUKE GO FIST YOURSELF

'This is how things go on an Ayahuasca retreat,' Gary is saying sternly, looking round at all of us individually as we sit on benches before him in this tiny hut. 'Day one is rest and relaxation. Day two is the preparation ceremony, day three is the first of three or four Ayahuasca ceremonies, which then take place every other day. There's no caffeine, no meat, no alcohol, and there's a strict diet enforced, in order to avoid introducing toxins into our systems.'

He pauses dramatically, making eye contact with Mark, Joe and me, sitting in a small group at the end of the row, and on to Marie and Anna, huddled beside us holding hands excitedly. Clara sits on the other side of them, looking nervous next to Craig/Greg, who is at the other end of the bench. He is still wearing that hat and it still feels like he's mocking Texans even though he is one.

'But . . .' Gary stops, grinning triumphantly before continuing. 'Screw all that! We're the unofficial branch of the Ayahuasca retreat tree. The mavericks, the rebels, the revolutionaries. We are District 12 taking on Capitol City. But with Ayahuasca.'

Clara twitches violently. I suspect she is a *Hunger Games* fan.

He continues. 'So let's all just chill the eff out, drink a bit of tree bark and – as for that no drinking alcohol rule—' he stops again, slowly pulling out a bottle of absinthe from behind his back. 'Fuck it! We'll take some Ayahuasca tonight, as the sun goes down, and in the meantime, let's get drunk and have some banter, yeah?!'

Oh God.

He said banter.

I am strongly anti-banter.

This is everything I feared it might be.

I guess I should've known when Mark and Joe told me it was their mate running things. Or at least known when Mark said Gary smuggled the drugs in up his bum. How am I here? What am I doing? Is this a total waste of my time here? Should I just leave?

183

Gary hands the bottle of green stuff to Mark and I watch as he and Joe snigger as they each take a swig.

I reach for it, and pause. Maybe I can still get something out of this process though. Gary and the rest of them don't have to take this retreat seriously, but I can.

My hand drops and I shake my head at the proffered liquid. It passes me, down to Marie and Anna who gladly take a drink, giggling gleefully at each other. They are just so sweet together, I can't handle it.

'Absinthe and Ayahuasca!' shouts Craig/Greg, woo-hooing as the bottle reaches him. 'Truly, Shaman Quam, you are a leader among men. Let's get this party started!'

The group starts chatting excitedly. Clearly, they had more of an idea what they were signing up for than I did. A Thai woman comes in the door of the hut. She offers around bowls of what look suspiciously like Doritos – tangy cheese tortilla flavour – and lingers over Mark, smiling widely. No one is immune to his looks. He politely takes a crisp, ignoring her admiring stare.

'Hey Jessica Jones,' Gary flops down on the bench beside me, almost landing in Marie's lap, who squawks in surprise. '*Scheiße!*' she says, adding, '*Achtung.*'

They are such healthy-sounding, satisfying words and I am suddenly desperate to learn German. Maybe they can teach me this week? I may as well get something out of my time here. And how long does it take, even, to learn a new language? Probably like a week?

'How's it going, Shaman Shaman?' I say conversationally, shuffling up to make room for him. He fists his hands under his chin, adopting a therapy pose and looking at me deeply.

'I am pure light and joy, Alice, that's how it is going. How are YOU though, my new friend?' he says in a sing-song voice. 'I feel like maybe you're not ready to open yourself up to this. I really need you to give yourself over to this process wholeheartedly. I need you to help me *help you*.'

'Which process is that, Gary?' I say, giving in to my irritation. 'The drinking heavily process? Or the one where you culturally appropriate and co-opt a traditional spiritual retreat to make money?'

He smiles. 'You should relax, my friend. It'll be great, I promise.'

The Thai lady passes by and I grab a handful of Doritos, nodding my thanks at her. 'I am incredibly fucking relaxed, thanks,' I say.

He sighs and turns to the group, his voice raised. 'Everyone gather round, let's get to know each other a little better, shall we? Has everyone had a drink? Keep passing the bottle along, it will help us with the bonding and the sharing of ourselves. Kohsoom, could you bring the stools in?' The Thai lady nods obediently, leaving the hut and returning with several tiny stools, clearly built for children. Clara, Mark and Joe all abandon the bench for the tiny seats, forming a circle, and for a moment we all just stare at each other, waiting.

Gary clears his throat. 'I'll start, then, shall I? I grew up in North Wales, on the Isle of Anglesey. I have six sisters and worked as an accountant for seven years before I discovered enlightenment during a trip to Phuket when I was thirty-two. Last year I retrained as a life coach and then set up shop here around Christmas.'

So he's been a guru for all of five months. How wonderful. How *authentic*.

Gary catches the look I am giving Mark – a not very nice look – and quickly adds, 'But even though I have not been running these retreats all that long, I have already had multiple conversations with the universe. Very deep conversations. I am enlightened and more than qualified to help you reach the same level as me. Plus, I think I'm the only one around here with a big pile of Ayahuasca in my bag, am I right?' He laughs and smiles nicely at me.

I smile back despite myself. He is obviously a total fraud, but at least he's open about it. I also have a kind of respect for the way he's changed his life so dramatically. It feels like there are so many people around – myself included – who sit there, buried in a life and job they don't like, always moaning and wishing for something else; dreaming big, but doing nothing to change anything. It is so boring and unsexy. Gary has, at least, done something about it.

The Texan clears his throat. 'Well folks, I'm Craig,' – or is it Greg? – 'I'm fifty-three and I live in Austin – the Lone Star State!' He pauses dramatically and I see Clara is very close to applauding. She grins across at me. He continues after a moment and suddenly looks a little vulnerable under his big hat. 'I'm going through a pretty hellish divorce right now, folks, and my life kinda sucks.' He sighs. 'You know, life can be hard and sometimes I just wish I could be Mike O'Donnell for a day.'

He looks at each of us expectantly and we all look at him blankly. Who the hell is Mike O'Donnell? Is he an American footballer or something? A US politician?

'Mike O'Donnell?!' he says, exasperated, looking at each of us. 'The lead character in the most important movie of the twenty-first century?'

Still nothing.

His voice is raised as he adds, 'Mike O'Donnell, played by iconic actor Zac Efron and Matthew Perry in two thousand and nine?'

Is he . . . is he talking about . . .

'*17 AGAIN*?' he shouts.

Clara sounds a little strangled as she asks, 'The comedy body-swap movie thing?' Craig/Greg stands up, incensed.

'It is more than a "body-swap movie *thing*"!' He seems genuinely outraged. 'It's about the choices we make and the regret we feel as we get older. It is groundbreaking, it is SEMINAL.' He is red in the face and I try not to burst out laughing.

To be fair, it is a great film, and from what I remember, Zac takes his top off a few times, so I am on board.

Gary clears his throat as Craig/Greg throws his hands up in the air. 'Um, thanks for sharing man, I'm sorry about the divorce. I hope this retreat gives you what you need. I truly hope this is your *17 Again* moment.'

Craig/Greg nods self-importantly as he sits down. 'Thanks man. You just *get me*, Shaman Quam.'

Crisis averted, Clara stands up next. 'Well, I'm actually here for some of the same reason . . .' Catching Craig/Greg's eye, she adds quickly, 'Not the *17 Again* thing. I mean I'm going through a divorce, too.' There is a slightly judgy silence around the circle as we all calculate how young she is. She cannot be more than mid-twenties, almost certainly younger. Sensing the mood, she stands taller, raising her chin. 'I know what you're all thinking, and yes, I am only twenty-three. It is young to be married, never mind divorcing, I'm well aware of that. But I don't need to justify my choices to you. I truly believed he was my soulmate, I really did. And I've had months of people making me feel like a foolish little child, so I don't need it here, too. I made a mistake, but life is full of mistakes, and I'm trying to believe I've been brave walking away from something I knew was wrong. I could've wasted twenty years on the wrong man. Instead I'm out here, travelling the world and figuring out who I am on my own again.'

I give her a tight nod. Good for you, Clara. Her brave face falters for a second, and she adds, 'But I am a little lost. I don't know what happens next, I don't know how to be sure, and I could really do with finding some clarity. I've tried a few different things . . .' she makes eye contact with me '. . . and nothing has helped so far.' Anna, beside her, reaches up and gives her a reassuring pat. Clara smiles at her gratefully before taking her seat.

Anna and Marie stand up together simultaneously and then laugh at their mirroring. These two are so in sync, I feel like they spend their whole days giggling and copying each other.

Anna begins slowly. 'We are Anna and Maria. I am seventy-seven and Maria is eighty-one. We have never done anything like this before!' She falls silent and Gary calls across the circle, encouragingly, 'Tell us about yourselves, the pair of you.'

Anna nods at Maria and her partner picks up the thread. 'We have been lovers for ten years . . .'

'But . . .' Anna interrupts, sounding sad, 'I am married to someone else.'

'I am Anna's mistress,' says Maria, a weird sort of pride in her voice. 'We spend time together whenever we can but this is our first-ever trip away.'

The circle is thick with judgement again – but, I would swear it was way judge-ier for Clara's divorce confession. People's standards for women continue to surprise me – cheating on a partner is apparently not so bad as making the wrong choices when you're young. Interesting.

188

'My wife doesn't know about Maria,' Anna adds, sounding slightly regretful. 'But we have been much happier in the last ten years, since Maria has been in my life. My wife and I were unkind to each other before, and now we love each other again.'

'I have helped,' Maria confirms.

'Love is complicated,' Anna sighs.

This much I can certainly agree with.

The pair sit down slowly and the group turn to me. I don't even stand up.

'Honestly, I don't really know why I'm here,' I say after a moment. 'It was my brother's idea.' I shoot him another dirty look. 'But everything kind of imploded in my life, at home in London. I turned thirty, I lost my job and my home and my best friend. And . . . some other stuff happened with my family. I'm trying to figure out what I want from life and what to do next.'

I trail off and Clara smiles nicely at me. I blink a few times and turn away. I feel oddly emotional, sharing even only that much with these strangers.

Joe stands next, looking excited. 'I'm on a voyage of self-discovery,' he pronounces, proudly. 'My life is great and fulfilling in lots of ways, but I want to be brave and I want to see new things. I want to ask the universe some questions about myself and about others. I want to be open to everything in my life, I want to find the strength to *try*.'

He glances down at Mark, and for a moment I think . . . maybe. Maybe . . .?

Mark stands up abruptly and Joe closes his mouth, taking his seat.

My brother takes a minute to start talking and when he does, he speaks quickly and robotically.

'I'm here because I'm really, truly miserable,' he says, and suddenly he looks it.

He is?

'It's been a rough couple of months,' he goes on. 'My step-dad recently had a major stroke. It was sudden, but not wholly unexpected. He'd been . . . ill for a long time.' He makes eye contact with me. 'He's still in hospital, and we don't know what's going to happen to him. Either he's going to die or he's going to come out of this and be a vegetable for the rest of his life. Maybe I want him to die, maybe I want him to be OK, I don't know. Maybe I even want him to suffer. He made all of us suffer a lot over the years. He even drove some of us apart . . .' His fists are in balls at his side and I feel very cold all at once.

He continues. 'And sure, Steven wasn't – isn't – a very good guy at times, but he was also the only dad I ever knew. So what do I do with that? He's my dad. And on top of that, my mum is a wreck, which makes me a wreck, and . . . I don't know how to feel.'

He breaks off, and I stare at his hands, clenching and unclenching. 'I am struggling. I am really struggling,' he continues at last. 'But I also don't feel like I'm allowed to struggle, because my mum needs me. Everyone needs something from me, and I have to be strong. I'm tired and sad. And probably the worst part is the way my closest, best friend – the one person who should get what I'm going through – won't talk to me about what is happening.'

He looks directly at me again and I swallow hard.

His voice is shaky as he continues, 'I feel like I'm in limbo. And I can't cry. I want to know how to grieve for someone I hate a lot of the time but also love. Someone I've had to love. Someone who has needed my love so much, but has never deserved it. I want to learn to forget but also remember. Life is too hard, I need something and I don't know what.'

I haven't seen Mark like this before and I glance down to see my hands are shaking. He continues in a rush, his eyes dark. 'I am sad and I feel like I have been sad for a long time. Probably before this happened to Steven. And I don't know how to not be sad any more. I hope this retreat helps me. I feel like I need help . . .'

Joe stands back up, placing an arm on Mark's shoulder. I reach across in the semi-darkness, but my brother sits down instead of taking my hand. Someone gives him the bottle of green liquid and he takes a long, hard drink.

He stares off into the distance, studiously ignoring me. I sit there, feeling cold and afraid, and furiously wipe away the tear making its way down my face.

20

29 May – 9.42 p.m.

Good evening, dream chasers,

Obviously I am here at this retreat to get away from life and re-connect with myself and with nature, but I also just have to say how impressed I am with the WiFi service here. Of course, I am very very rarely checking my phone – no more than every few minutes at the absolute most – but it is very helpful to have, as they have just announced this year's *Love Island* contestants and I am very keen to read more about which one used to go out with that soap star.

But this retreat is about escaping the rest of the world, which I am definitely doing. There are trees here and everything. I am also pleased to report all the other guests at this resort are very deep and meaningful humans and I am confident they will help me find myself. Any minute now. Tonight is a big, important night for connecting with myself and the universe, as well as the other amazing souls here. For the record and just to be very clear, there still won't be any drugs taken because that would be illegal. But if there were, this would be the night I take the most.

Love Alice x

PS. Do you think the soap guy is going to enter the villa to stir up drama????

#SpiritualRetreat #LoveIsland #LoveMyWiFi #TravelBlogger #GoneAWOL #AliceEdwardsBlog #BloggerLife #Blessed #Brave #DreamChaser

6 Comments · 2 AWOLs · 9 Super Likes

COMMENTS:

Hollie Baker
| Wow, I wanna go to this retreat!!!

Karen Gill
| if you get bored of connecting with your inner being n that, there is an amazing new crime thriller available on Netflix. He definitely didn't do it!

Seamus NaughtyLad678
| y u is waisting ur life on dis dumb websight, looser.

Alice Edwards
Replying to Seamus NaughtyLad678
| I can't argue with your logic, Seamus NaughtyLad678, you're dead right. Probably not going to stop though.

Hannah Edwards
Replying to Seamus NaughtyLad678 and Alice Edwards
| stay n touch sis

Sarah Sommers
| WiFi, eh? Downloading porn, much?

193

We are three days into our 'retreat' and have just begun our second Ayahuasca ceremony. The first go – that first night – was fairly uneventful in terms of making any giant connection with the universe. I mean, that's not to say *nothing* happened. It was, for example, deeply pleasant.

We all gathered in the main hut as the sun went down – a little sheepish after a day of drinking and oversharing – to sip from cups of this thick brown tea-like thing. It tasted like it looked and the gagging began pretty much straight away. Then we lay around for a while, each on our own little camp bed dotted around the room, waiting for something to happen.

Sure, I was sick a lot – a lot a lot – but that was sort of it for me. I felt a bit spacey, but that might've been the nausea. Some of the others had more luck. Clara couldn't stop crying and then laughing, and then crying again, while Texan Craig/Greg shouted for three hours straight about goddesses and monkeys and Zac Efron.

Lucky fuckers.

Mark was quiet after his emotional display earlier in the day, but seemed serene, lying there in his corner. He was certainly experiencing something, as was Anna. Sadly, Maria and Joe were like me – but worse. I guess they had even more toxins in their body that needed shedding than I did. We were up most of the night, half of us ill, the other half seeing some kind of God, and yesterday was mostly spent napping and staring into space, feeling weird.

I did try to speak to Mark.

I didn't know what to say, but I tried. I couldn't just leave it after everything he said to the group. I've never seen him like that. I had no idea he was struggling; no idea he was in trouble. And yes, I know, that's because I'm a selfish bitch. Always too wrapped up in how I'm coping to notice how he is. Always making everything about me. I feel terrible.

I guess predictably, he didn't want to talk to me about it. He wasn't horrible, but he was firm in his dismissals. He said I'd had plenty of chances to talk to him and now he wanted to spend some alone time with this experience and with Shaman Quam. They went off for a long walk earlier today and have both been totally silent ever since.

As we arrived at the hut tonight, I tried again, but Mark waved me off. Told me we could talk properly after all this was over.

Not that I want to.

I turn over on my camp bed now, sighing. Gary is singing something he called the *icaros*. He said it will enhance our *mareación* – our visions – but it's been about thirty minutes since I took my latest dose and nothing has happened yet. At least I'm not being sick! Yet! Actually, I'm really starting to suspect Shaman Gary has fed us placebos. Very toxic placebos.

I stare out the window. Sweet Jesus it's dark out there.

But of course it is. There are no street lamps or electric lights here – it's a national park. It's totally blank outside. The rain clouds are even covering any stars that might've provided some proof we're still a part of this world. It feels like it is a black universe out there. Just us, the incessant noise of birds and monkeys off in the distance, and a wall of blackness. It is incredibly surreal.

I am barely conscious of the warm sensation creeping up my spine before I blink and my head comes off. It floats above me, looking down at the figures huddled around me. They blink in and out of existence, flashing red, amber, green, like traffic lights. I am aware enough to know this is really fucking weird.

The music is suddenly so very loud and brightly coloured shapes are moving everywhere around me. It is fascinating and really quite wonderful. It is exciting and thrilling and also calming. I feel suddenly like I am happy and full of bliss. I float there forever, moving but not moving. Everything is good. Is this the universe? Because I am sure now that I am part of it and it is a part of me.

Maybe I should ask the universe for a selfie?

No, that's probably not OK.

It would be cool to have a selfie with the universe though! Imagine the likes on Instagram.

And then I am rushing through space, moving faster than any human has before. I have no body, I am just a blue light, the world rushing past me, unaware of my existence as I move faster and faster. It's scary now, I want it to stop, I don't like it any more. At last I slow, and then I rest. After years of moving, I am now in a familiar kitchen. It feels real – it *is* real – it is more real than anything else.

Mum is here.

My mum. Mummy.

She's in the kitchen and she's humming a tune. It's the tune Shaman Gary was playing all those years ago at the retreat. Or is it years *from* now? I am not sure. Mum is young, she looks younger than I've ever seen her. She is line-free and fussing over a little girl, who must be about four or five. It is my sister, Hannah, I can see that. There is also a little boy – around two – sitting in the corner, smashing his tiny fist into a brightly coloured book, its pages thick card. Hello Mark, I try to say, but I am not really there.

'Hannah,' Mum says to the little girl, and her voice is

bright and high. 'Go get the outdoor cushions. It's March today, they can go outside now.'

I laugh now. Wherever I am, I laugh so hard. I had forgotten how Mum did this, every year; prematurely taking the outdoor fucking cushions out to the outdoor fucking patio furniture. That ritual. Running in and out with the cushions at the beginning of spring, even though we all knew the rain would continue to come and go for at least another three months. Mum was always determined that spring was here, so optimistic with her outdoor sofa cushions.

I can see her more clearly now. She is pregnant. It is me, and I am suddenly inside her. In the womb, surrounded by pinkness. At first I panic and fight. I am so small and my breathing is all wrong. But then I am OK. It is small, yes, but it is not claustrophobic. It's nice, comfortable, happy. My mum loves me, I *know* it through and through. I am flooded with it. I can feel her stroking me through our shared skin and singing songs to me. Badly.

Outside of myself I am sweating and crying. Crying so much.

And then it is later and Steven is there. He's drunk, like he always was. Like he always is. Except he can't be drunk now, can he? Not now, lying in hospital with half his brain destroyed, waiting to see if death comes. He can't be drunk now. But even if he dies, he'll never be gone really, he'll always be hanging over things. Over my mum's life, over her destroyed relationship with me. He is staggering around now, shouting, breaking things. He is shouting at me, shouting at Hannah, shouting at Mark.

Shouting at Mum.

Why won't she leave him? Why won't she go? I'm begging her, crying, begging. Over and over for years. Why does she love him more than she loves us? Because that's what it comes down to: we love her, she loves him, and he loves the bottle. Why can't she see he will always choose that over her and over us? Why can't she make him go? This was our home, not his. He came in, took our mum away, got drunk every day, told us we were not wanted. Why is he here?

Then he is gone, and we are sitting around Mum on the settee, in the living room. She is weeping, inconsolable, because he has left again. On another bender, he will be gone for days on end. But I know he will be back because he always comes back eventually. He comes back covered in bruises, stinking from days sleeping rough, saying sorry sorry sorry. But watching Mum cry now, I wish with all I have in me that he won't come back. I wish for him to die. I wish for him to fall and hit his head and never come back. I want him to be gone for ever, however much it would upset Mum. I want him out of our lives. I want him away from us.

But now I am getting my wish and I can't stop wishing.

I can't forgive. I'm stuck in this rut, unable to forgive.

It's too late. He drove me away. He took my mum away from me. She chose him every time. I mattered less. Everyone leaves. Everyone abandons me eventually. I might as well push them away first, get in there before they leave.

And then everyone is gone and I am in a blackness all alone. It's what I wanted, isn't it? For everyone to go. But it doesn't feel good.

When I open my eyes, it feels like days have passed. I feel absolutely wretched. Broken open, like I've just had open heart surgery.

I'm sick.

Wiping my mouth feebly, I look around at everyone else.

Joe is sitting up in the dim lighting, looking pale and fragile. He looks like he's survived something major. Mark is beside him, crying quietly, his eyes closed.

Clara, Maria and Anna are standing by the doorway, laughing quietly, holding each other up. I make a move to join them, but feel too weak. Instead, I lie back down. I need to talk, but not just yet.

It feels like something has loosened inside me. Seeing everything like that – all my worst moments up close and so real – has done something. It was awful and intense and horrible. But those are my experiences; they are me, they are mine. And they're also long since over. I have survived them, I'm here and I'm OK. I can't let them keep controlling my life.

I fall asleep, completely wiped out.

AWOL.COM/Alice Edwards' Travel Blog: Living My Dream and Feeling Very #Blessed

3 June – 3.12 p.m.

GOOD EVENING, DREAM CHASERS,

I WRITE TO YOU THIS AFTERNOON IN CAPITALS BE-CAUSE MY EYES ARE OPEN. MY EYES HAVE BEEN OPENED.

I'll stop doing that now in case it loses its impact. But seriously, my eyes have been opened by this retreat. I feel so open and free. I have shed my previous life-skin and touched the universe. I am a whole new, better person, looking at the world through the new eyes that I mentioned a minute ago.

I have had the best week of my life. I have learnt so much, felt so much, gave so much. My retreat comrades will be my friends for life, we are bonded for ever. Thank you Mark, Joe, Clara, Craig, Anna, Marie and Guru Shaman Quam. I am lucky to call you my friends. We are blessed to know each other.

LONG LIVE AYAHUASCA. Yes, I did drink a tree bark and I don't care who knows!! NB. It's a very well-respected traditional remedy and should not be held against me if I happen to be up for a job in the future.

Sending love from this spiritual place,

Alice xxxx

#LOVEYOUALL #CAPS #MissYouAlready #Ayahuasca

#SeeYouHereAgainNextYear #TravelBlogger #GoneAWOL #AliceEdwardsBlog #BloggerLife #Blessed #Brave #DreamChaser

9 Comments · 3 AWOLs · 41 Super Likes

COMMENTS:

Hannah Edwards
| awwww, glad u r havin a g8 time. take care

Clara Weber
| Love you more! Thanks for all the big chats my giraffe friend. I feel wonderful!!

Karen Gill
| Have you been hacked?

Hollie Baker
| What is ayahuasca? Is it a restaurant?

Noah Deer
| More fun than LA?! I'm offended! Guess you should've spent more time with me, huh?

   Alice Edwards
   Replying to Noah Deer
   | You had four weeks to ask me out, you blew it, dude.

Noah Deer
| :(

Sarah Sommers
| Oh yeah?! Best week of your life?!!! I know what you've been up to, you saucy minx!!

Alice Edwards
Replying to Sarah Sommers

| You are more than this caricature, Sarah. I'm not doing the Slutty thing any more, it makes me uncomfortable. I love you, but no.

We are all crying, weeping into each other's armpits. Every time we try to break away from the group hug, one of us starts again, and we all lose it and pile back in.

It's been a very emotional few days.

Craig – because of course it is Craig and I am ashamed of myself for mocking his confusing pronunciation – is the worst of us. He has cried non-stop this whole week.

'I've had my Mike O'Donnell moment,' he keeps saying, before expanding: 'I know what's important now. I've got to stop living in the past and chasing my glory days. My glory days are ahead of me if I can only let them be.' It's super wise.

He says he's going back to Austin to beg his ex-wife to take him back. He wants to say sorry for everything he did, and I can confirm, he did do some shitty things, which we have discussed in intricate, awkward detail. He wants to fix things between them. But if she won't have him back, he has promised me he will respect her decision and let her live her life. Because it is my pet peeve how we teach men not to listen when a woman says no. Persistence is not romantic. If you've had an emphatic no – in whatever scenario – BELIEVE HER.

And it's OK because Craig has a back-up plan. He says if his wife isn't interested, he's going to try to woo Leslie Mann because she was 'really great in *17 Again*'. I told him she's married to a film producer but he didn't really understand and asked if a 'Juddapatow' was anything like Ayahuasca. I have also recommended he check out *Freaky Friday*, which he has apparently never seen, despite there being seven hundred different versions out there.

Anna and Marie surprised the group by announcing they've decided to go their separate ways. It was quite the shocker – they seemed so simpatico – but they have talked a lot and decided it is unfair to Anna's wife to continue without her knowing. The guilt they've been burying for so long has been exposed, and it is too raw, too much for them. Anna is going to tell her wife the truth and see what happens from there. I am sad for them and proud of them, and I very much hope it works out, however it's meant to.

Clara is joyous, crying with relief. She isn't going home to change her life like the others. She's already done that. The retreat has given her what she came for – confirmation that she is OK. That she has done the right thing. That she is great just as she is, and strong enough to survive everything she's going through. She is excited about her life once more. She's staying in Thailand for another few weeks, like me, but then she wants to get back to Denmark and she wants to hug everyone she loves. Which now includes all of us. I've talked to her about the possibility of me visiting Denmark for my third adventure. She's very keen. I think it could be great.

Joe has been bouncing off the walls. He says he's never had so much energy in his life. He saw Gods, he says – many of them. He keeps touching the walls and talking about unicorns. Honestly, I think he might've taken something else, along with the Ayahuasca. He says he wants to do it all again, right now. He is the only one though, because the rest of us are all fully broken apart. We've told him he has to wait, and he says he never wants to wait for anything again in his life. He wants to try it all and is impatient for all of life to happen now. He keeps looking at Mark while he talks at speed, and I wonder . . .

We have all talked and talked and talked.

Everyone, apart from Mark. Mark has been quiet. He has been involved, encouraging and warm, but quiet about his own stuff.

As have I, actually. I talked a bit about my experience with the blue light and the colours, but I didn't want to share all I'd seen with my mum and Steven. Especially not with Mark there. I don't know what he'd think. I don't know what *I* think. I've been slowly processing everything. It is overwhelming, and something is unravelling inside me. Something big. But I don't feel ready for it yet. I don't want it to unravel yet, I'm a little afraid that it's the only thing holding me together.

When the lot of us finally go our separate ways, all cried out, Mark, Joe and I trudge slowly and silently towards our bus stop. We are heading to a homestay in Koh Chang. I want to check out the night markets, because apparently they sell frozen frogs and roasted scorpion. There is also, I'm told – and this is far more exciting a prospect – Jacob's Creek wine available. Then we're going to get a car to the airport where we will fly to northern Thailand, where I want to do some relaxing things. I want to take boat trips. I want to scuba dive, and I want to scream in pain when I inevitably scrape my knee on coral.

I want to stare at some things and process.

The bus pulls up and we climb on board in single file. Mark sits next to me and Joe slumps down in the seats behind us, closing his eyes. He seems to be crashing hard. It is the most zapped I've ever seen him; he's usually puppy-levels of energy at all times.

I am exhausted too. It feels like I've never been this tired. I want to sleep for a day. I want to . . .

'Come on then,' Mark says suddenly, interrupting my thoughts. He is looking at me intently. He looks, um, angry.

'What is it?' I say, feeling defensive. 'Are you cross with me?'

'Should I be?' he says, cryptically.

'No!' I reply, my voice raised. 'Well, I don't know, should you?'

There is silence between us and I crack first. 'Look, Mark, I'm sorry, I'm really sorry you've been feeling so awful. I didn't know. I wish you had talked to me . . .'

'How was I meant to talk to you, Alice?' he says and it pierces something deep in me. 'You've refused to talk. Every time I've mentioned Mum or Steven – every time I've just asked to talk – you've run off or changed the subject. You literally left the country to avoid talking about it. You've left me and Hannah to deal with all of this on our own.'

I sigh. 'OK, yes, some of that is true, but it's only partly fair. Me leaving the UK was about way more than just . . . *that*. And you kept pushing me to talk about Ste . . . about him, when you knew full well I didn't want to. I didn't have any idea that you needed to talk about the situation. I would've tri—'

'Did you ask?' he interrupts, and his voice is raised.

I hang my head. 'No, I didn't.'

He shakes his head. 'I know you didn't mean to be, but you've been really selfish, Alice. Running away, hiding, no thought for anyone else.'

'I know that,' I say, but I feel combative. 'But you could've told me you needed me. You didn't have to hide it from me. You never share anything with me, and I want you to, you know I do. If you'd just told me you were miserable, I would've tried to help. I would've – would – do anything for you. You just need to ask me, Mark.'

There is a silence and he takes my hand. I think I am forgiven.

'Talk to Mum, then,' he says simply, and the anger is no longer in his voice.

I swallow hard.

I haven't spoken to my mum for five years. Nearly six. Which I know sounds terrible, but it was necessary. It was self-preservation. It was the only thing I could do.

My stepdad, Steven, came into our lives when I was about four. Mark was six, Hannah would've been about eight or nine then, I guess. I never knew my real dad, he left us when I was a baby, and at first it was thrilling having a big man-dad type around. We were finally like the other kids in the playground who had two parents. And he was better than everyone else's dads! He was always laughing and cracking jokes. He was always fun, always throwing us around and playing with us out in the garden. He was the life and soul of parties – and we were suddenly having parties all the time. We went from a one-adult household, to grown-ups everywhere constantly, chatting, laughing, dancing, having barbeques and all-night living room giggling. Mum seemed happier than we'd ever seen her.

It took about a year for everyone to realise why he was always the life and soul. Why we were always having sponta-neous parties that lasted all night and all weekend. Why he was always laughing and dancing.

Steven was an alcoholic.

It took Mum a long time to fully comprehend the extent of it because he was so very good at manipulating her, so good at making her feel crazy. She would find bottles hidden down the back of cupboards in the bathroom, or smell something on his breath in the morning and he would laugh and convince her it was nothing or that it was from one of their parties. Sometimes he would just plain make her feel like she was losing her mind.

At some point though, there was no way anyone could deny it any longer. Mum tried for a very long time to get him to cut down, she begged him to stop. And he would, sometimes, but it was never for very long. But, honestly, even then, it wasn't *so* bad – not for me, Mark and Hannah anyway. Steven was what they call a high-functioning alcoholic. He held down his day job on a building site, and was still fun to be around for us kids. He still played with us sometimes and made us laugh. It wasn't like before, but it was fine, y'know? So what if he was drinking from seven in the morning? So what if he smelt bad and his eyes were always red and swollen? We had a dad.

But things changed around about when I started secondary school. The beer became vodka. The loud laughing became loud shouting. He would disappear for days on end, and Mum would be frantic. I would watch silently from the hallway door as she cried down the phone to everyone she knew, asking if they'd seen him. I would watch as she rang round the local bars asking if he was there, begging them not to serve him any more. The police would often be in the living room when we got home from school, taking yet another missing persons report and looking bored. Sometimes they'd bring him home and I would hate them for that. Then Steven started being cruel. First to Mum, then to us. He was never physically violent, but he was nasty. A nasty drunk. We weren't wanted. We were in the way. He put up with us so he could fuck our mum. He took money from our piggy banks, he emptied out our drawers looking for more. He laughed at us when we cried.

And there was Mum, always in the middle. Always, always defending him. Always calling it an illness. Always excusing his behaviour. Always using our summer holiday money to book him into another rehab centre that he refused to attend, or would leave after a couple of days. She even re-mortgaged our family home to help him.

My mum, always choosing him over us.

When I turned eighteen, I moved away to London and tried to find my own life. But I called every day and visited my mum back in Hertfordshire religiously, once a week. I really, really wanted to save her, I thought I could. I would listen to Steven crashing around the house, looking for bottles, searching for money, breaking things. I pleaded with her to leave. I wanted her to move in with me – I even bought a sofa-bed for my room, so I could be ready for her. I gave her the details of women's refuges if she didn't want to stay with me. I only took temp jobs in case I ever needed to run away with her. But she never wanted to hear it, always waved away my speeches, told me he was poorly and she needed to look after him. She always let him off the hook.

The final straw came when I was twenty-four. I'd fallen in love with a boy called Kit – my first big, overwhelming, all-consuming love. It felt like the first time in my life that Mum and Steven weren't my priority. I liked it. He moved in with me after only six months. It was quick, but I liked that. I wanted it to be quick, I wanted him to save me from my family. I thought we were soulmates, I thought we were going to get married. I was sure of it, so certain, right up until the moment I came home early from work with the flu, and found him in bed with a woman from his office.

He didn't even try to say sorry, just laughed awkwardly while she scrambled around for her clothes. She said sorry. She said she didn't know about me. She was probably quite nice.

And, oh God, how I cried. I cried so much. I screamed at him to go and I lay on the floor of my living room, crying like I never had before. I wanted to die, and I wanted my mum. So much. I rang and rang, over and over. I left voicemails weeping down the line. I wanted her so much, I *needed* her. I'd never asked her to put me first before, I'd never asked her to drop everything and come to me, but I asked her to then. I was close to some kind of an edge and felt dizzy and sick and afraid. I needed my mother to save me.

She never called back. The next day, when I woke up passed out on the floor where I'd cried myself to sleep, there was a text from her. 'Sorry to hear about your break up. Just in the middle of something with Steven. Maybe chat next week?'

I didn't cry again after that – and I didn't speak to my mum again.

I know it sounds selfish, and I know it might sound harsh, but something in me snapped. I just couldn't do it any more. I couldn't be second place, watching idly on as my mum hurt herself choosing a man like that over her children. She did love us, I knew that, but I also knew she would just keep choosing him over and over again.

She tried to ring me a few days later, and I blocked her number. She emailed and texted me, several messages, and I deleted them all unread. Hannah and Mark both tried to talk to me, begged me to speak to Mum, but I said no. I was always the closest to Mum, the nearest to the pain epicentre, and they both know I had reached the end of my tether. They kept saying Mum didn't even understand what she'd done – which only made it worse. I couldn't explain how she let me down when I needed her most. It seemed silly and trivial after everything we'd been through already, but it was my breaking point. I couldn't articulate how it felt when she chose him, it was betrayal. I'd had my heart broken, first by Kit, then by my mum, all in the space of a day. It was too much. Every time I picked up the phone to call her, I thought again about what it must've taken for her to hear all my voicemails, crying like that, sobbing and talking about death – and still not come to me. I just couldn't.

And horrible as it is to say, in those days, weeks and months afterwards, I only felt better being away. Clearer, freer. Like it was the right decision and I was putting myself first. Of course I felt terrible ignoring my mum and I missed her badly. It was painful in many ways, but I also couldn't keep her in my life. Not while Steven was also in her life, wreaking his destruction everywhere he went. I had to save myself. Mum couldn't walk away from him, so I had to walk away from them both.

A couple of years ago, she and Steven moved to Australia, where his family are from. It was yet another attempt at a 'fresh start', and I'd guess Mum couldn't afford to keep our house any more. It was re-mortgaged a bunch of times to pay for his pointless rehab stints. But I knew the booze would follow them wherever they were. And at least them being so far away made things easier for me. Out of sight, out of mind, I told myself. I could at least pretend that was true. And I had an excuse when people asked me why I never saw my mum – she was on the other side of the world.

Mark is looking at me now, carefully, waiting. I feel my eyes watering.

'I can't,' I say at last, looking away. 'I'm not ready.'

He sighs and turns his body to the window to stare out. We don't talk again for a while.

**

from: Mark Edwards <markedwardscityboy@gmail.com>
to: Alice Edwards <SimplyTheBestAlice2003@hotmail.com>

Here you go. You should just ask her if you can be allowed back on the mailing list!

---------- Forwarded message ----------

from: Hannahtruthseeker@protonmail.com
to: Hannah Edwards
cc: Hannah Edwards
date: 4 June at 23.26
subject: MAY FAMILY NEWSLETTER: TOP SECRET
mailed-by: ProtonMail

EDWARDS FAMILY NEWSLETTER/MAY RECAP

Welcome, truthers,

Hannah here. As ever, I identify myself to you all with this month's code word so you know it's really me and not the government co-opting my family newsletters.

SNOWFLAKE

I have had a very busy few weeks on my Flat Earther quest. I have spoken at length to my whistle-blowers from NASA and finally have proof of everything I have previously proposed re 'the truth'. I have included links below to many very convincing videos showing definitively that Lorraine Kelly is secretly an alien who is running the country and is personally controlling the populace with chemtrails. Please watch them.

In other family news:
-Alice and Mark are now in Thailand, and they have seen many, many monkeys.
-Uncle Ned says to say thank you all for the links to hypnotherapy and Slimming World, but he says he would prefer the money please.
-Cousin Leon would like me to mention how disappointed he is that so few of the family made it along to Gertie's 17th birthday, but that he is now considering breeding her, if any if the family have dogs they would like to get involved. I can confirm that Gertie is very sweet-looking, despite the hump and inbred blindness.
-Little Jemima has requested that the family please stop sending her bras. She says her mum shouldn't have mentioned it and she has plenty of bras from Primark. I told her she would be better off going to M&S but she told me to stop being embarrassing. Such a shame.

Until next month, fellow Truth Seekers.
Hannah xx

This email is not for public consumption and the Edwards family have specifically asked to be disassociated from any views expressed. Hannah Edwards encourages you to click on all links but does not accept responsibility for any damage whatsoever that is caused by viruses being passed. Be advised that any use, dissemination, forwarding, printing or copying of this email is strictly prohibited. ESPECIALLY BY YOU, LORRAINE KELLY.

22

7 June – 6.40 p.m.

Good evening, dream chasers,

How do you guys actually feel about the dream chasers thing? I'm not sure whether to keep it. I thought it would be a cool signature intro but I think it might be rubbish. How about fellow voyagers? Or wander-lusters? That's a bit clunky, isn't it?

Anyway, sorry I haven't been very on it with this blog lately, I'm not sure what I'm doing with it. I have just posted a whole new bunch of monkey pictures though.

So this is just a quick update to say Mark, Joe and I have been island hopping in 'water taxis', and we're now looking for investors for our genius water Uber company. We want to make a billion, then we never have to come home.

Send money,

Alice xx

#WaterTaxis #DreamChasersOrNoDreamChasers #TravelBlogger #GoneAWOL #AliceEdwardsBlog

13 Comments · 9 AWOLs · 52 Super Likes

COMMENTS:

Mark Edwards

| Water Uber was my idea, you thieving whore!

> **Alice Edwards**
> **Replying to Mark Edwards**
> | Please don't use that word, it is offensive. I am a thieving sex worker.

>> **Jessica Sex4U**
>> **Replying to Alice Edwards and Mark Edwards**
>> | Give me a call some time ;) I have big dick and big tits for good price

>>> **Mark Edwards**
>>> **Replying to Jessica Sex4U**
>>> | The sex bots have landed!

>>>> **AWOL MODERATOR**
>>>> **Replying to Jessica Sex4U**
>>>> | Please everyone, please stop this. I can't keep doing this. It's too much. I can't. It's too much. Luke

>>>> **Jessica Sex4U**
>>>> **Replying to AWOL MODERATOR**
>>>> | I tell no one. our secret. dm me

Karen Gill

| Um, guys, this is genuinely a great idea. Let's get @Lord Sugar involved in this.

> **Mark Edwards**
> **Replying to Karen Gill and Lord Sugar**
> | Hi Sir Alan! We need an initial billion-pound investment to get started and also then to live off and not do any work because it's boring.

Guru Shaman Quam AKA Gary Porter
| This is another of my businesses! See my other AWOL account IslandHopWithAGuru

Piers Ned
| U r a hoe

AWOL MODERATOR
Replying to Piers Ned
| I don't even know if this is an insult, do you mean a literal garden hoe? If not, please please be respectful to our users. Please please please. I can't handle this any more. Do you know how little I get paid? My life is so empty. Luke

Hannah Edwards
| be careful water and mountains can be an edge

Joe Downe
| You are the cutest. Have you considered maybe just 'hello human beings'? :)))

'Have you ever noticed in straight people movies,' Joe begins thoughtfully, laying down his iPad where we've been watching an illegally downloaded Adam Sandler comedy. 'How missionary sex means love, and woman on top means one-night stand?'

I consider this. 'Oh yeah, that's true,' I say.

'Is it true in real life, though?' he says, facing me.

I nod. 'Oh absolutely. Anything other than missionary once you're in a loving heteronormative relationship is considered something akin to a satanic ritual.'

'Being straight sounds *awful*,' he says, awed.

'It is. But what about you, Joe?' I continue, turning to him.

216

'How is your love life these days? Have you had much on-top fun during this trip?'

He shakes his head and then turns to me, smiling slightly.

'No darling, but I'm not interested in anything casual any more. I've done all that.'

I sit up a little. 'You want to meet someone for real?' I say carefully and Joe's smile gets wider. 'No,' he replies simply, but there is more to it.

'Because . . .' I begin slowly. 'You've already met someone real?' I hold my breath.

'Oh Alice,' he says quietly. 'You know full well I am madly in love with your brother. Truly, madly, deeply.' We are still holding hands and I grip it tightly, tighter. He laughs a small laugh. 'You know it and I know it – and Mark knows it. But he doesn't see me like that, he never has.'

I bite my nail thinking of how hard my brother laughed when I mentioned the possibility. 'But maybe . . .' I try, 'maybe if you talked to him . . .'

Joe smiles again. 'I have. Many times. He is always kind about it but he's sure. I'm just not that person for him. He can't see me like that. I need to walk away really. I'll never get over him if I keep spending every waking moment with him. But it is so hard when all I want is to be with him, always.' His eyes are suddenly a little damp and we fall into a mournful silence.

I want to offer to speak to Mark for Joe. I want to shout at my stupid brother about how stupid he is not to love Joe. I want to hit him over and over until he agrees to love this man for ever. Who could fail to love Joe? He is so good and kind and handsome. How can Mark not see that?

But I am selfishly afraid. On the surface of it, my brother

and I have been totally fine since our little *moment* on the bus. We woke up the next day in our dorm room and pretended nothing had happened. We laughed and joked like normal. We planned our adventures. We spent our evenings exploring street stalls and visiting temples in the day. And it was brilliant. You have to take off your shoes in the temples because they're sacred places – even the loos, which is hard to get my head round, having seen the way most men piss. Anyway the guides give you flip-flops to wear inside and it made me laugh long and hard thinking back to just a few weeks before when I was wearing those lurid green flip-flops in very different circumstances.

LA and pedicures feel like so long ago already.

Mark and Joe also went off for an elephant ride yesterday, but I felt ethically ambiguous about it and worried I might try and orchestrate a large-scale elephant-nap if I saw any of them in chains, so Mark made a unilateral decision that I wasn't welcome. Then we went on this mind-blowingly incredible hike up to a waterfall and we all stood there for close to an hour, colourful butterflies circling us, just silently marvelling at how magical the whole thing was.

Then it rained a lot and felt less magical, but still, I will never forget the feeling of standing there, under that waterfall.

But, if I'm honest, wonderful as it all was, our bus conversation has been there between Mark and me that whole time. Underneath everything. Underpinning the joy.

Maybe that's why I'm feeling so disconnected and ... unfinished?

I haven't even really written my blog properly. Actually, to be honest, I'm starting to feel like it's all a bit silly and pointless. I've been trying to do this glossy shiny thing online, like Constance Beaumont does, and it is not working. I'm trying to make all of this travelling stuff sound so glorious and perfect, which it hasn't always been. It's been fun at times, but also messy and complicated. But people don't want to hear about the insect bites and the petty bickering, do they? Oh, I don't know.

We're going to spend another week here, and then we're heading up to north Thailand for the final week. And then . . . I still don't know. I just don't know where to spend my third month. I've been looking at a whole range of places but I haven't booked anything just yet. I'm considering India because – no disrespect to Shaman Gary – it would be nice to meet some proper gurus. Except I am worried that I will end up asking them for advice on my crappy love life, instead of bigger picture stuff about the world. I feel like that might not be cool and I don't want anyone who may or may not be in contact with a higher being to know how shallow a person I really am.

Constance Beaumont's latest post had her in Indonesia, which sounds incredible and isn't too far from here, in a global context. I'm very into that idea. I'm also really tempted by Brazil, Argentina – that area of the world. I could even attend a proper Ayahuasca retreat if I made it to Peru. But maybe I've had enough deep, intense looks into my being for now.

The idea originally was fun in LA, soul-searching in Thailand, and then maybe a physically arduous adventure for the third part? But now my deadline is fast approaching and I'm realising you probably kind of need to be fit or do some training to climb a mountain. Right? I could get on a boat and sail about, I guess, but again, I think you need to know, like, *stuff*. There are, I don't know, ropes and wheels and shit on boats, aren't there? Unless I got on a cruise? But that feels maybe forty years premature.

A minute passes as we silently watch Adam Sandler playing Adam Sandler.

'Look Joe,' I begin urgently. 'I—'

A voice in the doorway interrupts our moment.

'Hello you two,' Mark says, his voice giving nothing away. Joe and I exchange a look. How long has he been standing there?

He wanders in, passing the sink and absent-mindedly picks up my hairbrush. He twirls it in his hands. There is an expectant tension in the air.

'Al, have you decided what you're going to do next, yet?' he says, suddenly sounding a bit serious. 'You know, after Thailand.'

I sigh, glancing at Joe. 'No. Still no.' I pause. 'I was thinking maybe I could go do something super healthy? Some kind of fitness retreat. It'll be like going to jail – I'll get so fit and glow-y. I'll have a bunch of colonic irrigations, detox and return to the UK looking like a Pussycat Doll.'

'Just like prison,' Joe nods.

'That sounds like a reasonable goal,' Mark adds, but he seems distracted, fiddling with the brush. He turns to face me then, a determined look on his face.

'Look,' he takes a deep breath. 'I know you don't want me to do this, but I need to try one more time to convince you to change your mind about Mum. The last time I tried on the bus, I came in too hot, I know I did. I was angry, and I shouldn't have been, because this isn't about guilting you into forgiving her, this is about helping you. I want to help you.'

He stops and I look straight down. He's talking nonsense. *Help me?* I am helping me. Staying away from our family is all about helping me. That's what this whole estrangement thing is about. He sits down in the chair opposite and takes a deep breath.

Joe pulls the cover back and slips out of the bed. 'I'll give you guys a minute,' he murmurs, slipping out of the room.

For a moment Mark sits there quietly.

'Please listen to me,' he says suddenly, in a pleading voice. 'Forget about Mum for a minute, and forget about Steven lying in hospital. This is about you. You're holding in all this anger and resentment and it's making you into something you're not.'

I sit up straighter. Where is this coming from? I open my mouth to tell him to mind his own business and then stop. I've run away from this conversation for too long now. He's tried over and over to speak to me and I need to give him the chance to talk. Maybe if I can sit here quietly without getting angry – just let him make his dumb speech – we can get on with our trip in peace.

He continues quickly, sensing I want to stop him. 'Because it's obvious that your history with Mum is holding you back in so many different ways. Haven't you thought about it? Don't you think? You've got this shitty thing – this shitty *rift* – hanging over you all the time, never resolved, never settled. And it's embedded into you like some broken piece of glass in your foot. You're limping everywhere. Limping through your life, Al. You've let the pain and the sadness become a part of your personality, a part of who you are, where they never used to be. You're afraid of being abandoned, like you feel Mum did to you. It makes you push people away.' He raises his voice for the first time. 'Look at yourself, for fuck's sake, Alice. You can't even commit to a job! You're so afraid of intimacy, you've been a temp for ten years!'

I am shocked into silence for a moment, before letting out a short, sharp fake laugh. 'No, Mark,' I say, as lightly as I can. 'I've been a temp for ten years because I don't want to have any involvement in office birthdays. That is where I draw the line of decency.' I don't want to do this, I don't want to argue, I need him to stop talking in this serious tone.

He sighs, and continues: 'Look, I just had a really long chat on the phone with Eva about this whole thing and . . .'

What? This hits me like a slap in the face. He's been *gossiping* about *this*? With my best friend? The best friend I'm in a half-huff with? That is not OK, he knows that's not OK. If I want to talk to Eva about my family stuff, I will. He hasn't got the right to do it on my behalf! I am filled with fury at the two of them going behind my back like this, whispering about me, judging me.

'You cannot be serious?' My voice is louder than I expected. 'You had no right, no right!' I am suddenly furious with him and spitting my words. 'How *dare* you, how *dare you*?'

'Ali . . .' he starts.

'Don't you dare,' I say, and I am really upset. 'You had no right. This is such a betrayal, Mark.'

He raises his voice. 'Alice, stop it, for God's sake. You're not actually upset I spoke to your best friend about this, you're just trying to distract me and yourself from what I'm saying. You don't want to hear it, so you're making a fuss over something that isn't important.'

He's wrong.

He continues. 'You need to get over yourself, Alice, because this is tearing a lot of people apart. You've put me and Hannah in the middle of things for years and we're both sick of it.'

I nasty-laugh, 'You didn't have to be in the middle of this,

Mark, I never asked you to mediate. In fact, I've asked you not to, many times. I have only ever asked you to stay the hell out of this. It's between Mum and me. You made a choice and I want . . .'

'Stop making this all about you,' he snaps.

'Stop making it not all about me,' I snap back.

We glare at each other for half a second, panting furiously.

'So that's it, is it?' he says, anger in his voice. 'No discussion, no compromise. You're just never going to be a part of this family again? What if Steven dies? Will you still refuse to speak to Mum? Or is that what you're hoping for? The bad man dies and you get to play happy families again? It's all so black and white with you, isn't it, Alice? You can't see any nuance. You can't see that Mum has been torn apart all these years, trying to care for an alcoholic idiot she loves – and a stubborn idiot she loves.' He means me.

'Don't you dare compare me with him,' I say, my voice low and threatening.

'But you're both forcing Mum to choose, aren't you?' he spits back. 'Both demanding something from her that you know she can't give. Yes, fine, our mother is a weak woman and she should've thrown him out years ago, but she feels like she can't. She truly believes he needs her and that she can save him. And maybe she can. Maybe she has. We both know he would've been dead years ago without her.' He pauses while that sinks in before continuing. 'You know this is not a simple situation with a simple solution. There's no one answer. He's not all bad, Alice, you know that. He's just messed up, and Mum sees that. She wants to help him. And instead of loving her despite her weakness, and supporting her in whatever way you can, you've spent years punishing her.' He pauses to breathe heavily. 'She can't help the way she is. People are weak, Alice, you can't expect them all to be strong like you.'

'I won't be pushed into having someone in my life!' I explode and I am so mad. 'You don't get to dictate when and how I deal with things, Mark. I'm not ready. You're always telling me what to do, always bossing me around! You turned up over here, uninvited, crashing my trip. You made me change my plans and do everything your way. I was meant to be doing all this on my own, meant to be figuring things out for myself, but here you are, taking over and telling me what to do, as ever. And here I am – following you around like a lost fucking puppy, yet again. But not with this, Mark, you can't make me get over this thing with Mum by shouting at me.' I feel the bile in my throat as I add, 'Stop telling me what to do with my life, Mark, and hey, why not actually get a life for yourself? You say I'm limping through my life, but at least I have things to limp through. Your life is empty as fuck.'

A flash of pain crosses his face. We stare at each other again and something in me sinks. I've never seen him look so wounded. 'Great, fine, OK,' he snaps at last. 'Well, I'll leave then. Since I am not wanted here and never was. I was planning to go back to Australia soon anyway, so Joe and I will just go now. We'll let you have this time all on your own, like you wanted all along. I'll let you *find yourself*. Let's just hope you actually like the person you find in there after all this, eh? Because you're going to be all on your own with her.' His voice is mocking as he storms out. 'Have fun, Alice.'

He is gone, door slamming behind him and I collapse back on the bed. I didn't even realise I'd stood up at some point during the fight.

I am breathing hard, furious. Shit shit shit. Fuck him! I don't need Mark here. I'm glad he's going. I can finally get back to doing what I wanted to do all along. I don't need him here talking horseshit and trying to make me feel bad about how I'm living my life. I don't push people away! I'm not black and white! I know things with my mum are complicated, but why can't he see how complicated it is on my side, too? He hasn't got the first idea what he's talking about, he doesn't know how badly she let me down. He clearly doesn't know me at all. I'm glad he's leaving – I can't wait to get back to my travels on my own, just like I wanted. There are plenty of people who go about here alone.

I wanted this. It's fine. It's good.

Through the wall I hear Mark's raised angry voice telling Joe to pack up his stuff.

I roll over on the bed and cry because it seems like the right thing to do.

23

AWOL.COM/Alice Edwards' Travel Blog

13 June – 3.12 p.m.

Hey.

I know this is really lame and I hate it when people make a thing of doing this, but I think I'm going to come off social media and AWOL for a couple of weeks. I just need a bit of head space to think. But I didn't want anyone to think I was dead if I just disappeared without a word, so here it is. I'm fine, I just want to enjoy my last bit of Thailand in silence.

Bye for now.
Ax

3 Comments · 75 AWOLs · 84 Super Likes

COMMENTS:

Danny Boy
| GOOD RIDDINS STUPID COW

> **Karen Gill**
> **Replying to Danny Boy**
> | ↑ what he said. JK! Miss you already. Have fun and stay safe out there.

Hollie Baker

| Noooo! You and Constance Beaumont are my fave bloggers to follow!! Come back soon!!!

I am not too proud to admit this has been a tough few days.

So, yeah. Joe and Mark left.

Joe said an awkward goodbye, standing in the doorway, looking like he wanted to say so much more, but Mark just picked up his bag and went. I'd say he went silently but boy howdy did he slam that front door. It was awful.

I basically stayed in bed for a full twenty-four hours, and after forcing myself to get out of bed, I've mostly been wandering around feeling shitty and wondering what to do. I guess I should get back to my original itinerary?

It's not always been easy, being away from home for a long time – away from familiar things and familiar people – but this is the first time I've really, really wanted to quit.

The thing is, I wasn't mentally prepared for being alone for this part. I'd got used to having the guys around. Got used to having someone or some-two to bounce things off. I got used to having people there to go, 'Ooh, look at that pretty thing over there, isn't that pretty!' And now I am here without a safety net, and it feels like I'm free-falling. I'm suddenly realising how cut off I am. And looking at social media and AWOL made me feel even lonelier for some reason.

I am sad.

Making the whole thing worse is that all the drinking I've been doing these past few weeks – not to mention the jet lag and odd hours I've kept – has caught up with me all at once. My face has not been this acne-ridden since I went on the pill in 2007. And, as happens whenever I'm seriously run down, I have thrush. Bad thrush. Bad-bad, rubbing yourself on things, red, sore, cottage-creamy thrush. There's nothing to make you want to run back home like being around strangers, a million miles away from your home comforts with an itchy, burning vagina. *Believe me.*

I was really hoping it would go away on its own, but yesterday I couldn't take it any more, so went into a Thai chemist to beg for help.

'Do you speak English?' I half whispered at the girl behind the counter, who genuinely didn't look more than about twelve years old. She pulled a face, looking helpless, which I could only assume meant she didn't even understand the question.

I tried anyway, but I've never been good at charades.

'I need help. I have . . . um, thrush?' I said, half pointing at my crotch and waving in the air for some reason. She looked blank.

'Thrush? A yeast infection? You know, itchy-itchy, sore-sore, down there?' I kept going. 'Really red? Ow-y?'

She looked behind her shoulder, slightly alarmed.

'I'm really sorry,' I said, the mortification turning my face bright red.

I almost gave up at that point, but a searing pain radiating from my vagina kept me rooted to the spot.

'Bad vagina, evil vagina!' I said again, my voice a pitch higher, aware of a small queue of customers forming behind me. 'Bad thrush . . . in my pants. Thrush? You know? Thrush, like a small brown bird? But in my wizard's sleeve? Thrush?' I sighed, but she had started to look intrigued, so I continued.

'*Yeast* problem, y'know?' I said, loudly. 'Yeast? Like, as in bread? Or Marmite? Do you have Marmite over here?'

She looked at the floor, and I wondered if I should pull my trousers down and show her. But I had a feeling the other people in the shop might object. Things were bad enough without me getting arrested for flashing a chemist.

We stared at each other for a long moment and I took one last shot.

'FUNGUS? IN MY FANNY? FUNGUS FANNY?' I said, pointing aggressively at my undercarriage. It was at this point that a much older Thai man emerged from the back room. He caught my last couple of words and stopped short.

'Can I help you, miss?' he said in lovely English and then paused, adding a few quiet words to the girl who immediately left – giving me one last, haunted look.

'I'm sorry,' he turned to address me again. 'My daughter must do homework now. She is learning English at school, but I don't think she has learnt the word "fungus" yet. Or "fanny".'

Oh.

She actually literally was twelve.

I shouted at a small child about fanny fungus.

OK, cool cool cool cool cool cool cool cool cool.

I cleared my throat then, my face flaming with humiliation, as he came around the counter and picked something up from a shelf behind me.

Canesten. The same one we have in the UK. They have the brand name cream and pessary. And it was right there if I'd only looked.

Yep.

After that oh-so-rewarding experience with the locals, I returned back to the hostel, to find new tourists had taken over Mark and Joe's beds in the dorm room. I ignored them, climbing into bed and trying to sleep while the cream

– hopefully – started to work. That was about twenty hours ago, and I haven't got back up yet.

I just feel a bit like giving up. What's the point? Like, what am I *doing* here? If this has been about learning who I really am, I think I have, and honestly, I do not care for her. Mark was right, I suck. I'd rather go back into denial now. I'd rather not know what a selfish, unlikeable bitch I am.

And I really would quit and go back to England right now – this very fucking second – but it's not like there's anything waiting for me back at home anyway, is there? I have no home, no job, no family waiting for me. Mark's not talking to me. I don't even know for sure where he is – maybe Australia like he said. Or maybe he went home if he was really upset. Maybe he and Joe have even continued on the Thai adventure without me. And my best friend Eva isn't exactly desperately waiting for me to come back. She's busy talking behind my back with Mark, while building her lovely grown-up nest with Jeremy and the baby. She doesn't want me in the way, bothering her and interrupting her special family time. No one needs me, nobody wants me. I am a waste of space. Maybe I really have pushed everyone away.

I pull out my phone and tap a few buttons.

'Hey, are you awake?' I type. 'How are you? I kinda miss you and I am sad. Do you want to talk?' I pause, my finger hovering over the send button.

I am arguing with myself.

I've come so far. Do I really want to start this again?

I haven't messaged TD in weeks. I was finally feeling good about it. Over it. Do I really want to ruin that with this message? Get sucked back into his twat vortex? I don't – I really don't – but I am also so fucking lonely and there is no one else who will make me feel that familiar way. That safe, bad way I'm so used to feeling.

I just need to hear some kind words. I need to hear from someone that they care about me, even if it is meaningless and hollow and too complicated.

But will it make me feel better? Or just even worse?

I think I know the answer to that.

Defeated, I delete the un-sent message and throw my phone back under the covers.

My phone beeps and I pick it back up. It's my lovely Clara from the Ayahuasca retreat.

'You fancy a chat on the phone?' she's written, and a tear rolls down my face thinking how much I fancy that.

She picks up after one ring. 'I'm lonely,' she says by way of a greeting.

'Oh God, me too,' I say in a gulp. We both laugh, relieved to share the moment.

'I mean,' she explains, 'I am having a very wonderful time travelling, but I am also a human and I think it's OK to be lonely when you are on your own so much.' She pauses. 'The retreat taught me to say things like that out loud. It takes the power away. I feel less lonely now that I've said it out loud.'

I nod, even though she cannot see me. One of my room mates passes through the dorm, reaching for her bag, and glances over. She hesitates and I see myself through her eyes. A crazy-looking, red-eyed, blotchy, spotty lump who hasn't left her bed in a full day. She must be wondering if I am going to kill her.

She hurries out, not looking back.

Clara clears her throat on the line. 'Are you OK, Alice? You sound funny.'

Reluctantly I sit up.

'Yes, I'm OK,' I say, my voice husky. 'I've just been day-sleeping, I think I'm dehydrated. Hold on.' I reach for a bottle of water by my bed and take a long drink. It helps. My brain feels less fuzzy.

'It's so nice to hear your voice, Clara,' I say, really meaning it. 'I miss the retreat gang already. Have you heard from anyone much?'

'I miss you, too,' she sighs. 'Yes, I spoke to Anna and Maria yesterday! They were upbeat. They have told their truth to Anna's wife at long last. It was very difficult but Maria said she was feeling better than she has in years. Living with a lie is not ever a good idea.'

'Good for them,' I say, delighted. 'I hope it all works out for them, I really do. And Craig?'

She giggles. 'He sent me a selfie yesterday. I think it was meant to be of him with his wife, but it was just his entire hat. He said Shaman Quam is coming to visit him next summer; he wanted me to invite you. They're going to have a Zac Efron movie marathon.'

'I am definitely up for that,' I say happily.

'Hurray!' she says. 'And Mark and Joe must come too, how are they doing?'

The sound of their names takes me by surprise. I take a deep breath. 'They left me,' I say a little melodramatically. But then, I feel melodramatic.

'Oh Alice, I'm sorry, did something happen?' she says, sounding worried.

'Mark and I had a big fight,' I say after a beat. 'Family stuff. Things that have been hanging over us for a long time now. It was inevitable, I guess. But I'm all alone now.'

She is silent for a few seconds. 'You're not alone, Alice. You have almost eight billion people around you.' I laugh, but she sounds earnest as she continues. 'They are all outside your room, waiting to meet you. There is nowhere like being on the road for making new friends. If that's what you want.'

We are silent, but it is not an intrusive silence. After a moment I add, 'To be honest, Clara, I'm thinking about calling this whole thing off and heading back home.'

She sighs. 'Oh Alice. I'm sorry you have argued with your brother. But you should not give up on your journey, not until you get to where you want to get.'

'I was only going to be here another week or so anyway,' I say hurriedly. 'It felt like I was getting somewhere with all this travelling, but now it feels like I've gone backwards again.' She doesn't say anything for a minute, we just sit together on the phone. She is a very calming presence, even on the phone.

'That's how it works, I think,' she says at last. 'Everyone assumes there is an end point with life. I don't mean death, which is of course an end point. But I mean that "settled" point. Where everything is solved. Like, you age, you accumulate things, you stick to the path set out for you by everyone else, and then you will be happy. People think that is the end point. The idea is that you travel through life until you get *there*, and then you stop, give yourself up, and are happy forever.' She stops again, and I can hear her smiling down the phone. 'But it's not how it works. Rarely ever. Mostly, I think, we are all travelling around in circles. And it is often in different directions to other people. Sometimes it is backwards, sometimes it is forward, sometimes it is up, sometimes it's down. But that is not so bad.'

I think about this. It's a little confusing. We started talking about travelling around the world, and now we're talking about travelling through life.

Something in it makes sense though.

I've spent a lot of time resisting traditional life goals, but also questioning and resenting the fact that I haven't got there yet. It's a weird type of brainwashing. Like, I don't necessarily want that life, but I'm annoyed I don't have it.

'Anyway,' I clear my throat, speaking in a rush. 'I'm supposed to be heading on somewhere else after Thailand. I was going to do something spontaneous. I wanted to do something different and unexpected, but I cannot work out what. So maybe I should take that as a sign that it's time to head home and get my life back on track.'

'Maybe,' she says simply. 'What are your options if you keep going?'

I shrug. 'I had a thousand ideas, really,' I say. 'I wanted to go to France to learn a new language, or go to Italy to naked paddleboard like Orlando Bloom. I wanted to go to Bali to meet a medicine man. I wanted to do everything but nothing. I don't know.' I pause and she doesn't say anything so I continue. 'I thought I would connect with myself more out here. I thought being alone here would be peaceful. I thought I wanted solitude to figure out who I am. Maybe discover religion or something. But everything here feels so intense. It is too hard.' I break off suddenly, nothing left to say.

'Maybe it is working if it feels hard,' she says quietly. 'Things have to hurt and itch and scab over before they can heal.'

'That sounds like something Buddhist,' I say a little flippantly. 'My problem with Buddhism is that it preaches no self and I like being a self. I want to feel like I matter. Is it so bad to matter in this world?'

She laughs and her bracelets jingle down the line. 'I am not religious – unless you count Sheathology,' she laughs. 'So

I don't have any answers for you. But—' she pauses again and I hear her stand up, 'right now, I have to go, because I am getting on a bus with some new friends today. We're going to hike up a mountain and swim in a lake. Why don't you go outside and do something like that?'

I sigh before answering. 'To be honest with you, Clara, the only thing I really want right now is a cheesy Dolmio pasta bake and the eleventh series of RuPaul's *Drag Race* on Netflix.'

She laughs. 'Go outside,' she says sternly. 'RuPaul and pasta bake will still be there where you left them.'

She hangs up.

24

AWOL.COM/Alice Edwards' Incredibly Unimaginative Travel Blog

24 June – 4.34 p.m.

Hello human beings,

Firstly, I'm BACK. Not dead. Thanks for the messages asking if I'm dead, but no, to confirm: not dead.

Secondly, I want to apologise for previously calling you all dream chasers. I've realised just how patronising and meaningless that was. I only did it because I thought it sounded clever and cool. I'm realising now how much of my life I've spent saying things just because I thought they sounded clever and cool. I was trying to present myself in some dumb pretentious way I thought people wanted – and, let's face it, it's bullshit.

And while we're on the subject, what is this idea that we're all chasing dreams, anyway? Most of my dreams involve running away from something. So if I'm chasing that dream, then I'm chasing myself being chased. Seems kinda stupid, no? For real though, I don't like the idea that we're 'chasing' something, because that implies that it is unattainable and will always be out of reach. But my dream is just to be happy, and I can be happy. I know I can.

Anyway, to that end, I've decided to stay on in Thailand a little bit longer. There's too much to see and do. I want to be brave now – really, actually brave, not just #brave.

Yours,

Axx

7 Comments · 96 AWOLs · 89 Super Likes

COMMENTS:

Sarah Sommers
| YESSSSSSSS. PREACH GURL.

Hannah Edwards
| i am v glad u r happy

Karen Gill
| Very disappointing on the not-dead front. Mammy was all prepped to tell the Irish Sun all about it. She had her quotes typed up and everything.

Hollie Baker
| Yayyy! So happy you're back on AWOL, it wasn't as good without you!!!

Guru Shaman Quam AKA Gary Porter
| It's all about the happiness, Alice. Good for you.

Clara Weber
| I'm still here, too! You coming up to north Thailand at any point? Message me.

Joe Downe
| Now THIS is the kind of blog you should be writing, Ali! I love this, and I love you!!!! Sorry about . . . y'know, what happened. Miss you.

'No, pisssssss *in*,' I say again, enunciating, but knowing it is meaningless. 'Piss in the *piscine*.'

I'm trying to explain the moment back in Year 10 when our whole French GCSE class fell apart, hysterical for the whole hour's lesson. Our poor teacher, Mr Mitchells, had to go get the head teacher in the end – he'd wholly lost control. All because self-proclaimed 'class clown' Aaron Sullivan had pointed out that the word for swimming pool – '*piscine*' – sounded like 'piss in', which, he said, is what we've all done in the pool at some point.

Therefore, you piss in the *piscine*.

Fifteen years later, I'm starting to suspect the joke is not *that* funny. Or maybe you just need to understand some of the nuance of English slang? Which this group of French tourists I've just met definitely do not.

They continue to look at me blankly, but for some reason I keep going.

'Piss? You know, like wee? Urine? Whizz? Pee? Spending a penny? Isn't it funny how there are so many English words for having a wee? We're clearly obsessed!'

They are showing no signs of life, but I'm still talking: 'Tinkle? Going number one? Taking a leak? Or,' – I stop to laugh – 'as my super posh friend Eva says, "visiting the lavatory" ... ' I break off, suddenly really, urgently missing Eva.

We've barely spoken in the last couple of weeks. I've been avoiding her because I don't want to tell her what happened with Mark. I didn't want her to give me a pep talk and try to make me feel better about my shitty life. Not when everything is so great for her at the moment. But I feel a bit guilty suddenly, thinking about the messages she's sent that I've hardly replied to, and the Skype calls I've ignored. We haven't actually spoken on the phone or Skype since I was in LA. Which is unheard of for us.

Right. That's decided. I will call or Skype her as soon as we get off this bus – the airport will have WiFi, surely.

I'm flying up to north Thailand today. I've been here longer than I thought – snorkelling, swimming and wandering around talking to people. I've realised I really like human contact. All this talk about needing to be alone to truly 'find yourself' is kind of nonsense. Or at least, it doesn't really apply to me. I am a sociable, gregarious person – I get lonely! I'm allowed to say that, right? Because it feels a bit taboo sometimes. But shock-horror; humans like being around other humans at times. It's what Clara was saying on the phone – there are eight billion people out there, surely some of them are going through the same things as me. Surely some of them are looking for connections. Anyway, I feel stronger. I've spent time on my own and I've spent time with other people. Both have been good, both have been necessary.

And sure, yes, I miss Mark and Joe. I am worried about how I left things with my brother. I am scared we won't be able to work it out and I'll have lost yet another important person in my life. I am frightened. But I am also an excellent compartmentaliser. I have put our fight into a box and I am mostly ignoring it right now. Because what else can I do.

Plus, adventures do actually come easier when your dumb big brother isn't micro-managing your experience over your shoulder.

So now I'm adding another week to my Thai adventure so I can go up north to meet my Ayahuasca-Garfield buddy, Clara. She was so wise and soothing on the phone, I'm hoping she can help me figure out what I'm doing next. I don't know why I keep putting off the decision.

Actually, I do know why. I think that's obvious.

It's because of course I do know where I'm going next. But I'm not quite ready yet. I need more time. I need more time to think.

The French tourists are still staring at me blankly, so I give them a thumbs up and turn back towards the bus driver, Terry, who is laughing at me in the mirror. He's Scottish and I sat up the front so we could chat. He's brill, I really like him. I swear to God, he is a character ripped straight out of *Last of the Summer Wine*. Those old dudes were all so sassy.

Terry has been telling me all about his lovely family. He has a son 'about my age' who he wants to set me up with, and I've already given him my email address and AWOL handle because why not, eh. Maybe his son is hot.

'Are we nearly there yet, Terry?' I say, grinning at him in the mirror. He laughs at me again.

'You're a very impatient young lady, aren't you, Alice?' he says like every dad, ever.

'I am just excited to get to where I'm going,' I say and he shrugs.

'You need to learn how to enjoy the journey,' he replies, kindly. 'Stop always chasing what's next and embrace the now. That's what I tell my boys, and I'll tell you the same. Slow down and look around you, or you'll end up going round in circles. There are many ways of going forward, but only one way of standing still.'

'Ooh, Terry, that's dead wise,' I say, in awe.

'It's a Franklin Roosevelt quote,' he says, indicating and checking his blind spot. 'You have to be responsible for making your own life worth living, and choosing to be happy. There's no point waiting around for someone else to solve life for you and deliver happiness to your front door. You've got to live, not just exist.'

I am quiet, thinking about his words.

'Terry, I think you might be a genius,' I say at last.

'That's what they tell me,' he replies conversationally.

We pull up a few minutes later, and I grab my bag from the overhead compartment. It is so much lighter and I swing it onto my back with ease. It makes me laugh thinking what a literal weight it is off my shoulders.

I realised, when I was packing up, that I am an idiot. I've been carrying around so much unnecessary stuff since I got here. I had a whole make-up bag I've toted around Thailand for no reason. I haven't actually worn mascara since I left LA, never mind foundation, cover up, BB cream, powder, et al.

Obviously I am hideous, but who cares, really? You spend a few days wearing your patchy, discoloured, pale skin out in the world, and you get used to it. You realise nobody is really interested.

I also had an array of clothes and shoes I would never wear out here, because – shocking revelation coming up – Thailand is not a very 'stiletto' place.

I know, what a surprise.

And I had so many stupid pointless items I'd panic-packed at the start of this trip. It seems completely laughable now. A first-aid kit? Hair straighteners?? And I really don't know when I would ever really need Sellotape while travelling.

Anyway I packed it all up separately in a suitcase and had it sent back to my old flat – Eva and Jeremy's place.

I'm down to the basics now – a few t-shirts, some shorts

and skirts, a couple of pairs of flip-flops – and it is so freeing. I actually feel really wonderful.

I hug Terry goodbye and he promises to be in touch. It's so nice making these random connections. Whatever happens next, I want to do that more. I want to stay connected with the world around me. Strangers have so much to offer.

Inside the airport, I find a quiet corner and fire off a message to Eva.

Her reply is fast: 'YESSSS! I'm here!!! Waiting by the computer.'

I fire up Skype and the oxytocin floods me as we connect and her lovely round face fills my screen.

'Oh my God, Eva!' I say, laughing. 'You're pregnant!' She laughs too, and stands back, a bit awkwardly, away from the screen so I can see how her body has filled out in the last few weeks. Guilt flashes through my brain, realising how much I'm missing.

'Mum says I'm going to be huge,' she says, laughing, as she sits back down. 'She says she's very disappointed in me, as it's not the Slate way. We've been dainty pregnant women for generations apparently.'

'Dainty can eat my shit,' I say, smiling. 'No one has ever made a human being inside them elegantly.'

She laughs again. 'I think Mum did. She was still throwing tea parties for Mags a week before she had me.'

I cock my head. 'Mags?'

'Auntie Margaret.'

'You have an auntie Margaret?'

She looks sheepish. 'Sorry, I meant Princess Margaret. She was one of Mum's besties. They got up to all sorts. She says *The Crown* doesn't know the half of it.'

I snort. 'God your family is weird.'

She goes red. 'Anyway, you look amazing. You're actually a bit tanned!'

I shake my head, gesturing around me. 'I'm not, I think it's just the lighting in here.'

'It's good lighting then,' she says, studying me closely. 'You really do look great. How is it over there? I thought you were leaving Thailand this week? Where are you now?'

'I'm still in Thailand,' I confirm with a nod. 'I'm flying north today for one last week and then I will have to move on for my third and final trip.'

'Where to?'

'Not sure yet,' I hedge, looking away.

'If you're heading back to Europe, Cousin Penelope's Lake Como lodge is probably free?' Eva says eagerly. 'What does Mark think? Surely he has an opinion on your next adventure? Mark has never not had an opinion.'

I hesitate. Here we go, I guess.

'Actually, um, Mark's gone now,' I say casually.

'Oh?' she says, not looking too concerned. 'Did he have to get back to work?'

'Um, well, actually,' I take a deep breath. 'We kind of had a big fight and he stormed off with Joe. I haven't spoken to him in two weeks.'

She puts her hand to her face, looking upset. 'Oh Ali, I'm so sorry, that's so sad. Are you OK? What on earth happened? Oh no, it wasn't what me and him talked about, was it . . .?'

I wave my hand dismissively. 'It's not your fault, Eva. You know what he's like. He's such a dick. So sure of everything and always bossing me about, thinking he knows what's best for me. And yet heaven forbid he actually lets me into his personal life, or tells me anything about what is happening in his head.'

Eva looks at me sadly. 'I'm really sorry.'

I sit up straighter. 'Honestly, Eva, it's actually been great without him. I was upset for, like, a hot minute, and then I got back out there and started having fun again. My friend Clara helped put things in perspective, and so did a coach driver called Terry. People are amazing. And I've seen so many beautiful, stunning things, I can't even tell you. I feel so light and free.'

She smiles but looks a bit misty-eyed. 'That sounds so nice,' she says, but she sounds weird. 'I'm sad I never got to do anything like that. I could do with an escape from life myself.' She laughs now, a little shakily.

'Well, why don't you?' I say, inspiration suddenly striking. 'You could fly out here for a week. I could stay on an extra few days up in north Thailand. I've already changed my flight a bunch of times, they don't seem to mind that much. And it's not like I'm ready to move on to the next place yet anyway, so we'll have a holiday together. Come. Please Eva. Why not?'

She looks a little thrown.

'Oh, I couldn't. I'm nearly six months' pregnant . . .' she hedges, but I can see she is tempted.

'That's even more reason to do it, Eva,' I say, enthusiasm building in my voice. 'This is probably your last chance to do something this random and spontaneous for the next eight-een years! Soon you'll be trapped with Jeremy and the baby, with no exit or escape.'

That last bit was probably a bit harsh, but it is also true.

She looks thoughtful. 'I mean, I could . . .' she starts but then stops. 'No, no, I can't. What about work?'

'Surely they'd let you take a week or two off?' I try, but I can see I'm losing her. 'Oh, come on, Eva! Why not! I know what you're like. You never take your holiday entitlement, and your boss is nice, isn't she . . .? Listen, I really miss you, we haven't seen each other in months, and I think you actually need this.'

A sudden look crosses her face and she sits up straighter.

'I'm going to do it,' she says, determined. 'I'm coming.'

'Are you SERIOUS?' I shout, and people nearby shoot me a look. 'Do you mean it?' I say, quieter this time but I am jumping up and down inside.

She nods happily. 'I'm going to book a flight right now,' she says, and she is already tapping away at her computer. 'Send me the details of where I'm flying to. Can I stay with you?'

'Of *course*,' I crow, and I am so happy. 'We will have such a great time. We can take the slow-boat trip up the Mekong river, visit the Golden Triangle and stay overnight. I wanted to do it, but thought I'd run out of time. This is perfect!'

She claps her hands, thrilled. 'I can't believe I'm really doing this. Oh, I can't wait, Alice! I can't wait to see you and catch up. I've missed so much.'

We grin at each other.

25

AWOL.COM/Alice Edwards' Travel Blog

27 June – 7.19 p.m.

Oh HIYA!

Guess who's just arrived over here!!!!! My best friend in the universe, Eva, has come to see me in north Thailand, and she is currently sweating her way through her UK travelling clothes. She has never looked better. We're going to hook up with my fabulous pal Clara, and get on a boat. Thailand doesn't know what's coming.

Many, many blurry drunk selfies to come. No more monkeys though, I swear.

Love,

Axx

8 Comments · 145 AWOLs · 101 Super Likes

COMMENTS:

Sarah Sommers
| No way! The pair of you are going to rip up East Asia. So jel!!
Clara Weber
| I can't wait to meet you Eva, I've heard so much about you!!!

Eva Slate
Replying to Clara Weber

| Clara, I'm so excited to meet you, too!!

Kirpa Saul

| You paint such evocative images. I can just picture sweaty Eva in a scarf right now.

Eva Slate
Replying to Kirpa Saul

| Kirpa, I'm literally in a scarf, hahaha!

Seamus NaughtyLad678

| lol u have freinds? Yeh rite

Karen Gill

| Aren't you heavily prego right now, Eva?! Take it easy you two!

Eva Slate
Replying to Karen Gill

| Karen, yes I am just nearly six months!! But it's OK because pregnant women aren't broken or ill, lol!

'What are these?' Eva is pawing through my drawer, trying to find room for her stuff. She holds up my favourite grey pants.

I grab them off her. 'I have pared down my luggage,' I tell her self-importantly. 'I have learnt to value things for their internal importance rather than judging them on their external appearance, like *most* people.' I shoot her a supercilious look before adding, 'Plus, I am a Sheathologist now and have learnt to love my vagina and give it what it needs. And it *needs* giant, comfy, grey pants, so stop judging me.'

Eva giggles and dumps her casually expensive stuff out of

her bag into the drawer, on top of mine. We'll just share, I guess.

I still can't believe she's actually here. I stare at her for a moment, smiling my head off.

'Do I look awful?' she says, looking gloomy as she catches my adoring gaze. 'I feel awful. It's been so long since I felt out of control of my body like this.' She cups her protruding little stomach. 'I thought I'd just gain weight on my belly, like those celeb mums you see in the mags and on telly, but I've gained it everywhere. And like, I thought it would just be this perfect, neat little bump. But it's all lumpy and flabby. And I also didn't think it would be here yet! I'm six months gone, and I have a layer of blubber all over. It's everywhere. Al, I've even gone up a shoe size! And look at this . . .' She pokes at the skin showing through the rips on her jeans. 'I have blobs of fat poking through the holes. I swear this has only happened since I left England. Every day I wake up and my body has changed in another weird way.' She sighs and I give her a long hug.

'Eva!' I say, slightly scolding. 'Firstly, you are absolutely beautiful, I wish you could be less hung up on your weight. It's all just societal messaging brainwashing, telling you that you need to look a certain way. And your mum. But it is really meaningless. We might just as easily have decided a hundred years ago that being a size twenty was the ideal look. It's totally subjective.' She sighs again heavily, and I keep going. 'And secondly, *dude*! You are literally making another human being. Of course your body is going to change. I know it's weird and scary, but you are a fucking superhero. Your body is creating life, it is magnificent, you are magnificent.'

She smiles a little wanly and sits down heavily on the end of the bed. 'Ali . . . it's not just the body thing. It's been a rough few weeks.' She takes a deep breath. 'I don't know how to say this, so I'm just going to say it.' She pauses. 'Me and Jeremy broke up.'

'WHAT?' I say, too loudly. No! What? Did she really just say that? I'm flummoxed, I can't believe it. Where has this come from?

'What?' I say again in a lower voice, sitting down next to her and putting my arm round her. 'Oh Eva, no! I'm so sorry. No, you can't mean it. What's happened?'

She is silent for a full minute, staring at the floor. 'Things have just changed between us since we found out about the baby,' she says at last, her voice full of emotion. 'He doesn't seem to get it that things are going to need to be different. He's been out just as much as ever and I need him at home. I don't know how to say that without sounding like a needy nag, though. I don't know how to talk to him about how I feel. I knew my life would change, but, I don't know, I thought it would be more magical. It's all so unfamiliar and I don't know what is happening to me. I am so scared and everything is going to be so different. I am different, and I don't just mean with my body, but my mind.' She breathes in slowly. 'I don't know how to get my head round the idea that me and Jeremy are going to be responsible for a *person*. A whole person. If we get that wrong, if we mess her up, we're going to be to blame!' She is cradling her stomach protectively as her words rush out. 'I feel so overwhelmed with the information. I keep reading books, but they all just make me more afraid. There's so much you're supposed to know, and it keeps going on about maternal instinct, but what if I don't have that? I don't think I have it yet, so when does it kick in? Will I just somehow *know* how to change a nappy? And, oh, there are going to be so many nappies, Alice! Did you know a newborn needs to be changed *twelve* times a day?! And we're never going to get any sleep – you know how much I love my sleep – and there is just so much responsibility. I'm so, so scared.' Tears are rolling down her face and I pull her close as she finally stops for air. My poor, poor Eva.

'I want to talk to Jeremy, but I don't know how, and I know he won't understand it,' she swipes at her face but the tears keep coming. 'It's easy for the dad, they just have to take their kid to the park once a week and everyone hails them as some kind of a hero. People keep saying they're sure he'll be "helpful", as if he's a bonus rather than a parent who should do half. And I'm worried about leaving work. What if I forget everything or they realise they don't need me at all? I like working – what if they don't want me to come back? I mentioned to my mum about not taking my whole maternity leave and she laughed in my face. She said I probably won't ever want to go back and why should I. But no one expects Jeremy to stop working! Then Mum said it wouldn't be possible to go back to work early, what with breastfeeding, and when I admitted I wasn't sure how long I'd be doing that, or if I'd be able to breastfeed at all – Al, you know what tiny nipples I have! – she looked at me like I'd told her I was planning to drown my own baby. Then she started talking about hiring nannies but I don't want to do that either . . .'

She trails off and puts her face in her hands to cry properly.

Fucking hell. Being pregnant sounds *awful*. What is with all these dickheads telling her how to do everything? Eva is going to be a lovely mum! Surely the only thing that really matters is that the baby is really loved? And that's never going to be a problem for my kind-hearted Eva.

I don't know what to say. But I don't think this is one of

those conversations where Eva wants me to offer solutions or try to fix this, she just needs to talk and let it all out. It doesn't sound like she's been able to talk to anyone about any of this. Reading my mind, she continues in in a raspy, cried-out voice. 'I've tried so many times to tell Jeremy all that, but it's hard to explain, y'know? Then I told him I was coming here and we had a huge fight. It was horrible. He didn't understand why I was going. Then he even said he'd come too. He didn't get it, he didn't understand that I needed an escape from him. I told him I needed space and then we . . . then we broke up, Alice.' She pauses and I think she is going to properly lose it. She sobs, 'I am so, so tired from all this, so tired of trying to understand, and of trying to make him understand, Al. And you've been so far away . . .'

'Oh my God, Eva, I'm so, so sorry,' I say in a rush. 'I'm so sorry. I had no idea. I thought you were in your little pregnant love bubble. I thought you didn't want me around. I assumed you wouldn't want me getting in the way of your new life with Jeremy and the baby.' I pause and add slowly, 'I thought you didn't need me in your life any more.'

She looks up at me, eyes wide, the crying momentarily stopped. 'Did you really? Alice, I'm so sorry. I didn't realise.' She takes a deep breath. 'It was the opposite, I have needed you more than ever, but I didn't want you to feel like you couldn't get on with your own life or stop you having all this fun. Oh God, Al, have I been awful? Have I been shoving my relationship in your face? Have I been leaving you out? Am I one of those dreadful smug couples we used to moan about? Is it my fault you ran away? Is it because of the flat? Honestly Alice, you really didn't need to move out, I didn't want you to go. Certainly not yet. But you seemed like you wanted to go. I thought you couldn't wait to escape the boring pregnant lady and the idea of a screaming baby on its way. I'm so sorry, Alice.'

I feel terrible. She hasn't been awful. She's been wonderful. My wonderful, wonderful Eva. My warm, sweet, kind, lovely Eva. She has always been there for me. Always looking after me, caring for me, making sure I'm OK. Always understanding when I'm horrible and selfish and snappy.

I shake my head slowly. 'Eva, no,' I say quietly. 'You haven't been awful. I've been awful. I can't believe the way I've been acting. I've been a child. I pushed you away, like I do with everyone. Like I always do. I think I . . .' I hesitate, taking a deep breath. 'I think I was punishing you for being with Jeremy. Punishing you for having a baby. For moving on with your life. For going off and getting yourself a life without me. I didn't do it entirely consciously, but I think I've been out here, ignoring you, to make some kind of point. Not replying, not contacting you like before, to make you feel bad for "abandoning" me. And that makes me the most unbelievable selfish prick. I am so, so sorry. I hate myself.'

I'm crying too now, a lot. Eva reaches for me this time, pulling me closer. Even when she's in pain, going through hell, she's still the one comforting and reassuring others. The thought makes me cry even harder and I sob into her t-shirt as she whispers, 'It's OK Al, it's really OK.'

We cry together for a few more minutes, and when we pull apart we are both red and blotchy.

'I'll get a tissue,' I say, laughing weakly. She sniffs and smiles gratefully.

Returning from the loo, I hand Eva a wad of tissue and say quietly, 'I'm really so sorry about Jeremy.'

She smiles brightly, shaking the emotions away. 'Thank you, me too. But I'm OK. I think it's the right decision. We haven't been good together for months. It's changed between us. I love him so much, but if we can't get through this bit together, how will we cope when we're changing nappies on no sleep? Obviously it's not ideal with the baby coming. But I can be a single mum, can't I? Maybe I can hire one of Mum's nannies after all. And he'll still be a good dad. He's a really good man, Alice, he'll still be there for us. It'll be OK, I know it.'

I nod confidently. 'It will be OK, definitely, Eva.'

She's broken up with Jeremy. I can't believe it.

But shit, this is a good thing, isn't it? I knew they weren't right for each other, I knew it! I called it. I never liked lame old Jeremy.

Except . . . wasn't that all just the resentment and jealousy talking? Wasn't it just because he was the one making My Eva happy instead of me? Wasn't that just me being petty because I felt left out? And didn't he always treat her nicely? Didn't he always make an effort to be friendly to me and all our friends? Wasn't Eva always smiling when he was around? Didn't he make Eva happier than I'd ever seen her?

I push the thought away.

'You will be absolutely fine – great even,' I say emphatically again, sitting back down and dabbing at the mascara smeared all over Eva's face. 'Just because you two Frankensteined a baby together, doesn't mean he's the one for you, Eva. I think you just decided he was The One because your ex's penis looked like a ketchup bottle and Jeremy's was so normal in comparison.'

She nods, agreeing half-heartedly, but she still looks sad.

'I might go for a little walk on my own, if you don't mind too much?' she says after a minute, standing up. 'Clear my head, get a bit of air on these swollen eyes!'

'Are you sure?' I say, worried. 'I could come with you?'

'No, no,' she says nicely. 'I think I just need a little quiet time on my own. I need to stretch my legs after that massive flight, wedged into that middle seat – and then again in the taxi. I won't be long, and then we can get a drink and plan what we're going to do for the rest of this week. I'm excited! I promise I won't spend the whole time being a weepy, wail-y mess!'

She kisses me on the cheek, giving my arm a last squeeze and heads briskly for the door.

Eva has never liked getting emotional in front of me. Or anyone. I'm guessing she is going somewhere quiet to cry some more. I have learnt over the years to just let her go in these situations.

The door shuts and I sit heavily on the bed again. What a selfish bitch I've been. Just because my friend is doing new things with her life doesn't mean I have to lose her. Sure, things will change – that is life – but we will always have each other. And I am excited about being the best Auntie Alice ever.

But what about Jeremy? I can't believe I didn't realise things were this bad. Or bad at all! I've been swanning about, ignoring Eva when she needed to talk. Maybe if she had me to talk to, she wouldn't have needed Jeremy so much. We all need different people for different things in our lives, right? Without me around to talk to, and with Eva going through so much, how could things *not* start imploding with Jeremy?

A buzzing interrupts my thought process and I realise Eva's left her phone on the bed.

Caller ID says it's him. It's Jeremy. I take a deep breath and I answer.

'Jeremy?' I say and there is a pause on the end of the line. 'Alice?' he says, hesitantly.

'Yeah,' I say heavily, unsure. 'It's me.'

'Does Eva not want to talk to me?' His voice breaks and I clock how wretched he sounds.

'Oh, it's not that,' I say hurriedly. 'She's just popped out for a walk. She forgot her phone, she won't be long. Are you doing OK, Jeremy?'

There is a long, dark silence and I realise he's crying. 'Not really,' he says simply. 'I guess she told you she broke up with me?'

'Yeah. Yeah, she did. I'm really sorry.' I don't know what else to say.

'I didn't know anything was wrong!' he says through his tears. 'She has been a bit quiet lately, and I know she's found it strange with her body changing and everything, but I laughed that off. Of course her body was going to change! I didn't think she was being serious.'

For a moment I am annoyed with him. How could he not know his partner was going through a big thing? And how could he think it was just that simple! Isn't it his job to know she was suffering?

The flare of anger fades just as quickly as I realise I had no idea she was struggling either. I had no clue. She's very good at hiding things and I have no right to judge. If Eva wasn't talking – wasn't explaining how she felt – how was he supposed to help her or change things?

There's a weird onus we put on each other in relationships, an expectation that our loved ones should be able to guess what is wrong with us from tiny hints – but how? Really, how? How is anyone supposed to know what's happening in anyone else's head? Why can't we just talk to each other? Be honest and explain what we need? If we could start asking for help, the world would be a much better, easier place to live in.

'I think it's more than just her body changing,' I say quietly. 'It's about her whole life changing. I think she's afraid of things changing with you as well, Jeremy.'

He is silent and I think he might be crying again. 'I love her so much, Alice, I am so in love with her. You know that, don't you?'

And suddenly I do. I really do. Of course he loves her, and of course she loves him. Truly, madly, deeply. I can't believe it's taken me this long to fully understand that. I've been dismissing Jeremy as a time-killer boyfriend – as another boring, faceless man passing through our lives – but he's much more than that. Eva's not settling just because she's thirty. She hasn't chosen Jeremy just because he came along at the right time, or for any other mean-spirited reason I decided because I was jealous. She adores him. From the moment they met, they've made each other happy. I'm a stupid moron, a jealous cow. It's as simple as that. I had Eva all to myself before, and then I didn't any more, and I was a petty, spiteful little witch wanting things to go back to how they were before. It's pathetic and I am so, so ashamed of myself.

I sigh, feeling wretched. 'Jeremy, of course I know that, and I'm sorry if I've ever been less than welcoming to you. I know Eva loves you, too. I think she's just going through a thing right now.' I pause. 'I really hope you two can work it out. I mean that. But I promise I'll look after her while she's out here, I really will.'

There is another long silence on the phone, but this one is like a long-distance hug. An *entente cordiale* down the phone, after so many months of awkward civility.

'I'll tell her you called,' I say simply at last.

'Thank you, Alice,' he replies and we stay on the line a few more seconds before hanging up.

26

1 July – 10.23 a.m.

Too much fun to post properly. Just know that me, Eva and Clara are about to be trapped on a boat together for two days. Taking bets on who goes overboard first?

Axx

6 Comments · 132 AWOLs · 124 Super Likes

COMMENTS:

Hollie Baker
| Oh noooo! Please don't fall in! Lol!!

Kirpa Saul
| Put me down for a tenner on a three-way tie.

Sarah Sommers
Replying to Kirpa Saul
| Lol, three-way tie sounds hot.

Ayo Damiunse
| You. For sure.

Karen Gill
| Finally we're going to get a death out of this trip. Took you

long enough. Mammy says she'll chip in for a wreath.

Alice Edwards
Replying to Karen Gill
| That is so very generous, please tell her thank you.

'Do you think they have alcohol around here somewhere?' Clara stage-whispers, leaning heavily across the laps of a frightened-looking family of tourists wearing large, shapeless anoraks.

I look around the small boat at the twenty or so other passengers – none of them drinking – and shrug.

'Surely they do!' Eva says enthusiastically from four seats down.

I give her a thumbs up and she adds anxiously, 'Do you think I'd be allowed a sip of a Mai Tai?'

We were a bit late arriving at the dock this morning for our two-day trip along the Mekong river. We only just made it on board before it set sail, and so the three of us had to grab three separate seats only vaguely near each other.

A youngish boy in his late teens pipes up in a Polish accent from our right. 'They do have drinks for sale here, but I do not think they have got a cocktail. And there definitely will not be any fancy Mai Tai cocktails.' He sniggers and Eva blushes as Clara leaps up.

'Great news. I'll go find the bar,' she squeals, disappearing off towards the other side of the boat. She treads on the teen boy's foot on her way past, and he winces. I wonder if it was an accident or payback for mocking Eva.

Clara returns with two plastic cups of very yellow wine, and one coke, handing the last to Eva with a sympathetic look on her face. The wine is bound to be disgusting, but better than not drinking on a boat ride, right? I know it's not actually a booze cruise, but still, the beauty of nature is that much more beautiful viewed from the other side of a large yellow wine.

Apparently unfazed by the foot stomping, the teen boy reaches out to shake Clara's hand as she sits. 'I'm Jan, and this is Jakub,' he says, gesturing at another sullen-looking teenager on his right, who does not look up from his phone.

Oh huzzah, we're interacting! I'm really into interacting with strangers these days, even if these strangers happen to be rude teen boys. And I am fascinated by the eclectic group on board this slow boat. We're all going to spend two days together – stopping halfway up the Mekong river to stay at a hotel overnight – and I'm dying to get everyone's life story. I love a life story.

'Hello Jan,' she says enthusiastically. 'I am Clara, that is Alice, and the pregnant one over there is Eva.' Eva looks a bit put out by the dismissive description. We've only been together a few days out here, but already I've noticed how much you become only One Thing to people when you are pregnant. It's all anyone's talked to her about. It's truly strange. People touch her without permission and give her unsolicited advice about breastfeeding. She's already been told off multiple times by strangers for travelling abroad in her 'condition'. She has to keep explaining that her doctor said it was fine. It's been a bit tortured and I can really, totally see why she's having a life crisis and wanted to escape. But when it's your literal stomach causing the issue, it is a little bit impossible to get away.

I wave over at Jan and Jakub, adding, 'Nice to meet you! Where are you lads from?'

'Warsaw,' Jan says, 'but we are moving to Spain soon, where all the sexy ladies live.'

I choose not to take offence at this and continue, 'Oh, how very exciting for you. Are you at school at the moment?'

He shakes his head, irritated. 'We have left school – we are eighteen years old – and we are now training to be body builders. We are going to be big men. Then we move to Spain.'

I try not to react. Jan is very small and thin. I have not come into much close contact with body builders but he doesn't strike me as the right . . . shape.

The silence has gone on too long and he continues a little defensively. 'I am currently on the GOMAD protocol. I will soon be twice the size of this.'

'Um, what is the GOMAD protocol?' Eva says politely, looking alarmed.

'It is milk,' he says, looking at her like she is stupid. 'You drink a gallon of milk every day.'

'Are you serious?' I say before I can stop myself. 'A *gallon of milk*?'

He nods self-importantly. 'Everyone on the internet is doing it, you look it up. It is tricky because I am lactose intolerant but it will be worth it when I am big and all the sexy girls are sexing me.'

'You are lactose intolerant but you drink a gallon of milk *every day*?' I say slowly, trying not to let the incredulity too much into my voice.

He nods again. 'Yes, this is right. So I am spending a lot of time on the toilet, but yes, worth it.'

Cor.

Imagine being so obsessed with your weight that you'll voluntarily spend all day, every day, on the loo, liquid pouring out of your bum.

Wow. This man knows what it's like to be a woman.

I mean, I don't care that much about my weight – definitely not GOMAD levels – but I'd be lying if I said the messaging doesn't get to me on some level. More so in my teens and early twenties, for sure. But no lie, I think every woman out there has had, like, at least a low-key eating disorder at some point in her life.

Actually, I thought being out here travelling around strangers on beaches would bring that fear out in me more, but actually it's had the opposite effect. Having my fleshy, dimply body out on display as often as possible has made me care less. You get used to the sight of yourself, don't you? Your body normalises in your eyes, because you can't spend all your time hating on yourself. Not all your time. It's too tiring, and there are too many other things around to distract you from the self-loathing. You put it out there enough and you realise people don't *really* care. Your previously hated body becomes fine at long last, and that is such a joy and such a relief. And then maybe – after your shape normalises in your brain – maybe you even start to *like* it. Then – a long time after that – maybe, just maybe, you reach a point where you stop feeling ashamed – stop thinking that you are wrong and disgusting – for seeing your body as quite nice. It's a process. I'm working towards it.

I hope poor old Jan will get there one day, too.

'That does not sound healthy,' Clara says loudly and Jan shrugs.

'It will be worth it,' he says again. 'When I am drowning in the pussy.'

'Garfield,' Clara mutters and we make eye contact.

The frightened family sitting between us clear their throat.

'Shall we move up so you can all sit together?' says the dad and we ignore the blatant irritation in his voice as we nod happily and shuffle around.

'Come on Eva!' I say loudly, gesturing at her to come join us, which she does sheepishly, apologising to the group who have to move up on her side.

'Thanks everyone!' I say grinning and they smile begrudgingly back.

In the mess of seating rearrangement, Jan has managed to position himself between me and Clara, and he now turns his back on me to trap my young friend into conversation.

I catch her eye over his thin shoulders to ask – with my eyebrows – if she needs help. To my surprise she winks back at me, smiling coyly.

She fancies him! Gross. So I guess the foot stomping was *flirting*! How bizarre. But good for the pair of them, I suppose?

I turn my attention back to Eva, who is sipping her Coke and looking a little glum.

'Are you OK?' I say gently, and she nods a little too vigorously, smiling.

She has been uncharacteristically quiet since she got out here. Not surprising, of course, with everything that's going on back at home, but I am still very worried. When I've tried to get her to talk about Jeremy, she's brushed me off, saying she doesn't want to spoil our lovely holiday. Jeremy has tried to ring many more times since that first day, and I've tried to encourage her to answer, but as far as I know, she has not. Nor has she called him back. But now she's trapped with me on a boat for another four hours and it's enough now. I need to talk to her.

'Eva,' I say softly and I slip my arm around her back. She leans into me, and I feel her sag a little on my shoulder.

'Listen, my darling wonderful Eva,' I say in a clear but low voice. 'I'm going to make a little speech now, and you don't have to say anything, but I want you to listen.' Her breathing stills against me.

'Eva,' I begin. 'I know you are struggling. I know you are worried and more scared than you've ever been in your life. I know you are, and it only makes you human, so I want you to know it's OK that you feel that way. But I also want you to know that you are not on your own. I swear you're not. I haven't been a good friend to you recently – or maybe ever – but I will be. I want to be. And I am going to help you as much as you want or need when our little girl comes along.' I feel the breath catch in her throat on the word girl. I keep going. 'But I need you to start talking, Eva. I need you to start asking. You need to tell me when you're feeling afraid, and when you want me to be there. Because I will do everything I can to be there for you, like you've always been there for me. I love you so much, my friend, and so will your child. I promise you, Eva, you're going to be the most wonderful mummy ever, and this kid is going to be the luckiest little thing in the universe to have you. It's going to love you so damned much. I know it's scary, but I swear to you, you're going to be brilliant.'

She doesn't say anything, but I can feel she is crying quietly. I clear my throat.

'And, Eva, I know you're scared of sharing yourself this much with Jeremy, but you need to start talking to him, as well. He is not a mind reader, so you need to tell him what you need and what you're feeling. He is a lovely, kind, sweet person, and he will listen. Kindness is a more important personality trait than almost anything, and it's really rare, Eva.' I pause. 'He wants to make you happy, I know he does. And he also loves you something crazy. I honestly don't think anyone

264

has ever loved anything or anyone like Jeremy loves you. And, Eva, I think you feel the same. You're just hiding your head in the sand, like you do sometimes, because you're scared. It's understandable, but it's time to stop hiding away, please, my lovely, lovely Eva.'

There is a long silence while she sobs quietly into my neck.

She speaks at last, in a cracked voice. 'Oh, Alice.' She pulls a tissue from her pocket and wipes her nose before adding, half laughing, 'You know, it's funny, I didn't think you really liked Jeremy very much.'

'What?' I say, outraged. 'Of course I do! I adore him. He's brilliant and sexy. When you are fifty and can't stand each other, I plan on having an affair with him, Eva.'

She giggles. 'That would be fine, but I genuinely don't think I will ever not be able to stand him. I love him so much,' she says. 'But maybe we could have a group affair?'

'That sounds agreeable to me,' I say blithely.

She takes a deep breath and I feel her heat on my shoulder as she wipes the last remaining tears from her eyes.

'Thank you, Alice,' she says quietly, adding in a dramatic voice, 'You are the wind beneath my wings.'

'I'm fucking what?' I shout and she bends forward, laughing.

'I love you,' she says simply, warmly, and looks up at me at last. Her eyes are red and shiny, but she looks happy. She looks content and calm. For the first time in days, she looks like she is OK. I know she'll be OK. She has Jeremy and she has me, and soon we'll all have a little extra person, too. We are all going to be OK.

27

AWOL.COM/Alice Edwards' Travel Blog

2 July – 8.58 a.m.

HIYA,

About to get back on a boat with the world's worst hangover. Is there a classy way of throwing up over the side of the boat, do you think? If anyone is near the Golden Triangle, please bring me wet wipes.

Love,

Axx

8 Comments · 142 AWOLs · 167 Super Likes

COMMENTS:

Hannah Edwards

| It might be satellite signals making u ill. They use them to track ur movements x

Seamus NaughtyLad678

| fuckin gumpa baboon

AWOL MODERATOR
Replying to Seamus NaughtyLad678

| THAT IS IT. I AM FUCKING DONE. I'M NOT DOING THIS ANY MORE. I'M SO SICK OF IT.

Seamus NaughtyLad678
Replying to AWOL MODERATOR
| alrite luke chill out mate

Isabelle Moore
| I have wet wipes!

Ethan Winkleman
Replying to Isabelle Moore and Alice Edwards
| Actually I used the last of them up last night ;)

Isabelle Moore
Replying to Ethan Winkleman and Alice Edwards
| What?! But I was so careful not to spill a drop ;)

Alice Edwards
Replying to Ethan Winkleman and Isabelle Moore
| I have now vomited on my phone, thanks a lot, you two.

We are all a bit crumpled and tired as we file back on board our boat for the second day of exploring the Golden Triangle along the river.

My hangover is colossal but I have to admit, it was a great night. We got to the hotel in the early evening, after a day on the water. It was up a hill, and we were a bit drunk, so there was a lot of pushing each other up and falling over giggling.

After checking into the hotel, there was this amazing ceremony outside, where a bunch of local kids performed a traditional dance for tourist tips. We sat in a circle watching them, and staring up at the sky contemplating our existence.

Like, what does anything matter, really? Why do we get

so bogged down and bothered about the small boring Life Things like paying bills and bleeding radiators, when this kind of magic exists in the world? Not that I've ever bled a radiator in my life – is that still a thing adults are meant to do?

Afterwards, Clara said she was going off with Jan, so I insisted on seeing his passport to check he was definitely actually eighteen. I didn't want any statutory things interrupting my trip. Or y'know, young people being exploited or whatever. As soon as they'd gone, Eva excused herself to call Jeremy. We were sharing a room and I could tell she needed space to talk things through properly, so I stayed in the bar downstairs. Luckily, there was a massive group of Canadians in there, all on a stag do and they invited me to join them. So I latched onto them and had a great night losing at foreign drinking games. It was fun.

Less so this morning, which has been a hard, hungover slog.

Eva was asleep by the time I finally got up to bed, and I haven't had a proper chat with her yet this morning – but I suspect the conversation with Jeremy went well. I'm guessing there was huge amounts of happy crying because her eyes are swollen to fuck. She is glowing with joy and I'd hazard a guess that they're back together and all is right in the world.

As Eva and I take a seat on the boat, tired but happy, Clara and Jan reappear, looking shagged, in all the different senses.

'Morning you two,' I say loudly, grinning. 'Nice night?' The family from the day before – still wearing their matching waterproof anoraks – glance over anxiously, aware of the direction the conversation is likely going.

Clara takes a seat beside us, not smiling, and Jan sits beside her. They don't answer my teasing question and the cloud of anger hovering over them is opaque. They are very clearly mid-fight.

Well, that honeymoon didn't last very long.

Eva and I exchange an awkward grimace. A frosty silence falls across our group and I clear my throat, staring off into the middle distance. Anorak Family look uncomfortable.

The boat pulls away from the dock and my internal organs make a protesting groan. I can actually feel my liver pickling inside me. I think I'm done with the binge drinking for a while. I've put in my time, I've committed to it, I think I've earned a few weeks off.

Eva shifts in the plastic seat next to me. No one knows what to say. Clara coughs aggressively, like she didn't need to cough but she wanted to make the point that she was there and she was angry.

Jan gets up abruptly. 'Does anyone want a drink?' he snarls and stomps off before we can answer.

I mean, he *stomps* as much as anyone who weighs, like, seven stone can.

It's actually really elegant.

'Are you OK?' I murmur to Clara.

She shrugs, clearly not. 'We had such a lovely night together,' she says unhappily. 'We stayed up most of the night and he kept saying how much he liked me and that he could not believe I wasn't Spanish. I know he is a few years younger than me, but he seemed so mature and sweet, didn't he?'

I make a non-committal noise that I hope both conveys support for Clara and also distances myself from the idea of finding him attractive. This being the kid who yesterday spoke at length about shitting himself. Each to their very own.

She sighs. 'We finally fell asleep wrapped up in each other's arms. It was magical. Until I woke up and he was on his phone. I glanced up and he was on Tinder speaking to someone else. He was sexting some other random woman while I was asleep next to him, post-coitus.'

'They have Tinder here?' I say, startled. She shoots me a murderous look because of course that is not really the point.

Eva chips in, 'Or maybe he's just got his distance settings really wide? Like, to cover the entire world?'

She has missed the point, too.

I quickly put my arm around Clara. 'I'm so sorry, lovely. What a prick! What did you say? Did you have a fight?'

She nods, looking a bit tearful. 'Yes, I went mad at him, and he didn't even say sorry. He just got really defensive, saying he can do what he likes. He shouted at me that he doesn't need anyone and is better off alone. That he didn't owe me anything and I was just a one-night stand. But that's not what he'd said at all the night before – he had practically been telling me he loved me! And then he shouted that I was just being a "bunny boiler". I don't really know what that means but I am a vegetarian, so then I got really cross.'

'Ugh,' I say. 'Bunny boiler is a disgusting, sexist thing that gaslighting men say just to hurt and dismiss women. Men should know better than to use that term any more.'

She looks even more confused. 'Gaslighting? Because of his problem with the bowels? He only went to the toilet three or four times last night, it was not an issue. It didn't ruin any of the sex.'

I shake my head, feeling sick again. 'No, gaslighting is a thing people – narcissists – do, where they make you feel crazy when you are having legitimate human feelings. Like, when someone is cheating on you and they make you feel like you're going mad to cover up their lies, instead of being honest. It's like a levelled-up type of negging.'

'TD used to do that to you a lot,' Eva says confidently, beside me.

'He did?' I say, surprised, turning to her.

Did he?

She looks at me, shocked. 'Of course he did!' she says. 'You know that, don't you, Alice? Didn't you? He did it constantly. Since day one. He would tell you you were being silly – he would laugh at you – when you were upset over yet another horrible thing he'd done. Then you'd feel like you were overreacting and forgive him. It was really hard to watch.'

She looks contemplative for a minute. 'I think it was to keep you confused and vulnerable so you'd keep coming back, no matter what he did to you.' She pauses and we look at each other before she adds in a low voice, 'He isn't a very nice person.'

I let her words sink through my skin.

She's right. He did do that. All the time. And it worked every time. I would constantly question myself and feel stupid for getting upset over 'nothing'. He'd make me feel like I was nuts for asking about our relationship status after a year. Or made out like I was the biggest weirdo ever for being upset when he didn't text me back for three days.

But even if I was overreacting – and finding another woman's toothbrush in your boyfriend's bathroom is surely not something you can ever *underreact* to – if someone loves you, they should still listen to how you're feeling, shouldn't they? They shouldn't mock you or make you feel stupid for having emotions. Wherever the feelings are coming from, they're still your feelings – you're still sad – and a real, emotionally kind partner should hear you and try to empathise. Not make you feel stupid.

Actually, my first boyfriend, Kit, used to do that, too.

Fuck, I had no idea just how stupid I'd been.

I have always thought of myself as such a strong feminist. I read so much about these things and never thought I would fall for an idiotic narcissist's tricks. I suddenly feel very foolish and very relieved I didn't send that text to TD a couple of weeks ago.

I prod myself. Is there anything left in me that still wants him?

Nothing.

The relief is palpable. Absolutely nothing. I don't even hate him any more. I just feel sad for him. He's a miserable person who is going to spend his life trying to make women feel insecure because he thinks that's the way to ensure they stay. Isn't that sad? And isn't it sad that I let it happen to me for so long?

But I can't punish myself for what's done. Because that's another vicious circle. You hate yourself for being so weak, and the hatred makes you feel unworthy of real love – so you go back. But not any more. I take a deep, slow breath in.

'Clara,' I say, my head swimming. 'Lovely Clara, try not to be sad. Jan is very young and stupid. Of course he doesn't mean any of it, he's just a fucking moron. And if he spends his whole life pushing people away, being cruel and unkind, pretending he doesn't need anyone else, he's going to end up so completely alone, with no one . . .'

I trail off, my own words smacking me in the face.

That's what I've been doing. Shit. That's what I've been doing for years.

Jan's furious voice interrupts my realisation.

'All right, Erin Brocker-bitch, have you finished trying me in your feminist court?' he shouts, and the Anorak Family fully stand up, ushering their children away from us.

Oh crap, he heard me calling him a fucking moron even though he definitely is one and many other words.

'Listen, Jan,' I begin in a conciliatory tone. I should try to smooth things over. We are, after all, going to be trapped on a boat together for another few hours.

'Get fucked, shit for brains,' he interjects. 'Why would I listen to anyone else? I'm doing fine on my own, I don't need some goth chubster—'

Wait, is that me?

'—telling me what's good for me. Other people just hold me back. I'm going to be a body builder, living it up in Spain. I am on this road to success all on my own . . .'

His loud rant continues, more like a speech. Everyone on the boat is his audience. It briefly occurs to me that this is a performance piece arranged by the organisers, and Jan is an actor hired to entertain the guests.

But I guess sleeping with Clara would be quite a long game in terms of entertainment.

Clara jumps up shouting, and the pair of them perform their set, yelling for the cheap seats at the back.

I turn to Eva, ignoring them. 'LeFou, I'm afraid I've been thinking . . .' I say, and she adds automatically, 'A dangerous pastime . . .'

'I know,' I nod. 'Really though, I've thought a lot about it, and I've decided it's time for my third adventure. Enough now, I'm ready.'

She cocks her head at me, but she is smiling because she knows what is coming. 'I'm going to Australia,' I say, grinning back at her. 'I think it's probably time, don't you?'

She nods, and leans across giving me a long hug.

Australia

28

AWOL.COM/Alice Edwards' Travel Blog

5 July – 9.07 a.m.

Hey everyone,

After staying in Thailand much longer than I intended, I've finally moved on. This next bit of my journey is going to be tough, but – I hope – pretty special and important.

Anyway, I just popped on here to say thank you so much to Eva and Clara for being incredible people. I had a truly great time with you both and I can't wait to see you again soon.

But that's not to say it was all good. There's good and bad in everything, always. Just wanted to add that point.

That's it for now.

Axx

3 Comments · 149 AWOLs · 157 Super Likes

COMMENTS:

Jeremy Stail
| Thank you for everything, Alice. Good luck with where you're going. x

Eva Slate
Replying to Jeremy Stail

| Miss you, Alice. Thank you so much for this past week, you know what it meant to me.

Hannah Edwards
| where r u now?!!!!!!!!

I am standing outside an unfamiliar door, with all too familiar people inside. But I cannot knock. I've been standing here for twenty-five minutes and I can't do it. I can't remember the last time I was this afraid. It seems silly to say I am afraid to be unafraid, but that's all it is. Being a coward is safe, I want to stay there. I don't want to be brave. But my heart cannot take much more of this. I can feel it thumping loudly in my chest every time I reach for the door. Panic seizes me again and I step back.

OK, I can't stand here forever. This is it now. I can do this.

I reach again for the door, but as I do, I hear movement inside – and I bolt. I run away, away, away, away, and I don't slow down until I am out of breath, red-faced and sweating.

Which, to be fair, only took about forty seconds but still, it is long enough to be out of sight of my mum's house.

Jesus, what's wrong with me?

I came all this way, am I really not strong enough to see this through? To see her? To say sorry? Am I that pathetic?

I glance around and spot a coffee shop across the road. I will have a coffee. That will help calm me. Calm me in a much twitchier, pug-eyed, too-much-caffeine kind of way.

Opening the door, I stop short at the sight of a young woman at the nearest table. She is on her laptop and for a second I think we must've gone to school together. She is familiar, but unfamiliar. Someone I know very well, but also not at all.

OH MY GOD. I know who it is! It's Constance. Constance Beaumont. THE BLOGGER. Ohmygod, she is amazing, I love her so much.

Except, she is a bit greyer than in her pictures. She's in a thin tracksuit and glasses. Not exactly her usual floaty Coachella-type style. I mean, I'm not a total idiot, I knew there would be filters and quality control on the shots, but – wait – her eyes aren't even green. How did she do that?

She's still beautiful and cool though, still glowing. Do I dare speak to her? I want to tell her how much she's inspired me. I want to tell her about my recent travels. I want to impress her.

'Um, excuse me?' I say timidly, aware she must get this all the time and probably hates it. She turns and looks at me blankly.

Definitely not green eyes.

What filter or app is that, because I want it.

'I'm so sorry to bother you, it's just . . .' I am lost for words. 'I can't believe it's you. I love your travel blog so much. I've basically been copying your trip, I'm obsessed, I love you. Me and my friend Eva love everything you do.'

She sighs. 'Well it's all a load of shit, you shouldn't,' she says, but it is not said unkindly. 'What's your name?'

'Er, Alice. What do you mean it's a load of shit? It's not . . . it's not shit! It's wonderful, you're wonderful!'

'Hi Alice,' she says wearily. 'It's really nice to meet you and I'm sorry to shatter your illusion. I'm just having a bad day and you caught me in a moment where I'm really totally sick of it all. Sick of pretending. My life is shit, and my travel stories are mostly bullshit. I haven't been out of Australia in three years, it's all old stuff from my twenties.'

'But . . . but . . .' I am lost. She's not in her twenties? I thought she was about twenty-three.

She goes on, not seemingly able to stop. 'I'm sorry but I'm sick of it, I'm sick of having to be this slick, glistening *thing* all the time. Nobody cares about the real me. They don't care that I have neck acne and a bad back from years of hostel beds. They don't care about my irritable bowel syndrome from all the food I've eaten that wasn't cooked properly from faraway places. Nobody cares that I really want to be a science fiction author, writing novels about zombies. My management says I can't do it because it doesn't fit with my *brand*. They say my sponsors will pull out if I don't stay on message, and then how will I live? I'm too old to do anything else now, and I have a five-year gap on my CV.'

She pauses to take a long drink from her takeaway cup of coffee. The smell wafts towards me and I realise it is decidedly not coffee. I gape at her like a dumb fish.

'I'm just miserable, y'know?' she continues. 'But I'm not allowed to be sad, because that's not *cool*. Actually, no, that's not true. It is actually cool to be sad for, like, five minutes. It's cool to write a really poignant, "honest" post about feeling low, and how everyone gets sad. That will get you praise and maybe a feature with, like, the *Guardian*. But then you are meant to get better and stop moaning because everyone is bored of hearing about it. The internet – my followers – don't want to know how I really feel every day. They follow me for escapism. They want to believe their life can one day be perfect – like mine. But fuck it, fuck them, fuck everything. That isn't real life.'

She stops to wobble on her coffee-shop stool, pulling at her joggers, like she cannot get comfortable.

I don't know what to say but I suddenly feel for her so intensely. I am one of those people she's describing. I didn't want Constance Beaumont to have flaws. I wanted her to be a 2D shimmering Mary Poppins. Practically perfect in every way. She is meant to represent what we all could've won if we'd been so beautiful, so rich, and so privileged – like her.

'Oh, Constance, I'm . . .'

She interrupts me. 'You know Constance Beaumont isn't even my real name? It's a made-up name my management chose for me because they thought it sounded cool. Do you want to know what my real name is? Janet Morris. Do you want to know what my middle name is?'

'I mean . . .' I hedge but she is on a roll.

'It's Janet,' she spits. 'My name is Janet Janet Morris. My parents called me Janet Janet Morris.'

'Well that's, er, nice . . .' I try.

'No, it's not!' she exclaims. 'It's fucking unimaginative and ridiculous. But the stupid thing is that I *want* to be bland. I dream of being bland. I want to be Janet Janet Morris again. I liked bland Janet Janet Morris!'

There is silence and I put my hand gently on her arm.

She looks at it like she doesn't understand the gesture. After a moment she continues. 'Sorry Alice, you seem really nice, and I'm sure you didn't want to hear all this. You caught me at a bad moment, is all. I was debating whether to post a picture of my cat. I've been sitting here for thirty minutes, trying to work out if I can post a picture of my sodding cat. It's not a beach or a chic, previously undiscovered B&B, so I don't know if I'm allowed. I don't want to ask my management because they always say no. But I want to post a picture of my cat! It shouldn't take me half an hour to work this out. That isn't a life, is it?'

I shake my head.

She sighs. 'I just want to sit at home, eating Toblerones

– PLURAL – and not sharing pictures of FUCKING BEACHES. I don't even like beaches! I hate sand! It gets everywhere. In your bag, in your clothes, in your knickers, in your butthole. I hate it.'

'Um, well, I know this is easy for me to say,' I start slowly. 'But . . . screw it, Janet—' That is so weird to call her '—I think you can take a chance and post a picture of your cat. And maybe even a Toblerone. Maybe a cat lying down near a Toblerone? And I don't want to freak you out, but maybe you could even . . .' I pause dramatically, '. . . not post anything at all.'

She looks at me and for a moment I think she might start crying. Instead, she bursts out laughing. I start laughing too, and we laugh together.

'I'm really sorry,' she says at last, wiping her eyes. 'The truth is, I do have a lovely life, and I do know how lucky I am. And I mostly quite like travelling! But I think people see it as this magic answer to all their problems. They will travel to Phuket, discover their true self, have some kind of spiritual awakening and everything will be perfect in their sad little lives at long last.'

All right Janet Janet, no need to get personal.

'And sure, it can be loads of fun, and a great time away from real life,' she continues, unaware of how close to the bone she's getting. 'But when you get home, you're still going to be you, aren't you? You're still going to be the same person, with the same obsessions and worries and insecurities. You can change the setting around you for a while, but if you're sad, you'll still be sad lying under a palm tree, won't you? Things aren't going to be magically solved. Life is so much more complicated than we think, isn't it? And so am I. I want to be multi-faceted, Alice. I want to be a whole person, not just a travel automaton with dewy skin.'

'Well that's fair enough, Janet!' I say, defiantly. 'And I promise you, I'll still follow you on Instagram if you post cat pictures. I'll even stick it out if you post ones with your real eye colour.'

She laughs again, gratefully. 'You noticed that, huh?' She sighs. 'Thank you. I know you're right. It's just hard. I know I need to change things and I think I might sack my management. They're kind of shitty to me. I reckon they just see me as a money-making product on their books. They don't want to risk me changing and chance losing that fifteen per cent. But damn them! I want to be the real me! And maybe I could use a pen name or something for the sci-fi writing?'

'That's a great idea!' I say enthusiastically.

There is a pause while we look at each other, smiling. Two strangers. Two idiots just trying to get through this weird, messy life.

She stands up.

'So,' she says, and she sounds like she has something important left to say. 'Do you, like, want a selfie or something?'

29

5 July – 2.13 p.m.

HELLO.

I think it's time I blocked some dickheads on here. This is your last chance to get in some insults before I say goodbye to you for ever. I really don't know why I've ignored it for so long, it's like I enjoy being punished by awful people. But I'm done with that now.

Bye,

Axx

18 Comments · 157 AWOLs · 140 Super Likes

Seamus NaughtyLad678

| it's cos you love the attention stupid ho

Alice Edwards
Replying to Seamus NaughtyLad678

| Nice knowing you Seamus NaughtyLad678, BLOCKED.

Eva Slate

| Yay! Good for you. Life is too short to let these idiots go unblocked.

Danny Boy

| U CAN BLOK US BUT UR STILL FAT

Alice Edwards
Replying to Danny Boy
| Great point, well made, Danny Boy! BLOCKED.

Hannah Edwards
| good girl

Piers Ned
| Whore slut.

Alice Edwards
Replying to Piers Ned
| That is sex worker aspiring slut to you, Piers! BLOCKED.

Ryan T
| lol lol lol, u think ur better than us? C u on 4chan bitch

Alice Edwards
Replying to Ryan T
| No you won't, Ryan T! BLOCKED.

Paul ProudDadtoDaughters
| rabid feminists are wat is wrong wiv this country

Alice Edwards
Replying to Paul ProudDadtoDaughters
| I'm sad you feel that way Paul, because feminism is about helping men, too. I hope you understand that one day, and that your daughters grow up to be proud feminists. BLOCKED.

Randy Howels
| pathetic. can't even take a bit of banta

Alice Edwards
Replying to Randy Howels

| I don't think the word banter should be used as an excuse for being cruel to each other, Randy. BLOCKED.

Hollie Baker
| I am afraid to block people on here, what if they get angry?

Alice Edwards
Replying to Hollie Baker
| Ah, Hollie, we don't know each other but I want you to be brave. I want you to not care if strange men are angry with you for standing up for yourself. It's not easy I know. I know that as women we are conditioned to be nice at any cost, to run around making sure we are not upsetting the men we meet, for fear of retaliation. But you are worth more than being called a bitch on the internet for no reason. Block block block!

AWOL MODERATOR
| Hi Alice, thank you for doing this, and I'm sorry I haven't been able to stem the tide of trolls. It's too much – too hard. My bosses won't let me block them, I'm just supposed to encourage trolls to be nicer using pally corporate speak. I have never said 'bantz' or 'chill pill' in my life, but there is a script. I can't keep it up though. How is this a life? Trawling a website for badly spelled abuse and begging people to stop being pricks? I hate myself. Luke

Alice Edwards
Replying to AWOL MODERATOR
| You deserve better than this, Luke.

Looking around, my insides hurt from longing for this place. Not the house itself – but everything it represents. A family home. A safe space. The things themselves, too, so old and familiar. So full of my childhood. So full of memories I'd forgotten.

The picture on the wall of me smiling widely at school sports day, and how I cried forever after it was taken because I dropped my egg minutes before the egg and spoon race.

Those chairs over there, which Mum used to build a den for us, draping sheets across them, and jumping out to surprise us when we got home from school. And then Hannah saying she was too old to play, but caving ten minutes later when she saw KitKats being brought in.

That clock in the corner that belonged to my grandma. We were all convinced it was haunted so Mark and I did a ouija board underneath it once, and ran out screaming when a 'demon' came through called – with hindsight fairly suspiciously – 'Mark'.

The ancient computer in the corner – the 'family computer' – that I would bet good money still operates on a dial-up modem. Just looking at it, I can hear the sounds it would make. That awful, shrieking, whirring noise it made as it climbed slowly, tortured, online. I can still feel the excitement of waiting for it, waiting to visit chat rooms to flirt with teenage boys, who were definitely actually predatory fifty-year-old men living in studio flats.

Even the crisps Mum has just brought in – emptied out into the 'special visitor bowls' – are making me emotional. I blink hard as I remember Mum shouting at the three of us that time for raiding the pantry a week before Christmas. We had opened the 'Christmas crisps', bought to be consumed only in that vacuum time period between Christmas Eve and New Year's Eve. Even though we never once got through all the food she'd bought for the festive period.

And yes, there are the bad memories here, too. The ones

I don't want to remember. But I'm realising now that I have blocked out all the good memories along with the bad. I have blocked out how much my mum loved us.

I came straight here after my encounter with Constance/ Janet Janet and standing on the doorstep again, I found that the fear was gone. I was suddenly way more afraid of staying in my safe space. Afraid of never moving forward or changing things. We all get so stuck – trapped – in fear-glue. It's such a human thing to stay forever in a miserable position rather than chance changing things.

I felt sorry for Janet Janet back there, but it also hit me so hard that she could change her life if she wanted. She's put up all these barriers in her mind. She's convinced herself there is no escape from her lovely prison, but of course there is. She has so many choices and options if she took a step back and actually looked at her life, instead of just focusing on feeling sorry for herself. And maybe she will change things, but I suspect not.

It's like me. For years I've been so sure ignoring my mum – pretending she didn't exist – was the only right way, the only answer. I've felt so very sorry for myself. I have comforted myself by pretending I am the only sad one in this situation. I told myself that I was the only one brave enough to take the right and only path. But of course there are so many answers – so many right and wrong paths. Everything is right and everything is wrong.

And now I want to try making things better. Which also might be the wrong thing! Maybe I won't ever be able to truly forgive my mum – maybe she won't ever be able to truly forgive me – but I want to try.

*

It was Hannah who answered the door when I finally knocked, and I have never seen her so slack-jawed.

'Alice ...' she said, utterly bewildered. 'What are you ... are you really here?'

I smiled, tight-lipped, trying not to cry. 'I'm really here, Hannah.'

Still she didn't move. 'But how ... when ...?' she trailed off and then she suddenly leaned forward out of the door, looking around me suspiciously. 'Are *they* forcing you to come here?' she said in an urgent whisper. 'Are you being held hostage, Alice? Blink twice if you need help.'

I blinked once, in slow-motion, before I burst out laughing, pushing past her. 'Hannah you dick, stop reading Reddit.'

Mum looked up as I came through the living-room door, and promptly dropped her full cup of tea all over the carpet. The ensuing running about for a 'blue cloth' rather distracted from the moment, but Hannah – who had followed me in – quickly took control of the situation.

'Mum, stop,' Hannah said simply, and she did. Freezing in place on her knees, mid-mopping at the huge stain across the thick beige carpeting, Mum sat back on her heels, down there on the floor, and looked at me, properly this time.

And then she doubled over and cried.

For a moment, I didn't know what to do. And then of course I knew what to do. I took three steps across the carpet to my mum, knelt on the floor beside her – next to the giant tea stain – and I cried too.

We knelt there for ages, side by side, holding each other, clinging on, and crying so hard. We didn't say anything, because what do you say in situations like that? Sorry? That's not the right word. Of course I know we are both sorry, but we are also both not sorry. We both did what we needed to do, what we had to do, and it tore us apart. But we still love each other. That wasn't in doubt.

After a few minutes I was vaguely aware of Hannah near us, silently clearing up the mess, while Mum and I cried it all out. The years of sadness and distance took a while to drain away.

I was the first to stop, my head aching fiercely. I was already dehydrated from the flight's air-con and, after crying harder than I had in years, I'm pretty sure there was no liquid left in me.

Mum reached for my hand, simultaneously wiping her face with her blouse. We studied each other intensely then, for the first time in years.

She looked the same, but also different. A little older, of course, but also plumper. It suits her. She was always so thin – so thin with the stress of Steven. I don't know what has gone on these last few months – or last few years – but she has found a way to eat. Maybe him being incapacitated has freed her at last. Maybe she has finally felt able to eat more Christmas crisps.

'Hello,' I said shakily, half laughing with the strangeness of the word.

'Hello Alice,' she said, and her eyes welled up again.

'Don't,' I said with a wobble. 'You'll set me off again.'

'I can't believe you're here,' she breathed and squeezed my hand so hard.

We stared at each other for another long second and then I looked down.

'I'm sorry about Steven,' I said at last, and I meant it.

Because Steven wasn't – isn't – a bad man. Not really. That's what I have realised in the last couple of months.

People aren't bad or good, everyone is both, and everyone is trying to do what they think is right in their own small, selfish way. Steven didn't want his life to go the way it did, of course he didn't. Nobody would want that. He was powerless, just like the rest of us.

I've spent a long time sneering at the idea that alcoholics have an 'illness'. When you're up close and personal with something like that for a long time, it feels so much like that person is choosing the bottle over you, but it's never that simple. I know Steven didn't want this to happen, just like I didn't want it to happen. Sure, he was weak, and so was Mum, but weakness is something I understand. I understand it all too well. It is so hard, so tiring, to be strong. We have to be strong through so much of our lives. Being strong all the time is so much, too much, to ask of human beings.

She nodded. 'I'm sorry about Steven, too,' she said in a quiet voice and she didn't mean his stroke.

I helped her up on her feet, and we laughed as we shook off the pins and needles in our legs.

'Let me get some snacks,' she said, dabbing her eyes again and shaking off the hysteria that had threatened to overwhelm the both of us. 'You must be hungry.'

That's when she went to get the crisps because she is a mum, and mums know snacks can heal everything.

'How is he?' I say slowly, munching on a ready-salted own brand as we finally sit down together on the sofa a few minutes later. It still has the same old familiar blanket thrown over the back, and it still smells the same.

Mum clears her throat. 'We don't have to talk about Steven, if you'd rather not?' she says kindly.

I consider it. 'No,' I shake my head. 'I want to. I've spent too long pretending he isn't a part of my life – a part of my family – but he is. I'm not saying I want to forgive and forget everything, but I do really want to know how he's doing.'

She nods, smiling carefully. 'I understand, my love.' She pauses. 'He is awake,' she says and I breathe in, unsure how to feel. 'He woke up a couple of weeks ago, but he's still at the hospice. He can't talk or move much yet. It's going to be a long road to recovery, and we won't know for a while just how bad it'll be. But the doctors say he's out of danger of . . . passing away now.'

I bite my nail. I don't know if this constitutes good news or not, really.

'Are you doing OK?' I say and Mum takes my hand again, giving a quick nod.

'It's been very difficult,' she says, her voice breaking a little. 'Emotionally difficult, I mean.' She pauses. 'Actually, to be honest, in a lot of ways, it's been easier without him here because . . .' she falters. 'Well, you know.'

I do know. I can imagine very well the difference between being a full-time carer to a life-long alcoholic and the full-time carer of a life-long alcoholic who is in hospital, barely conscious.

Mum lifts her head up and continues. 'At the moment, Steven can't do much, but the doctors say it is possible he'll get better. It's a long process, waiting to see how much his brain can repair itself and make new pathways. But I'm hoping to be able to bring him home soon. I want to have him here if I can, I want to be able to look after him.'

'Like always,' I say simply, but there isn't any resentment in my voice. I know that Mum will always do that for him. I can't punish her for that.

She looks at me. 'What happened?' she asks, sounding so sad. 'You were there one minute and gone the next. I lost you. What happened?'

I stare at the floor, at the wet patch from the tea.

'It was everything,' I say at last. 'The years of watching you suffer . . . I couldn't do that forever. But the final straw was the day I broke up with Kit and you wouldn't come. I needed you and you wouldn't come. You chose Steven, when I was more heartbroken than I'd ever been before. I've never needed my mum more than that day and you wouldn't come. I knew then that you'd never be there for me like I needed. I don't blame you any more, but it felt impossible to keep going on that road.'

She frowns. 'But I didn't know you needed me,' she says, sounding perplexed. 'You didn't tell me. You sent me that one text saying you'd split up, but I didn't even know you loved him. Why didn't you tell me how upset you were? I tried to call you, I emailed, I texted . . .'

I shake my head, trying not to get angry. 'I did call you!' I raise my voice, upset at the memory. 'I called and messaged you so many times. I was a mess. It was humiliating.'

She takes my hands in hers, and she is shaking.

'Alice,' she says carefully, her white face close to mine. 'You listen to me.' She breathes in deeply, shakily. 'You didn't. You texted me once, saying you'd broken up with Kit, and that you were OK – that I shouldn't worry. I would've come, of course I would have. I would always be there for you. If I'd known you needed me. You didn't give me the chance to choose you. You are remembering this wrong, my darling. I didn't even know you were serious with that boy until Mark told me, weeks later. And by then, you wouldn't answer my messages.'

We fall silent. Is that right? Have I really built this up in my head over the years into something it wasn't? I was such a mess in those weeks after I broke up with Kit. My head was all over the place. I remember sending that first text to Mum and then . . .? But I must've . . . I was so used to protecting her by then, maybe I did tell her not to worry. I was sure she had failed me but what if I didn't give her the chance? How could I be so stupid.

'I'm so sorry,' Mum says, watching my face. 'I'm so, so sorry, Alice. I can't . . . I had no idea. I would've been there, I swear I would've . . . Oh, my darling girl, I'm so sorry you had to go through that alone. I can't believe . . .' Her voice breaks and I squeeze her hand.

'It's my fault,' I say simply. 'I had this idea that you should be able to tell I needed you. And I didn't think you would come anyway, I didn't trust you to come, so I didn't tell you. And then I think I built it up in my head over the years to protect myself. To stop myself from ever having to be the one at fault.'

I look again around the room, at all the mementos of our lives before all this. Photos, keepsakes, souvenirs. Evidence of my mum's love.

'I'm really sorry,' I say, shaking hard, as the tears start rolling down my face again. She reaches up to wipe them away with her thumb and the gesture is too much. I cry hard and she pulls me in.

'You're really here,' she murmurs into my ear. 'You're really here. This makes everything better, Alice. There is nothing I can't do with you back here by my side, back as a part of my life. My Alice, my wonderful Alice.' Her voice is thick. 'I don't know if this is real, is this real? I don't know if you are.' She touches my face and a tear makes its way down her creased cheek.

'You are,' she whispers. 'You are real, and you're really here. I've missed you so much, my darling child.'

We sit there for a long time then, crying and holding hands.

30

AWOL.COM/Alice Edwards' Travel Blog

6 July – 9.45 a.m.

Someone is going to need to explain to me how this is 'winter' in Australia. I'm sweating my balls off.

  Axx

5 Comments · 76 AWOLs · 135 Super Likes

COMMENTS:

Kirpa Saul
| Nothing like a Brit abroad for moaning about lovely weather.

Hollie Baker
| Lol, lol! You don't have balls!! Do you??

Karen Gill
| Meanwhile, it's July in the UK and three degrees Celsius.

   Alice Edwards
   Replying to Karen Gill
   | I miss three degrees. I miss wearing socks.

Hannah Edwards
| haha u will get used 2 it! sooo happy ur here.

I have barely slept.

And I feel better than I have in years.

Mum and I stayed up all night, talking. Not about The Bad Stuff, but about our lives, about who we are now, and the things we have missed. I wanted so much for her to *know* me, to know everything about me. I told her all the stupid inane stuff about my life without her: what time I get up in the morning; what I have for breakfast; how my favourite shoes are too small for me but how I still wear them because they have a pineapple embroidered on the front. I told her about the work I'd been doing for the dodgy politician – and how I'd ruined it all with my drunken thirtieth life-crisis text. I left nothing out. I even told her how my last dentist appointment went (only one filling but I made a huge fuss).

It was like I'd been storing everything up for her, holding it ready for this reunion. She listened, enraptured for hours, firing questions when I left out any detail, asking what the weather was like on any one day I was describing so she could better picture it. She didn't let go of my hand the whole time.

And we talked about her, too. I'm finally able to talk about Steven without wincing and we did talk about him. A lot. Mum told me about the move over here. How things have still been difficult these last few years, but that he has been slowly getting better. He had managed to cut down on the drinking; he was not disappearing on benders so much. He was more loving, he was shouting less, he was going to meetings. He was more grateful for Mum's love. Maybe he was softening with old age, or maybe the fresh start in a new country had finally shaken him free of something. Not altogether of course – he was still drinking every day – but what they had between them was on its way to being something almost like a life. But then of course, just as hope was beginning to flower, the

297

stroke happened. For Mum, that has been the hardest part of all this. Just when she thought she might get her Steven back – after twenty years of slow-burn devastation – this new kind of devastation happened.

But she is hopeful. And she is also very used to being a carer. So she will be OK if and when he comes home. And I get it. I understand. Life is not black and white.

We finally crashed out together on the sofa at about 5 a.m., and I woke up with a dry mouth, feeling like I had the worst hangover ever. But also feeling great.

I didn't want to leave Mum this morning, and she was on the verge of calling in sick to her work as a receptionist at a local school, but I said no.

I had to go see Mark.

He's here, staying at a nearby hotel. I don't know if Hannah's told him I'm here, too, but I have to go see him. I need to make up with him and make sure we're OK. Our fight has been hanging over me for weeks, following me around Thailand like a bad smell. We've never gone this long without talking and it all seems so silly and pointless now. Of course he was right, I needed to forgive Mum, but I also had to get there – here – on my own. We both knew I was coming here eventually, but I had to do it slowly. I had to figure it out for myself.

Hannah gave me the hotel address with Mark's room number, and – standing outside yet another door, feeling the same nerves in my belly as I knock – I almost burst out laughing.

Mark opens up immediately, and doesn't look surprised to see me.

He doesn't dramatically spill tea on the floor, or anything.

'Hi,' I say, feeling weird because I never say hi to my brother. He's my brother. Usually we enter a room immediately halfway through a sentence. We don't need formalities or small talk, we have history.

He smiles tightly and nods for me to follow him in.

I clear my throat and begin as I take in his room. 'So I think maybe I'm the favourite child now,' I say, aiming for a light, teasing tone but my voice comes out a bit strained. 'Mum's insisting I stay at the house while I'm in Oz. Meanwhile you're stuck here, in this lame-ass hotel.'

He laughs, and flops down on a sofa at the foot of his bed. 'True enough, but your beloved status is only temporary,' he says casually as I take a seat next to him. 'Once the novelty of your reappearance wears off, she'll be back to worshipping at the feet of her darling only son and heir.'

I snort and then we smile nicely at each other.

Phew. Things are going to be OK.

'I really . . .' I start and then my phone loudly beeps from my coat pocket.

We laugh at the interruption.

'Get it,' he says, and I reach in my pocket.

It's a text.

From LA Noah. The producer.

'Woah!' I exclaim and Mark leans in, excited. I show him the name. 'It's that guy. LA Noah! The one who seemed so keen when I was there – texting me every day – but then just never asked me out.'

Mark is nodding, he remembers.

'I haven't heard from him in ages,' I muse.

'For the love of fuck, just open it already,' he says, exasperated. I click on the message and start reading it silently. It's long.

'Out loud,' he snaps and I clear my throat.

'So, hi,' I read. 'It's me, Noah, that guy you've already forgotten about from your first night in LA. I hope this isn't too unwelcome a message. I don't know if you want to hear from me, but – forgive me this cliché – I felt like there was some unfinished business between us.'

Mark interrupts me with a whoop, which I ignore. This is a lengthy message and we're just getting started.

'I know my behaviour was kind of weird when you were in LA,' I continue reading. 'But I'll be honest and hope this doesn't sound like some stupid line; I was in a bad place after my divorce. The fact is, I really liked you, I wanted to talk to you all night and I haven't felt a connection like that in years. And believe me, I kept wanting to ask you out during those next few weeks. I loved our text conversations, they made me laugh so much. But I kept chickening out. I knew my head was in too much of a mess. And you were only there a few weeks. It sounds heavy, but I didn't want to risk falling for you. It was too much to chance when I was still so fragile.'

Mark lets out a low whistle and I stop to stare at him, open-mouthed. This is so out of the blue. I can't believe it.

There's more.

'Listen Alice, I know this seems ridiculous, and out of nowhere, but things are a lot better with my head these days. I've been having therapy (I live in LA so of course I've been having therapy). It's helped a lot. I feel much more sorted, and I at least wanted to explain myself to you. The cliché applies: It wasn't you, it was me. And I'm sorry for that. There is one more thing . . . I'm coming to the UK for work in September and I wondered if I could finally take you out on a date?' He's finished with a sweet single x.

Mark shrieks. 'Is that the end of it? Essay much, Noah?' I

nod, completely flummoxed. He takes the phone off me and silently re-reads the text. His eyebrows shoot up as he reaches the end.

'Phew,' he says, putting the phone down at last, his perfectly arched brows on the ceiling.

'So, what do you think?' he says, before adding, 'This guy actually sounds pretty on the level to me. The message is a bit OTT, but feels heartfelt and honest, don't you think? How do you feel?' He looks at me expectantly and I giggle.

'Um,' my head is spinning. 'I don't really know. He's so good-looking, and we had some great chats on WhatsApp. He makes me laugh, but . . .' I pause. 'I think he might bore me, to be honest.'

Mark cocks his head at me. 'Why?' he says, looking puzzled.

Why? That's an interesting question. Why do I think Noah might bore me?

Mark continues, not waiting for me to get to the answer myself.

'Do you think it might be because you're used to dickheads?' he says, and his tone is a little cold. 'Do you think it might be because you have decided somewhere inside you that "nice" – someone who doesn't treat you like pond scum – must be boring? You've decided that a relationship without drama isn't a real relationship. That "love" has to be traumatic and awful? You've been so trained by that prick TD and Kit before him – so brainwashed into thinking *that* is love – you think that someone who is simply kind and sweet to you can't be serious or real?'

Oof. I guess there is some residual resentment here between us, after all.

'Like, that shitty Bumble date you told me about in LA,' he says, and he's suddenly very angry. 'Why the fucking fuck

301

did you not leave the moment he called you *fat*? I know you don't care about that word, but that's not the point, is it? He was trying to be cruel and you took it, happily. It's like you want to be punished, like you wanted to stay and be flagellated some more. You even told me beforehand that he was a dirtbag – you actually said that's what you wanted – and then you complained when that's exactly what he was. It's absolute bullshit, Alice.'

'All right, Jesus!' I say, my voice raised. 'Don't hold back, will you? Do you want to dissect my faults any more? I left the date eventually.'

He grabs me by the shoulders and looks at me sternly. 'Alice, I'm serious. You specifically choose men who fuck you over. You stick around and let them treat you like shit. You even did it with the trolls on your dumb pretentious blog. How long did it take you to block all those losers calling you names and threatening to rape you? Months! Why? Because somewhere early on – naming no names, er, MUM – you watched a relationship where a woman was treated badly and used up by her partner, and you learnt *that* was love. You learnt that you didn't deserve something decent and good.' He is almost shouting.

Everything in me is fighting back against his words. My chest is tight and my hands are shaking. I don't want to listen; I don't want to hear it. Tears start rolling down my cheeks, but he doesn't stop.

'I've had enough of watching you push people away – I'm sick of it,' he says and he does sound sick of it. His whole voice is weary and sick. 'You have the patience of a saint when it comes to shitty people like TD, but you walk away from the people who actually care about you. Or you're mean to them, like you are with Eva.'

'What?' I am shocked. 'I'm not mean to Eva!'

'You can be, Alice,' he insists, but he says it a little more kindly. 'You say things harshly and laugh at her when she mentions her horoscopes or memes. She would never tell you this herself, but it hurts her when you're critical of her. When you mock her family. I've seen that look on her face when you laugh at her. You have a tendency to be overly critical. You don't seem to realise that things can really cut. You push people away because something in you thinks they're going to leave you, and you figure you might as well shove them off the cliff before they jump.'

I am reeling. That's not true. I tease Eva, but it's how we've always been. We joke around. I don't *push* her off *cliffs* for God's sake! Except I did push her away, didn't I? I know I did, I admitted to it. The moment it seemed like she might be leaving me, I left her. OK, so yes, I am afraid of people leaving me. But isn't everyone?

'What about you then, Mark?' I say and I am fighting back tears. I thought I was all cried out last night, but apparently not. 'Because yes, I might push people away or date idiots occasionally, but you avoid love altogether. Is that any better? Pretending that part of life doesn't exist at all – is that healthy? You haven't dated anyone in twenty years, Mark. Is that normal?'

'Better than going out with morons, like you do,' he spits.

'Maybe, maybe not, Mark,' I say, but some of the fight has drained out of me. All of a sudden I just feel tired and sad. 'It isn't even the lack of dating, Mark,' I say quietly. 'If you were happy on your own, I wouldn't care about it, but you never even talk to me about it. It makes me feel so awful that you don't want to share that part of your life with me. We are so close and I've never wanted to push you into talking about things if you didn't want to, but I feel really crap about it.'

There is silence between us, and at last he reaches over and takes my hand.

'Stop making this all about you,' he says at last, and he sniggers.

'Stop making it not all about me,' I laugh at the callback to our last fight in Thailand. The tension between us eases. I sniff loudly. 'I know you're right about me pushing the good people in my life away,' I admit, slowly. 'But I'm working on it. And I'm done with the shitheads, I promise. I blocked the online trolls, didn't I? I haven't even thought about TD in weeks. I think I'm genuinely over him, at last. And I'll go on a date with Noah back in London I promise. You're right, I have this shitty brainwashing thing that tells me love can only be fucked up. He isn't actually boring, he's nice.'

I pause. 'And I'll stop being mean to Eva. I feel awful, I didn't realise it bothered her.'

He nods. 'I don't think it does, not really,' he concedes. 'She adores you, and you are a good friend. She's just so sweet and innocent, I sometimes worry that you will hurt her without realising. You're so smart, Alice, and I don't think you notice how your words can be hurtful.' There is a heavy silence, while we both consider things.

'And I'm sorry I haven't talked to you about my love life,' he says at last, staring at the floor. 'I don't know how or why I've ended up here. As this person. I guess . . . well, I was shy – a late starter – when it came to accepting myself. I was afraid of what being gay meant. Steven's Neanderthal tendencies didn't help. When he got drunk he would use nasty words, call me a "fag" and stuff, so I was scared to actually come out to him and Mum for a long time. And then I think *not talking* became a habit. I have been afraid of sharing things. Plus,

Mum and Steven's dysfunctional relationship affected me, too, of course it did. You only went out with awful men – that was your take home from them. Me, I assumed all men were awful and avoided them altogether. Neither of us have been very healthy when it comes to our relationships, have we?'

He smiles at me now, my cocky, silly, funny brother.

I shake my head slowly and lean my head on his shoulder.

'Right,' he takes a deep breath. 'Enough of this shouting at each other. We're both fucked up, but who isn't, right? And let's make a pact to make more of an effort to be ever so slightly *less* messed up in future. You're going to stop pushing people away and be kinder. I'm going to start dating, and actually talk to you about my romantic endeavours. And if we can't manage not to be dicks, we'll at least always talk to each other about it, OK?'

'OK, agreed,' I say, feeling emotional but happy.

'So then, what are you going to reply to Noah?' he says decisively, taking my phone off me. 'Let's compose a text, and then . . .' he takes another big, deep breath. 'Then, I think you should help me write a text.'

I look up at him, my smile getting bigger.

'To Joe?' I say hopefully and he nods shyly.

'To Joe,' he confirms.

31

Update from AWOL's CEO, Kyle: Hey guys! Just a quick message as many of you have contacted our moderators to say you're worried about AWOL's Troll Police Chief, Luke. Not to worry, he has been temporarily taken off duty for R&R and further training, but he will soon be back online to handle any of your probs!!!! Cheers for listening, all you AWOLers out there!!!! Take it easy guys, and I'm here if you want to chat, chill or blue sky. Kyle x

AWOL.COM/Alice Edwards' Travel Blog

12 July – 1.22 p.m.

HULLO.

I'm still in Australia and it's still hot.

I'm just here to say that I've put my mum on AWOL because I thought it would be funny. Everyone follow her @FionaEdwards, but please don't send her porn because that wouldn't be funny. Or would it?

6 Comments · 153 AWOLs · 239 Super Likes

COMMENTS:

> **Alice Edwards**
> **Replying to Alice Edwards**
> | For real tho, it wouldn't be funny.

Eva Slate

| Welcome to AWOL, @FionaEdwards! So glad you're here with us.

> **Alice Edwards**
> **Replying to Eva Slate and Fiona Edwards**
> | I'm glad too :)

Fiona Edwards

| Dear Alice, I hope you are well. Thank you for helping me to join the AWOL. I am now following @MariahCarey and @kanyewest and have asked them to message me about a possible duet. I will let you know when they reply to me. Yours lovingly, your mum xxxxxx

> **Alice Edwards**
> **Replying to Fiona Edwards**
> | I'm sure it'll be any second now.

Karen Gill

| Right, that's it, I'm putting Mammy on here. We can have an AWOL mammy-off.

'HELP ME I'M GOING TO FALL,' Mum is screaming from the rock face, sweating as she clings on, frozen and clammy-faced. Except she is maybe two and a half feet up, and nobody told her to climb up it.

'OK, down you get,' I say as nicely as I can, pulling her off by her backpack. She collapses dramatically to the ground.

'I don't think we should rock climb, after all,' she says, as I offer her my hand and hoist her up.

'Good idea, Mum,' I say, trying not to laugh.

Driving to the Blue Mountains National Park was her

idea, but if I'd known she was going to be such a mad person, I'd have left her at home.

It has been a slow, careful and brilliant week. Mum and me have been moving around each other like new friends on a playground. Circling each other warily, sharing eager smiles whenever our eyes meet, spending long nights talking until the early hours.

The big thing is that we both want this to work so much. We are being kind to each other, and both trying really hard. It's so good, so nice. I can't describe how I feel every time I look at her. *Hope* is probably the closest to it.

For the first few days we just hunkered down together in her living room, doing a lot of normal mum-daughter stuff: watching daytime telly, drinking sherry at six o' clock in the evening, and generally worrying about sofa cushions not being plumped enough. But we eventually decided to get out there and do things. So we went to look at Sydney Harbour and the Opera House, where we bickered over whether it looked more like a shark or a toilet roll holder. Cultural chat, y'know.

Then this morning, I woke up to find her and Hannah grinning from ear-to-ear, dressed in what they obviously thought hiking gear looks like. By which I mean, very expensive trainers and khaki-coloured jumpers. Hannah is also wearing what can only be a bee-keeper hat.

'It's dual purpose,' she told me when I asked. 'It keeps out the mosquitoes, but also blocks government radio waves. I bought it online from my NASA contacts.'

'Is your NASA contact also a part-time bee-keeper?' I asked innocently but she ignored me.

The Blue Mountains are an hour's drive from my mum's house in Sydney and I was promised waterfalls, forests, hiking tracks, cliffs, canyons and caves. But mostly so far it's just been Mum trying to do dangerous things and then falling over. Bless her, I think she's trying to impress me.

'C'mon you two,' I say as Mum brushes herself down. 'Let's just go get on the cable car. That's probably enough exertion.'

'Cable cars are too easy to track,' Hannah mutters from underneath her bee-hat.

I pull up the map on my phone to figure out where we are, as Mum strides on ahead, still eager to impress me with her obvious wilderness skills.

I watch her disappear into the trees and feel a surge of love and gratitude. I am so happy we're here together, slightly lost, laughing together. It's so nice.

There have been moments, of course, these last few days, when it hits me how much time we've lost. The guilt screams through me and I am wracked with it. But I refuse to let regret ruin this time. I can't let what's been lost too far into my head. We all make choices, and they are the ones we make. There's no point looking back and wondering what if. We do what we had to do in those moments. I just have to be relieved I was able to overcome my own stubbornness and be here now.

I mean, it's not totally *there* between us. We're not inside a fairy tale, so of course it can't be perfect. A happily ever after is whatever we make it and it takes work. We've missed a lot and there is still a lot left to work through. I know I still have things I need to forgive, and so does Mum. And, honestly, I still don't know really how I feel about Steven. I feel weird every single morning when Mum calls or visits the hospice. I'm not ready to see him because I'm not ready to feel sorry for him, to pity him. I'm not sure if I ever will be ready. Mum says that's OK, and I hope she means it.

Life is complicated but we're trying, which is what matters.

'Oh! Hello there!' she shouts now, from up ahead. Hannah and I follow, almost tripping over a group of people sitting in a clearing, mid yoga class.

'God, sorry to interrupt you . . .' I begin but the instructor is smiling benignly, waving off my apologies.

'Can we join in?' Mum says eagerly, already throwing her bag off her shoulders.

'They're in the middle of things!' I protest weakly but several lotuses have already shouted yes, waving us over and into their midst.

Mum bends forward into a stretch a bit professionally, as I pull off my coat. 'Oh, a bit good, are you?' I say, amused.

'Well actually,' she replies coolly, 'I'm a fully trained yoga teacher.'

She is? Wow, I really have missed a lot. Before I have a chance to reply, the instructor has leapt up. 'That's wonderful news!' she shouts at Mum. 'I've pulled something in my leg, so I'm struggling to effectively lead this class. There's only fifteen minutes left, could you finish them off for me?'

Mum gapes at her, her mouth opening and closing as the limping woman bustles her up to the front.

'It's mostly ashtanga, with just a bit of Iyengar,' she tells Mum casually, waving her hands at the group of thirty-strong yogis. 'And then I was thinking I might end with some core work to release the kundalini energy? Thanks so much!'

She positions my gormless-looking mum at the front, and she looks directly at me, like a rabbit in headlights. It is in that moment that I understand. Of course.

She was faking it. She's not a yoga teacher. It was more of the rock-climbing stuff – more showing off to try and impress me.

I watch in slow motion as Mum gets whiter and whiter, staring dumbly round the expectant group.

She suddenly looks at me again, standing up straighter, a new expression in her eyes. Determination.

Oh fuck.

'Right,' she says, clearing her throat. 'Let's do this then, shall we?'

There is a long pause.

I am seized with panic. What should I do? I glance frantically at Hannah for help, but she doesn't seem worried. She's sitting cross-legged, waiting expectantly. She's still got her bee-keeper hat on.

Mum clears her throat again. 'Right,' she says once more, her voice only faintly shaky. 'OK, you lot. Everyone on all fours.'

The group responds obediently.

She's really doing it, she really is. That's it, Mum's on her own.

'Now,' her voice is high. 'Do a . . . forward roll.'

I spot a couple of people glancing nervously at each other. Three of the teacher's pets at the front do it without question. I couldn't even do a forward roll when I was a kid, so I just sit back and watch.

'Ow,' says a muffled Hannah beside me, who is halfway through the exercise, bee-keeper hat trapped under her boobs.

'Great, er, very well done, everyone,' Mum says, regarding the group again. Off at the side, the original teacher is starting to look a bit nervous.

'Up next,' Mum is nodding confidently now, even smiling a bit. 'Is the downward . . . crouching, um, camel.'

A young woman at the front sticks her hand up like the

goodie-two-shoes she definitely always was at school.

'Excuse me, could you demonstrate that one for us?' she says, looking blank.

Mum stares at her, a little bit hostile. 'I could,' she replies at last. 'But then . . . how will you learn?' She nods over in my direction, like I get it.

'But . . .' the woman looks confused. 'But . . .'

'Oh fine,' Mum snaps impatiently. 'If you really do need babysitting, you can show the class. Stand up on your knees, quick, quick.'

The class suck-up jumps to attention.

'Then . . . just, um, lean right back, into the . . . camel,' Mum says waving vaguely. 'Further, further. Keep going. Now, let me . . .' She reaches for the woman, already stretched oddly, to press on her shoulders.

I see it coming and yet I still sit there, doing nothing, watching it happen. Unable to say anything.

We all hear the crack.

32

12 July – 8.22 p.m.

Hey.

    Does anyone know if Australia has a similar healthcare system to the UK? I mean, just as an example, if we were to, say, dump a person outside an A&E department and drive away, would they get treated for free or turned away for not having insurance? Asking for a friend.

    Ta, Axx

3 Comments · 94 AWOLs · 145 Super Likes

COMMENTS:

> **Eva Slate**
> | What have you been up to?!!

> **Fiona Edwards**
> | Dear Alice, do not worry about a thing, I slipped $30 into her sports bra. Love mum xxxxx

> > **Alice Edwards**
> > **Replying to Fiona Edwards**
> > | So we can add sexual assault to the list of crimes we will be charged with. Great.

'I'm walking in right now,' I type. 'And it's very difficult to walk and type, the only reason this makes any sense is autocorrect. So please stop messaging me, I AM COMING RIGHT NOW.'

I'm not even late for God's sake. Honestly, there was no way I'd be late. I'm too happy and excited about it.

I'm about to meet up with Joe and Mark.

Joe got to Sydney yesterday and they've had a full twenty-four hours together to talk things through and probably do other things – wink. I'm trying not to be too over the top with my enthusiasm because I don't want to scare Mark. He's only just starting to let me into this part of his life and I don't want him running back into his repressed hidey-hole. But I can tell he's happy. Even just on his texts, urging me to hurry up and get to the hotel already, there is an irrepressibly jaunty tone to his sentences. Like he is smiling and he can't help it.

I think, y'know, that he might be in love.

So the other day he finally filled me in on *Joe and Mark's Relationship: The Back Story*.

They've been friends forever, this much I knew. I also knew Joe was madly in love with Mark, but I had no idea for how long. Basically, every now and again, Joe would drunkenly confess his feelings and want to talk about it. But Mark would brush him off, refusing to even discuss the possibility of their friendship becoming something more. He laughed the whole thing off, much like he did with me when I brought it up. So yeah, Joe dated other people and tried to move on, but just ... couldn't. He knew deep down that this was it for him. Mark was his lobster. And for some reason he hung on in there all this time, hoping. Which I swear to God would've never worked for a straight woman, desperately waiting for a man to change his mind – but this is not the time for a rant about sexist double standards and toxic masculinity.

Anyway, it's actually happening at last.

I would really like to be able to take all the credit for sparking this whole love-revelation in Mark – believe me, I tried to take the credit – but, to be honest, it sounds like he'd already pretty much reached the obvious conclusion on his own.

They'd become so much closer travelling around Thailand together, and with hindsight, I think a lot of Mark's grumpiness on the trip was to do with the creeping realisation of his feelings. I guess he was frustrated with himself and struggling to comprehend things. He'd been in denial for so long. But then we went to that Ayahuasca retreat and he says pretty much all of his experiences and hallucinations were centred around Joe.

Which made me feel way better. Sure, maybe I tried to get a selfie with the universe, but at least I didn't waste my experience mooning over a boooooooy.

Either way, it rather forced a more intensive internal conversation for my brother. He could no longer deny how much Joe meant to him.

But because Mark is Mark, still, he fought it.

It was only when me and him had that huge row at the hostel and he stormed off, dragging Joe along with him, that things reached a kind of breaking point. After they left me, they checked into a hotel nearby, where they had their own big fight. Mild-mannered, lovely, ever-patient Joe told Mark that he was being a dick, and that they should never have abandoned me in the middle of Asia. He said it was laughable that Mark told me off for being in denial, when he's been in his own world of denial for years and years. He said he was done, for good this time, and was going to head off to Australia on his own, to travel up the east coast and 'cool off'. He packed his bag and left, telling Mark on his way out that things were going to change between them. He wasn't prepared to be his adoring puppy-dog any more.

Mark told me he sat in that hotel room, fuming and ranting in the mirror about the both of us, before finally coming to some kind of self-realisation. He followed Joe to Australia and waited in Sydney for his true love to come back to him.

I added the true love part, and *je ne regrette rien*.

By the time I arrived in the city and shouted at him about never giving love a chance, he was already ninety-nine point nine per cent of the way there.

Oh, but I'm still going to make a speech at the wedding and tell everyone their relationship is down to me.

Anyway, I'm genuinely thrilled, and can't wait to see the two of them together properly at long last.

I'm bouncing on the spot as I scan the hotel bar and spot them sitting in a corner booth. They are holding hands in that casual way people who have been touching non-stop for days at a time tend to do. It takes me a moment to register the third, random person sitting there in the booth with them, and as I get closer I stop and fully gasp in the middle of the room.

They hear me – apparently I gasp loudly – and all four of us stare at each other from across the room, unblinking.

Shut up.

It is not.

What the fuck. What is GOING ON?

What the fuck is he *doing* here? It is him, isn't it?

This can't actually be real? How is he . . .?

Mark half smiles at me and I can tell he is as baffled as I am.

I slowly make my way over to their booth, but don't sit down.

'What on earth are you doing here?' I say, and my voice doesn't sound like my own.

'I came to see you,' he says simply.

It's Uber driver Dom and I do not understand how it's him on any level.

'What?' I say dumbly and he gestures at me to sit down.

'Hello,' he smiles and after another long moment of silence, he adds, 'OK, don't freak out, I haven't gone full stalker. I have a friend's wedding in Sydney but I probably wouldn't have accepted the invite if not for you. I saw you tagged into this hotel on Instagram, so assumed you were staying here.'

I flop heavily into the booth, no clue what to say as he continues, 'I spotted your brother here in the bar, I recognised him from your pictures. So I came over and introduced myself.'

'I can't believe you're actually here,' I say dumbly. This is so weird. My head is spinning. What is going on? First a message from Noah asking me out, then Dom is here, out of nowhere.

Am I . . . am I secretly a fucking goddess? Guys, I think that must be it.

Or, wait . . . it's way more likely he's got a terrible STD and wants to tell me face-to-face. What would be the worst one to have? Gonorrhoea? That's the one that's popular with footballers, right? I don't know what it does but it's a fucker to spell, so it must have some terrible symptoms.

'Hello you,' Joe interrupts my shock, jumping up and giving me a long hug. He pulls me closer and whispers in my ear protectively, 'Is he nuts? Want me to escort him out?'

'Um, maybe?' I murmur back, still not sure what to think. 'Give him five minutes and then we'll reassess.' He starts to pull away and I grip him closer again. 'It's really good to see you, Joe,' I add, my voice thick with emotion. I haven't forgotten why I'm here. He gives me an acknowledging squeeze. I can feel his happiness radiating off him. He deserves this more than anyone.

I clear my throat as I slide into the booth beside Dom, no idea what to do next. To his credit, Dom does look uncomfortable. Like he regrets making an impulsive and bizarre decision without thinking it through.

The thing is, I did actually hear from him a couple of times after he had that tantrum on the rollercoaster and stormed off like a child. We actually settled things, we left it on goodish terms. He said he was sorry for his jealous rage and I told him it sucked but it was OK. Then he'd said something about wanting to see me again before I left LA and I pointed out that I'd already long-since left LA. I also reminded him that, fun as it was spending time with him, it was only ever meant to be a short-term thing and that it was best to draw a line under it now. We could be pals on Facebook or whatever – and then never speak again, like every other person in the world who's had a holiday fling.

And I meant it. So I'm not sure what he's doing here now.

'Shall I get us some drinks?' I say into the awkward silence.

Mark nods and Dom pipes up, 'I'll come with you.'

We wander towards the bar and I half automatically reach for the keys in my handbag. Just in case. Because maybe I've misjudged the fuck out of this dude. Maybe he's actually insane? You never really know someone, do you? You always see these wives on telly being like, 'I had no clue my husband was holding seventy-two women captive in our basement, I thought it was cats down there and the excessive electricity bill was because of our outdoor heater.'

I spent weeks with this man, day in, day out, but what do I really know about him? Like, does he have seventy-two women in a basement somewhere? *Does he have an outdoor heater?*

'Seriously, Uber Driver,' I clear my throat, stopping just short of the bar. 'What are you doing here? Did you get an international fare that was too good to miss?' I say, keeping my tone light, but gripping the keys between my fingers. I'm so glad Mark and Joe are nearby.

'It's the big romantic gesture, isn't it?' he says, grinning. 'Like in the movies. I'm here to declare that I'm in love with you and we should be together.'

I laugh, I can't help it. What the hell is he talking about?

'You're not in love with me, you moron! We had a few weeks of sex!' I say, waving my hand. 'It's the chemicals and blue balls talking.'

'It's not!' he shakes his head. 'I know you didn't mean what you said in that text, I know you really like me.'

'Dom,' I take a deep breath, 'I wasn't, like, *testing* you when I said that I wasn't interested. It wasn't me playing hard to get or trying to upset you. It wasn't a *ploy* to make you try harder. I've realised I hate all those kinds of games, they're boring and get you nowhere. I've spent years doing that with my ex and I hate it. Never again. I sent that message because I wanted to be honest with you. We had a fun time and, sure, I like you as a person – occasional jealous rages aside – but I was only ever there for a month. It was what it was, nothing more. I'm sorry.'

Ugh, I hate that we teach men that persistence will get them whatever they want. That 'no' means, 'keep trying', and that it is 'romantic' to stalk a woman halfway across the world after she's already said she doesn't want to date you. I just really want to live in a world where men believe a woman when she says nah.

'OK, just hear me out,' he says, undeterred. 'Alice, I understand what you're saying, but I think you're wrong. You must see it too – it's so obvious that we're right for each other! I know it.' Inspiration strikes him and he adds, 'We're both 3.5s! Our Uber rating! We are life's 3.5 types. We will never be rich or famous or particularly cool. We are middle-of-the-road people, average. We are the same level, the same type! And that's why we should be together. We need each other because we are a 3.5 match. The 3.5s belong together.'

I consider this.

I'm a 3.5? Am I though? Is that how he sees me?

Hold on.

OK, maybe I am a 3.5, but I want to meet someone who sees me as a full five stars. Or more! I want to meet someone one day who sees me as worth more stars than the Uber system is capable of awarding. That doesn't seem like too low a bar to set. And here is Dom, telling me we should settle for each other because we're both only OK. I get it, it makes some kind of warped sense – and if this were three months ago, I think I would've jumped on the offer. Something in me would've liked that he was putting me down and offering to keep me down. But not any more. Getting a 3.5 offer is not enough for me. It shouldn't be enough for anyone.

'I see what you're saying,' I tell him slowly, kindly. 'But I don't want to be a 3.5. If you and me settle for each other, we will always stay at that level. We won't ever try to be better versions of ourselves. If I'm with someone, I need them to be someone who brings out the best in me – a guy who makes me a five, Dom. And more than that, I want to be a five on my own.'

He looks defeated. 'But I . . .'

'Thank you for your interest,' I add robotically like a sales assistant. 'But no, thank you.'

He sags but nods. 'OK Alice,' he says nicely. 'I understand, and thanks, I guess, for being honest with me. I'm really sorry for turning up like this. I know I seem all over the place. I just felt like such a fool for the way I acted, and wanted to do the grand gesture thing. I feel a little silly now.' He laughs nervously.

'Don't feel silly!' I say. 'It's nice to see you – as a friend – and if you don't have to rush off, it would be great to have a catch up. My brother and his boyfriend over there are celebrating, and you're very welcome to join us!' I pause and add, 'Seriously, Uber Driver, I had such a wonderful time with you. I'll never forget it. You made my LA adventure something really special. Plus . . .' I laugh, '. . . I will always be grateful to you for helping me realise there is more out there than my stupid ex.'

He smiles but it is a thin smile. 'You know,' he says sighing. 'It really hurt me every time you openly texted him in front of me. And the way you would joke about using me to get over him?'

I am stung. 'Huh? But you always laughed! I thought it was part of what we were doing? It was, y'know, part of our shtick!'

He sighs. 'I smiled because it hurt, Alice. Don't you know anything about human behaviour? We smile through our pain. We laugh when we are hurt.'

Well that is true enough. And stupid enough.

'Oh my God, Uber Driver, I'm so sorry,' I say, meaning it. 'I've been realising lately that sometimes I can be thoughtlessly mean and unkind. I'm working on it.'

'Also, please don't call me Uber Driver,' he says a little haughtily. 'My name is Dom. Calling me Uber Driver is very dehumanising.'

'Oh, cripes, I'm so sorry.' I am mortified.

'And never say "cripes" again,' he says, but now he is smiling properly. 'Because that is really embarrassing.'

'Right, yes,' I smile back. 'I don't know where that came from. Sometimes Americans bring out the British in me.'

'Yeah,' he says laughing. 'I didn't think Brits ever really said "gosh" until I met you. You are one of a kind.'

'To be fair, they don't,' I confirm. 'I only say things like "cripes" or "gosh" in America, never in England. It's like a chat-up line to make the Yanks melt.'

We grin at each other and it is OK. I am relieved. The grip on my keys loosens and I step towards the bar.

'Let's get drunk together one last time,' I say, leaning towards the barman to order shots.

33

25 July – 1.47 p.m.

Hello out there, if anyone is listening.

I know I haven't been posting proper blogs lately, and I don't really have an excuse. Life? Busy-ness? Intense laziness?

(Copy and paste those excuses for literally everything.)

The truth is, I'm realising blogging is probably just not me. I can't spell for shit, I use thesaurus.com at least twice a day, and I still don't know how to upload a photo that isn't upside down. It's not *me*.

Ha.

Not that I know who or what 'me' is – does anyone? God, we spend so much time chasing this idea of *finding yourself*. But aren't all selves a bit of everything? My *me* changes every day. Some days I am a kind, nice, happy person. Other days I'm a selfish, heinous, miserable bitch. Just like everyone, surely? I am not one thing, and it was silly to think I could find a box to put myself in.

I also wanted to say sorry for all that pretentious, forced stuff I wrote before. I thought it was what I was supposed to do as a blogger. It was stupid, but also, most of what I wrote was non-sense. Yes, this trip has been fun and an adventure, but it's also been rubbish at times. I've been bored and disappointed a whole bunch – just like I was at home – and all my problems were still waiting for me at the end of it. I've realised that travelling is great as an experience in and of itself – a great distraction – but it can't *fix* you. It can't fix problems when the problems are inside.

So anyway, this is my last post on here. I'll go back to Instagram, where I almost post something every day and then chicken out because at the last second it doesn't seem worth posting. Yay.

In the meantime, me, Hannah, Mark, Joe and Mum are off up the east coast for some scuba diving. Hannah and Mum have lived here for years and never visited the Great Barrier Reef because they are clearly straight up monsters. I feel fairly confident my first time underwater I will hyperventilate, run out of air, get a nose bleed, and be eaten by a shark. So this was probably going to be my final blog either way.

Bye everyone. Thanks for listening, look after yourselves.

Alice x

15 Comments · 385 AWOLs · 326 Super Likes

COMMENTS:

Mark Edwards
| I'm going to push you off the boat at the first hint of a shark nest.

Alice Edwards
Replying to Mark Edwards
| Obviously my official party line is: please don't do that. But off record: omg how cool would that be as a way to die.

Karen Gill
Replying to Alice Edwards and Mark Edwards
| Finally. Me and mammy have been waiting months for this.

Hannah Edwards
Replying to Mark Edwards
| there's a boat?? no 1 told me there was a boat???? i am not going on a boat

> **Alice Edwards**
> **Replying to Hannah Edwards**
> | Hannah, what did you think a reef was?

> > **Eva Slate**
> > **Replying to Alice Edwards**
> > | Isn't it marijuana????

> > **Alice Edwards**
> > **Replying to Eva Slate**
> > | You're thinking of a reefa, and only if this was 2003.

Fiona Edwards
| Hello Alice. And hello @DanniiMinogue and @kylieminogue. Any advice on what to see in Cairns? We will be staying in the area for a week if you are free for a coffee. Love, Fiona Edwards xx

Clara Weber
| If you're diving, swim on back to Thailand please. Miss you.

Hollie Baker
| G8 barrier reef is supposed to be really pretty!

Ayo Damiunse
| Tourists like you are ruining nature and killing the wildlife.

Isabelle Moore
| Have fun! Just don't trust anyone during your travels because you'll only get betrayed.

Alice Edwards
Replying to Isabelle Moore
| u ok hun :(

Noah Deer
| When are you going to be back in the UK already?!

Alice Edwards
Replying to Noah Deer
| Soon enough Noah. Now stop trying to flirt with me on AWOL, it's too attention seeking and my mum is watching.

Oh my God, Mum is screaming at the top of her lungs. It is seriously eardrum-perforating levels.

It's the karaoke staple, *You're So Vain*, and she is off-key in the extreme. She is so into the chorus – her eyes screwed up and sweat beading her forehead – that she forgets the song has a whole other verse. The music bops along nonetheless and she looks around her, suddenly helpless. Off stage, the karaoke compere hisses the next bit of the song at her.

Joe bounces up on stage to save Mum and they find the words just in time for the final chorus to pick up again. The pair of them fully howl the final 'don't-yous', looking down happily at me, Mark and Hannah who are dancing like mad. We are all grinning our heads off.

I have to say, this is a side of my mum I was not expecting to discover during my time here in Australia.

It's been a busy, family-filled couple of weeks in Sydney. Lovely, full-on, intense, exhausting, meaningful, combative, annoying, important family time.

Mum and me have already had a couple of minor-league

squabbles over important things, like which dishcloth I'm meant to use for hand washing, which one is just for drying plates and which ones are purely decorative. But I think it's a good thing. It means we're starting to feel comfortable with each other. Comfortable and secure in our new-found – old-found – relationship. We're able to risk disagreeing without being afraid. I don't know that we'll ever be fully normal, but I'm OK with it if this is our new normal. We are happy to be back in each other's lives and we're hugging a lot.

She's also delighted with her new son-in-law, Joe, who she's treating like he is Prince fucking Harry. I am actually feeling a bit huffy about it because I was meant to be the big-ticket item during my time here ferfuxache. But, no, apparently Joe is the favourite and all Mum does is fuss and preen over her darling 'new son'. Mark and I bitch about them together in corners, while Joe sucks up, helping Mum make endless cups of tea for everyone, as Hannah reads us alarmist propaganda she finds on the dark web.

The five of us have become quite the #squadgoals (Mum is Taylor, I'm Lena, Joe is Selena, Mark is Gigi), and we decided for my last two weeks in the country – the final stage of this life sabbatical – that Mum would take time off work so we could all travel up to Cairns together. We agreed we could book ourselves on a boat trip, learn to scuba dive around the Great Barrier Reef, and – apparently – all get tipsy and do unprovoked karaoke.

The hospice told Mum she should go, she needs the break. Steven is awake now, and he'll be coming home in a few weeks. He can't walk or talk properly and is going to need a lot of looking after. There will be professional carers and support, but this is still going to be a big thing.

I still haven't seen him. It is a life loose end that I haven't been able to tie up neatly. I want to want to forgive him, but my feelings are too complicated to boil down and examine just yet. Maybe it will be forgotten in time, or maybe Steven and I will never resolve things fully. Maybe it will remain a pebble in my shoe for the rest of my life. But existence is complicated and family is even more so. And I think it's OK to leave that question unanswered for the time being.

Joe and Mum climb down from the stage, people slapping them on the back jovially. They are buzzing and giggling.

'Did you hear me up there, Alice?' Mum says as if literally anyone between here and Papua New Guinea could've missed it. I nearly make a joke about how pieces of Ayers Rock are currently crumbling into oblivion thanks to the vibrations, and then I stop myself.

'You were brilliant, Mum,' I say. Because I'm totally kind now.

She beams. 'I always sing that song for karaoke, I love Kate Hudson,' she says and I cock my head at her.

'Kate Hudson?' I am bewildered. 'The actress?'

Mum nods, 'Yes, but she's a singer, too, isn't she? I saw her sing it on *Top of the Pops* years ago. She was wearing a yellow dress.'

It takes me a minute.

'Mum, I think you're thinking of the film, *How to Lose a Guy in 10 Days*, starring Kate Hudson. She sings "You're So Vain" in it, but the song is by Carly Simon.'

'Oh,' she looks stumped. 'Is that right? Well, she was very convincing playing a singer though.'

I smile widely. 'You're awesome, Mum, you know that?'

She smiles back, delighted. 'I think you're the awesome one.' She sighs, a little sadly. 'I really don't want you to go home, but I know I can't keep you here for ever. You're sure it's OK to visit over Christmas? I'm booking my flights tonight. You won't be able to get rid of me that easily, my wonderful girl.'

'I can't wait,' I say, beaming back and meaning it.

I feel so sad that my trip is coming to an end. But also, secretly a bit excited. I feel ready for things. Ready to embrace my life a bit more. I even feel ready for a full-time job. I've been thinking about it and decided I was actually pretty good at that last temping role (faux-sexting my boss aside). I like fixing things and shouting at people, so I'm going to start applying for things in that same area. Maybe PR? Maybe marketing? Maybe there's even a job out there called 'Troubleshooting for your deviant boss'? It's been a while since I had a proper look at the job market, but it feels like that is a role this world would need. The gaps on my CV will be fine because I will just lie. That is the honourable thing to do.

I feel so tingly about the possibilities of my life now.

I know it sounds cheesy, but I feel different, I really do. And it's not just making up with my mum – although that has been such a huge weight off my mind – it's everything.

The thing is, things have changed. And it's not because of travelling. Honestly, it's not like this journey has helped me discover who I am and fix myself, because the truth is, I've always been able to see my own flaws and problems. It's just that before, I thought those flaws defined me. I thought that was just who I was. I've spent my life telling myself over and over that I am not that great. That there was no point trying to escape people like TD because he was who I deserved. I told myself I was too weak to walk away and there was no point fighting it. I told myself that was just who I am – that they are entrenched personality traits – and I just had to live with disliking that side of me. But I think this is a problem we have as humans. We get bogged down telling ourselves something over and over until we can't see anything else. I got stubborn about staying where – and who – I was in life.

The thing is, if you're genuinely in a happy rut, that's great – stay there! Why not! But I wasn't. I was in a self-hating, miserable rut. Travelling took me outside of myself and let me see how shut down I've been – to people and to possibilities. And OK, fine, I have some abandonment issues thanks to a vaguely complicated childhood, but who hasn't had something in their lives to be sad about? At some point? Everyone has something! I don't need to spend my whole life carrying all that around with me. I don't need to use it as an excuse to push good people away or bash them over the head. And I definitely shouldn't use my childhood as an excuse to chase after awful men who don't care about me.

I think we all have a tendency to let the wrong people into our lives at vulnerable moments, and then we get too tired and worn down to remove them.

But I'm done with all that.

I can't stop thinking about my thirtieth birthday party, where I was so angry with everyone. So angry with the world for moving on around me and without me. But I wasn't prepared to move on myself. I stomped around that party – where a lot of kind people had given up their time and money to come along – acting like I deserved better. I behaved so badly. I was a moody bitch for no reason and it's a wonder I have any friends left – never mind ones as wonderful as Eva, Joe and Mark. I'm deeply ashamed.

I had a re-read of that drunken note I wrote to myself on

my phone late that night, where I was moaning incomprehensibly and shouting at Future Alice about things she had to do. I thought I was being so wise and clever, but re-reading it now, I can see it's utterly stupid drivel. And there was also a bit at the bottom I'd missed the first time I'd read it, when I was all hungover and in denial.

'Nobody fucken cares about u alice NO ONE and u hav to lok out for urSELf. TD is a dik but he is prob the only 1 who GETS u, proly going to end up together. he understas u, he noes the real u and likes you anyway. Despite wat a shitty perso u r.

soulmate????

This was ur 30ieth and everythin iz ging to be different now. u r differnt and u have yo make ur own way now. fuk evry1 else u don't need them.'

It makes me so embarrassed to read it back now. Because *of course* people care about me. They'd tried so hard to show me that, and I'd thrown it back in their faces. The ridiculous part is that the only person who truly didn't care about me back then was TD.

But this is what happens when you're unhappy. Things get distorted around you. Things get out of perspective and you project that unhappiness on other people. I thought I was being treated badly because I was sad. I tried to force people around me to be what I wanted them to be – to stop moving on without me – and that was wrong. You can't make people into anything. They just are who they are. Like with Constance Beaumont – or, sorry, Janet Janet Morris – it's not her fault she isn't what I had decided in my head that she was. It's not her fault everyone needs her to be this perfect glossy thing with a perfect life and perfect green eyes. I can't be disappointed when people are not what I have created out of thin air.

Ultimately, you have to figure out how to be happy for yourself because you can't expect other people to create the happy for you. What I've realised in the last few months is that happiness comes and goes. No one is happy all the time. And that's fine. Life is about feeling all of it and enjoying the journey. It's what Terry the coach driver said – instead of always chasing what's next, I need to learn how to make the most of what was happening around me.

And smile more.

My phone buzzes and I look down to see Eva is trying to FaceTime me. It's too loud in here, but I want to talk to my lovely best friend. I want to make time for her.

I wave my phone at my family and run outside to answer.

'Hello you,' I say at her beautiful smiling face.

'Aah, Alice, I miss you,' she says, skipping the greeting.

'Me too,' I grin affectionately. 'How are things back home with Jeremy and the bump?'

'Really good,' she says, beaming contentedly. 'I promise I'm talking to him properly about everything, like you told me to. He's so kind, I was silly to think he couldn't handle hearing what I was worried about. I'm still scared, but I think we're going to be OK.'

'I'm so glad, Eva!' I say, smiling widely. 'I can't believe you'll soon be a mum! It's so amazing that you're making a person in there.'

She nods. 'I know, it's so clever.'

'And only a tiny bit like the plot of *Alien*,' I add and she giggles.

My phone beeps and a message drops down on the screen.

'It's Isy,' I tell Eva, tapping on it.

'Is she OK?' she asks and I grimace. 'I had a chat with her last night, and she's ended things with Ethan, that wanker producer. He tried to get her to have a threesome, and she was almost insecure enough to do it. She backed out at the last minute, thank God, but of course he was shitty about it and said he was going to find someone else to make up the third. So she dumped him.'

Eva makes a sympathetic face. 'Poor thing, I know she liked him a lot.'

'She did,' I agree, 'but she got an advert out of it, which paid her big bucks and she said she's already had some auditions off the back of that project. I reckon she's going to move more into telly and commercial stuff now. She says she's proved herself in the theatre world and this is a new and important challenge for her art.'

We both stifle a giggle. Typical Isy.

'Anyway, I'm sad she is sad,' I say, pulling myself up because I am the new, kinder Alice Edwards. 'But I was trying to tell her about the joys of being single and then she made some random murmur-y noises, before confessing that she's been spending a lot of time with my AirBnB host-pal, Patrick.'

Eva throws her head back and laughs.

'Good for her!' she says, wiping her eyes.

'I know right!' I say, laughing too. 'I'm happy for them both, they'd make beautiful babies.'

We smile at each other and she grins. 'I am so excited you're coming home soon, Alice.'

I make a face I don't really mean and she adds, 'Aw, sorry. I guess you must be really bummed about coming back here to this grey British summer and real life. Have you got the travelling bug now? Will you be off on another adventure immediately?'

I make a face like I'm considering it but I already know the answer.

'No,' I say, shaking my head and laughing. 'I've had such an amazing time these last few months, and I'm going to enjoy this last bit as much as I can, but I've realised I'm definitely not a traveller at heart. I miss expensive shoes and my GHDs. I miss home-cooked junk food, and deciding what temperature to have the thermostat on, y'know? I like being at home – wherever that will be next – and I'm excited to just lie in bed watching Netflix for a week without feeling guilty about wasting the sunshine. And oh my God I miss having a Boots nearby.'

She laughs. 'Really?! I thought you were having the time of your life.'

'Oh, I have had an incredible time,' I say quickly. 'And I've learnt so much and figured so much stuff out. But I don't think it was necessarily the travelling that did that. It's more about the people I met. I think people are what make up the fun parts of life and experiences. And the thing is, I wasn't really going away to travel and see the world, was I? I left to escape because I thought I had a shitty life that wasn't worth sticking around for. I went away to avoid living my life because I felt sorry for myself. But there is so much to be at home for and so much I can do and see back there.'

She breaks into a grin, looking down at her belly, and I laugh. 'Yes, indeed, becoming an honorary auntie is definitely one of them,' I confirm, pausing then before I continue. 'I still want to take trips and go on wonderful holidays in the future, but I think probably just a week or two in Tenerife-type adventures. I don't need to do any more faux self-discovery stuff really. Don't get me wrong, I do like beaches and joy. I like the joy of seeing things, the joy of meeting people, the joy of showing off about it online because why not. But I can do that in smaller ways.'

Eva giggles.

'I'm excited about what's going to come next,' I say, 'because I have no idea what it is. But whatever it is, I do think I'm going to be OK.'

She smiles at that. 'You know, Alice? I think you are, too.'

***

from: Hannahtruthseeker@protonmail.com
to: Hannah Edwards
cc: Hannah Edwards
date: 15 August at 10.15
subject: JUNE/JULY FAMILY NEWSLETTER: TOP SECRET
mailed-by: ProtonMail

EDWARDS FAMILY NEWSLETTER/JUNE/JULY RECAP

Good afternoon, all.
Hannah here. This month I identify myself with another new
code word to prevent government forgery and hacking into my
newsletters.

SULTANA

Firstly, apologies for the lack of newsletter last month. I know many of you were concerned I had finally been tracked down by the 'man'. But it's fine, it has just been a very eventful time. We have had my sister staying with us for the whole month here in Sydney. Alice is now back on the mailing list by request, but do not concern yourself, because she has been vetted and briefed about all safety precautions.

We have had a lovely time as a family these past few weeks. We did some sight-seeing around Sydney, and visited the Blue Mountains where we did yoga. We travelled up the east coast to Cairns, where we learnt to scuba dive and went on a boat trip. For those worried, I can confirm there are no Earth edges next to Australia. But I will continue to investigate this subject and report back.

Alice has now returned to the UK, where she is planning on renting a flat on her own in London!!!! I have asked her to check in with me twice a day so she doesn't fall through the cracks of the system, and she's promised it is near her best friend Eva Slate so she can babysit.

I have also added another name to the mailing list: Joe Downe, who is Mark's boyfriend. We met Joe in Sydney and he came with us to see the Great Barrier Reef. I have had many great conversations with him about the moon landing and how Stevie Wonder can actually secretly see. He is very funny and nice. We are glad he is part of the family.

Speaking of AWOL, my first few months infiltrating the blogging network has been a success. I am keeping an eye on the government there, and giving them no information. Please follow me because I only have six followers right now.

In other family news:
-Uncle Ned has had his gastric bypass this week. The surgery went well but he would appreciate you all not sending so many boxes of chocolates as a gift because he cannot eat them.
-Little Jemima finally got her first period two weeks ago, and even though she asked me not to say anything, I will just say: we are all so proud of you kiddo, and welcome to womanhood. But everyone else? Please do stop sending bras. Especially you, Aunt Mildred, because Jemima is nowhere near a 48GG.

-Cousin Leon's dog, Gertie, has now had the snip, and is no longer humping people, so he would like me to pass along that people can come visit again, if they'd like. Although FYI Leon's budgie is still attacking people who get too close.

-Mum would also like me to pass along her thanks to everyone for all their support this year. It has been a difficult one in many ways, but positive in others. Steven is coming home this week and has already regained some of his speech. Doctors are hopeful he will make a lot more progress with the help of regular physical therapy. We all know Steven was and is a troubled man, but Mum has been with him a long time and we are all human beings who don't always have all the answers.

Apart from the pod people who have replaced thirty per cent of the human race and do actually have all the answers.

Until next month, fellow Truth Seekers.
Hannah xx

PS. DO NOT FORGET TO COVER YOUR CAMERA ON THE COMPUTER SCREEN, THEY CAN READ THIS EMAIL FROM IT.
PPS. Also don't forget to get rid of all your Harry Potter books. As I have mentioned before, JK Rowling does not really exist, she is a government front for magic propaganda.

The Edwards Family have requested that no one read this email at all.

Epilogue

NINE MONTHS LATER

What's on your mind, Alice?

3 hrs · London · Friends only

I am so happy Facebook is back in fashion!! I knew I was right not to delete my account. Spoiler alert: this is going to be a long, slightly drunk, award-show-type speech. I just got back from my 31st birthday party where there was both booze AND food – and I must be growing up because I genuinely loved it. I want to say thank you so so so so much to everyone who came, I have the actual best pals in the universe. Special shout out to Eva, Jeremy (and baby Olivia, who made a particularly cute cameo via FaceTime), Mark, Joe, Hannah and Mum. Love you guys. A still-in-shock-thanks to Clara, Maria, Anna and Craig who all travelled from far and wide to surprise me. I was so glad to see you and hear about how well your lives are going. I'm so glad you're all happy – #Ayahuas-caPalsForever? – and see you tomorrow for brunch. Thanks to my new friend and work colleague, Luke, for popping along, too. I've only been working for AWOL a couple of months, but I already love it so very much. For those who don't know, Luke and I are now heading up AWOL's troll-busting avenging angel team. Who knew shouting at online dickheads and hitting a button marked 'block' all day would be so satisfying? (Everyone. Everyone knew that.) It's an excellent outlet for my, er, let's say *snappier* side. Anyway it's brilliant, and I'm loving it. Finally happy to have a job with a CONTRACT.

Anyway, a lot has happened in the last year – travelling, making new friends, reuniting with loved ones, and my stepdad coming home after his illness – and I want everyone to know how grateful I am that you all stuck by me. Life isn't always easy or straightforward, but I've learnt to embrace all of that. It's about the journey, not the destination. Remember that it's all too easy to get stuck in an unhappy rut, waiting for someone to come along and fix you. But happiness is about taking risks and forgiving people for being people. So I'm going to forgive myself for this slightly cheesy moment and also forgive myself for getting fish and chips all over my duvet as I write all this in bed. Byeeeeeeee.

Checked in at: Infernos, London
Like   Comment
245 likes

Mark Edwards
When did you get so open and honest with your feelings?

Alice Edwards
Around about the same time as you did. Don't think I didn't see you and Joe snogging your faces off in the middle of the dance floor, buddy.

Joe Downe
Your brother is a changed man, Alice :)

Noah Deer

You coming to LA again this year? Maybe we can finally get that date in!

Alice Edwards

Maybe one day, Noah!

Eva Slate

You're not leaving the country any time soon, sorry, I forbid it. I need you.

Isabelle Moore

Aw, so sorry I missed your party!!! But Patrick and I can't wait to see you in June for our Tenerife holiday!!!!

Alice Edwards

Yay! Me tooooooo! So happy.

Dan Heam

THIS USER HAS BEEN BLOCKED AND HIS COMMENT DELETED.

Acknowledgements

The first person I would like to thank is my best friend Beyoncé. Beyoncé has been my best friend for many years now and she has definitively never said otherwise and you can't prove anything. Bey, thank you for all the love and support you have given me, by not specifically saying you didn't want me to have your love and support.

Remember that really amazing night out we had together that one time? Where you looked amazing and everyone stared at you for hours and where you were singing the whole time and were also on stage and it was in the O2 Arena and I was in the audience. Let's do that all the time.

Remember how we cried together over *Lemonade* in that I was crying and you sounded sad as you sang about Becky with the good hair. Even though we are best friends I still don't know which Becky you mean – is it my sister Becky? Because her hair isn't even good, it's really, really thin. Either way, I'm always here to cry with you over *Lemonade* until the Spotify adverts start up because I'm not paying £9.99 a month for Premium, you can forget about it.

I would also like to thank all those people I've left behind since becoming best friends with Beyoncé. My family: Mum, Nigel, Dad, Liz, Dale, Lisa, Carey, Nick, Phil, Becky, Ros. Thank you all for making me have Christmases with you when I know Bey would've wanted me there with her and the kids so we could immediately leave them with Jay and go get drunk at Kelly's house.

And thank you to all the nieces and nephews I no longer care about: Frankie, Charlotte, Ali, Sam, Leon, Charlie, Lola, Tilly, India, Flo. None of you mean anything like as much to me as Blue Ivy, Rumi and Sir do.

Thank you to all my lesser friends; Sarah Cook, Fred Attrill, Lyndsey Heffernan, James Doris, Isla, Finn, Ciaran, Tara, Clair Terry, Hayden Green, Emma Patterson, Jo Usmar, Kate Dunn, Katie 'Horse' Horswell, Daniel K, the Paw Walker gang, the School for Dumb Women lads, Daisy Buchanan, Laura Jane Williams, Angela Clarke, Karen Gill, Mike Townsend, Emma Ledger, Kate Wills, Caroline Corcoran. Special thank you to Abi Doyle, who talked to me at length about her own travelling and was much better at it than Alice. Also thanks to Olivia Newhouse because it'll annoy Abi. Thank you to Lucy for Family Pilates (I'm better than the others, right?). And thanks to Ivy and Teddy, who lay at my feet being so fucking adorable while I wrote this.

And thank you, Jeremy Vine because Always.

Thank you most of all to everyone at Orion. Even though you have not yet let me write a book about my friendship with Beyoncé which just seems weird to me but hey, I suppose you are the experts at books. Thank you dream team: my phenomenal editor-cum-genius Clare Hey, the awesome and seriously-where-is-my-Dictaphone Poppy Stimpson, marketing genius and she-of-that-hair, Jen Breslin (miss you already), awesome, clever, cool Olivia Barber, Jen Wilson, Georgina Cutler, Paul Stark, Susan Howe, Krystina Kujawinska, Richard King, Jessica Purdue, Hannah Stokes, Ruth Sharvell, Rabab Adams, and all the other incredible humans who work there. Also, can I have another selfie, Katie Espiner?

Thank you always and forever to my agent Diana

Beaumont, you remain a Goddess. Would it be OK if I called you Beyoncé?

This joke was only meant to be one line, but I really got into it.

THANKS BUBYE.

Discover your next laugh-out-loud read from Lucy Vine

Hot Mess [n.] – *someone attractive, who is often in disarray*

Have you ever shown up to Sunday brunch still smelling of Saturday night?

Chosen bed, Netflix and pizza over human contact?

Stayed in your mould-ridden flat because it's cheap?

Meet your spirit animal, Ellie Knight. Her life isn't turning out exactly as she planned. She hates her job, her friends are coupling up and settling down, and her flatmates are just plain weird.

Some people might say she's a hot mess, but who really has their sh*t together anyway?

Available in paperback and ebook now

'Truly, the Bridget Jones for our generation'

Louise O'Neill

What do you get if you cross a dozen drunk hens with one shiny Butler in the Buff?

Meet Lilah Fox. She's on the hen do from hell. Then she gets a message (44 of them, actually) from her best friend with big news: she's getting married in six months. Oh, and Lilah's her maid of honour. Which means she just got signed up for:

- A military schedule of wedding fairs and weekly planning meetings

- Excel spreadsheets and endless hen emails

- All the enforced, expensive fun you can imagine...

What fresh hell is this?

Available in paperback and ebook now